Mistress B

Jules Gabriel Verne

Volume 36 of 54 in the

"Voyages Extraordinaires"

First published in 1891.

2013 Reprint by Kassock Bros. Publishing Co.

Printed in the United States Of America

Cover Illustration By Isaac M. Kassock

ISBN: 148401250X
ISBN-13: 978-1484012505

Jules Gabriel Verne (1828-1905)

The Extraordinary Voyages
of
Jules Verne
~

Table of Contents

MISTRESS BRANICAN

Jules Verne

PART ONE

CHAPTER I - THE *FRANKLIN*

There are two chances of never again seeing the friends we part with when starting on a long voyage; those we leave may not be here on our return, and those who go may never come back. But little heed of these eventualities was taken by the sailors who were preparing for departure on board the *Franklin* in the morning of the 15th of March, 1875.

On that day the *Franklin*, Captain John Branican, was about to quit the port of San Diego, in California. on a voyage across the Northern Pacific, A fine vessel of nine hundred tons was this *Franklin* — a barquentine fully canvassed with gaff sails, jibs and staysails, and with topmast and top-gallant-mast on the fore.

Long and narrow in the bow, finely modelled in the quick-works, and with a good clean run, her masts gently raking and strictly parallel, her standing rigging of galvanized wire as stiff as iron bars, she was of the most modern type of those elegant clippers which the North Americans find so well adapted for their ocean trade and which compete in speed with the best steamers of their mercantile marine, The *Franklin* was so well built and efficiently commanded that not a man of her crew would have shipped on another vessel — even with the assurance of obtaining higher pay. All were preparing to start content in their double confidence in a good ship and a good captain.

The *Franklin* was to make her first voyage on behalf of William H. Andrew, and Co. of San Diego. She was bound to Calcutta by way of Singapore with a cargo of American goods to return with Indian products to one of the Californian ports.

Captain John Branican was a young man of nine and twenty, with an attractive but resolute face, his features telling of unusual energy; he possessed in the highest degree that moral courage so superior to physical courage — that "two o'clock in the morning courage," as Napoleon called it. — that is to say, the kind that faces the unexpected and is ready for action at any moment. His head had more character than beauty, with his rough hair, his eyes animated with a keen, frank

2

look which flashed like a dart from their black pupils. It would be difficult to imagine a man of his age more robust in body or constitution. That was clear enough in the vigour of his handshakings which indicated the ardour of his blood and the strength of his muscles. But what we have particularly to note is that the spirit contained in this body of iron was a good and noble spirit, ready to sacrifice its life for its kind. John Branican was of the character of those rescuers whose coolness enables them to perform heroic acts without hesitation. He had given proof of this early in life. One day, among the broken ice of the bay on a capsized boat, he had saved children like himself; and later on he had not belied the instincts of self-sacrifice which had marked his youth.

A few years after John Branican had lost his father and his mother, he had married Dolly Starter, an orphan, belonging to one of the best families of San Diego. The girl's dowry was a modest one, and suitable for the position, equally modest, of the young sailor, then a mate on a merchant vessel. But there was reason to think that Dolly would one day be the heiress of a very rich uncle, Edward Starter, who lived a farmer's life in the wildest and most out-of-the-way part of Tennessee. Meanwhile it would have to be enough to live on for two, or even for three, for little Walter — Wat, by abbreviation — came into the world in the first year of the marriage. Thus John Branican — and his wife understood it — could not dream of abandoning his profession as a sailor. In the future he would see what he could do, when the fortune came by inheritance, or by his enriching himself in Andrews' service.

Besides this, the young sailor's promotion had been unusually rapid. He had advanced quickly, and he had advanced straight. He was a captain at an age when most of his colleagues were only mates. If his abilities justified this promotion, his advance was explained by certain circumstances which had properly drawn attention to him.

In fact, John Branican was popular at San Diego, and at the different ports on the Californian coast.- His acts of self-sacrifice had been noted with applause, not only by sailors, but by the merchants and shipowners of the Union.

A few years before, a Peruvian schooner, the Sonora, had come ashore at the entrance to Coronado Beach, and the crew would have been lost if communication had not been established between the ship and the shore. But to take a rope out through the breakers was to risk one's life a hundred times. John Branican did not hesitate. He threw himself amid the waves which came rolling in with extreme violence on to the reefs and then came beating on to the beach in a terrible surf. In sight of the death which he would have faced without thinking of the danger, the people would have held him back. He resisted; he hurried himself towards the schooner; he succeeded in reaching her, and, thanks to his bravery, the Sonora's crew were saved.

About a year afterwards, during a storm which broke some five hundred miles out in the Pacific, John Branican had another opportunity of showing what might be expected from him. He was mate on the Washington when the captain was washed overboard by a wave at the same time as half the crew. Remaining on board a disabled ship with half a dozen seamen, most of them injured, he took the command, and although the vessel had lost her rudder, he managed to handle her, and brought her into San Diego under jury masts. This almost unmanageable hulk contained a cargo worth five hundred thousand dollars, and belonged to Andrews.

Great was the young sailor's reception when the Washington was moored in the port of San Diego. As the chances of the sea had made him captain, there was not a voice among the whole population against confirming him in his rank.

It was under these circumstances that Andrews built the *Franklin* and offered him the command. He accepted it, for he felt himself equal to the post, and could pick and choose his crew, for people had confidence in him. And that is how it came about that the *Franklin* was beginning her first voyage under the orders of John Branican.

4

The departure was an event for the whole town. Andrew's was justly considered one of the most honourable firms in San Diego. Of the highest character for the security of his business relationships and the strength of his credit was Mr. William Andrew, who directed its affairs with a sure hand. This worthy ship-owner was not only esteemed, he was loved. And his behaviour towards John Branican was unanimously applauded.

There was thus nothing to be astonished at if during this morning of the 15th of March, a numerous gathering of spectators — in other words a crowd of friends, known and unknown, of the young captain — appeared on the quays of the Pacific Coast Steamship Company to greet him with a last cheer at his departure.

The crew of the *Franklin* consisted of twelve men in-

cluding the boatswain, all, however, good sailors belonging to San Diego and happy to serve under the orders of John Branican. The mate was an excellent officer, named Harry Felton. Although he was five, or six years older than his captain he was in no way offended at having to serve under him, nor was he in any way jealous of the position his captain held. He considered that. John Branican deserved his position, he had sailed with him before and they mutually appreciated each other. Besides, what Mr. William Andrew did must be well done. Harry Felton and his men were devoted to him body and soul. Most of them had already sailed in some of his ships. It was, as it were, a family of officers and sailors — a numerous family devoted to its chief, which constituted its maritime staff and did not cease to increase with the prosperity of the house.

And it was without apprehension, or rather with ardour, that the crew of the *Franklin* were entering on this new campaign. Fathers, mothers, relatives, were there to say farewell, but to say it to those whom they would soon see again. "Good-bye, and see you again soon, shall we not?" It was only a six months' voyage, a simple passage during the fine season between California and India, there and back between San Diego and California, and not one of those expeditions of commerce or discovery which keep a" ship for long years on the most dangerous seas of the two hemispheres. The sailors had been many other such voyages, and their families had been present at many more disquieting departures.

The-preparations would soon be complete. The *Franklin* at her anchor in the middle of the harbour was already clear of the other vessels, whose number bore witness to the importance of San Diego as a port. From the. place she occupied she would have no need of a tug to take her out to sea. As soon as her anchor was short apeak, it would be enough for her to fill her sails, and a beautiful breeze would take her rapidly out of the bay without her having to go about Captain John Branican could not have wished for better weather, nor a more favourable wind, over the sea which glittered under the rays of the sun around the Coronado islands in the offing.

At this time — six o'clock in the morning — it need scarcely be said that all the crew were on board. None of the sailors could return to the shore, and as far as they were concerned the voyage had already begun. A few of the harbour boats were at the starboard gangway waiting for the people who were bidding the last good-bye to their friends and relatives. These boats would take them to the quay as soon as the *Franklin* hoisted her jibs. Although the tides are not strong in the Pacific, it was quite as well to go out with the ebb which would soon begin.

Among the visitors we must particularly notice Mr. William Andrew and Mrs. Branican, accompanied by the nurse carrying little Wat; they were accompanied by Mr. Len Burker and his wife, Jane Burker, Dolly's cousin- german. Harry Felton, the mate, having no family, had no one to bid him good-bye. The good wishes of Mr. William Andrew were not wanting on the occasion, and he asked no more than that those of John's wife should be added to them — of which he was assured in advance.

Harry Felton was on the forecastle where half a dozen of the men were shortening in the cable at the capstan amid the metallic clatter of the pawls. The *Franklin* had already begun to move as the chain came grinding in through the hawse-hole. The house flag with Andrew's initials floated at the main-mast head, while the American flag fluttered in the breeze from the peak, and displayed the Stars and Stripes. The square sails were all ready for setting as soon as the ship was under way under jibs and staysails.

On the front of the poop so as to lose nothing of what was being done, John Branican received the final instructions from Mr. William Andrew relative to the manifest, that is, the detailed statement of the goods which constituted the *Franklin*'s cargo. Then the ship-owner gave the young captain the papers, and added, —

"If circumstances oblige you to change your course do the best you can for our interests, and send me news from the first land you touch at. The *Franklin* may perhaps put in at one of the Philippines, for you have doubtless no intention of going through Torres Straits?"

"No, Mr. Andrew," said John, "I should not think of taking the *Franklin* into the dangerous seas to the north of Australia. My road should be to Hawaii, the Ladrones, Mindanao of the Philippines, Celebes, and the Strait of Macassar, so as to reach Singapore by the Java Sea. From there to Calcutta the road is clear enough. I do not think the route will have to be changed on account of the winds we shall meet with in the Western Pacific. If you have anything of importance to telegraph to me send it to Mindanao, where I shall probably put in, or to Singapore, where I certainly shall."

"That is agreed. On your part let me know as soon as you can the state of the market at Calcutta. It is possible that it may oblige me to change my intentions regarding the return cargo."

"I shall not fail to do so, Mr. Andrew," said John Branican.

At this moment Harry Felton approached, and said, —

"The anchor is apeak, sir."

"And the ebb?"

7

"Is just beginning to be felt."

"Hold on."

Then addressing Mr. William Andrew, the captain, full of gratitude, repeated, —

"Once more, Mr. Andrew, I thank you for having given me the command of the *Franklin*. I hope I shall justify your confidence."

"I have no doubt of it whatever," said Mr. Andrew; "and I could not leave the business of my house in better hands."

The ship-owner shook hands with him heartily and moved towards the stern.

Mrs, Branican, followed by the nurse and the baby, rejoined her husband with Mr. and Mrs. Burker. The moment of separation had come. Captain Branican had now but to receive the last farewells of his wife and family.

Dolly, as we know, had not been married two years, and her child was hardly nine months old. Although the separation caused her profound grief, yet she would not let anything of it be seen, and restrained the beating of her heart while her cousin Jane, of weak nature and without energy, could not conceal her emotion. She was very fond of Dolly, and in being near her had often found some alleviation of the sorrows caused by the imperious and violent character of her husband. But if Dolly concealed her anxieties, Jane was none the less aware of what she felt in all its reality. Doubtless Captain Branican would be back before six months, but at least it was a separation — the first since their marriage — and if she was strong enough to restrain her tears it could well be said that Jane wept for her. As to Len Burker, the man whose look no tender emotion had ever softened, his eyes were dry, and with his hands in his pockets he moved about inattentive to what was going on, and thinking of one knows not what. Evidently he had no ideas in common with the visitors whom sentiments of affection had brought on board the ship at her departure.

8

Captain John took his wife's two hands between his, and drawing her towards him said, in a gentle voice, —

"Dear Dolly, I must go. I shall not be long away. In a few months you will see me again. I will find you again, Dolly, never fear. On my ship with my crew, what have we to fear from the dangers of the sea? Be strong as a sailor's wife should be. When I come back our little Wat will be fifteen months old. He will be a big boy. He will be able to talk, and the first word I hear on my return — "

"Will be your name, John!" said Dolly. "Your name shall be the first he will learn." We will both talk of you and always! Dear John, do write to me at every opportunity. And tell me all you have done, and all you think of doing. Let me feel that thoughts of me are!n all your thoughts."

"Yes, dear Dolly, I will write to you. I will keep you posted- up in the events of our voyage. My letters shall be like a log, with all my tenderness to the good!"

"All! John. I am so jealous of this sea which n taking you away so far. How much I envy those who love and whom nothing in life can separate! But no; I am wrong to think of that."

"Dear wife, say to yourself that it is for our child that I go — for you also, to give both of you comfort and happiness. If our hopes of the future are one day realized, we shall never again separate."

Here Len Burker and Jane came near. Captain John turned towards them.

"My dear Len," he said, "I leave you my wife; I leave you my son. I entrust them to you as being the only relations they have in San Diego."

"You can depend on us, John," said Len Burker, endeavouring to soften the harshness of his voice. "Jane and I are here, and we will take care of Dolly."

"And we will console her," said Mrs. Burker. "You know how much I love you, my dear Dolly! I will see you often.' Every day I will spend a few hours with you. We will talk about John."

"Yes, Jane," answered Mrs. Branican, "for I shall not cease to think about him."

Harry Felton again came to interrupt the conversation.

"Captain," said he, "it will be time — "

"All right, Harry," said John. "Up with the inner jib and mizen."

The mate went off to execute the orders, which meant an immediate departure.

"Mr. Andrew," said the captain to the owner, "the boat will take you back to the quay with my wife and her relations as soon as you like."

"Now, John," answered Mr. Andrew, "and once more — a pleasant voyage!"

"Yes! a pleasant voyage!" said the other visitors as they went down into the boats on the starboard side of the *Franklin*."

"Good-bye, Len! Good-bye, Jane!" said John, clasping their hands in his.

"Good-bye! good-bye!" said Mrs. Burker.

"And you, my Dolly, you must go," added John; "the sails are filling."

And in fact the sails were giving a slight heel to the *Franklin*, while the sailors sang, —

"Here goes one,

A bouncing one,

One will go,

She will, oh!

But two come home, they will, oh!

Here goes two, A bouncing two,

Two will go, ihey will, oh!

But three come home, they will, oh!

Here goes three — "

And so on.

During this the captain had led his wife to the gangway, and as she put her foot on the ladder, feeling "himself as incapable of speaking to her as she was of speaking to him, he could only clasp her tightly in his arms.

And then the baby, which Dolly had just taken from the nurse, stretched out its arms towards its father, shook its little hands as it smiled, and this word escaped from its lips, —

"Pa — pa! Pa — pa!"

"My John," exclaimed Dolly, "you have heard his first word before separating from him."Self-controlled as was the young captain, he could not restrain the tear which rolled down on to little Wat's cheek.

"Dolly!" he murmured, "Good-bye! good-bye!"

Then, —

"Are you clear?" he called in a loud voice, to put an end to this painful scene.

A moment afterwards the boat was off and heading for the wharf where its passengers would immediately land.

Captain Branican was busy getting under way. The anchor began to mount towards the hawse-hole. The *Franklin*, free from her last fetter, already felt the breeze on her sails, which were shaking violently. The big jib was almost close home, and the guyed mizen caused the ship to

11

huff a little so that she could pass clear of a few vessels moored at the entrance of the bay.

At a new order from Captain Branican the mainsail and foresail went up together with a simultaneous precision that did honour to the arms of the crew. Then the *Franklin*, coining round on the port tack, stood off out to sea.

From the wharf the numerous spectators could admire these different manoeuvres. Nothing could be more graceful than this elegantly shaped vessel when she heeled to the capricious gusts of the wind. During the evolution she approached the end of «the wharf where Mr. William Andrew, Dolly, Len and Jane Burker stood within less* than half a cable length; and consequently the young captain again had a glimpse of his wife and her relations and friends.

They all replied to his voice which was clearly heard, and to his hand which he stretched out towards those from whom he was going away.

"Good-bye! Good-bye!" said he.

"Hurrah!" shouted the crowd of spectators, while the handkerchiefs waved in hundreds.

Liked by all was Captain John Branican 1 Was he not the townsman of whom the town was most justifiably proud? Yes! they all would be there on his return when he appeared outside the bay.

The *Franklin*, which was already at the mouth, had to huff to avoid a long mail boat just coming in. The two ships saluted by dipping their American ensigns.

On the wharf Mrs. Branican stood motionless gazing at the *Franklin* rapidly sailing away under the fresh breeze from the north-east. She would follow her with heir eyes as long as her masts were visible over Island Point.

But the *Franklin* was soon round the Coronado Islands outside the .bay. For a moment the house flag at the masthead was visible through a gap in the cliffs. Then she disappeared. — -

"Good bye, John. Good-bye!" murmured Dolly. And why was it that an inexplicable presentiment prevented her from adding, "Au revoir?"

CHAPTER II - FAMILY MATTERS

It is necessary to speak in more detail of Mrs. Branican, whom the different events of this history will bring into fuller light. At this time, Dolly — an abbreviation for Dorothy — was one and twenty. She was of American birth. But without going very far back in her pedigree, there could be found the generation which allied her to the Spanish or rather Mexican race, from which the chief families of this country are descended. Her mother, in fact, was born at San Diego, and San Diego was already founded while Lower California still belonged to Mexico. The vast bay discovered about three and a half centuries before by the Spanish navigator, Juan Rodriguez Cabrillo, was at first named after San Miguel, but received its new name in 1602. In 1846 the province changed its tri- coloured flag for the Stars and Stripes and since then it has formed one of the States of the Union.

Of middle height, with a face lighted up by eyes large and deep and black, a warm complexion, abundant hair of rich dark brown, with hands and feet rather strongly made, as is generally the case in the Spanish type, a walk firm and graceful, a physiognomy denoting energy of character and goodness of heart — such was Mrs. Branican. She was one of those women who cannot be looked upon with indifference, and before her marriage Dolly had the reputation among the girls of San Diego — where beauty is not at all rare — of being the one most worthy of attention. She was of a serious, reflective turn of mind, in its larger sense, and was of enlightened views, gifts which marriage would assuredly develop in her.

Yes! under whatever circumstances, grave as they might be, Dolly, now Mrs. Branican, would know how to do her duty. Having frankly looked straight at life and not through the deceitful surfaces of a prism, she possessed a noble spirit and a strong will. The love with which her husband had inspired her rendered her more resolute to accomplish her task. If the case required it — and this is not an empty phrase when applied to Mrs. Branican — she would give her life for John, as John would give his for her, and as both would give for the child born to them in the first year of their union. They adored this baby, which had just lisped the word "papa" at the moment the young captain was separated from him and his mother. The resemblance which little Wat bore to his father was striking — in the features at least, for he had the warm complexion of Dolly. Of vigorous constitution he had nothing to fear from childish ailments. Besides, he was so carefully looked after. Ah! what dreams of the future, the paternal and maternal imagination had already dreamt for this little being whose life had barely begun.

Assuredly Mrs. Branican would have been the happiest of women, if John's position had allowed him to abandon his trade as a sailor, of which the least of the drawbacks was this necessity of separation from each other. But when the command of the *Franklin* had been offered to him, how could she even think of keeping him from it? And besides, had she not to think of the necessities of housekeeping, and providing for a family which might not always consist of this one child? Dolly's dowry was hardly enough for the needs of the house as it was. Evidently John Branican might reckon on the fortune which the uncle would leave to his niece, and very unlikely things would have to occur for this fortune to escape him, for Mr. Edward Starter was almost a sexagenarian and had no other heiress than Dolly. In fact, her cousin, Jane Burker, belonged to the maternal branch of the family, and was in no way related to her uncle. Dolly would be rich — but ten years, twenty years might pass before she came into her inheritance. And so John Branican was obliged to. work at present, if he had no reason to be anxious about the future; and he had done well in continuing in Andrews' service, in addition to the interest which had been given him in the results of the *Franklin*'s voyages. And as besides being a sailor he was a merchant well acquainted with trading affairs, there was every chance of his acquiring by his work a certain degree of comfort while waiting for the heritage of Mr. Edward Starter.

One word concerning this American — whose "Americanism" was quite original. He was the brother of Dolly's father and consequently her uncle. It was her father, the elder by five or six years, who had so to speak brought up the younger, for both were orphans; and the younger

15

Starter had always retained for him a lively affection augmented by gratitude. Circumstances favouring the elder he had followed the steady road to fortune, while the younger brother had wandered along the crossroads which rarely lead to anything. He had gone off to engage in lucky speculations in buying and clearing vast extents of land, in the State of Tennessee, but he had never broken off communications with his brother, whom business kept in the State of New York. When he had become a widower he had settled at San Diego, the native place of his wife, where he died just after the marriage of Dolly with John Branican had been decided on. The marriage took place when the mourning was over, and the young couple's entire fortune was the very modest heritage left by Starter senior.

A short time afterwards there had arrived at San Diego a letter addressed to Dolly Branican by Starter junior. It was the first he had written to his niece, and it was to be the last.

In substance this letter said, in a form as concise as it was to the point: although Starter junior was a long way away from her, and although he had never seen her, yet he did not forget that he had a niece, his own brother's daughter. If he had never seen her it was because Starter senior and Starter junior had never met since Starter senior had taken to himself a wife, and because Starter junior lived near Nashville In the remotest part of Tennessee while she dwelt at San Diego. Between Tennessee, and California there were several hundred miles which it was in no way convenient for Starter junior to travel, and if Starter junior found the journey too fatiguing for him to go and see his niece, he thought it would be no less fatiguing for his niece to come and see him, and he begged her not to think of taking any trouble in the matter.

In reality Starter junior was a regular bear — not one of those American grizzlies with claws and fur, but one of those human bears who are specially fitted to live outside all social relationships. But that was no concern o-f Dolly's. She was the niece of a bear — be it so! But this bear possessed an uncle's heart. He did not forget what was due

16

from Starter junior to the brother's daughter who would inherit his fortune.

Starter junior said that this fortune was already worth having. It was then worth 500,000 dollars, and could not but increase, for clearing speculations were prospering in the State of Tennessee. As it consisted of land and cattle it would be easy to realize at good prices, and there would be no difficulty in finding buyers.

If this was said in that positive and somewhat brutal fashion which is peculiar to Americans of the old type, it was said all the same. The fortune of Starter junior would go entirely to Mrs. Branican and her children; but in the event of the death of Mrs. Branican, without descendants, this fortune would revert to the State, which would be very happy to accept it.

Two things more.

1, Starter junior was a bachelor. He would remain a bachelor: "the folly he had avoided between the years of twenty and thirty he would avoid at sixty," so his letter said. There was nothing then to turn aside this fortune, as he desired formally to impress upon her, and she would have it for her household use as certainly as the Mississippi flows into the Gulf of Mexico.

2. Starter junior would use every effort — superhuman, indeed — to enrich his niece at the most distant date possible. He had no intention of dying till he was at least a centenarian, and would use all the obstinacy of which he was capable to prolong his life to the utmost possible limit.

Finally, Starter junior begged Mrs. Branican, and even ordered her, not to reply. There was but little communication between the towns and the forest region in the depths of Tennessee. And for his part he would not write again unless it was to announce his death, when the letter would not be in his own hand.

Such was the singular letter received by Mrs. Branican. That she would be the heiress, the universal legatee of her Uncle Starter, there could be no doubt. She would one day possess a fortune of 500,000 dollars, which would probably be greatly increased by the work of this clever clearer of forests. But as Starter junior clearly expressed his intention of living till he was a hundred — and one knows how tenacious these Americans are — John Branican had wisely decided not to abandon the sea. His intelligence, his courage, and his determination would probably help him to acquire a certain affluence for his wife and child long before Uncle Starter had started for another world.

Such was the position of the household when the *Franklin* sailed for the Western Pacific, and which it was necessary to explain in order that what follows may be understood. And now for the only relations of Dolly Branican at San Diego, Mr. and Mrs. Burker.

Len Burker, an American by birth, was then in his thirty-second year, and had only during the last few years settled in the capital of Lower California. This New England Yankee, cold in face, hard in feature, strong in body, was very determined, very active, and very close, allowing nothing to be known of his thoughts, and saying nothing of his actions. His was one of those natures which resemble closed houses, the door of which is opened to nobody. However, at San Diego there had been no unfavourable rumours concerning this uncommunicative man, whose marriage with Jane Burker had made him John Branican's cousin. There is nothing surprising in John's having entrusted Dolly and his child to the Burkers, for he had no other relations; but in reality it was .more particularly to Jane that he entrusted them, knowing that the two cousins had a profound affection for each other.

And it would have been different had John known the truth about Len Burker, if he had known the knavery which he dissimulated behind the impenetrable mask of his physiognomy, or the unceremoniousness with which he treated the social proprieties, respect for himself and the rights of others. Deceived by his somewhat seductive exterior, by a sort of dominating fascination he exercised over her, Jane had married him five months before at Boston, where she was living with her mother, who died a little time after the marriage, the consequences of which were to become so regrettable. Jane's dowry, and the maternal inheritance, would have sufficed for the young couple to live upon if Len Burker had been a man to follow the usual road and not the by-paths. But he did nothing of the sort. After having run through his wife's fortune, Len Burker had been bankrupt at Boston, and had to leave that city. On the other side of America, where his dubious reputation had not followed him, the new countries offered him chances he could not have in New England.

Jane, who now knew her husband, readily seconded this plan of departure, happy to get away from Boston, where Len Burker's position, led to disagreeable comments, and glad also to be with the only relative she had left to her. They had come to San Diego where Dolly and Jane became friends again. For three years they had lived in the town, and Len Burker had given rise to no suspicions, owing to his hiding his difficulties with so much ability. Such were the circumstances which had again brought together the two cousins at the time when Dolly was not yet Mrs. Branican. The young wife and the girl became close friends.. Although it would seem that Jane should have influenced Dolly, the contrary was the case. Dolly was strong, Jane was weak, and the girl soon became the wife's support. When the union of John Branican and Dolly was decided on, Jane showed herself very pleased at the match — a marriage which in no way promised to resemble hers! And in the intimacy of this young household what consolation she might not have found if she had told the secret of her troubles. But subdued under her husband's domination, she had never dared to say a word.

But Len Burker's position was becoming more and more serious. The little that remained to him of his wife's fortune when he left Boston had almost entirely gone. This gambler, or rather this reckless speculator, was one of those people who leave everything to chance, and await the event. Such a character, incapable of listening to reason, could not but bring about deplorable results.

On his arrival at San Diego, Len Burker had opened an office in Fleet Street — one of those offices like dens from which every idea, good or bad, is made a starting-point for business. Clever in putting the best appearance on everything, quite unscrupulous as to the means he employed, an adept at treating quibbles as arguments, much inclined to look on the property of others as his own, he launched out into a score of speculations which would gradually end in disaster, but not without leaving him a few pickings. At the opening of this history Len Burker was reduced to many shifts, and discomfort was in his house; but he still enjoyed a certain amount of credit, owing to his keeping his affairs quiet, and this he employed in making new dupes. The position, however, could only end in a catastrophe. The hour could not be distant when the claims would come in. Perhaps this adventurous Yankee, transplanted to Western America, would have no other resource but to leave San Diego as he had left Boston, although in a time of such enlightenment and such powerful commercial activity, the progress of which increased from year to year, an honest and intelligent man would have found a hundred opportunities of success. But Len Burker had neither honourable feelings, just ideas, nor honest intentions.

But it must be understood that neither John Branican nor William Andrew had any suspicion concerning the affairs of Len Burker. In the world of industry and commerce no one knew that this adventurer — and would to heaven he merited that name only — was approaching a disastrous end. And even when the catastrophe came about the world might see in him merely a man little favoured by fortune, and not one of those persons without morality, to whom every way of making money must be right. And so, without having taken a great liking to him, John Branican had conceived no mistrust towards him; and it was in all good faith that he reckoned on the kindness of the Burkers to his wife. If anything happened to make Dolly have recourse to them she would not go in vain. Their house was open to her, and she would there find a welcome due not only to a friend but to a sister.

In this respect there was no cause to suspect the sentiments of Jane Burker. The affection she entertained towards her cousin was without

20

restraint or calculation. Far from blaming the sincere friendship which united these two young women, Len Burker had encouraged it, on the contrary, doubtless with a confused notion of the future, and the advantages which this connection might bring. He knew, too, that Jane would never say a word she ought not to say, and that she would maintain a, prudent reserve regarding her personal position that she was ignorant of the blameworthy undertakings on which he had entered, of the difficulties amid which his housekeeping had to struggle on. And Jane was silent, and not a word of recrimination escaped her. She was completely overawed by her husband, and submissive to his absolute influence, although she knew him to be a man without conscience, destitute of any moral sense, and capable of committing the most unpardonable acts. After so many disillusions how could she retain the least respect for him? But — and this is the essential point — she feared him, she was like a child in his hands, and at a sign from him she would follow him, if his safety obliged him to fly to no matter what part of the world. But for her own self-respect she allowed no one to know her misery, not even her cousin Dolly, who perhaps suspected it without being taken into her confidence.

The relative positions of John and Dolly Branican on the one hand, and that of Len and Jane Burker on the other, is thus sufficiently clear for the understanding of the occurrences that followed. In what way would this position be altered by the unexpected which was so soon and so suddenly to happen? No one could have foreseen.

CHAPTER III - PROSPECT HOUSE

Thirty years ago Lower California — about a third of the State of California — contained only about thirty-five thousand inhabitants. To-day its population is one hundred and fifty thousand. At that time the land of the province was almost uncultivated and was deemed only fit for cattle- raising. Who would have divined what the future had in reserve for a region then so abandoned that the only means of communication by land was the roads rutted with cart-wheels, and by sea a solitary line of packet-boats calling at every port on the coast?

But ever since 1769 the embryo of a town existed a few miles in the interior to the north of the Bay of San Diego, which town has the historical claim of being the most ancient settlement on Californian soil.

When the new continent, attached to old Europe by the simple colonial ties which the United Kingdom thought to tighten, had been given a violent shock, these ties were broken, and the union of the States of North America was founded under the flag of independence; but in those days California belonged to the Mexicans, and it continued in their possession until 1846. In that year, after receiving its freedom, the municipality of San Diego, formed eleven years before, became what it should always be — American.

The bay of San Diego is magnificent. It has been compared with the bay of Naples, but the comparison would be more exact if made with the bays of Vigo or Rio Janeiro. Twelve miles long and two miles wide it gives enough space for the anchorage of a merchant fleet as well as for the manoeuvres of a squadron, for San Diego is considered to be a military port. Forming a kind of oval, opening to the westward by a narrow mouth between Island Point and Loma or Coronado Point, it is sheltered on all sides. The winds from the open sea respect it, the swell from the Pacific hardly troubles its surface, ships get away from it without difficulty, and come alongside the quays in a minimum of twenty-three feet of water. It is the only port, safe, practicable, suitable for putting in at, south of San Francisco and north of San Quentin.

With so many natural advantages, it was evident that the old town would soon be found too small as at first laid out. Already barracks had been built for the installation of a detachment of cavalry on some adjoining ground which was covered with brushwood. Owing to Mr. Horton's initiative a suburb to this was begun, and this has now become the city which now stands on the ridges at the north of the bay. The expansion took place with that celerity so familiar to Americans. A million of dollars sown on the ground germinated as private houses, public buildings, offices and villas. In 1885 San Diego contained fifteen thousand inhabitants, to-day it has thirty-five thousand. Its first railroad dates from 1881. At present the Atlantic and Pacific, the Southern California, and the Southern Pacific put it in communication with the continental network, and the Pacific Coast Steamship Company gives it constant intercourse with San Francisco.

It is a handsome, comfortable town, airy and healthy, with a climate beyond eulogy. In the vicinity the country is of incomparable fertility. The vine, the olive, the orange, the citron grow side by side with the fruits and vegetables of northern climes. We might call it a Normandy combined with a Provence.

The town itself is built with that picturesque freedom of position and private fancy which is conducive to health when there is plenty of space. If progress under all its forms is not to be met with in a modern city, more especially when this city is American, where should we look for it? Gas, telegraph, telephone — the inhabitants have but to make a sign to be lighted, to exchange messages, to speak in each other's ears between one quarter of the town and another. There are even masts a hundred and fifty feet high which shed the electric light over the streets of the town. If the milk is not yet distributed under pressure by the General Milk Company, if moving footpaths running four miles an hour are not yet working at San Diego, this will certainly be done — eventually.

To these advantages we must add the different institutions in which is controlled the vital movement of these great agglomerations — a custom house, the importance of which increases daily, two banks, a chamber of commerce, an emigration society, vast offices, numerous counting houses, in which an enormous trade is carried on in timber and flour; churches for different denominations, three markets, a theatre, a gymnasium; three large schools for poor children, the Russ House, the Masonic and the Odd Fellows'; a number of establishments in which studies are carried on for the gaining of university diplomas — and we can imagine what will be the future of a city, still young and compulsorily careful of its moral and material interests, within which are accumulated so many elements of prosperity. Are newspapers unknown to it? No! It possesses three daily sheets, among others the Herald, and these papers have each a weekly edition. Is there any fear of tourists being unable to find comfortable quarters? Without counting the hotels of inferior order, are there not at their choice the three magnificent establishments — the Horton House, the Florence Hotel, and the Gerard Hotel with its hundred rooms, and on the opposite side of the bay, overlooking the beach at Coronado Point, on an admirable site amid charming villas, a new hotel which has not cost less than five million dollars'?

From all the countries of the old continent and from all points of the new, come tourists to visit this young and lively capital of Lower California, where they are hospitably welcomed by its generous inhabitants, and in no way regret the voyage — unless it be that they thought it too short.

San Diego is a town full of animation and well organized in all. the confusion of its business like the majority of American cities. If life is shown by movement, one can say its people live in the most intense sense of the word. They have scarcely time enough for their commercial transactions. But if that is so for the people whose instincts and habits throw them into the whirlpool, it is no longer true of those whose existence drags on in interminable leisure. When the movement stops the hours cannot go too slowly!

And thus did Mrs. Branican feel after the departure of the *Franklin*. Since her marriage she had helped her husband in his work. Although he did not go to sea, his business with Andrews' gave John a good deal to do. Besides the commercial transactions in which he took part, he had had to superintend the building of the ship to which he was to be appointed. With what zeal, we might almost say with what love, did he look after the smallest details. He gave it all the incessant care of a man building the house in which he is to pass his life. And more so, for the ship is not only a house, or a mere instrument of fortune, but an assemblage of wood and iron to which is confided the lives of so many men. Is it not as it were a detached fragment of the native soil to which it returns to leave it again, and which unfortunately destiny often forbids from finishing its maritime career in the port in which it was born?

Frequently would Dolly accompany Captain John to the shipyard. This framework, which rose on the sloping keel, the curves arranged like the ribs of a gigantic mammifer, the planking which was to go on; this hull of complex form, this deck with the large openings in it destined for loading and unloading the cargo; the masts laid on the ground until they are in place, the poop and its cabins, could not all this interest her? It was John's life and that of his companions that the *Franklin* would defend from the surges of the Pacific. Could there be a plank, therefore, to which Dolly did not in her thought attach some chance of safety, a hammer stroke, amid the noise of the shipyard, which did not echo in her heart? John explained everything to her, told her the destination of each piece of wood or metal, and showed her how the progress accorded with the working drawings. She loved this ship of which John was to be the soul, the master, after God! And sometimes she would ask, when she did not go with John, why he did not take her with him, why she did not share with him the perils of the journey, why the *Franklin* did not take her as well as him from San Diego? Yes! She wished never to be separated from her husband. And had not seafaring households, afloat for many years, existed for a long time among the people of the north?

But there was Wat, the baby, and could Dolly abandon him to the cares of a nurse far away from maternal caresses? No! Could she take him to sea, exposing him to the eventualities of a voyage so dangerous for such little creatures? - Not at all. Therefore she must stop at San Diego with the child, to preserve the life that had been given him, without leaving him for an instant; surrounding him with affection and tenderness in order that as he blossomed forth in health he might smile when his father returned. And the captain would not be away more than six months. After taking in a new cargo at Calcutta the *Franklin* would return to her port of registry. And, besides, was it not advisable for a sailor's wife to become accustomed to these inevitable separations?

It was necessary to become resigned to it, and Dolly did resign herself to it. But after John's departure, as soon as the movement which was life to her had ceased around her, how vacant, monotonous and desolate her life would have been if she had not been absorbed in her child, if she had not concentrated on him all her love.

John Branican's house was on one of the upper levels of the heights which surround the shore of the bay. It was a sort of chalet, standing in a little garden, planted with orange trees and olive trees, enclosed with a wooden fence. A ground floor with a path along the front, on to which opened the door and the windows of the drawing and dining rooms, a first floor with a balcony the whole length, and above it the graceful gables of the roof — such was this very simple and attractive dwelling. On the ground floor were the drawing and dining rooms, modestly furnished. On the first floor were two rooms occupied by Mrs. Branican and the child, behind the house a small annexe for the kitchen and offices; that was the interior plan of the chalet. Prospect House rejoiced in an exceptionally fine position owing to its southern aspect. The view extended over the entire town, and across the bay to the buildings on Loma Point. It was rather too far away from the business quarter undoubtedly; but this slight disadvantage was amply compensated for by the chalet's position in a good atmosphere, exposed to the southerly breezes, laden with the saline odours of the Pacific.

26

It was in this house that the-long hours of absence for Dolly were to be passed. The baby's nurse and a domestic were the only servants. The only persons who visited it were Mr. and Mrs. Burker — Len rarely, Jane frequently. Mr. William Andrew, according to his promise, often called on the young wife to acquaint her with all the news of the *Franklin* which might reach him directly or indirectly. Before any letters could come the maritime journals would record the vessels spoken with, their arrival in port, and the different shipping news of interest to shipowners. Dolly would thus be kept up to date. As to the people around and her neighbours, she was accustomed to the isolation of Prospect House and had never sought acquaintanceship. One thought occupied her life, and even if visitors had crowded to the chalet, it would have seemed empty to her, for John was not there, and it would remain empty until his return.

The first few days were very sad for her. Dolly never went out of the house when Jane Burker came to see her.

They Spent their time with little Wat and in speaking of Captain John. Generally, when she was alone, Dolly would spend a part of the day on the balcony, looking out beyond the bay, beyond Island Point, beyond the Coronado Islands, beyond the horizon. The *Franklin* was far away, but in thought she was on board of her and near her husband. And when a ship came into view and sought the harbour she would say to herself that one day the *Franklin* would also appear, and grow larger as she neared the land, that John would be on board.

But little Wat's health would not be improved by rigid seclusion within Prospect House. In the second week after the departure the weather had become very fine and the breezes tempered the growing heat. So Mrs. Branican deemed it necessary to go out. She took with her the nurse to carry the baby. They went for a walk as far as the outskirts of San Diego, as far as the houses of the Old Town. That was of great benefit to the child, who was fresh and rosy, and when the nurse stopped he clapped his little hands and smiled at his mother. Once or twice, for longer excursions a pretty chaise, hired in the neighbourhood, took out the three, or rather the four, for Mrs. Burker formed one of the party. One day they went as far as Knob Hill, which rises near the Florence Hotel, from which the view extends beyond the islands to the west. Another day the drive extended to Coronado Beach, on which the furious sea beat like thunder. Then they visited the Mussel Beds, where the high tide covers the superb rocks with its spray. Dolly touched with her foot this ocean, which bore as it were an echo from the distant regions where John was then sailing — this ocean, the waves of which were perhaps dashing against the *Franklin* thousands of miles away. And she stood there motionless, seeing the young captain's ship in the flight of her imagination, and murmuring the name of John.

On the 30th of March Mrs. Branican was on the balcony when she perceived Mrs. Burker coming towards Prospect House. Jane was hurrying along, and signalled joyfully with her hand, a proof that she brought no bad news. Dolly immediately went downstairs to meet her at the door.

"What is the matter, Jane?" «he asked.

"Dear Dolly," replied Mrs. Burker, "I have something to tell you which will please you. I have come from Mr. William Andrew to tell you that the *Boundary* came in this morning and has spoken the *Franklin*."

"The *Franklin*?"

"Yes! Mr. William Andrew had just heard it when he met me in Fleet Street, and as he could not come on here until the afternoon, I hurried on in his place to tell you."

"And is there any news of John?"

"Yes, Dolly."

"What? Tell me."

"Eight days ago the *Franklin* and the *Boundary* passed each other on the sea and communicated with each other."

"Was all well on board?"

"Yes, dear Dolly. The two captains were near enough to shout to each other, and the last word heard on the *Boundary* was your name."

"My poor John!" exclaimed Mrs. Branican, with tears of love in her eyes.

"I am so glad, Dolly," said Mrs. Burker, "to have been the first to bring you the news."

"And I thank you!" said Mrs. Branican. "If you only knew how happy you have made me! Ah! If every day I could hear of my John — my dear John! The captain of the *Boundary* has seen you. John has spoken to him — it is like another good-bye he has sent me!"

"Yes, dear Dolly, and I tell you again that all was well on board the *Franklin*!'

"Jane," said Mrs. Branican, "I must see this captain of the *Boundary*. He will tell me more in detail. When did the meeting take place?"

"That I do not know," said Jane, "but the log book would tell us, and the captain of the *Boundary* will give you full information."

"Well, Jane, let me put on my things and we will go off together at once."

"No. Not to-day, Dolly," said Mrs. Burker; "we cannot go on board the *Boundary*."

"And why not?"

"Because she only arrived this morning, and she is in quarantine."

"For how long?"

"Oh! For twenty-four hours only. It is merely a matter of form, but no one can — "

29

"And how did Mr. William Andrew come to know about this meeting?"

"Through a message sent through the custom house by the captain. Dear Dolly, be easy. There is no doubt at all about what I have told you, and you can have the confirmation of it to-morrow. I only ask a day's patience."

"Well, Jane, to-morrow," replied Mrs. Branican. "Tomorrow I will be at your house at nine o'clock in the morning. You will then come with me on to the *Boundary*?"

"Willingly, dear Dolly. I will go with you to-morrow, and then, as the quarantine will have been raised, we can be received by the captain."

"Is not Captain Ellis a friend of John's?" asked Mrs. Branican.

"Yes, Dolly, and the *Boundary* belongs to Andrews'."

"Then it is agreed, Jane. I shall be with you at the time named. But the day will be very long for me. Will you have luncheon with me?"

"If you like, my dear Dolly. Mr. Burker is away until this evening, and we can spend the afternoon."

"Yes, dear John, and we will talk about John — always about him — always!"

"And little Wat? How is the baby?" asked Mrs. Burker.

"He is very well!" said Dolly. "He is as happy as a bird. How glad his father will be to see him again! Jane, I have a great mind to take him and his nurse with us to-morrow! You know I don't like to be separate from my child even for a few hours. I should never be easy if he were out of my sight — if I did not have him with me."

"You are right, Dolly," said Mrs. Burker, "it is a good idea. Little Wat will be all the better for the outing. It is fine weather, the bay is calm. It will be his first sea voyage, the dear child! Is it agreed?"

"It is agreed!" said Mrs. Branican.

Jane remained at Prospect House until five o'clock in the afternoon. Then, as she left her cousin, she repeated that she would expect her at nine o'clock next morning to accompany her on board the *Boundary*.

CHAPTER IV - ON BOARD THE "BOUNDARY"

In the morning they were up early at Prospect House. The weather was superb. The breeze off the land blew the last mists of the night away out to sea. The nurse dressed little Wat, while Mrs. Branican was busy at her toilette. It had been agreed that she would lunch with Mrs. Burker; and so she contented herself with a light meal which would last her till noon, for very probably the visit to Captain Ellis would take two good hours. Everything the brave captain told her would be so interesting.

Mrs. Branican, and the nurse with the child in her arms, left the chalet as the clocks of San Diego were chiming half-past eight. The wide streets of the upper town, bordered with villas and gardens, were descended at a good pace, and Dolly reached the narrower streets more crowded with houses, which form the business quarter. Len Burker lived in Fleet Street, not far from the wharf belonging to the Pacific Coast Steamship Company. In short, Mrs. Branican had made a good passage, for she had come right through the city, and it was just nine o'clock when she entered Jane's house.

It was a small house and of rather melancholy aspect, with its Venetian shutters generally closed. Len Burker's friends were almost always men of business, as he had no acquaintances with his neighbours. Little was known of him even in Fleet Street, and his business frequently kept him away from morning till night. Often, too, he went on journeys, and most frequently to San Francisco, on matters of which he never spoke to his wife. This morning he was not in the office when Mrs. Branican arrived. Jane Burker made an excuse for her husband not being able to accompany them in their visit to the *Boundary*, adding that he would certainly be back to lunch.

"I am ready, my dear Dolly," said she, after kissing the baby. "You do not want to wait?"

"I am not tired," said Mrs. Branican.

"You do not want anything?"

"No, Jane. I am anxious to see Captain Ellis. Let us be off at once, please."

Mrs. Burker had but one servant — an old woman, a mulatto whom her husband had brought from New York when he had come to San Diego. This mulatto, whose name was No, had been Len Burker's nurse. Having always lived in his family, she was entirely devoted to him, and still talked to him as if he were a child. This uncouth, imperious creature was the only one who had ever exercised any influence over Len Burker, who had completely handed over to her the management of his house. Often Jane had had to put up with a domination almost exceeding bounds, "and of which her husband entirely approved. But she submitted to the domination of the mulatto as she did to that of her husband. In her resignation, which was nothing but feebleness, she left matters to themselves, and Nô consulted her in nothing as to the management of the household.

Just as Jane was going away the mulatto advised her to be back before noon, for Len Burker would return for lunch, and certainly would not wait for her. Besides he wished to see Mrs. Branican on important business — so said No.

"What is it about?" asked Dolly of her cousin.

"And how should I know?" answered Mrs. Burker. "Come, Dolly, come!"

Mrs. Branican and Jane Burker, accompanied by the nurse and the child, left the house and walked towards the wharf, where they arrived in a few minutes.

The *Boundary*, whose quarantine had just been raised, had not yet come alongside the berth reserved for Andrews' ships. She was moored in the bay about a cable's length from Point Loma. It was thus necessary to cross the bay to get on board the vessel, which would not move up for two hours. This meant a passage of about two miles, which the steam launches started on every half hour.

As soon as they arrived Dolly and Jane took their places in the steam launch with about a dozen other passengers. Most of them were friends or relatives of the crew of the *Boundary*, who were taking advantage of the first opportunity to visit them on board the vessel. The launch let go her painter, sheered off from the wharf, and under the impulse of her screw headed obliquely across the bay, puffing at every stroke.

In the limpid clearness of the weather, the bay was visible all round, with the amphitheatre of the houses of San Diego, the hill dominating the Old Town, the mouth open between Island Point and Loma Point, the immense Coronado hotel of grandiose architecture, and the lighthouse which rayed forth its light over the sea after the setting of the sun.

There were several ships moored here and there, which the launch avoided cleverly, as she did also the boats coming in the opposite direction, and the fishing boats going close-hauled so as to fetch the point in one tack.

Mr. Branican sat near Jane on one of the seats aft. The nurse, near them, held the child in her arms. The baby did not sleep, and his eyes filled with the light which the breeze seemed to brighten with its breath. He jumped when a couple of gulls passed over the launch, uttering their sharp cry. He was blooming with health, with his fresh cheeks and his rosy lips, still humid with the milk he had drawn from the bosom of his nurse before he had left the Burkers. His mother regarded him with emotion, bending over him to kiss him, while he smiled in return.

But Dolly's attention was soon attracted by the sight of the *Boundary*. Lying apart now from the other vessels, the three-master, clearly outlined at the end of the bay, was flying her flags against the sunny sky. She was swinging with the tide, her bow to the westward at the extremity of her straining cable, on which the last undulations of the surge were breaking.

34

All Dolly's life was in her look. She thought of John, carried away on a ship the sister of this one, so much were they alike. And were they not both children of the house of Andrew? Were they not both of the same port? Were they not both built in the same yard?

Dolly, beset by the charm of the illusion, her imagination stimulated by the remembrance, abandoned herself to the idea that John was there on board, that he was waiting for her, that he would stretch out his hand to her when he saw her, that she would be able to jump into his arms. His name rose to her lips, she called him, and he answered by uttering her name.

Then a gentle cry from her child recalled her from sentiment to reality. It was the *Boundary* towards which she was going, and not the *Franklin*, which was far, far away, thousands of leagues from the American shore.

"She will be there — one day — in that very place!" she murmured, looking at Mrs. Burker.

"Yes, dear Dolly," answered Jane. "And it will be John who will welcome us on board."

She was conscious that a vague uneasiness was wringing the heart of the young wife when she asked about the future.

However, the steam launch had in a quarter of an hour covered the two miles which separate the San Diego wharf from Point Loma. The passengers landed on the pier at the beach, and had then to return towards the *Boundary* a little more than a cable's length away.

At the foot of the pier in charge of two sailors was a boat plying to and from the three-master. Mrs. Branican hailed it, and the men put it at her disposal to take her to the *Boundary* as soon as she was assured that Captain Ellis was then on board.

A few strokes of the oars were enough, and Captain Ellis having recognized Mrs. Branican, came to the side as she was coming up the ladder, followed by Jane, not without having cautioned the nurse to hold on tight to the baby. The captain took them to the poop, while the mate began the preparations to take the ship alongside the wharf at San Diego.

"Mr. 'Ellis," said Mrs. Branican at once, "I hear you met the *Franklin*?"

"Yes, madam," said the captain, "and I can assure you she was in good condition, as I have already reported to Mr. William Andrew."

"You have seen — John?"

"The *Franklin* and the *Boundary* passed so close on different tacks that Captain Branican and I were able to exchange a few words."

"Yes! You saw him!" repeated Mrs. Branican, as if she were talking to herself and seeking a reflection of the sight of the *Franklin* in the captain's eyes.

Mrs. Burker then asked several questions, to which Dolly listened attentively, although her eyes were turned towards the horizon of sea.

"On that occasion," said Captain Ellis, "the weather was very favourable and the *Franklin* was running free under all plain canvas. Captain Branican was on the poop, his telescope in his hand. He had bluffed a point so as to approach the *Boundary*, for I had not been able to change my course, being as close to the wind as I could haul without shivering my sails."

Mrs. Branican doubtless did not understand the full meaning of Captain Ellis's terms, but what she remembered was that he had spoken with John, who had exchanged a few words with him.

"When we were alongside each other," added he, "your husband, Mrs. Branican, waved me a salute with his hand and shouted: 'All's right with us, Ellis! As soon as you get to San Diego give news of me to my wife, to my dear Dolly!' And then the two vessels parted, and in a few minutes were a long way from each other."

36

"And what day was it that you met the *Franklin*?" asked Mrs. Branican.

"On the 23rd of March," answered Captain Ellis, "at 11.25. a m."

It was then better to go into detail, and the captain pointed out on the chart the exact point at which the ships had crossed. It was in 145 deg. of longitude and 20 deg. of latitude that the *Boundary* had met the *Franklin*, that is to say, at seventeen hundred miles from San Diego. If the weather continued favourable — and there was a chance that it would with the fine season now becoming established — Captain John would make a quick and fortunate passage across the North Pacific. And as he would find a cargo as soon as he arrived at Calcutta, he would stay but a short time in the capital of India, and his return for America would promptly take place. The *Franklin*'s absence would thus be limited to five or six months, as foreseen and expected by her owners.

While Captain Ellis answered sometimes Mrs. Burker, sometimes Mrs. Branican, Dolly, carried away by her imagination, figured to herself that she was on board the '*Franklin*. It was not Ellis — it was John who was telling her these things. It was his voice she was listening to.

At this moment the mate mounted the poop and told the captain that the preparations were almost complete. The sailors on the forecastle were only waiting for the order to weigh the anchor.

Captain Ellis then offered to set Mrs. Branican ashore, unless she preferred to remain on board, in which case she could cross the bay on the *Boundary* and land when she was alongside the wharf, which would be in about two hours.

Mrs. Branican would have very willingly accepted the captain's offer; but she was expected to lunch at noon, when Len Burker would have returned. She knew that Jane, after what the mulatto had said, would rather be at home at the same time as her husband. She therefore asked

Captain Ellis to put her ashore at the pier, where she could get away in the first launch.

Orders were given in consequence. Mrs. Branican and Mrs. Burker took leave of the captain, after he had kissed little Wat's cheeks. Then the two cousins, preceding the nurse, descended into one of the ship's boats, and in a few minutes reached the pier.

While waiting for the steam launch which had just left San Diego, Mrs. Branican observed the manoeuvres of the *Boundary*. To the rugged song of the boatswain, the sailors shortened in the cable and the three-master came up to her anchor, while the mate hoisted the jib, the forestay- sail and the mizen. Under this canvas she would easily move up to her station with the incoming tide.

Soon the launch came in. Then she gave a few puffs of the whistle to call the passengers, and two or three dilatory ones had to hurry coming over the point in front of the Coronado Hotel. The launch waited only five minutes. Mrs. Branican, Jane Burker, and the nurse took their seats on the bench on the starboard side, while the other passengers — about twenty in number — moved about from the front to the after-part of the vessel. There was a final whistle, the screw was put in movement, and the launch left the shore It was but half-past eleven. Mrs. Branican would thus be back at the house in Fleet Street in time, for the crossing of the bay only took a quarter of an hour. As the launch moved away her eyes were fixed on the *Boundary*. The anchor was apeak, the sails had caught the wind, and the vessel had begun to leave her anchorage. When she was moored at the wharf Dolly could visit Captain Ellis as often as she liked.

The steam launch sped along swiftly. The houses of the town grew larger on the picturesque amphitheatre which they occupied at different levels. It was only a quarter of a mile now to the landing-place.

"Look out! Look out!" shouted one of the sailors posted in the bow.

And he turned to the man at the helm who stood on a little bridge in front of the funnel.

38

Hearing the shout, Mrs. Branican looked away to port where something was taking place which also attracted the attention of the other passengers, most of whom had gone to the bow of the launch.

A large brigantine was coming out from the line of vessels along the quays with her bow directed towards Island Point. She was being assisted by a tug which would take her out to sea, and was already moving at some speed.

At the moment the brigantine was just in the course of the steam launch and so near that it was necessary for the launch to pass under her stern. It was this which caused the sailor to shout to the man at the helm.

A certain anxiety seized upon the passengers — an anxiety all the more justifiable as the harbour was crowded with ships moored here and there at their anchors. And by a very natural movement they drew back towards the stern.

It was clear what ought to be done. The launch ought to stop and give way to the tug and brigantine, and resume its progress when the course was clear. A few fishing boats running before the wind made this course more difficult as they crossed in front of the wharves of San Diego.

"Look out!" said the sailor at the bow.

"All right!" said the man at the helm. "There is nothing to fear. I have room enough!"

But embarrassed by the sudden apparition of a large steamer coming in, the tug made an unexpected movement, and fell away to port.

There were loud shouts, to which were added those of the brigantine's crew, endeavouring to help the tug by steering in the same direction.

There was hardly twenty feet between the tug and the steam launch.

Jane, very frightened, had stood up. Mrs. Branican, by an instinctive impulse, took little Wat from his nurse's arms and clasped him in hers.

39

"Port! Port!" shouted the captain of the tug to the helmsman of the launch, motioning with his hand the direction he should take.

The man had not lost his coolness, and suddenly put down the helm with all his might, so as to get out of the way of the tug, which could not stop, owing to the brigantine having begun to yaw and give signs of sidling on to her.

At the lift of the helm, which was very powerful, the launch shot over sharply to port, and, as frequently happens, the passengers losing their equilibrium were all thrown to the same side.

There was another shouting, this time a shout of terror, for it looked as though the launch was about to capsize.

At this moment Mrs. Branican, who was standing near the rail, could not recover her footing, was hurled overboard and disappeared with her child.

The brigantine was then almost grazing the launch as she passed, and all danger of collision was over.

"Dolly! Dolly!" screamed Jane, whom one of the passengers caught as she was falling.

Suddenly a sailor from the steam launch jumped over the rail on the side where Mrs. Branican and the child had just disappeared.

Dolly, kept up by her clothes, was floating at the surface of the water with little Wat, whom she held in her arms, when the sailor came near her.

The launch having stopped, it would not be difficult for the sailor, a strong man and good swimmer, to get back with Mrs. Branican. Unfortunately, as he was seizing her by the waist, the arms of the unfortunate woman opened while she struggled, half suffocated; and the baby rolled out of them and sank.

When Mrs. Branican was lifted on to the launch and laid on the deck she had quite lost consciousness.

Again the brave sailor — a man of about thirty, named Zach Fren — threw himself into the sea, dived several times, and searched in the water about where the launch lay. It was in vain; he could not find the child, which had been borne away by an undercurrent.

Meanwhile the passengers were giving Mrs. Branican all the attention her state required. Jane, distracted, the nurse, frantic, endeavoured to bring her to consciousness. The steam launch, motionless, waited until Zach Fren had given up all hope of recovering little Wat.

At length Dolly began to recover her senses; she murmured the name of Wat, her eyes opened, and her first cry was, —

"My child!"

Zach Fren came on board for the last time. Wat was not in his arms: "My child!" again cried Dolly. Then she rose, and pushing aside those who surrounded her, ran towards the stern.

And if she had not been stopped, she would have thrown herself overboard; and they had to hold her while the steam launch resumed its journey towards the wharf.

With her face convulsed, and her hands clenched, she had fallen on the deck. A few minutes afterwards the launch had reached the landing-place, and Mrs. Branican was taken to Jane's house. Len Burker, who had just come in, sent the mulatto out for a doctor.

The doctor came almost immediately, and it was not without trouble that Dolly again came to.

And then looking with a fixed stare she said, —

"What is the matter? What has happened? Ah! I know!"

Then with a smile —

"It is my John! He returns! He returns!" she cried. "He has come back to his wife and child! John I There is my John!"

Mrs. Branican had lost her reason.

41

CHAPTER V - THREE MONTHS ELAPSE

HOW can we describe the effect produced in San Diego by this double catastrophe of the death of the child and the madness of the mother? We know the people's sympathy with the Branicans, the interest they took in the young captain of the *Franklin*. He had been gone scarcely a fortnight, and he was no longer a father. His wife was mad. On his return, in his empty house, he would find neither the smiles of his little Wat nor the tendernesses of Dolly, who would not even recognize him. The day the *Franklin* returned to port he would not be saluted by the cheers of the town.'

But it was not necessary to wait for John Branican's return to inform him of the horrible misfortune that had just occurred to him. Mr. William Andrew could not leave Captain John in ignorance of what had passed, and at the mercy of some fortuitous circumstance to hear of the terrible catastrophe. He would immediately send off a letter to one of his correspondents at Singapore. In this way John would know the awful truth before reaching India.

But Mr. William Andrew wished to delay the sending of this message. Perhaps Dolly's reason was not irremediably lost? Perhaps the care with which she was being nursed would restore her to her senses? Why strike John a double blow, in telling him of the death of his child and the madness of his wife, if this madness was to be only short-lived?

After talking the matter over with Len and Jane Burker, Mr. William Andrew resolved to wait until the doctors had pronounced a definite opinion as to Dolly's mental state. In these cases of sudden .alienation was there not more hope of cure than in those due to a slow disorganization of the intellectual life? Yes; and it would be better to wait a few days, or even a few weeks.

The town, however, was plunged in consternation. Crowds came to the house in Fleet Street for news of Mrs. Branican. Meanwhile the minutest search had been made in the bay to recover the body of the child, but without success. Apparently it had been borne away on the flood, and then taken out to sea by the ebb. The poor little child would not even have a grave, at which his mother could pray if she recovered her. reason.

At first the doctors reported that Dolly's madness was of the form of a gentle melancholy. There were no nervous crises, none of those unconscious outbreaks of violence, which compel us to put the afflicted under restraint, and render all movement impossible. There seemed, therefore, no necessity to take precautions against the excesses which mad people frequently commit on others or on themselves. Dolly was merely a body without a mind, an intelligence in which there remained no remembrance of the horrible misfortune. Her eyes were dry, her look lifeless. She seemed not to see; she seemed not to hear. She was. not of this world. She lived only the material life.

Such was Mrs. Branican's state during the first, month after-the accident. There had been a consultation as to the advisability of putting her in an asylum where special attention would be given her. This was the suggestion of Mr. William Andrew, and it would have been acted on had it not been for a proposal made by Len Burker.

One day Len Burker went to call on Mr. William Andrew, and spoke to him as follows: "We are now pertain that Dolly's madness is not of a dangerous character necessitating her being put under restraint, and as we are her only relatives, we wish to keep her with us. Dolly is very fond of my wife, and Jane's nursing might probably be of greater effect than that of a stranger? If a crisis occurs later on, we can then consider the matter, and take our measures accordingly. What do you think, Mr. Andrew?"

The worthy ship-owner did not reply without a certain amount of hesitation, for he had no confidence in Len Burker, although he knew nothing of his precarious position and had no suspicion of his honesty. After all, the friendship between Dolly and Jane was real, and as Mrs. Burker was her only relative, it evidently seemed better that Dolly should be entrusted to her care. The main point was that the unhappy

43

woman should be constantly and effectually Looked after in the way her state required.

"If you are willing to take this trouble," said Mr. William Andrew, "I see nothing, Mr. Burker, against Dolly being entrusted to her cousin, of whose affection there is no doubt."

"An affection which will never fail!" said Len Burker. But he said it in a cold, positive, displeasing tone which he could not throw off.

"I approve of your offer," said Mr. William Andrew. "But there is one thing I must say. I am not certain that in your house in Fleet Street, in the noisy business quarter of the town, poor Dolly would find herself under favourable circumstances for her return to health. She wants quiet,- good air."

"Quite so," answered Len Burker. "Our intention is to take her to Prospect House and there live with her. The chetlet is familiar to her, and the sight of objects to which she is accustomed may perhaps exercise a salutary influence on her mind. There she will be away from all worry. The country is at her door. Jane can take her out for walks in the neighbourhood, which she knows and which she used to take with her child. Would not John approve of this proposition were he here? And what will he think when he comes back if he finds his wife in a lunatic asylum entrusted to mercenary hands? Mr. Andrew, we should neglect nothing which might be of a nature to exercise an influence on the mind of our unfortunate relative."

This reply was evidently dictated by good feeling. But why did this man's words always appear to inspire distrust? Nevertheless his proposal, in the way it was offered, was deserving of acceptance, and Mr. William Andrew could only thank him for it, adding that Captain John would be deeply grateful to him.

On the 27th of April, Mrs. Branican was taken to Prospect House, where Jane and Len Burker installed themselves the same day. The course received general approval.

Len Burker's motive can be guessed. The very day of the catastrophe he had, it will be remembered, intended to consult Dolly on certain business. This business was simply to borrow some money from her. But since then the situation had changed. It was probable that Len Burker would be appointed her trustee, and in that way would become possessed of resources, illicit no doubt, which would enable him to gain time. This was exactly what Jane had feared, and although she was happy at being able to devote herself entirely to Dolly, she trembled at the suspicion of the plan her husband proposed under cover of a feeling of humanity.

Life, then, began under new conditions at Prospect House. Dolly was installed in the same room from which she had gone forth to meet with her dreadful misfortune. It was no longer the mother that returned, but a being deprived of reason. This chalet so loved, this drawing- room in which a few photographs recalled the memory of the absent one, this garden in which the two had passed so many happy hours, told her nothing of the past. Jane occupied the next room to Mrs. Branican, and Len Burker had taken possession of the room on the ground floor, which had been John's work-room.

From this day Len Burker resumed his usual occupations. Every morning he went down into San Diego, to his office in Fleet Street, where he continued to carry on his business. But it was noticeable that he never failed to return in the evening to Prospect House, and only went out of the town on short absences.

The mulatto woman had of course followed her master to his new dwelling, where she was what she had been everywhere and always, a person on whose entire devotion he could count. Little Wat's nurse had been discharged, although she had offered to stay and look after Mrs. Branican. As to the servant, she was temporarily continued on at the chalet so as to help No, who was not quite equal to all the work of the household.

No one could have been more assiduous than Jane in her affectionate care of Dolly. Her friendship was increased, if possible, since the death of the child, of which she accused herself as being the primary cause. If she had, not come to Dolly at Prospect House, if she had not suggested the idea of the visit to the captain of the *Boundary*, the baby would still be with his mother and consoling her during the long hours of absence; and Dolly would not have lost her reason.

It doubtless entered into Len Burker's calculations that Jane's attention should appear sufficient to those who were interested in Mrs. Branican's position. . Even Mr. William Andrew acknowledged that the unfortunate woman could not be in better hands. In the course of his visits his first care was to discover if Dolly's state showed any tendency towards amelioration, wishing still to hope that the first message sent to the captain at Singapore or Calcutta would not announce the double misfortune of his child dead — his wife — And was it not as if she were dead, she also? Well, no! He could not believe that Dolly, in the strength of her youth, with her enlightened mind and energetic character, had been irretrievably deprived of her intelligence! Was it not only a fire hidden in ashes? Surely some spark would one day kindle again? But five weeks had now gone by and no flash of reason had dissipated the darkness. In a case like this of calm, reserved, languishing madness, with no physiological excitement, the doctors seemed to have but the very slightest hope, and they soon began to leave off their visits. Soon even Mr. William Andrew, despairing of cure, began to come less frequently to Prospect House, it being painful to him to find himself in the presence of this unfortunate woman, who was unable even to recognize him.

When Len Burker was obliged for one reason or another to be away for a day, the mulatto was ordered to keep a careful eye on Mrs. Branican. Without seeking to interfere with Jane in any way, she rarely left her alone, and faithfully reported to her master all she had remarked in Dolly's condition. She exercised her ingenuity in getting rid of the few people who called in search of news at the chalet. It was contrary to the doctor's orders, she said. Absolute quiet was necessary. These interruptions might occasion serious consequences. And Mrs. Burker herself sided with Nô when she got rid of visitors and nuisances who had no business at Prospect House. And so Mrs. Branican became isolated.

"Poor Dolly!" thought Jane. "If her state gets worse, if her mania becomes violent — they will take her away — they will shut her up in an asylum, and I may very likely see her no more. No! Heaven leave her to me. Who would look after her as lovingly as I do?"

During the third week of May, Jane tried a few walks in the neighbourhood, thinking it would do her cousin a little good. Len Burker made no objection, but on condition that Nô should accompany them. This, however, was only prudent. The walk, the fresh air, might have an effect on Dolly and suggest to her mind the idea of flight; and Jane would not be strong enough to prevent her. Everything was to be feared from a madness which might even end in self-destruction. It would not do to expose her to another misfortune; Many times Mrs. Branican went out leaning on Jane's arm. She allowed herself to be led as if, she were a passive being, and took no interest in anything.

From the commencement of these walks, if nothing else happened, at least the mulatto woman noticed a change for the better in Dolly's state. Her habitual calm gave place to a certain exaltation which might have serious consequences. Several times the sight of children she met made her utter a nervous cry. Was this in remembrance of him she had lost? Did little Wat return to her thoughts? Whatever it might be, even admitting that it was a favourable symptom, there followed- a cerebral agitation of a disquieting nature.

One day Mrs. Burker and the mulatto had taken Mrs. Branican to the heights of Knob Hill. Dolly had turned towards the horizon, but it seemed that her brain was as void of thought as her eyes were vacant in look. Suddenly her face lighted up, a shudder shook her, her eye gave a strange glance, and with a trembling hand she pointed to a spot shining out at sea.

"There! there! "She exclaimed.

It was a sail clearly distinguished against the sky, on which the sun's rays fell.

"There! there!" repeated Dolly.

And her voice was quite changed and did not seem to belong to a human creature.

While Jane regarded her with anxiety, the mulatto shook her head in sign of dissatisfaction. Seizing Dolly's arm, she said, —

"Come! — come!"

Dolly did not hear her.

"Come, Dolly, come!" said Jane.

And she endeavoured to draw her away, to distract her attention from the sail moving on the horizon.

Dolly resisted.

"No, no!" she cried.

And she repulsed the mulatto with a strength of which she did not believe her capable.

Mrs. Burker and Nô became very anxious. They saw that Dolly might escape from them". If she were irresistibly attracted by this disturbing vision, in which John's memory predominated, might she not descend the slopes of Knob Hill and rush towards the beach which was swept by the waves?

But, suddenly, the excitement calmed down. The sun had just vanished behind a cloud, and the sail no longer appeared on the face of the ocean.

Dolly again became inert, her look became vacant and she was no longer conscious of what was going on. The sobs which had convulsively shaken her chest had ceased, as if life had departed from her. Then Jane took her by the hand, and she allowed her to lead her away without resistance, and peacefully went back into Prospect House.

From that day Len Burker decided that Dolly should take her walks only within the Prospect House enclosure, and Jane had to conform to this injunction.

It was at this time that Mr. William Andrew made up his mind to inform Captain John that the mental state of Mrs. Branican left little hope of improvement. It was not to Singapore, which the *Franklin* ought already to have left, but to Calcutta that the message was sent for John to receive as soon as he arrived in India.

But although Mr. William Andrew had no hope concerning Dolly, the doctors thought some change might still be produced in her mental state if she experienced some violent shock — for instance, when her husband reappeared before her eyes. This chance was, it is true, the only one left, but, feeble as it was, Mr. William Andrew took it into account. ' And in his message he had begged John not to abandon himself to despair, but to hand over the command of the *Franklin* to,the mate, Harry Felton, and come home by the quickest route. If it had been necessary, this excellent man would have sacrificed his dearest interests to try this last experiment, and he asked the young captain to telegraph back to him on this subject.

When Len Burker heard of this message, which Mr.

William Andrew had thought it right to communicate to him, he approved of it, though he expressed his fear that John's return would be powerless to produce a shock from which any salutary effect could be gained. But Jane held to the hope that the sight of John might bring Dolly back to reason, and Len Burker promised to write to him to this effect, in order that there might be no delay in his return to San Diego — a promise, however, he did not keep.

During the following weeks there was no change in Mrs. Branican's state. If her physical life was in no way troubled, if her health left nothing to be desired, the alteration in her face was only too apparent.

Although she had not yet reached her twenty-first year, her features were ageing and the warm colour of her complexion was fading, as if the fire of life were dying out within her. And it was only seldom she could be seen, unless in the chalet garden, seated on some bench, with Jane walking near and looking after her with indefatigable devotion.

At the beginning of the month of June the *Franklin* had been gone from San Diego two months and a half. Since her meeting with the *Boundary* there had been no news of her. By this, after putting in at Singapore, she ought, barring accidents, to be on the point of arrival at Calcutta. No exceptionally stormy weather had been reported in the North Pacific or Indian Ocean which would delay a well- equipped sailing-ship.

But Mr. William Andrew could not help being surprised at this want of news. He did not understand why his correspondent had not informed him of the arrival of the *Franklin* at Singapore. To suppose that she had not put in there was impossible, for Captain John had had precise orders to do so. But at any rate they would know in a day or two, when he arrived at Calcutta.

A week went by. The 15th of June came and there was no news. A message was then sent to the correspondent asking for an immediate reply regarding John Branican and the *Franklin*.

The reply arrived two days afterwards. Nothing was known of the *Franklin* at Calcutta. The American barquentine had not been spoken up to then either in the Indian Ocean or in the Gulf of Bengal.

Mr. William Andrew's surprise became changed to anxiety, and as it was impossible to keep the telegram secret, the report soon spread that the *Franklin* had not yet arrived at either Calcutta or Singapore. Was the Branican family to be struck with another disaster — a disaster which would also fall on the San Diego families to whom the crew of the *Franklin* belonged?

Len Burker did not show much concern when he learnt these alarming news. However, his affection for Captain John had never been very demonstrative, and he was not the man to be troubled by the misfortunes of others, even those of his own family. But it was evident that from the day people began to be seriously uneasy as to the fate of the *Franklin*, he appeared more gloomy than usual, more careworn, more reserved to all his friends — even in business. He was rarely seen in the streets of San Diego, at his office in Fleet Street, and he kept within the enclosure at Prospect House. As to Jane, her pale cheeks, her eyes red with tears, her deeply dispirited face showed that she was in great trouble.

Just about this time a change took place in the staff of the chalet. Without any apparent motive Len Burker sent away the servant he had kept to help No, and who had given no cause for complaint. The mulatto remained in sole charge of the house. With the exception of her and Jane, no one had access to Mrs. Branican. As to Mr. William Andrew, his health having suffered from these strokes of ill fortune, he had left off visiting Prospect House. In the event of the probable loss of the *Franklin* what could he say, what could he do? Besides, now that the walks had been stopped, he knew that Dolly had recovered all her quiet, and that her nervous troubles had disappeared. She lived, or rather she vegetated, in a state of unconscious tranquillity, which was the true character of her affliction, and her health required no special care.

At the end of June Mr. William Andrew received another message from Calcutta. The maritime agencies had had no report of the *Franklin* from any of the points she ought to have passed, among the Philippines, Celebes, the Java Sea, and the Indian Ocean; and as the vessel had left San Diego three months before, it was to be supposed that she had been totally lost, either by collision or shipwreck, before even reaching Singapore.

CHAPTER VI - THE END OF A SORROWFUL YEAR

The concurrence of serious events of which the Branican family had become the victim afforded Len Burker an opportunity to which our careful consideration should be directed.

It will not have been forgotten, that if the pecuniary position of Mrs. Branican was very modest, she would yet be the sole heiress of her uncle, Edward Starter. In retreat in his vast forest domain, banished, so to speak, in the most inaccessible part of the state of Tennessee, this eccentric man had absolutely refrained from sending any news of himself. As he was still but fifty-nine his fortune might be a long time coming.

Perhaps even Edward Starter would have changed his intentions had he known that Mrs. Branican, his only direct relative, had been struck with mental alienation after the death of her child. But he knew not of this double misfortune, he would not even hear of it, having always refused to receive letters as well as to write them. Evidently Len Burker could have broken this prohibition had he chosen to do so, in consideration of the changes that had come over Dolly's existence, and Jane had given him to understand that it was his duty to communicate with Edward Starter; but he had imposed silence on his wife and kept his own counsel.

It was his interest to be silent, and between his interest and his duty he was not the man to hesitate for an instant. His affairs daily took too .serious an aspect for him to sacrifice the sole chance of fortune the future offered.

The position was indeed a simple one: if Mrs. Branican died without children, her cousin Jane was the only- relative who could inherit her property; so that by the death of little Wat Len Burker had certainly seen an improvement in the chances of his wife's coming into possession of Edward Starter's fortune; and his wife's chances were his own.

And were not events all tending to bring him this fortune? Not only was the child dead, not only was Dolly deranged, but according to the opinion of the doctors the only thing that could change her mental state was John's return.

And the fate of the *Franklin* was the cause of the liveliest anxiety. If news failed to come during the next few weeks, if John Branican were not met with on the sea, if Andrews did not learn that their ship had put in at some port, it would mean that neither *Franklin*, nor crew would ever again return to San Diego. Then there would only be Dolly, deprived of reason, between the fortune and Len Burker. And when driven desperate, what might not tempt this man without a conscience, when the death of Edward Starter would put Dolly in possession of her rich inheritance.

But evidently Mrs. Branican could only inherit the property on condition of surviving her uncle. It was Len Burker's interest to keep her alive until Edward Starter's fortune had come to her. There were at present but two chances against him: either Mrs. Branican's death might occur too soon, or Captain John might return after being shipwrecked on some unknown island. But this last eventuality was a very unlikely one, and the total loss of the *Franklin* might already be considered as certain.

Such was Len Burker's position, such was the future he had in view, and that at the moment he was reduced to the last expedients. In fact, if justice intervened in his affairs he would have to meet a charge of embezzlement. Part of the money entrusted to him by imprudent investors, or which he had obtained the use of by his manoeuvres, was no longer within his reach; the claims would inevitably have to be met in the long run, although some of his new liabilities had been incurred in paying off old debts. Ruin was approaching, and worse than ruin, dishonour, and what particularly appealed to him, his arrest on serious charges.

Mrs. Burker doubtless suspected that her husband's position was much threatened, but she had no idea that the end would be in the intervention of the law. Besides, no sign of pecuniary embarrassment had yet been visible at Prospect House.

And for this reason.

Since Dolly had gone out of her mind a trustee had had to be appointed for her in the absence of her husband. Len Burker had been clearly pointed out as the man for the post owing to his relationship to Mrs. Branican, and to him had been entrusted the administration of her property. The money left by John for household expenses was at his disposition, and he had used it for his personal needs. It was not much, certainly, for the *Franklin*'s voyage was not expected to last more than six months; but this patrimony which Dolly had brought at her marriage, although it consisted of some two or three thousand dollars, would help Len Burker to meet pressing claims, and gain time — which was of the utmost importance to him.

And this dishonest man did not hesitate to abuse his position as trustee. He misappropriated the securities in his charge, and owing to these illicit resources was able to obtain a little respite and plunge into new speculations. Having entered on the road leading to crime, Len Burker would, if needful, follow it to the end.

The captain's return was less and less to be feared. The weeks rolled by, and Andrews' received no news of the *Franklin*, whose presence had nowhere been reported for six months. August and September passed. Neither at Calcutta nor at Singapore had the correspondents received the least information relative to the American three- master. She was now looked upon as lost, and there was public mourning at San Diego. How had she perished? There was little difference of opinion, for all was conjecture. Since she had sailed several trading vessels bound to the same ports had taken the course she should have taken; and as they had found no trace of her, the only likely hypothesis was that she had been caught in one of those terrible storms, those irresistible tornadoes which are the scourge of the Celebes Sea and the Java Sea, and had gone down with all on board. Not a man probably had survived the disaster. On the 15th of October, 1875, the *Franklin* had been gone from San Diego seven months, and there was every reason to believe she would never return.

The town had become so convinced of this that a subscription list had been opened in favour of the families so unfortunately smitten by this catastrophe. The crew of the. *Franklin*, both officers and seamen, belonged to San Diego, and had left behind them wives, children and relatives who needed assistance.

The initiative in this subscription was taken by Andrews, who headed the list with a large amount. As he was interested in the matter, and for prudential reasons, Len Barker also contributed to this charitable work. The other firms in the town, the landowners, the retail dealers, followed the example; and the result was that the families of the lost crew were to a large extent assisted, and the consequences of this maritime disaster considerably alleviated.

On his part, Mr. William Andrew looked upon it as a duty that Mrs. Branican should have enough to live upon. He knew that Captain John had at his departure left enough for her requirements calculated on an absence of six or seven months. But thinking that the resources were coming to an end, and not wishing that Dolly should be a burden to her relatives, he resolved to consult with Len Burker on the subject.

On the 17th of October, in the afternoon, although his health was not completely re-established, the ship-owner set out for Prospect House, and after reaching the high part of the town, appeared before the chalet.

Outside there was no change, except that the shutters on the ground floor and first floor were closed. It looked like an inhabited house, but silent and mysterious.

Mr. William Andrew rang at the gate in the fence. No one came. It seemed as though the visitor had neither been seen nor heard.

Was there anyone at home? He rang a second time, and then followed the noise of a door opening at the side.

55

The mulatto appeared, and as soon as she recognized Mr. William Andrew she could not restrain a gesture of vexation, which, however, he did not notice.

No came towards him, and before the gate was opened he spoke to her over the fence.

"Is not Mrs. Branican at home?" he asked.

"No, Mr. Andrew," answered No, with a peculiar hesitation visibly mingled with fear.

"Where is she, then?" asked Mr. William Andrew.

"She is out for a walk with Mrs. Burker."

"I thought they had given Up their walks, which excited her, and might bring on a crisis?"

"Yes, doubtless," said No. "But for some days Mrs. Branican has gone out. It seems to be doing her good — "

" I am sorry you did not let me know," replied Mr. William Andrew. "Is Mr. Burker at home?"

"I do not know."

"Then see; and if he is, tell him I wish to speak with him."

Before the mulatto could reply — and probably she would have been much embarrassed for a reply — the door on the ground floor opened. Len Burker appeared on the steps, crossed the garden, and advancing, said, —

"Please come in, Mr. Andrew. In the absence of Jane, who has gone out with Dolly, allow me to receive you."

And this was not said in the hard tone so habitual to Len Burker, but in a voice that was evidently slightly troubled.

As it was especially to see Len Burker that Mr. William Andrew had come to Prospect House, he entered the gate. Then, without accepting

56

the offer made to him to go into the drawing-room on the ground floor, he sat down on one of the seats in the garden.

Len Burker, beginning the conversation, confirmed what the mulatto had just said: for some days Mrs. Branican had resumed her walks in the neighbourhood of Prospect House with great advantage to her health.

"Will not Dolly be back soon?" asked Mr. William Andrew.

"I do not think Jane will bring her home before dinner," answered Len Burker.

Mr. William Andrew looked much disappointed, for he had to return to his office before post time; and Len Burker gave him no invitation to wait for Mrs. Branican's return.

"And you have not yet noticed any improvement in Dolly's condition?" he asked.

"No, unfortunately, Mr. Andrew. It is to be feared we are dealing with the sort of derangement that neither care nor time can cure."

"Who knows, Mr. Burker? That which hardly seems possible to men is always possible to God!"

Len Burker shook his head like a man who scarcely admitted Divine intervention in the things of this world.

"The worst of it is," said Mr. William Andrew, "that we can no longer look forward to the captain's return. We must give up the hope of the change that the return might have had on poor Dolly's mental state. You are aware, Mr. Burker we have given up all hope of again seeing the *Franklin*?"

"I am quite aware of it, Mr. Andrew, and it is one more misfortune on the top of the others. But — even though Providence may not interfere — " said he in an ironical tone, very much out of place at the moment, "there would be nothing extraordinary in John's coming back after all."

"Now that seven months have gone by without news of the *Franklin*" said Mr. William Andrew, "and the inquiries I have made have had no result?"

"But there is nothing to prove that the *Franklin* has gone down at sea," replied Len Burker. "Can she not have been wrecked on one of the numerous reefs in the sea she was to cross? Who knows if John and the sailors have not taken refuge on a desert island? "And if so, these resolute and energetic men will know how to get back to their country. Can they not build a boat with the remains of their ship? Can their signals not be seen by a vessel passing in sight of the island? Evidently a certain time is necessary for these things to happen. No, I do not despair of John's return — in a few months, if not in a few weeks. There are a number of examples of shipwrecked people who have been thought inevitably lost, and who have returned to port."

Len Burker had spoken with a volubility which was not usual with him. His face so impassive, was now animated. It seemed as. though in expressing himself in this way, in adducing more or less specious reasons regarding the safety of the shipwrecked, it was not to Mr. William Andrew he was replying, but to himself, to his own anxieties, to the fear he would experience if although the *Franklin* might not reappear off San Diego, another ship might come in, bringing Captain John and his crew. That would mean the collapse of the system on which he had built his future.

"Yes," said Mr. William Andrew, "I know there have been almost miraculous escapes. All that you say, Mr. Burker, I have said to myself, but it is impossible for me to retain the least hope. In any case — and this is what I have come to see you about to-day — I desire that Dolly should not be any expense to you — "

"Oh! Mr. Andrew — "

"No, Mr. Burker; and you will allow me to see that the salary of the captain shall be at his wife's disposal as long as she lives."

"On her behalf I thank you," said Len Burker. "This generosity — "

"I think it is only my duty," said Mr. William Andrew. "And as I suppose that the money left by John before his departure must in a great measure have been spent — "

"Undoubtedly, Mr. Andrew," replied Len Burker. "But Dolly is not without relations whose duty it also is to come to her help — and was it not from affection — "

"Yes; I know I can reckon on Mrs. Burker's devotion. Nevertheless, allow me to interfere in a certain measure to assure John's wife — perhaps his widow — ;the comfort and the care which I am certain will never be wanting on your part."

"That is as you please, Mr. Andrew."

"I have brought you, Mr. Burker, what I look upon as legitimately due to Captain Branican- since the departure of the *Franklin*, and in your position as trustee you can draw every month what I have to-his credit."

"As you wish," said Len Burker.

"Perhaps you will give me - a receipt for the money I have brought?"

"Willingly, Mr. Andrew."

And Len Burker went to his desk to write the receipt in question.

When he returned to the garden, Mr. William Andrew, who much regretted not having met Dolly and not being able to wait for her return, thanked him for the interest he and his wife were taking in their unfortunate relative. It Was to be understood that the least change in her state was to be reported by Len Burker to Mr. William Andrew, who then took his leave, waiting for a moment at the gate to see if he could see Dolly returning to Prospect House in Jane's company, and then he went down into San Diego.

As soon as he Was out of sight Len Burker called the mulatto to him.

"Does Jane know that Mr. Andrew has just been?"

"Very likely, Len. She saw him come and she saw him go."

"If he should come here — and he is not likely to do so for Some time — he must not see Jane, nor particularly Dolly. You understand, no?"

"I will take care, Len."

"And if Jane insists — "

"Oh, when you have said, I will not have it," said No, "it is not Jane who will defy you."

"Be it so, but we must guard against a surprise! Chance may bring about a meeting — and — -at this moment — that would be to risk losing everything."

"I am here," said the mulatto, "and you need fear nothing, Len! No one shall enter Prospect House as long — as long as it does not suit you."

And, as a matter of fact, during the two months that followed, the house remained more shut up than ever. Jane and Dolly no longer showed themselves in the little garden. They were not seen either under the verandah or at the windows of the first-floor rooms which were invariably closed. The mulatto only went out on household matters for the shortest time possible, and never in the absence of Len Burker, so that Dolly was never left alone with Jane. It was also noticed during the last months of the year that Len Burker went but very seldom to his office in Fleet Street. Even weeks went by without his appearing there, as if he were endeavouring to withdraw from business while preparing for some new venture.

And it was under these conditions that, thus ended the year 1875, which had been so disastrous for the Branican family — John lost at sea, Dolly deprived of reason, and their child drowned in the depths of San Diego bay.

CHAPTER VII - VARIOUS MATTERS

There was no news of the *Franklin* during the early months of 1876. There was no trace of her presence in the seas of the Philippines, of Celebes, or of Java; neither was there in the neighbourhood of Northern Australia, but how could it be supposed that Captain John would have ventured through Torres Straits! Once only to' the north of the Sunda Islands, thirty miles from Batavia, a piece of wreckage was picked up by an American schooner and brought to San Diego under the impression that it belonged to the vanished ship. But after careful examination, it was shown that the wreckage was of much older wood than the materials employed by the builders of the *Franklin*.

Besides, the fragment could only have been knocked off if the ship had been thrown on some reef or collided at sea. In the latter case the secret of the collision could hardly have been so well kept for no news to come regarding it — at least, unless the vessels had both foundered. But as there had been no report of the disappearance of another ship during the twelve months, the idea of a collision had to be abandoned, as also the supposition of a wreck on the coast, to return to the simplest explanation that the *Franklin* had gone down in one of the tornadoes which are frequent in the seas of Malaysia, and which no sailing vessel can resist when caught within their sphere of activity.

A year had elapsed since the *Franklin's* departure, and she was definitely classed among the vessels lost, or supposed to be lost, which figure in such large numbers in the annals of maritime disasters.

This winter — that of 1875-76 — was very severe even in the fortunate region of Lower California, where the climate is generally moderate. With the excessive cold that prevailed up to the end of February, no one could be astonished that Mrs. Branican had not left Prospect House, even to take the air in the little garden.

But if this seclusion were prolonged it might become suspicious to the people, who lived in the neighbourhood, although it might be asked if Mrs. Branican's malady had not become worse rather than supposed that Len Burker had any interest in keeping Dolly out of sight. Mr. William Andrew was confined to his room during a. great part of the winter, but impatient to see for himself in what state Dolly was, he made up his mind to go to Prospect House as soon as he could get out.

In the first week of March Mrs. Branican resumed her walks in the environs of Prospect House accompanied by Jane and the mulatto. A few days afterwards, in a visit to the chalet, Mr. William Andrew saw for himself that the young woman's health gave no cause for anxiety. Physically her state was as satisfactory as possible; mentally there had been no amelioration — she 'was unconscious of what was going on around her, and had neither memory nor intelligence as is usual in these cases of mental degeneracy. During the walks abroad which might have recalled certain remembrances, in the presence of the children she met on the way, before- the sea and the distant sails, Mrs. Branican did not even betray the emotion which had formerly so deeply troubled her. She no longer tried to get away, and could now be left in Jane's charge. All idea of resistance, all desire of reaction being extinct, she lived in the most absolute resignation added to the completest indifference, and when Mr. William Andrew saw her again he thought her madness incurable.

By this time Len Burker's position had become quite hopeless. Mrs. Branican's patrimony, which he had applied to his own uses had been insufficient to fill the abyss opened under his feet. His last struggle was at the point of ending with his last resources. A few months yet, a few weeks perhaps, and he would be wanted by the police, and his only safety lay in his leaving San Diego.

Only One thing could save him, but that did not seem likely to happen — at least in time to be of use to him. In fact, if Mrs. Branican was alive, her uncle, Edward Starter, was also alive, and very healthy as well. With infinite precaution, lest the source of the inquiry should be recognized, Len Burker had obtained news of this Yankee from the depths of Tennessee.

Robust and vigorous, in the plenitude of his mental and physical faculties, and just upon sixty, Edward Starter spent his life in the open air and the forests and prairies of this immense territory, hunting and shooting over the land well stocked with game, fishing in the numerous rivers that water it, rushing about on foot and on horseback, managing his vast estate all by himself. Evidently he was one of those rough North-American farmers who die centenarians, and for whose death at all there never seems to be a reason.

It was only too clear that an early arrival of the inheritance was not to be counted on; and there was every chance that the uncle would survive the niece. Len Burker's hopes on that head were clearly vain, and before him rose the inevitable catastrophe from which Edward Starter's death could alone have saved him.

Two months went by — two months, during which his position went from bad to worse. Disquieting rumours concerning him began to be current at San Diego. Letters with threats of legal proceedings were received by him from people who could obtain nothing from him. For the first time Mr. William Andrew heard of the state of his affairs, and, in great alarm for the position of Mrs. Branican, he resolved to call on her trustee to produce his accounts. If necessary, Dolly's interest could be transferred to some representative more worthy of confidence, although this in no way reflected on Jane Burker, who was deeply devoted to her cousin.

At this time, two-thirds of Mrs. Branican's patrimony had been devoured, and of her whole fortune all that remained in Len Burker's hands was a few hundred dollars. Amid the claims pressing him on all sides, this was as a mere drop of water in San Diego bay; but that which was insufficient for him to meet his obligations with was enough if he made up his mind to disappear to put him safe beyond pursuit. But there was only just time.

In fact, proceedings had already been begun against Len Burker, proceedings charging him with swindling and abuse of trust. Soon a warrant was issued against him; but when the police presented

63

themselves at his office, in Fleet Street, he had not been seen there since the day before.

The . police then went to Prospect House. Len Burker had left the. chalet in the middle of the night. Whether she liked it or not, his wife had been compelled to accompany him. Only the mulatto woman remained in charge of Mrs. Branican.

An active search was immediately ordered in San Diego, then at San Francisco, and at different places in the State of California, in the hope of getting on his track; but these had no result.

As soon as the rumour of his disappearance had spread in the town, an outcry was raised against this worthless man of business, whose defalcations it was soon apparent would amount to a considerable sum.

On that day, the 17th of May, very early in the morning, Mr. William Andrew had been to Prospect House, and discovered that none of Mrs. Branican's securities were left. Dolly was absolutely without resources. Her faithless trustee had not left her the wherewithal for her urgent needs.

Mr. William Andrew immediately did the only thing he could. He took Mrs. Branican to an asylum where she would be safe, and dismissed No, whom he seriously mistrusted. If Len Burker, had hoped that the mulatto would remain near Dolly, and keep him informed of any change in her health or fortune, he was in this way checkmated.

No, being under orders to leave Prospect House, went away that very day. Her idea was, doubtless, to rejoin the Burkers, and the police kept her under observation for some time. But she was very cautious and artful, and managed to outwit them by soon disappearing without their knowing what had become of her. And now it was empty, this house in which John and Dolly had lived so happily, and where they had had so many dreams for their child's happiness.

It was in Dr. Brumley's asylum that Mrs. Branican had been placed by Mr. William Andrew. Would her mental state take notice of the change which had occurred in her life? It was vain to hope so. She remained as indifferent as she had been at Prospect House. The only symptoms worth notice seemed to be a sort of natural instinct which supported her amid the wreck of her reason. Now and then she would murmur a little baby song as if she were hushing to sleep a child in her arms. But the name of little Wat never escaped her lips.

During the year 1876 there was no news of John Branican. The few persons who still hoped that if the *Franklin* did not come back her captain and crew might nevertheless do so, had had to give up even this hope. Confidence could not indefinitely resist the destructive action of time; and now the chance of recovering the shipwrecked crew grew feebler from day to day, and was reduced to nothing when the year 1877 neared its end and eighteen months had gone by without anything being heard relative to the vanished ship.

It was the same with regard to the Burkers, the search continued to be useless. It was not known to what country they had gone or in what place they were hiding, doubtless, under a false name. And Len Burker must have bewailed his ill luck when, two years after his disappearance, the hope on which he had built his plan became realized; he had, so to speak, foundered in sight of port.

About the middle of the month of June, 1878, Mr. William Andrew received a letter addressed to Dolly Branican. This letter informed her of the unexpected death of Edward Starter. The Yankee had been killed accidentally. A bullet fired by one of his hunting companions had ricocheted, struck him full in the chest, and killed him on the spot.

When his will was opened it was found that he had left the whole of his fortune to his niece, Dolly Starter, the wife of Captain Branican. The condition in which the heiress was, in no way altered his intentions, for he knew nothing of her attack of madness, as he knew nothing of Captain John's disappearance. No such news had penetrated into Tennessee, into that wild and inaccessible region where, in accordance with Edward Starter's wish, neither letters nor newspapers came.

In farms and forests, in cattle, in industrial property of various kinds, the testator's fortune was estimated to amount to 2,000,000 dollars.

Such was the heritage which the accidental death of Edward Starter had just passed on to his niece. With what joy would San Diego have applauded this enrichment of the Branican family if Dolly had still been a wife and a mother in full possession of her intelligence, if John had been there to share this wealth with her. What use the charitable woman would have made of it! What misfortunes they would not have alleviated 1 But no! The revenues of this fortune would be put aside and accumulate without profit to any one. In the unknown retreat in which he had taken refuge did Len Burker know of Edward Starter's death, and of the considerable wealth he had left behind him? It is impossible to say. Mr. William Andrew, acting as Dolly's trustee, resolved to sell the lands in Tennessee, farms, forests, and prairies, which would have been difficult to have managed at such a distance. A number of buyers presented themselves, and the sales were effected under advantageous conditions. The amounts produced, converted into first-class securities, added to those which formed an important part of Edward Starter's bequest, were deposited in the strong room of the Consolidated National Bank at San Diego. The maintenance of Mrs. Branican at Dr. Brumley's could absorb but a small part of the dividends which would be annually credited to her, and their accumulation would end in forming one of the largest fortunes in Lower California; but, notwithstanding this improvement in her position, there was no question of removing Mrs. Branican from Dr. Brumley's care. Mr. William Andrew did not consider it necessary. The house afforded her all the comfort and care her relatives could have wished for. There, then, she would remain, and there, probably, she would end her miserable, her useless existence, from which it seemed the future withheld every chance of happiness.

But if time went on, the remembrance of the misfortunes which had overwhelmed the Branican family was always vivid at San Diego, and the sympathy for Dolly was as sincere, as profound as on the first day.

The year 1879 began, and those who thought it was going to roll by like the others, without bringing any change in the position were completely deceived.

During the early months of the new year, the doctor and his assistant were greatly struck by the changes evidently taking place in the mental state of Mrs. Branican. That dispiriting calm, that apathetic indifference to the details of existence were gradually giving place to characteristic agitation. These were not crises followed by reaction in which the intelligence was more deeply shattered than before. No! It seemed as though Dolly was beginning to want to return to her intellectual life, and her mind was seeking to break the bonds which prevented it from expanding to the surface. Children brought before her received a look, almost a smile. It will not have been- forgotten that at Prospect House, during the first period of her madness, she had had these outbursts of instinct which vanished at the crisis. Now, on the contrary, the impressions had a tendency to persist. It seemed as though Dolly were in the position of a person questioning himself and seeking in his mind for distant recollections.

Was Mrs. Branican about to recover her reason? Had a work of regeneration begun within her? Was the fullness of her mental life to be restored to her? Alas! At present, when she had neither child nor husband, was it to be wished that this cure, we might say this miracle, should manifest itself when it could only make her more miserable!

Whether it were desirable or not, the doctors were prepared for the possibility of obtaining this result. Measures were taken for producing on the mind and heart of Mrs. Branican a series of durable and salutary shocks. It was even thought desirable to take her away from Dr. Brumley's, to bring her into the garden at Prospect House, to again let her occupy her room in the chalet. And when that was done she was certainly conscious 'of the change in her way of living, and appeared to take some interest in finding herself amid these new surroundings.

With the first days of spring — it was then April — walks were recommenced in the neighbourhood. Mrs. Branican was many times taken to the beach at Island Point. The few ships passing out at sea she followed with her look and with her hand stretched out towards the horizon. But she did not try to run away, as she formerly did, to escape from Dr. Brumley who accompanied her. She was not excited by the noise of the tumultuous waves covering the beach with their spray. Was there any reason for thinking that her imagination was bearing her along the route followed by the *Franklin* in leaving the port of San Diego, at the moment the upper sails disappeared behind the, heights of the cliff? Yes! Perhaps! And her lips, one day, distinctly murmured the name of John!

It was obvious that Mrs. Branican's malady was entering on a period the different phases of which would have to be carefully studied. Gradually as she became accustomed to live at the chalet she was recognizing the objects which had been dear to her. Her memory was being built up amid the surroundings which had been hers so long. A portrait of Captain John, hung on the wall of the room, began to fix her attention. Every day she looked at it more persistently, and a tear still unconscious occasionally escaped from her eyes.

Yes! If there had been a doubt as to the *Franklin*'s loss, if John were just coming home, if he were to appear suddenly, Dolly, perhaps, might recover her reason! But John's return could not be reckoned on.

And so Dr. Brumley decided to give the poor woman a shock which was not without danger. He wished to act before the improvement observed in her mental state began to subside, before she again fell into that indifference which had been characteristic of her madness for the last four years. As it seemed that her mind was still vibrating at the breath of memory, it would be well to give it a vibration intense enough to permit of the former Dolly again entering into this comparatively lifeless being.

This was also Mr. William Andrew's opinion, and he encouraged Dr. Brumley to make the experiment. On the 27th of May they both went to call on Mrs. Branican at Prospect House. A carriage waiting at the gate took them through the streets of San Diego down to the wharves, and they stopped at the landing place from which the steam launch started for Loma Point.

Doctor Brumley's intention was not only to reproduce the scene of the catastrophe, but to put Mrs. Branican in a position exactly similar to that when she had so suddenly lost her reason.

As she stopped at the landing stage Dolly's looks began to brighten up wonderfully. She was evidently strangely agitated. Her. whole being seemed astir.

Doctor Brumley and Mr. William Andrew led her to the launch, and hardly had she stepped on the deck than they were still more surprised at her behaviour. Instinctively she went to the very place she had occupied at the corner of the starboard seat when she held her child in her arms. Then she looked out into the bay, away towards Loma Point, as if she were seeking the *Boundary* at her moorings.

The passengers on the launch had recognized Mrs. Branican, and Mr. William Andrew had informed them of what it was proposed to do, so that all were under the influence of excitement. Were they to be the witnesses of a resurrection — not the resurrection of a body, but the resurrection of a mind?

It need not be said that every precaution was taken in case, in a paroxysm of madness, Dolly attempted to throw herself overboard.

The launch had already gone half a mile, and Dolly had not yet lowered her eyes to the surface of the bay. All the time she looked towards Point Loma, and when she turned aside it was to observe the manoeuvres of a trading vessel in full sail which had appeared at the entrance of the mouth to take up her station in quarantine.

Dolly's face was as if transformed. She rose, she looked at the ship.

It was not the *Franklin*, and she did not mistake it for her. But shacking her head, she said, —

"John! My John! You also will come back soon! And I will be there to welcome you."

Suddenly her looks seemed to search, in the waters of this bay she had just recognized. She gave a heartrending shriek, and said, turning to Mr. William Andrew, —

"Mr. Andrew — you — and him — my little Wat — my child — my poor child! There! There! I remember! I remember!"

And she fell on her knees on the deck, her eyes drowned in tears.

CHAPTER VIII - A DIFFICULT POSITION

MRS. BRANICAN restored to reason was like a dead woman restored to life. Seeing that she had stood the test of this remembrance, of this evocation of the past, seeing that the flash of memory had not injured her, could it be hoped that her recovery would take place? Was her intelligence to succumb a second time when she learnt that there had been no news of the *Franklin* for four years, and that it was believed the ship had gone down with all on board, and that she would never again see her husband?

Dolly, completely prostrated by the shock, had been taken back immediately to Prospect House. Neither Mr. William Andrew nor Doctor Brumley would leave her, and from the women in the latter's service she received all the care her state required.

But the shock had been so severe that an intense fever came on. She was even for a few days in a state of delirium, which gave the doctors much uneasiness, although she recovered the fullness of her intellectual faculties. It is true that when the time came to acquaint her with the whole extent of her misfortune, many precautions would have to be taken.

To begin with, Dolly asked how long she had been deprived of reason.

"Two months," replied Dr. Brumley, who was prepared for the question.

"Two months only!" she murmured.

And It seemed as though a century had passed over her head!

"Two months!" she added. "John could not have come back yet, for It is only two months since he went away. Does he know that our poor little child — "

"Mr. Andrew has written," replied Doctor Brumley without hesitation.

71

"And is there any news of the *Franklin*? ""

The reply was that Captain Branican was to write from Singapore, but the letters had not come to hand. But at the same time, according to the shipping intelligence, the *Franklin* would soon reach the Indies, and telegrams would shortly be received.

When Dolly asked why Jane Burker was not with her, the doctor answered that Mr. and Mrs. Burker were away travelling, and had not yet announced the date of their return.

It was left to Mr. William Andrew to tell Mrs. Branican the fate of the *Franklin*. But it was agreed to say nothing until her reason had been sufficiently re-established to support the blow, and to be careful in revealing the facts little by little, in order that she might gradually be led to conclude that no survivor of the wreck remained.

The news of the inheritance which had come to her, through the death of Edward Starter, was also kept back. Mrs. Branican would know soon enough that she possessed this fortune, which her husband could no longer share with her.

During the fortnight which followed, Mrs. Branican had no communication with the outside world. Mr. William Andrew and Dr. Brumley alone had access to her. The fever, which was very high to begin with, began to diminish, and would soon, doubtless, disappear. As much from the point of view of her health, as from that of not having to reply to definite and embarrassing questions, the doctor had forbidden the patient from talking. And every allusion to the past was avoided, as was everything that could lead her to suspect that four years had elapsed since the death of her child and the departure of her husband. For some time yet it was advisable that the year 1879 should be for her only 1875.

But Dolly had only one desire, or rather a very natural impatience, and that was to receive a first letter from John. She calculated that the *Franklin* being at the point of arrival at Calcutta, if she were not there already, Andrews' ought soon to hear of her by telegraph. Then she herself, as soon as she had strength, would write to John. Alas! what would she say in her letter — the first she would write to him since their marriage, for they had never been separated until the departure of the *Franklin*? Yes! What sad things this first letter would tell!

And then thinking of the past, Dolly reproached herself for having been the cause of her child's death! That unhappy day of the 31st March returned to her memory! If she had left little Wat at Prospect House he would still be alive! Why had she taken him out to the *Boundary*? Why had she refused the offer of Captain Ellis, who had proposed her staying on board until the ship's arrival at the wharf of San Diego? The terrible misfortune would not have occurred! And why also had she in a thoughtless moment taken the child from the nurse's arms at the moment the launch was suddenly checked to avoid a collision! She had fallen, and little Wat was no longer in her arms! Poor child, who had not even a grave over which his mother could go and weep!

These fancies, too vividly called up in her mind, caused Dolly to lose the calmness which was so necessary to her. Several times a violent delirium, due to the increase of the fever, made Dr. Brumley extremely uneasy. Fortunately these crises grew less acute, less frequent, and finally disappeared. There was now no fear for the mental state of Mrs. Branican. The moment was approaching when Mr. William Andrew might tell her all.

As soon as Dolly had unmistakably entered upon the period of her convalescence she obtained permission to leave her bed. She was placed in a long chair at her bedroom window, whence she could look out over the Bay of San Diego, and even far out beyond Loma Point to the very horizon. There she remained motionless for many long hours.

Then Dolly wished to write to John; she wanted to tell him of their child he would never see again, and she poured out her grief in a letter John never would receive.

Mr. William Andrew took this letter, promising to send it with his mail to the Indies, and that done, Mrs. Branican became calm again, living only in the hope of receiving news of the *Franklin* directly or indirectly.

However, this state of things could not last. Evidently Dolly would learn sooner or later what they were hiding from her — by excess of prudence, perhaps. The more she concentrated herself in the hope that she would soon receive a letter from John, that with each day his return grew nearer, the more, terrible would be the blew.

And that appeared but too evident after an interview which Mrs. Branican had with Mr. William Andrew on the 19th of June.

For the first time Dolly had gone down into the little garden of Prospect House, where Mr. William Andrew found her seated on a bench before the steps of the chalet. He went and sat down close to her, and taking her hands, clasped them affectionately.

In this last period of convalescence Mrs. Branican had begun to feel quite strong again. Her face had resumed its former warm colour, although her eyes were always humid with tears.

"I see your recovery makes rapid progress, my dear Dolly," said Mr. William Andrew. "You are getting on well."

"Certainly, Mr. Andrew," replied Dolly, "but it seems to me that I have aged considerably during the two months! How much my poor John will find me changed when he comes back! And I am waiting for him alone! He will only find me — "

"Courage, dear Dolly, courage! I forbid you to be so depressed. I am now your father. Yes, your father! and I insist on your obeying me!"

"Dear Mr. Andrew!"

"Be it so."

"The letter I wrote to John has gone, has it not?" asked Dolly.

"Doubtless — and you must wait for his reply with patience! Sometimes there are long delays in the Indian mails! You are still crying! I beseech you not to cry any more!"

"I cannot help it, Mr. Andrew, when I think. And am I not the cause? — I — "

"No, poor mother, no. Providence has struck you cruelly, but all grief has an end."

"Providence!" murmured Mrs. Branican; "Providence will bring me back my John!"

"My dear Dolly, have you. seen the doctor to-day?" asked Mr. William Andrew.

"Yes, and he thought me better! I am getting back my strength, and I shall soon be able to go out."

"Not before he says you may."

"No, Mr. Andrew. I promise to do nothing imprudent."

"And I reckon on your promise."

"You have not yet received anything relative to the *Franklin*, Mr. Andrew?"

"No, and I am not surprised. Ships take some time occasionally to get to the Indies."

"It seems to me John might have written from Singapore? Did he not call there?"

"Very probably, Dolly! But if he missed the mail by a "few hours it would make a delay of a fortnight in his letters."

"And so you are not at all surprised that John has not yet sent you a letter?"

"Not at all," answered Mr. William Andrew, who felt the conversation becoming embarrassing.

"And have not the shipping journals noticed his voyage?" asked Dolly.

"No. Since he spoke the *Boundary* — it is about — "

"Yes; about two months. And why should he have spoken her? I should not have gone on board the *Boundary*, and my child — "

Mrs. Branican's look suddenly changed, and tears rolled down from her eyes.

"Dolly — my dear Dolly," answered Mr. William Andrew. "Do not cry. I beg you, do not cry!"

"Ah! Mr. Andrew. I do not know — a presentiment sometimes comes to me. It is inexplicable. It seems to me that a new misfortune — I am uneasy about John!"

"There is no need to be, Dolly! There is no reason for being anxious — "

"Mr. Andrew," asked Mrs. Branican, "could you not send me a few newspapers with shipping intelligence in them? I should like to read them."

"Certainly, my dear Dolly; I will do so. But if anything were known concerning the *Franklin*, if she had been met with on the sea, if her approaching arrival in India had been reported, I should be the first to hear of it, and immediately."

But it was advisable to give another turn to the interview. Mrs. Branican would notice the hesitation with which Mr. Andrew replied, and the way in which his look sank before hers when she questioned him more directly. And so the worthy ship-owner began to speak for the first time of the death of Edward Starter, and the considerable fortune which had fallen to his niece. And then Dolly asked, —

"Jane Burker and her husband are on a voyage, they tell me; have they been away long from San Diego?"

"No. Two or three weeks."

"And ought they not soon to be back."

"I do not know," replied Mr. Andrew. "We have received no news —
"

"Does nobody know where they have gone?"

"Nobody knows, my dear Dolly. Len Burker has been engaged in very important — very adventurous — matters, he has been called away — very far away."

"And Jane?"

"Mrs. Burker had to accompany her husband — and I do not know how to tell you what happened — "

"Poor Jane!" said Mrs. Branican. "I had a great affection for her, and I should be glad to see her again. Is she not the only relation I have left!"

She did not give a thought to Edward Starter, nor of the family tie which united them.

"How is it that Jane has not once written to me?" she asked.

"My dear Dolly, you were very ill when Mr. Burker and his wife left San Diego."

"Just so, Mr. Andrew, and why write to one who could not understand? Dear Jane, she is to be pitied! Life will be hard for her! I was always afraid that Len Burker would launch into some speculation which would turn out badly! Perhaps John thought so too!"

"But," said Mr. William Andrew, "no one expected such a regrettable ending."

"Was it then on account of some bad business that Len Burker left San Diego?" asked Dolly quickly.

And she looked at Mr. Andrew, whose embarrassment was only too visible.

"Mr. Andrew," she continued, "speak! Do not leave me in ignorance! I desire to know all!"

"Well, Dolly, I do not wish to hide from you a misfortune you are sure soon to know! Yes! In the end Len Burker's affairs became very bad. He could not meet his engagements. Claims came in; and, threatened with arrest, he had to take safety in flight."

"And Jane went with him?"

"He certainly had to compel her to do so, and you know she had no will of her own where he was concerned."

"Poor Jane! Poor Jane!" murmured Mrs. Branican.

"I pity her, and if I had been well I should have helped her — "

"You could have done it!" said Mr. Andrew. "Yes — you could have saved Len Burker, if not for himself, who deserves no sympathy, at least for his wife."

"And John would have approved, I am sure, of the use I would have made of our humble fortune."

Mr. William Andrew carefully abstained from saying that Mrs. Branican's patrimony had been devoured by Len Burker. That would have been to have shown that he had been her trustee, and she might have asked how so much could have happened in the short time of two months.

And so Mr. Andrew at once answered, —

"Say no more about your humble position, my dear Dolly; that is all altered now."

"What do you mean, Mr. Andrew?" asked Mrs. Branican.

"I mean that you are rich, extremely rich!'

"I?"

"Your Uncle Edward Starter is dead."

78

"Dead? He is dead! And since when?"

"Since — "

Mr. William Andrew was on the point of betraying himself by giving the exact date of Edward Starter's decease, nearly two years before, which would have revealed the whole truth. But Dolly's only thought was that the death of her uncle and the disappearance of her cousin left her without relations. And when she learnt that owing to the relative she had hardly known, whose wealth she and John had not expected to inherit until a remote future, her fortune now amounted to two millions of dollars, her only thought was what good she could do with it.

"Yes, Mr. Andrew," she said, "I ought to go to Jane's help! I ought to save her from ruin and disgrace! Where is she? Where can she be? What has become of her?"

Mr. William Andrew had to say that the efforts to discover Len Burker had had no result. He had either taken refuge in some distant part of the United States, or else had left America, but it was impossible to say.

"But if it is only a few weeks since Jane and he disappeared from San Diego," said Mrs. Branican, "we may learn — "

"Yes — a few weeks!" said Mr. William Andrew hastily.

But at this moment Mrs. Branican could think of nothing else than that, thanks to Edward Starter, John need no longer be a sailor. He could now leave the sea. This voyage in the *Franklin* for Andrews would be his last. And was it not his last, since he would never come back?

"No, Mr. Andrew," exclaimed Dolly. "Once John comes back, he will never go to sea again! His taste for sea life he will give up for my sake. We will live together — always together! Nothing shall separate us again."

At the thought that this happiness would be shattered at a word — a word that soon would have to be uttered — Mr. William Andrew could hardly control himself. He hastened to bring the interview to a close, but before taking his leave he obtained Mrs. Branican's promise that she would commit no imprudence, that she would not run the risk of going out, that she would not resume her customary life until the doctor had given her permission. On his part he repeated that if directly or indirectly he received any news of the *Franklin* he would immediately send it on to Prospect House.

When Mr. William Andrew reported this conversation to Doctor Brumley, the doctor made no secret of his fear that some indiscretion would put Mrs. Branican in possession of the truth. That her madness had lasted for years, that for four years no one had known what had become of the *Franklin*, that she would never again see John — Yes; it would be best for her to learn this either from Mr. William Andrew or from himself after taking all possible precaution.

It was therefore decided that in a week, when there could be no longer a plausible motive for preventing Mrs Branican from leaving the chalet, she should be told everything.

"And may Heaven give her strength to bear the trial," said Mr. William Andrew.

During the last week of June Mrs. Branican's life at Prospect House continued to be what it always had been. Thanks to careful nursing she recovered both physical strength and mental energy. And Mr. William Andrew found it more and more embarrassing when Dolly pressed him with questions to which he could not reply.

In the afternoon of the 23rd he came to see her, in order to put at her disposal an important sum of money, and account to her for her fortune which had been deposited in reliable securities in the Consolidated Bank at San Diego.

Mrs. Branican paid very little attention to the subject of Mr. William Andrew's conversation, and hardly listened to him. She could only talk about John, she could only think of him. What! Not a letter yet! That was most disquieting! How came it that Andrews' had not even received the telegram announcing the arrival of the *Franklin* in India?

The ship-owner tried to calm Dolly by telling her he had just telegraphed to Calcutta and would receive a reply in a day or two. But if he succeeded in diverting her thoughts he was considerably troubled when she asked, "Mr. Andrew, there is a man of whom I have never spoken until now — that is the man who saved my life and could not save my child's. That sailor — "

"That sailor?" said Mr. William Andrew, with visible hesitation.

"Yes; that courageous man — to whom I owe my life. Has he been rewarded?"

"Certainly, Dolly."

And he really had been.

"Is he at San Diego, Mr. Andrew?"

"No, my dear Dolly — no! I heard he had gone to sea."

Which was true.

After leaving the bay the sailor had gone on several trading voyages, and now was away at sea.

"But at least you can tell me his name?" asked Mrs. Branican.

"His name is Zach Fren."

"Zach Fren? Good! I thank you, Mr. Andrew," said Dolly.

And she said no more about the sailor whose name she had just ascertained.

But from that day Zach Fren never ceased to occupy Dolly's thoughts. Henceforth he was indissolubly bound up in her mind with the remembrance of the catastrophe of which San Diego bay had been the theatre. She would find out Zach Fren at the end of his voyage. He was in a San Diego ship, without doubt. The ship would return in six months — in a year — and then — assuredly the *Franklin* would be back before he was. She and John would be of one mind as to rewarding him — as to paying him their debt of gratitude. Yes! John would not delay in bringing back the *Franklin* and he would resign the command of her. They would never again separate from each other.

"And that day," she thought, "why should our kisses be mingled with tears!"

CHAPTER IX - REVELATIONS

But Mr. William Andrew desired and feared this interview in which Mrs. Branican would learn of the disappearance of the *Franklin* and the loss of her crew and her captain — a loss of which no one doubted at San Diego. Could her reason, which had once succumbed, be equal to this last blow? Although more than four years had gone by since John's departure, it would seem as though his death had occurred but yesterday. Time which had passed over so many human sorrows had not moved on in her case!

While Mrs. Branican remained at Prospect House they could hope that no indiscretion would be prematurely committed. Mr. William Andrew and Dr. Brumley had taken their precautions, and prevented any newspapers or letters arriving at the chalet. But Dolly felt strong enough to go out, and although the doctor had not given her permission to do so, could she not leave Prospect House without saying anything about it? And so they resolved to hesitate no longer, and Dolly would soon be told that she could no longer reckon on the return of the *Franklin*.

But after the conversation she had had with Mr. William Andrew, Mrs. Branican had made up her mind to go out without telling her maids, who would have done their utmost to dissuade her. And if this expedition were free from danger in the actual state of her health, it might nevertheless bring about deplorable results in the event of some accident acquainting her with the truth without previous precaution.

In leaving Prospect House, Mrs. Branican proposed to make some inquiries regarding Zach Fren. Now that she knew the sailor's name, only one thought possessed her.

"They have seen about him," she said. "Yes! a little money has been given him, without my having anything to say in the matter. Zach Fren has been away about five or six weeks. But perhaps he has a family, a wife, children — poor people, undoubtedly! It is my duty to go and visit them, to minister to their wants, to assure them of comfort! I will see them, and will do what I ought to do for them!"

And if Mrs. Branican had consulted Mr. William Andrew in the matter, how could he have dissuaded her from this act of gratitude and charity?

On the 21st of June, Dolly went out of the enclosure about nine o'clock in the morning without being noticed. She was dressed in mourning — mourning for her child, whose death she thought had taken place but two months before. It was not without deep emotion that she went out of the gate of the little garden — alone for the first time.

The weather was fine, and the heat already great in these first weeks of the Californian summer, although it was tempered by the sea breeze.

She went along among the houses and gardens of the upper town. Absorbed in thought of what she was going to do, she did not notice the changes which had taken place in the neighbourhood, the new buildings which ought to have attracted her attention; or at least she had but a vague perception of them. Besides, these changes were not important enough to interfere with her finding her way along the roads down to the bay. She did riot notice two or three people who recognized her and looked at her with a certain amount of astonishment.

In passing a Catholic chapel not far from Prospect House, of which she had been one of the most assiduous frequenters, she felt an irresistible desire to enter. The officiating priest had begun the mass as she knelt on a low chair in a dark corner. There she poured out her soul in prayer for her child, her husband — for all those she loved. The few faithful who attended the mass had not noticed her, and when she retired they had already left the chapel.

It was there that she noticed something which could not but surprise her. It seemed that the altar was no longer that before which she was accustomed to pray. This altar was richer, and of a new kind, and stood in front of an apse which appeared to be of recent construction. Had the chapel been made larger?

But this was only a fugitive impression which fled as soon as Mrs. Branican began to descend the streets towards the business quarter in which the animation was great. But at any moment the truth might break on her — a poster with a date — a railway time-table — a steamboat notice — the announcement of a fete or an entertainment bearing the date 1879; and then Dolly would suddenly learn that Mr. William Andrew and Doctor Brumley had deceived her, and that her insanity had lasted four years, and not a few weeks; and that in consequence it was not two months, but four years, since the' *Franklin* had left San Diego. And if they had hidden it from her that John had not come back — it was because he would never come back!

Mrs. Branican was hurrying towards the wharves when the idea occurred to her of passing Len Burker's house, which would only take her a little out of her way.

"Poor Jane I" she murmured.

When she arrived in front of the office in Fleet Street she could hardly recognize it, and this caused her more than a gesture of surprise, a vague and disturbing uneasiness.

Instead of the narrow, gloomy house she knew, there was an important building of Anglo-Saxon architecture, of many storeys, with high windows, and iron bars on the ground floor. On the roof was a lantern, from which floated a flag, bearing the initials H. W. Near the door was a plate, on which could be read these words, in golden letters, —

"Harris, Wadanton and Co."

Dolly at first thought she was mistaken; she looked to the right, to the left. No! it was here, at the angle of Fleet Street, that the house stood to which she came to see Jane Burker.

She put her hands to her eyes. An inexplicable presentiment chilled her heart. She could not account for what she felt.

Mr. William Andrew's house of business was not far off. Dolly, hurrying along, saw it at a turning out of the road. At first she thought of going there. No — she would go there as she came back — when she had seen Zach Fren's family. She intended to get the sailor's address at the steam launch office, near the landing-stage.

With her mind bewildered, her eyes irresolute, her heart palpitating, Dolly continued her walk. She now looked closely at the people she met. She felt an irresistible want to go to these people to interrogate them, to ask them — what? They would have taken her for a lunatic — but was she sure that her reason had not left her for a second time? Were there not gaps in her memory? Was she completely in possession of herself?

Mrs. Branican reached the wharf. Beyond, the bay lay revealed throughout its extent. A few ships were gently rolling at their anchorage. Others were preparing to depart. What memories this life in the harbour' recalled! Two months ago she was at the end of this wharf; it was from this spot that she had seen the *Franklin* go about for the last time to leave .the bay; it was there she had received John's last adieu; there the vessel had doubled Island Point, the upper sails had for a moment been seen above the cliff, and the *Franklin* had vanished into the distances of the high seas.

A few more steps, and Dolly found herself at the steam launch office near the landing-stage. One of the boats was going away at the moment, heading for Loma Point.

Dolly followed it with her eyes, listening to the noise of the steam which panted from the end of the black tube.

To what sorrowful remembrance did she then abandon herself? The remembrance of her child, whose little body the waters had not even yielded up, which attracted her — fascinated her. She felt herself fainting, as if the ground were failing her. Her head turned. She was on the point of falling.

A moment afterwards Mrs. Branican entered the steam launch office.

As he caught sight of this woman with her features drawn, and her face bloodless, the clerk who was sitting at a table arose, handed her a chair, and said, —

"You are ill, madam?"

"It is nothing, sir," said Dolly. "A moment of weakness. I feel better."

"Will you sit down and wait for the next launch? In ten minutes at most — "

"Thank you, sir," said Mrs. Branican. "I have only come to ask you for some information. Can you give it me?"

"What is it?"

Dolly sat down, and, putting her hand to her forehead to collect her ideas, —

"Sir," she said, "you had in your service a sailor named Zach Fren?"

"Yes," said the clerk, "he was not with us long, but I remember him perfectly."

"He it was, was it not, who risked his life to save a woman — an unhappy mother?"

"I remember her — Mrs. Branican — yes! that was the man."

"And now he is at sea?"

"At sea." .

"On what ship is he?"

"The Californian."

"Of San Diego?"

"No, of San Francisco."

"Where is he bound for?"

"For Europe."

Mrs. Branican, more fatigued than she believed herself to be, was silent for some seconds, and the clerk waited for her to ask him some more questions. When she had recovered a little, she said, —

"Does Zach Fren belong to San Diego?"

"Yes."

"Can you tell me where his. family lives?"

"I have always understood that Zach Fren was alone in the world. I do not think he has any relations, either at San Diego or elsewhere."

"He was not married?"

"No."

There was no reason for doubting the reply of this clerk, to whom Zach Fren was well known.

Nothing, therefore, could be done, for the sailor had no family, and Mrs. Branican would have to wait .until the Californian returned from Europe.

"Is it known how long Zach Fren's voyage will last?" she asked.

"I cannot tell you that, for the Californian is on a very long cruise."

"Thank you, sir," said Mrs. Branican. "I should have had great satisfaction in meeting Zach Fren, but some time will elapse, doubtless."

"Yes."

"But it is possible that there will be news of the Californian in a few months, a few weeks?"

"News?" said the clerk. "But the San Francisco house to whom she belongs has already had news of her several times."

"Already?"

"Yes."

"And several times?"

And as she repeated the words-Mrs. Branican rose, and looked at the clerk as if she had not understood him.

"Look, madam," he replied, handing her a newspaper. "Here is the Shipping Gazette. It says the Californian left Liverpool eight days ago."

"Eight days!" murmured Mrs. Branican, taking the newspaper and trembling.

Then, in a voice so completely broken that the clerk could hardly hear her, —

"How long is it since Zach Fren went away?" she asked.

"Nearly eighteen months."

"Eighteen months!"

Dolly supported herself against the angle of the desk. Her heart ceased to beat during some seconds.

Suddenly her looks were caught by a bill hung against the wall, and which gave the times of the steam launches for the summer season.

At the head of the bill were the word and the figures-

"March, 1879."

March, 1879! They had deceived her! Her child had been dead for years — four years since John had left San Diego! She had been mad these four years! Yes! And if Mr. William Andrew, if Doctor Brumley had allowed her to believe that her madness had only lasted two months, it was because they wished to hide from her the truth about the

Franklin. It was four years since there had been any news of John and his ship.

To the great alarm of the clerk, Mrs. Branican was seized with a violent spasm; but with a supreme effort she controlled it, and, rushing from the office, walked quickly through the streets of the lower town.

Those who saw this woman pass, with her pale face and haggard eyes, may have thought she was mad. And if she were not, was she not going to be so?

Where was she going? Towards Andrews', where she arrived almost unconsciously in a few minutes. She went through the offices, she passed among the clerks who had not time to stop her, and she pushed open the door of the private office where she found the ship-owner.

At first Mr. William Andrew was thunderstruck at seeing Mrs. Branican enter, and terrified at her agitated features and her frightful pallor.

But before he could say a word, —

"I know — I know! "she exclaimed. "You have deceived me. I have been mad for four years."

"My dear Dolly — be calm!"

"Answer! The *Franklin*? She has been gone four years, has she not?"

Mr. William Andrew bowed his head.

"You have had no news — for four years — for four years?"

Mr. William Andrew remained silent.

"You think the *Franklin* is lost! None of her crew will return — and I shall never see John again!"

Tears were Mr. William Andrew's only reply.

Mrs. Branican fell suddenly into an arm-chair. She had fainted.

Mr. William Andrew called one of the women of the house, who did all she could to bring Dolly round, while one of the clerks was hurried off to Doctor Brumley, who lived not far off and made haste to come.

Mr. William Andrew told him what had happened. By some indiscretion or accident, he did not know which, Mrs. Branican had just learnt everything. Whether at Prospect House, or in the streets of San Diego, did not matter. She knew now! She knew that four years had elapsed since her child's death, that for four years she had been deprived of reason, that four years had passed without receiving any news of the *Franklin*.

It was not without difficulty that Doctor Brumley succeeded in bringing back Dolly to life, while he asked himself if her intelligence had resisted this last blow, the most terrible of those with which she had been struck.

When Mrs. Branican returned to her senses she knew all that had been revealed to her. She returned to life with all her reason. And through her tears her look interrogated Mr. William Andrew, who held her hands, and knelt close to her.

"Speak — speak — Mr. Andrew!" were the only words that escaped her lips.

Then, in a voice broken with sobs, Mr. William Andrew told her of the anxiety that had at first been caused by the failure of news as to the *Franklin*. Letters and telegrams had been sent to Singapore and the Indies, where the vessel had never arrived. An inquiry had taken place with regard to the *Franklin*'s course; but no trace of her wreck had been found.

Motionless Mrs. Branican heard with her mouth silent, her look fixed. And when Mr. William Andrew had finished his recital, —

"My child dead — my husband dead," she murmured. "Ah! why did not Zach Fren let me die!"

Then' her face suddenly became animated, and her natural energy manifested itself with so much power that Doctor Brumley was alarmed.

"Since the last search," she said in a resolute voice, "nothing has been heard of the *Franklin*?"

"Nothing!" replied Mr. William Andrew.

"And you consider her as lost?"

"Yes! Lost!"

"And of John and his crew you can obtain no news?"

"None, my poor Dolly, and now we have no hope."

"No .hope!" said Mrs. Branican in a tone almost ironical.

She rose and stretched out her hand towards one of the windows through which she could see the horizon of sea.

Mr. William Andrew and Doctor Brumley looked at her with dismay, fearing for her mental state.

But Dolly was in full possession of her faculties, and with glowing look, she said, —

"No hope! You say no hope! Mr. Andrew, if John is lost for you, he is not lost for me! This fortune which belongs to me, I care not for it without him! I will devote it to searching for John and his companions of the *Franklin*. And by Heaven's aid I will find them] Yes! I will find them I"

CHAPTER X - PREPARATIONS

A new life was about to commence for Mrs. Branican. If she had absolute certainty of the death of her child, it was not so regarding John. John and his companions might have survived their wreck on one of the numerous islands of the seas of the Philippines, Celebes or Java. Was it impossible that they were held prisoners by some native race, and that it was impossible for them to escape? It was to this hope that Mrs. Branican clung from the outset, and with a tenacity so extraordinary that she soon provoked a change in the public opinion of San Diego on the subject of the *Franklin*. No! She would not believe, she could not* believe that John and his crew had perished, and it may be that to the persistence of this idea she owed the keeping of her reason. At least, as some were inclined to think, it was a species of monomania, a sort of madness which is called "the madness of desperate hope." But this was not the case, as we shall soon see. Mrs. Branican had resumed full possession of her intelligence, and had recovered that sureness of judgment which had always characterized her. One object she had for life, to find John, and she pursued it with an energy which circumstances occurred to stimulate. As Heaven had permitted Zach Fren to save her from the first catastrophe, and reason had been returned to her when she had at her disposal all the means of action fortune gives, if John were alive he should be saved by her. This fortune she would employ in incessant searches, she' would squander it in rewards, she would spend it in expeditions. There was not an island, not an islet, in the localities traversed by the young captain which should not be reconnoitred, visited, searched. "What Lady *Franklin* had done for John *Franklin* Mrs. Branican could do for John Branican, and she would succeed where the widow of the illustrious admiral had failed.

From this day Dolly's friends were those who could help her in this new period of her existence, encourage her in her investigations, and join their efforts to hers. And one of them was Mr. William Andrew, although he had but little hope of a happy result of these attempts to discover the survivors of his wrecked ship, and he became the most ardent adviser of Mrs. Branican, supported by the captain of the *Boundary*, whose ship was then at San Diego dismantled. Captain Ellis, a resolute man on whom they could depend, and a devoted friend of John, received an invitation to confer with Mrs. Branican and Mr. William Andrew.

There were frequent interviews at Prospect House. Rich as she now was, Mrs. Branican had no wish to leave the modest chalet. It was there John had left her when he started, it was there he should find her when he came back. Nothing should be changed in her mode of life until her husband returned to San Diego. She would live the same life with the same simplicity, spending nothing more than usual except for the expenses of her searches and her charities.

This was soon known in the town; and in consequence there was a redoubling of sympathy for this valiant woman who would not be John Branican's widow. Without any mistrust they became enthusiastic about her; they admired her, they even venerated her, for her misfortunes justified their going as far as veneration. Not only did a number of people pray that she might succeed, but they believed in her eventual success. When Dolly came down into the lower town to visit Andrews' or Captain Ellis, when she was seen serious and sombre, clad in her mourning garb, looking ten years older than she was, and she was then scarcely five-and-twenty, hats were raised in respect and people bowed as she passed. But she saw nothing of these deferences which were addressed to her.

During the interviews between Mrs. Branican, Mr. William Andrew and Captain Ellis, the first consideration bore on the course the *Franklin* should have followed. It was at the outset important to fix this with rigorous exactitude.

Andrews' had sent the ship to Calcutta with a call at Singapore, and it was in this port she had to discharge a portion of the cargo before proceeding to India. Thus, in sailing from the west coast of the American continent the probabilities were that Captain John would sight the Hawaiian or Sandwich archipelago. After traversing the zones of Micronesia, the *Franklin* would pass near the Mariannes and the Philippines; then by the Sea of Celebes and the Strait of Macassar she would gain the Sea of Java, bounded on the north by the Sunda islands, and thus reach Singapore. At the western extremity of the Straits of Malacca, formed by the peninsula of that name and the Island of Java, lies the Gulf of Bengal, in which, beyond the Nicobar islands and the Andaman islands, there was no refuge for shipwrecked men. Besides, it was beyond a doubt that John Branican had never appeared in the Gulf of Bengal; for as he had failed to reach Singapore it was evident he had not got beyond the Java sea and the Sunda islands.

No sailor would admit that the *Franklin*, instead of taking the Malaysia route, had endeavoured to reach India through the difficult channels of Torres strait and along the coast of the north of the Australian continent. Captain Ellis affirmed that John Branican would never commit such a useless imprudence as to risk his ship amid the dangers of this strait. This hypothesis was absolutely put aside; it was only in Malaysia that search should be made.

In fact, in the seas of the Carolines, of Celebes and of Java islands and islets can be counted in thousands, and it was there only, if they had survived an accident on the sea, that the crew of the *Franklin* could be abandoned or detained by some tribe, without means of returning home.

These different points established, it was decided that an expedition should be sent into the seas of Malaysia, and Mrs. Branican made a proposition to which she attached great importance. She asked Captain Ellis, if it suited him, to take command of the expedition.

Captain Ellis was then free, because the *Boundary* had been dismantled by her owners, and although he was surprised by the unexpectedness of the proposal, he did not hesitate to put himself at Mrs. Branican's disposal, with the acquiescence of Mr. William Andrew, who thanked him cordially.

"I am only doing my duty," he said, "and all that I can do to find the survivors of the *Franklin*, I will do. If Captain John is alive — "

"John is alive!" said Mrs. Branican, in so affirmative a tone that the most incredulous dared not contradict her.

Captain Ellis then entered into discussion on different points which ought to be settled. To engage a crew worthy of seconding his effort was not difficult. But there was the question of the ship. Evidently there could be no thought of using the *Boundary* for an expedition of this nature. It was not a sailing vessel that could carry out such a campaign, but a steam vessel.

There were then in the harbour of San Diego a certain number of steamers well suited for the purpose. Mrs. Branican instructed Captain Ellis to buy the fastest of these steamers, and put the necessary funds for the purchase at his disposal. A few days afterwards the affair was concluded, and Mrs. Branican was the owner of the *Davit*, the name of which was changed to *Dolly Hope* of happy augury.

She was a screw steamer of nine hundred tons, designed to carry a large quantity of coal in her bunkers, so that she could take long voyages without having to fill up often with fuel. Rigged as a three-masted schooner, provided with a considerable sail spread, her engines were of 1200 horse-power, and drove her at an average of 15 knots an hour. In these conditions of speed and tonnage the *Dolly Hope*, handy and seaworthy, would answer all the requirements of a voyage through narrow seas strewn with islands, islets and reefs; and it would have been difficult to have made a more appropriate choice for this expedition.

It only took three weeks to get the *Dolly Hope* ready for sea, to inspect her boilers, test her engines, repair her rigging and sails, adjust her compasses, take in her coal, and lay in provisions for a voyage which might last a year. Captain Ellis had resolved not to abandon the region in which the *Franklin* might have been lost without exploring every part of it. He had given his word as a seaman, and he was a man who kept his engagements.

To give a good ship a good crew was to increase the chances of success, and Captain Ellis could only congratulate himself on the crowd of the maritime population of San Diego, from which he had to choose. The best sailors offered to serve under his orders; and there was quite a dispute among those who were anxious to go in search of the victims, who all belonged to the families of the port.

The *Dolly Hope* had two mates and a boatswain, a quartermaster and twenty-five men, including engineers and stokers. Captain Ellis was certain of obtaining all he wished from the devoted mariners, no matter how long or difficult the voyage in the seas of Malaysia. It need not be said that during these preparations Mrs. Branican did not remain inactive. She assisted Captain Ellis by her constant intervention, solving all difficulties with money, and seeing that nothing was neglected to insure the success of the expedition. . In the meanwhile this charitable woman had not forgotten the families which the disappearance of the ship had left in poverty or misery, although in that she had only to complete the measures already taken by Andrews' and supported by public subscription. Henceforth the sub-

sistenee of these families was sufficiently cared for, until the attempt of Mrs. Branican had given, them back the men wrecked in the *Franklin*.

What Dolly had done for the families so cruelly tried by disaster, would she not also do for Jane Burker? She now knew how good Jane had been to her during her illness. She knew that Jane had never left her for an instant. And at this moment she would still be at Prospect House sharing in her hopes, if the deplorable affairs of her husband had not obliged her to leave San Diego, and doubtless the United States. Whatever reproaches Len Burker deserved, it was certain that Jane's conduct had been that of a relation, whose affection extended to entire devotedness. Dolly had thus retained for her a profound friendship, and in thinking of her miserable position her keenest regret was in not being able to show her gratitude by going to her aid. But in spite of all Mr. William Andrew's diligence, it was impossible to discover what had become of the Burkers. It is true that if the place of their retreat had been known, Mrs. Branican could not have summoned them back to San Diego, for Len Burker was under the most overwhelming charges of embezzlement, but she could have hastened to convey to Jane the help of which the unfortunate woman stood in need.

On the 27th of July the *Dolly Hope* was ready to start. Mrs. Branican went on board in the morning, so as to beg Captain Ellis for the last time to omit nothing that might discover traces of the *Franklin*. She had, however, no doubt that he would succeed. They would bring back John; they would bring back the crew. She repeated these words with such conviction that the sailors clapped their hands. All shared in her faith, as did their friends _ and relatives, who had come to see the departure of the *Dolly Hope*.

Captain Ellis then addressed Mrs. Branican at the same time as he spoke to Mr. William Andrew, who had accompanied her on board.

"Before you, madam," he said, "before Mr. William Andrew, in the name of my officers and my crew, I swear, yes! I swear to recoil from nothing either in danger or fatigue to discover Captain John and the men of the *Franklin*. The ship you have fitted out is now called the *Dolly Hope*, and she shall justify her name."

"By the aid of God, and the devotion of those who put their trust in Him!" said Mrs. Branican.

"Hurrah! hurrah! for John and Dolly Branican!"

The shouts were repeated by the whole crowd who thronged the wharves.

Her hawsers were cast off, and the *Dolly Hope*, obedient to the first revolutions of the screw, moved out to leave the bay. As soon as she was through the strait her head was laid south-west, and under the action of her powerful engines she was soon out of sight of the American coast.

CHAPTER XI - THE FIRST CRUISE IN MALAYSIA

ON the 27th of July, after a run of two thousand two hundred miles, the *Dolly Hope* sighted the mountain of Mouna-Kea, which towers for fifteen thousand feet above the island of Hawaii, which is the most southerly of the Sandwich group. Independently of the five large and three small islands, the group includes a certain number of islets on which there was no need to search for traces of the *Franklin*. It was evident that the wreck would long ago have been known if it had taken place on any of the reefs of this archipelago, even those of Medo-Manu, although they are only frequented by innumerable sea birds. In fact, the Sandwich islands are well populated — there are over a hundred thousand inhabitants in Hawaii alone — and through the missionaries the news of the disaster would soon have reached the Californian ports.

Besides, four years before when Captain Ellis had met the *Franklin*, the two ships were already beyond the Sandwich group. The *Dolly Hope* therefore continued her course to the south-west across that admirable Pacific Ocean which well merits its name during the few months of the warm season.

Six days later the speedy steamer had crossed the conventional line which geographers have traced from south to north between Polynesia and Micronesia. In this eastern part of the Polynesian seas, Captain Ellis had no investigation to make. But beyond, the Micronesian seas swarm with islands, islets and reefs, where the *Dolly Hope* would have the dangerous task of discovering some indications of the wreck.

On the 22nd of August the *Dolly Hope* dropped anchor at Otia, the most important of the Marshall group, visited by Kotzebue and the Russians in 1817. This group extends about thirty miles from east to west, and thirteen miles from north to south, and includes about 65 islets or atolls.

The *Dolly Hope*,-which, could have replenished her water tanks in a few hours, remained here five days, while Captain Ellis in the steam launch was able to assure himself that no wreck had occurred on the reefs within the last four years. He found a little floating timber along the Mulgrave islets, but this consisted of trunks of pines, palm trees, and bamboos brought by the currents from the north or the south, and which the natives used to build their canoes with. Captain Ellis also learnt from the chief of Otia Island that, since 1872, there had been only one vessel wrecked on the eastern atolls, and. that was an English brig, the crew of which was eventually taken home.

After leaving the Marshall archipelago the *Dolly Hope* shaped her course for the Carolines. Captain Ellis went in the launch to Olan island as he passed it, but the exploration yielded no result. On the 3rd of September he entered the vast archipelago which extends between the twelfth degree of north latitude and the third degree of south latitude, in one part or another,: between the hundred and twenty-ninth degree of east longitude, and the hundred and seventieth degree of west longitude, or two hundred and twenty-five leagues from north to south on both sides of the equator, and about a thousand leagues from east to west.

The *Dolly Hope* remained for about three months among the Carolines, which are sufficiently well known through the works of Lutke, the bold Russian navigator, added to those of the Frenchmen Duperrey and Dumont D'Urville. No less time was required for visiting the principal groups which form this archipelago, those of the Pelews, the Dangerous Sailors, the Martyrs, the Saavcdras, the Sonsorols, the Marieras, the Annas, the Lord Norths, etc.

Captain Ellis chose for the centre of his operations Yap or Gouap, which belongs to the Carolines proper, which consist of five hundred islands. It was from here that the steamer pursued her investigations to the further points. Of how many shipwrecks has this archipelago been the theatre, among others those of the Antelope in 1793, and the American, Captain Barnard, on the Morty and Lord North islands in 1832?

During this period the way in which the men of the *Dolly Hope* did their work was beyond praise. None of them took notice of the dangers or fatigues occasioned by this navigation amid innumerable reefs and through narrow channels, whose beds bristled with coral. And the bad season had begun to trouble these regions, in which the winds are unloosed with frightful impetuosity, and in which disasters are still so numerous.

Every day the ship's boats explored the creeks where wreckage might be deposited by currents. When the sailors landed they were well armed, for these were not such explorations as were carried on in the desert countries of the Arctic regions by Admiral *Franklin*. These islands were for the most part inhabited, and Captain Ellis's task consisted in manoeuvring like Entrecasteaux when he explored the atolls, where it was thought La Perouse had been lost. It was necessary for him to put himself in communication with the natives. The crew of the *Dolly Hope* were often received by hostile demonstrations among some of the natives, who are anything but hospitable to strangers. There were attacks which it was necessary to repel by force. Two or three sailors were even wounded, but fortunately not seriously.

It was from this archipelago of the Carolines that Captain Ellis's first letters could be sent to Mrs. Branican by ships bound to the American coast. But they contained nothing relative to traces of the *Franklin* or her crew. The attempts which had failed in the Carolines were to be resumed in the west, and comprise the vast system of Malaysia. There in reality were better chances of discovering the survivors of the catastrophe, perhaps on one of the numerous islets, the existence of which is not yet recorded in hydrographical books, even after the three expeditions which have been at work on this part of the Pacific Ocean.

Seven hundred miles more to the west of the Carolines, on the 2nd of December, the *Dolly Hope* reached one of the large islands of the Philippines, the most important group of the Malay archipelagos, and also the most considerable of those the position of which has been fixed by geographers in Malaysian hydrography, and even in the whole of

Oceania. This group, discovered by Magellan in 1521, extends from the fifth to the twenty-first degree of north latitude, and from the hundred and fourteenth to the hundred and twenty-third degree of east longitude.

The *Dolly Hope* did not go to the large island of Luzon, also called Manilla. It was not likely that the *Franklin* had got up so high as the China seas on her way to Singapore. For this reason Captain Ellis preferred to make his centre Mindanao in the south of the archipelago, that is to say on the same line as John Branican would certainly have followed to reach the Java sea.

At this date the *Dolly Hope* was moored off the southwest coast in the port of Zamboanga, the residence of the governor in charge of the three alcaldes of the island.

Mindanao is in two divisions, one Spanish, the other independent under the rule of a Sultan, who has his residence at Selangan.

Captain Ellis made his first inquiries of the governor and alcaldes with regard to the wreck of which the coast of Mindanao might have been the site. The authorities very obligingly put themselves at his disposal; but in the Spanish region of Mindanao, more or less, there had been no maritime disaster for five years.

On the coast of the independent portion of the island inhabited by Mindanais, Caragos, Loutas, Soubanis, and a few other savage races, very justly suspected of cannibalism, disasters might occur and never be heard of, for the people had every reason to say nothing about them! There are even a number of Malays who get their living as pirates. With their light vessels they give chase to merchant vessels, driven by the westerly winds on their coast, and when they capture them they destroy them. Such might have been the *Franklin*'s fate, and assuredly it would not have been reported to the government. The only information he could give relative to the portion of the island under his authority was thus judged insufficient.

And so the *Dolly Hope* had to leave these dangerous seas during the winter season. Many times she sent her boats to different parts of the coast, and the sailors ventured into the forests of tamarinds, bamboos, mangroves, black ebonies, wild acacias and iron woods, which form part of the wealth of the Philippines. Amid these fertile regions, where the products of the temperate zone mingle with those of the tropics, Captain Ellis and his men visited certain villages, where they hoped to find some indication, some fragments of wreckage, some prisoners detained by the Malay tribes; but their operations were fruitless, and the steamer had to return to Zamboanga much tried by the bad weather, and only by a miracle having escaped the submarine reefs in these seas.

The exploration of the Philippine archipelago lasted two months and a half. More than a hundred islands had to be visited, among them the chief, after Luzon and Mindanao being Mindoro, Leyte, Samar, Panay, Negros, Zebu, Marshate, Palawan, Catanduanes, &c.

After exploring the group of Basilan, by the south of Zamboanga, Captain Ellis steered for the Sooloo archipelago, where he arrived about the 25 th of February, 1880.

This was a veritable nest of pirates, in which the natives swarm among the numerous islets which are covered with a network of jungle, and extend from the southern point of Mindanao to the northern point of Borneo, There is but one port which is occasionally frequented by ships crossing the China seas, and the Malaysian waters, the port of Basilan, situated on the principal island which has given its name to the group.

It was at Basilan that the *Dolly Hope* put in. There communications were established with the Sultan and the datous, who govern a population of six or seven thousand inhabitants. Captain Ellis was not sparing of presents eitherin money or kind. The natives put themselves on the track of the different shipwrecks of which these islands, defended by their girdles of coral, had been the site. But amongst the wreckage that was collected nothing was recognized as having belonged to the *Franklin*; and either the men had died or gone home.

The *Dolly Hope*, which had filled up her coal bunkers at Mindanao, was already running short at the end of this cruise among the meanderings of the Sooloo group. Enough remained, however, to take her through the Sea of Celebes, towards the Marantonba Islands, and down to Bandjer Massing, which is situated in the south of Borneo.

Captain Ellis proceeded down this sea which is shut in like a lake between the large Malaysian islands, but it is badly sheltered, and in spite of the natural obstacles against the fury of the storms, it is desolated by the typhoons which cast a shadow over the lovely picture of the splendour of the waters which swarm with zoophytes of startling colours, and molluscs of a thousand species, making the sea a bed of liquid flowers.

Of its stormy nature the *Dolly Hope* had an experience on the night of the 28th and 29th of February. During the day the wind had gradually freshened, and although it had dropped a little towards evening, enormous clouds of livid hue were piled up on the horizon and betokened a troubled night.

The storm broke out with great violence about eleven o'clock, and the sea rose in a few minutes with an impetuosity quite extraordinary.

Captain Ellis, justly alarmed for the *Dolly Hope*s engines, and careful to prevent any accident which might endanger his cruise, lay to so as to require of the screw only enough speed to give the vessel steerage way.

Notwithstanding these precautions the tornado broke with such violence, and the waves beat with such fury round the *Dolly Hope* that several formidable seas boarded her. In some of them quite a hundred tons of water were hurled on to her deck, staving in the skylights and accumulating in the hold. But the strong bulkheads stood the pressure and kept it out from the boiler room and engine room; which was fortunate, for if the fires had been extinguished the *Dolly Hope* would have been left defenceless to the strife of the elements, and, being unable to steer, would have rolled in the hollows of the waves until she was lost.

The crew showed as much coolness as courage in these critical circumstances, and valiantly assisted their commander and officers, and proved themselves worthy of the captain who had chosen them from among the best of the sailors of San Diego. The ship was saved by the skill and precision with which it was handled.

After fifteen terrible hours the sea calmed down, falling almost suddenly as they approached the large Island of Borneo, and in the morning of the 2nd of March the *Dolly Hope* sighted the Maratouba islands.

These islands, which geographically belong to Borneo, became the object of minute exploration during the first fortnight of March. Encouraged by the gifts which were not spared, the chiefs did their best to aid in the search, but it was impossible to procure the least information relative to the disappearance of the *Franklin*, and as these regions of Malaysia are frequently infested by pirates it was to be feared that John Branican and his crew had been massacred to the last man.

One day Captain Ellis, talking over these things with the mate, said, — "It is quite possible that the loss of the *Franklin* was due to an attack of that nature. That would explain why we have not as yet discovered any trace of the wreck. Pirates do not boast of their exploits. When a ship disappears the catastrophe is credited to a typhoon, and there is an end of the matter."

"That is only too true, captain," said the mate. "Pirates are plentiful enough in these seas, and we shall have to keep a sharp look out as we go down the Straits of Macassar."

"Undoubtedly," said Captain Ellis, "but we are in a better position than John Branican to escape the rascals. With irregular and shifty winds a sailing vessel cannot be worked as you please; but so long as the engines work no Malay boat can get at us. Nevertheless, we must keep a good look out."

The *Dolly Hope* entered the Straits of Macassar which separate Borneo from the capricious coast of Celebes. During two months, from the 15th of March to the 15th of May, after coaling at Damaring, Captain Ellis explored all the .eastern creeks.

This Island of Celebes, which was discovered by Magellan, is not less than ninety-two leagues long and twenty- five wide. It is of such a shape that geographers have compared it to a tarantula whose enormous legs are represented by the peninsula. The beauty of its landscapes, the richness of its products, the convenient arrangement of its mountains make it equal to superb Borneo. But its numerous gulfs and creeks offer so many refuges to pirates that the navigation of the strait is really dangerous.

Nevertheless Captain Ellis accomplished his work with all desirable precision. With his boilers always under pressure he visited the creeks in his boats ready to return to the ship at the least appearance of danger.

As she neared the southern extremity of the strait the *Dolly Hope* could proceed under less alarming conditions. In fact, that part of the Island of Celebes is under Dutch rule. The capital of these possessions is Macassar, formerly Wlaardingen, which is defended by the fort of Rotterdam. It was there that Captain Ellis dropped anchor on the 17th of May to give his crew a little rest and to fill up with coal. If he had discovered nothing that could put him on the track of John Branican, he learnt in this port some very important news regarding the course taken by the *Franklin*, for on the 3rd of May, 1875, the ship had been signalled ten miles off Macassar heading towards the Java sea. It was therefore certain that she had not perished in the dangerous waters of Malaysia. It was beyond Celebes and Borneo, that is to say in the Sea of Java, that he must renew his investigations and continue them on to Singapore.

In a letter which he addressed to Mr-s. Branican from this extreme point of the Island of Celebes, Captain Ellis informed her of this circumstance, and renewed his promise to keep her acquainted with his investigations, which would now be localized between the Sea of Java and the Sunda islands.

In fact, the *Dolly Hope* would not pass the meridian of Singapore, which would be the limit of her cruise to the westward. She would complete her cruise by returning along the southern coast of the Java sea and visiting the chaplet of islands that border it; and then by the way of the Moluccas she would regain the Pacific and return to America.

The *Dolly Hope* left Macassar on the 23rd of July, crossed the narrow strait which separates the island of Celebes from the island of Borneo, and put in at Bandjer Massing-. At this port resides the governor of Borneo, or rather Kalematan, to give it its true geographical name. There the shipping records were minutely searched, but no mention could be found of the *Franklin* having been seen in those parts; but that could be explained by supposing she had kept well out in the Java sea.

Ten days afterwards, Captain Ellis, having steered southwest, dropped anchor at Batavia, at the end of the large Island of Java, which is essentially of volcanic origin, and is nearly always overhung by the flames from its craters.

A few days were enough for the crew to revictual in this great city, which is the capital of the Dutch possessions in Oceania. The governor-general, whom the shipping news had made acquainted with the efforts of Mrs. Branican to discover the castaways, received Captain Ellis with cordiality. Unfortunately he could give no intelligence as to the fate of the *Franklin*. The opinion of the Dutch sailors was that the American vessel had foundered with all on board in some tornado. During the first six months, of 1875 they mentioned several vessels which had not been heard of, and which had vanished in the same way without the least trace of them being thrown on the coast.

After leaving Batavia the *Dolly Hope*, leaving on the port hand the Strait of Sunda, which affords the communication between the Sea of Java and the Sea of Timor, stood off for the islands of Billiton and

Banca. Formerly the approaches to these islands were infested by pirates, and the vessels which came for cargoes of iron and tin only avoided attack with difficulty. But the maritime police had effectually cleared the sea of them, and there was no reason to think that the *Franklin* and her crew had been the victim of their aggressions.

Continuing to the north-west, visiting the islands on the coast of Sumatra, the *Dolly Hope* doubled the extremity of the peninsula of Malacca and reached Singapore in the morning of the 29th of June, after a passage much retarded.

Repairs to the engines obliged Captain Ellis to remain a fortnight in this port, which is situated to the north of the island. Of little extent — some two hundred and seventy square miles only — this possession, which is of such importance in the trade between Europe and America, has become one of the richest in the east since the day the English founded their first house there in 1818.

It was at Singapore, as we know, that the *Franklin* had to deliver a part of her cargo on account of Andrews', before she proceeded to Calcutta; and we also know that the American vessel had never appeared there. At the same time Captain Ellis resolved to put the delay to good use by obtaining all the information he could regarding the disasters in the Java sea during the last few years.

The *Franklin* had on the one hand, been reported at Macassar; on the other, she had not arrived at Singapore; consequently she must have been wrecked somewhere between these points; that is, unless Captain Branican had left the Java sea through one of the straits which separate the Sunda islands and entered the Sea of Timor. But why should he do this if his destination were Singapore? It was inexplicable, it was inadmissible.

The inquiry regarding the disasters in the Java sea during the previous five or six years having given but negative results, Captain Ellis could only take his leave of the governor of Singapore, and begin his return to America.

On the 25th of August he started in very stormy weather. The heat was excessive, as it generally is in the month of August in this part of the torrid zone, which is only a few degrees below the equator. The *Dolly Hope* experienced very rough weather during the last week of the month; but in cruising past the Sunda islands not a place was left unexplored. One after the other, Madura island, one of the twenty regencies of Java, Bali, one of the busiest of these possessions, Lombok, and Sumbava, with its volcano then threatening the island with an eruption as disastrous as that of 1815, were visited. Between these different islands opened many straits, giving access to the Timor sea, and the *Dolly Hope* had to be carefully handled to avoid the powerful currents, which are of such impetuosity as to bear away the vessels, even in the teeth of the western monsoon. It will be understood from this, how full of danger navigation is in these seas, particularly for sailing vessels, which have no power of locomotion in themselves, and hence the maritime disasters so frequent within the Malaysian zone.

Leaving the Island of Floris, Captain Ellis followed the thain of the other islands to the south of the sea of the Moluccas, but in vain. After so many failures, it is not to be wondered that the crew was discouraged. But there was no reason for giving up all hope of discovering the *Franklin* until the exploration had been finished. It was possible that Captain Branican, instead of descending the Strait of Macassar, had crossed the archipelago and Sea of the Moluccas, to reach the Java sea, and thus had appeared off Celebes.

But time, went on, and the log continued to be silent regarding the fate of the *Franklin*. Neither at Timor, nor in the three groups which constitute the Moluccan archipelago, the group of Amboyna, the residence of the governor-general, which includes Ceram and Bouro, the Banda group, nor the Gilolo group, could any information be obtained regarding a vessel that should have been lost among these islands in the spring of 1875. From the 23rd of September, the date of the *Dolly Hope*'s arrival at Timor, to the 27th of December, the date of her arrival at Gilolo, three months were occupied in investigations which the Dutch assisted to the best of their ability, and nothing was discovered to throw light on the disaster.

The *Dolly Hope* had finished her cruise. At this island of Gilolo, which is the most important of the Moluccas, terminated the circle which Captain Ellis had undertaken to follow round the Malaysian region; the crew then had a few days' rest to which they were well entitled. And if any new clue had been discovered, what would not these brave men have attempted, even at the cost of greater dangers!

Ternate, the capital of Gilolo, which commands the Moluccan seas, and which is the headquarters of the Dutch . Resident, furnished the *Dolly Hope* with all that was necessary in the way of provisions and coal for the return voyage. There ended the year 1881, the sixth which had elapsed since the disappearance of the *Franklin*.

Captain Ellis weighed anchor in the morning of the 9th of January, and steamed off to the north-east.

It was then the bad season. The crossing was not easy, and unfavourable winds occasioned long delays. It was not until the 23rd of February that the *Dolly Hope* was signalled by the semaphores of San Diego.

This cruise in Malaysia had lasted nineteen months. In spite of the efforts of Captain Ellis, in spite of the devotion of his crew, the secret of the *Franklin* remained buried in the mysterious depths of the sea.

CHAPTER XII - ANOTHER YEAR

The letters which Mrs. Branican had received in the course of the expedition made her doubt that the attempt would be crowned with success. And so after the arrival of the last, she retained but little hope regarding the search of Captain Ellis in the Moluccan archipelago.

As soon as she learnt that the *Dolly Hope* was in sight of San Diego, Mrs. Branican, accompanied by Mr. William Andrew, went down to the harbour, and as soon as the steamer came to an anchor they went on board.

The looks of Captain Ellis and his crew said clearly enough, that the second half of the cruise had been no more successful than the first.

Mrs. Branican, after shaking hands with the captain, stepped up to the men so severely tried by the fatigues of the voyage, and said in a firm voice, —

"I thank you, Captain Ellis, and I thank you, my friends 1 You have done all I could expect from your devotion! You have not succeeded, and perhaps you despair at success? I do not despair! No! I do not despair of again seeing John and his companions of the *Franklin*! My hope is in God — and God will realize it!" These words were uttered with such extraordinary assurance, they testified to such rare energy, they said so resolutely that Mrs. Branican would never give in, that her confidence should have been communicated to all hearts. But if the men listened with the respect that her attitude commanded, there was not one who doubted but that the *Franklin* and her crew were inevitably lost.

But could they have done better than yield to that special intuition with which .a woman is naturally endowed? When a man clings only to the direct observation of facts and their consequences, it is certain that woman has occasionally a juster prevision of the future, thanks to her intuitive qualities. A kind of instinct of genius guides her and gives her a certain prescience. Who knows if Mrs. Branican would not one day be justified in her opposition to the general opinion?

Mrs. Branican and Mr. William Andrew then passed into the *Dolly Hope*'s cabin, where Captain Ellis gave them a detailed account of the expedition. The charts of Polynesia and Malaysia were spread upon the table and permitted them to follow the course of the steamer, her anchorages at the numerous points explored, the observations collected in the principal ports and native villages, the searches instituted among the islands and islets with minute patience and indefatigable zeal.

In conclusion, said Captain Ellis, —

"Allow me to call your attention specially to this: The *Franklin* was seen for the last time at the southern end of Celebes on the 3rd of May, 1875, about seven weeks after she left San Diego, and from that day she has never been met with. As she never arrived at Singapore it is beyond doubt that the disaster occurred in the Java Sea. How? There are only two hypotheses: The first is that the *Franklin* went down under all sail or perished in a collision without a trace of her being left; the second is that she was dashed to pieces on the rocks, or destroyed by Malay pirates, and in either ease it would have been possible to find some wreckage. But in spite of all our efforts we have found no material proof of the *Franklin*'s destruction."

The conclusion derivable from their argument was that it was more logical to admit the first hypothesis — that which attributed the *Franklin*'s loss to one of the tornadoes so frequent in Malaysian waters. In fact, for the second supposition, that of the collision, it was so seldom that one of the two ships continued to keep the sea, that the secret of the meeting would have been known sooner or later; and therefore, no hope remained.

This is what Mr. William Andrew understood, and he sadly bowed his head before Mrs. Branican, who did not cease to question him. "Well, no!" she said, "no! the *Franklin* has not foundered! No! John and his crew have not perished!"

113

And the interview continuing at Dolly's request, it became necessary for Captain Ellis to make his report in most circumstantial detail. She returned to the matter again and again, questioning and discussing without yielding in her opinion in any way.

This conversation lasted for three hours, and when Mrs. Branican was about to go, Captain Ellis asked if it was her intention for the *Dolly Hope* to be laid up.

"No, captain," she answered, "I should be sorry to see your crew and yourself dismissed. There may be something new arrive. which will make another expedition necessary; if then you consent to retain the command of *Dolly Hope'*.'

"That I would do willingly," answered Captain Ellis, "but I belong to Andrews', Mrs. Branican, and they may require my services."

"Do not let that stop you, my dear Ellis," said Mr. William Andrew, "I shall be happy for you to remain at Dolly's orders if she wishes it."

"I am at your orders, Mr. Andrew. My crew and myself will not leave the *Dolly Hope.*"

"And I beg, captain," said Mrs. Branican, "that you will take care the ship is always ready for sea."

And in giving his consent, the ship-owner had had no other thought than to defer to Dolly's wishes. But neither he nor Captain Ellis doubted that she would give up a second campaign after the useless results of the first. If time had not weakened in her the memory of the catastrophe, it would at least end in destroying the hope that remained.

And so, in conformity with Mrs. Branican's desires, the *Dolly Hope* was not dismantled. Captain Ellis and his men continued to figure on her books and receive their wages as if they were at sea. There were important repairs to make after nineteen months in the trying seas of Malaysia; the hull required careening, the rigging required partial renewal, the boilers had to be replaced, and several parts of the engine required changing; and when the work was done, the *Dolly Hope* shipped her provisions, filled up with coal, and was ready for sea when ordered.

Mrs. Branican had resumed her habitual life at Prospect House, where, with the exception of Mr. William Andrew and Captain Ellis, no one was admitted to her friendship. She lived only in remembrances and hopes, having always present in her thoughts the double misfortune which had fallen on her. Little Wat would have been seven years old at this time — the age when the first rays of reason illuminate impressionable young brains — and little Wat was no more. Then Dolly's thoughts returned to him who had risked his life to save hers, to Zach Fren, whom she wished to know and who had not yet returned to San Francisco. . But that would soon happen. Many times the shipping intelligence had contained news of the Californian, and the year 1881 would probably not finish before he came back to his native place. As soon as he arrived, Mrs. Branican would call him to her and pay him her debt of gratitude, which would assure his future.

Meanwhile Mrs. Branican did not cease to help the ' families suffering from the loss of the *Franklin*. It was only to visit their humble homes, to soothe their cares, and do some work of charity that she left Prospect House and went down into the lower town. Her generosity showed itself in all forms, and extended to the mental requirements as well as the material wants of her friends; and it was in the earlier months of this year that she consulted Mr. William Andrew regarding a project she was eager to put into execution.

She desired to found a hospital to receive children that had been abandoned, or orphans having neither father nor mother.

"Mr. Andrew," said she to the ship-owner, "it is in memory of our child that I wish to found this institution, and endow it with the resources necessary for its maintenance. John will no doubt approve of what I do when he returns. And what better use could I make of our fortune?"

Mr. William Andrew, having no objection to make, put himself at Mrs. Branican's disposal with regard to the preliminaries that were required in the creation of an establishment of this nature. One hundred and fifty thousand dollars were devoted to it, first for the acquisition of a convenient building, and then for the payment of its annual expenses.

The affair was very quickly concluded, owing to the assistance given to Mrs. Branican by the municipality. No buildings were necessary. A vast edifice situated in a good atmosphere, on one of the slopes of San Diego, near the Old Town, was secured. An able architect adapted the edifice to its new purpose, and altered it so as to provide a home for fifty children, with a staff sufficient to educate and look after them. -Surrounded by a large garden, shaded by beautiful trees, watered by running streams, and including all the sanitary systems approved by experience, it had everything to make it healthy.

On the 19th of May this hospital — which received the name of Wat House — was inaugurated amid the applause of the whole town, which on this occasion sought to shower on Mrs. Branican the most striking testimonies of its sympathy. But the charitable woman did not appear at the ceremony, as she did not care to leave her chalet. As soon however, as a certain number of children had been received at Wat House, she went every day to visit them as if she had been their mother. The children could remain in the hospital until they were twelve years old. As soon as they were old enough they were taught to read and write, and received a moral and religious education at the same time as they were taught a trade according to their abilities. Some of them belonged to families of sailors and showed a taste for the sea, and these were destined to be shipped as cabin boys or apprentices. And in truth it seemed that Dolly felt more personal affection for them than for the rest — doubtless in remembrance of Captain John.

At the end of 1881 no news of the *Franklin* had been received at San Diego or elsewhere. Although a considerable reward was offered to whoever brought the least clue, it had not been possible to send the

Dolly Hope on a second cruise. But still Mrs. Branican did not despair. That which 1881 had not given, 1882 might give.

What had become of Mr. and Mrs. Burker? Where had Len Burker taken refuge to escape the pursuit ordered against him? The Federal police had given up all inquiry in the matter, and Mrs. Branican had to abandon all thoughts of knowing what had become of Jane.

But this was a deep affliction for her who was so much distressed at the position of her unfortunate relative. She was astonished at never having received a letter from Jane — a letter which she might have written without in any way endangering her husband's safety. Were they both unaware that Dolly, restored to reason, had sent a ship in search of the *Franklin*, and that the expedition had had no result? It was inadmissible. Had not the newspapers of both worlds followed the different phases of the enterprise, and could it be imagined that Len and Jane Burker had not heard of it? They could not even be ignorant that Mrs. Branican had become rich by the death of her uncle Edward Starter, and that she was in a position to come to their assistance. But, all the same, neither one nor the other tried to enter into correspondence with her, although their position must have been very precarious.

January, February, March passed, and it seemed as though the year 1882 would bring no change in the state of things, when something happened that appeared to throw some light on the fate of the *Franklin*.

On the 27th of March, the steamer Californian, on board of which was Zach Fren, came to an anchor in the bay of San Francisco, after a cruise of several years in the seas of Europe.

As soon as Mrs. Branican heard of the ship's return she wrote to Zach Fren, who was then boatswain on board the Californian, and invited him to come immediately to her at San Diego.

As Zach Fren had intended to return to his native town to take a few months' rest, he replied that as soon as . he could get ashore he would come to San Diego, and his first visit would be to Prospect House. This was a matter of a few days.

117

But at the same time a rumour spread which would make considerable noise in the States if it proved to be true.

It was said that the Californian had brought home some wreckage which appeared to belong to the *Franklin*. One of the San Francisco papers added that the Californian had found the wreckage off the north of Australia, in the region between the Timor Sea and the Arafura Sea near Melville Island, west of Torres Island.

As soon as this news arrived at San Diego, Mr. William Andrew and Captain Ellis, who had had the news by telegram, hurried to Prospect House.

At the first Word they said on the subject, Mrs. Branican became very pale. But her tone denoted absolute conviction as far as she was concerned.

"After the wreckage they will find the *Franklin*," said she, "and after the *Franklin* they will find John and his companions."

The discovery of this piece of wreck was a fact of importance.

It was the first time that any relic of the lost ship had been met with. For a search for the site of the disaster Mrs. Branican now possessed a link in the chain which bound her to the past.

Immediately she had brought a map of Oceania. Then Mr. William Andrew and Captain Ellis could study the question of another cruise, for she wished a decision in the matter to be come to on the spot.

"And so the *Franklin* did not go straight to Singapore on her way through the Philippines and Malaysia," said Mr. William Andrew.

"But that is improbable; it is impossible," said Captain Ellis.

"But," continued the ship-owner, "if she had followed that course, how could this wreckage have been found in the Arafura' Sea to the north of Melville Island?"

"That I cannot explain and cannot understand, Mr. Andrew," replied Captain Ellis. "All I know is that the *Franklin* was seen south-west of

Celebes after leaving the Straits of Macassar; and if she came down those straits she must have come from the south and not from the east. She was therefore unable to come through Torres Strait."

The question was discussed for some time, and it had to be admitted that Captain Ellis was right Mrs. Branican listened to the objections and replies without making any observation. But a vertical fold in her forehead indicated with what tenacity and obstinacy she refused to admit the loss of John and his companions. No! She would not believe it until some proof of their death was forthcoming.

"Agreed!" said Mr. William Andrew. "I think as you do, my dear Ellis, that the *Franklin* crossed the Sea of Java on her way to Singapore."

"Some part of it, at least, Mr. Andrew, for it was between Singapore and Celebes that the wreck took place."

"Be it as you say. But how could the wreck be drifting off Australia, if the *Franklin* was lost on some reef in the Sea of Java?"

"That can only be explained in one way," said Captain Ellis, "by admitting that the wreck drifted through the Straits of Sunda, or one of the other channels leading into the Timor and Arafura seas."

"Would the currents take it in that direction?"

"Yes, Mr. Andrew, and I may add that if the *Franklin* had been disabled in a storm, she might be carried down one of the straits, to be finally lost on the reefs of the Australian coast."

"Quite so, my dear Ellis,", said Mr. William Andrew, "and that is the only plausible explanation, and in that case if a wreck has been met with off Melville Island six years after the disaster, it is because it has been recently detached from the reefs on which the *Franklin* was lost."

This hypothesis no sailor would have contested.

Mrs. Branican, whose look was never taken off the map that lay before her, then said, —

119

"If the *Franklin* were really lost on the coast of Australia, and the survivors of the wreck have not reappeared, it is because they were taken prisoners by the natives."

"That, Dolly, is not impossible — but — " said Mr. William Andrew.

Mrs. Branican was about to protest with energy against the doubt implied in Mr. William Andrew's reply, when Captain Ellis intervened with, —

"It remains to be seen if the wreckage fished up by the Californian really belonged to the *Franklin*"

"And do you doubt it?" asked Dolly.

"We shall soon know," said Mr. William Andrew, "for I have given orders for it to be sent on."

"And I," said Mrs. Branican, "give orders that the *Dolly Hope* is got ready to sail."

Three days after this interview, the boatswain, Zach Fren, who had just arrived at San Diego, presented himself at Prospect House.

At this time he was about thirty-seven years of age, strong and resolute in appearance, with his face tanned by the wind and sea, frank and cheery in look. He was one of those sailors who inspire confidence in others because they have confidence in themselves, and who always go straight to the point.

The welcome he received from Mrs. Branican was so full of gratitude that he did not know what to say.

"My friend," said she to him, after giving utterance to the first outpourings of her heart, "it is you — you who saved my life, you who did all you could to save my poor child. What can I do for you?"

The boatswain said that he only did his duty. That a sailor who did not act as he had done would not be a sailor — he would only be a soldier. His only regret was that he had not been able to restore the baby to its mother. But he did not deserve anything at all. He thanked Mrs.

Branican for her good intentions regarding him; and if she would allow him, he would call and see her whenever he came ashore.

"For years, Zach Fren," said Mrs. Branican, "I have been waiting for. your return, and I hope you will be near me on the day Captain John returns."

"The day Captain John returns!"

"Zach Fren, can you believe — "

"That Captain John has perished? No, I do not!" said the boatswain.

"Yes! You have hope?"

"I have more than hope, Mrs. Branican; I am sure of it.- Is a captain like Captain John to be lost like a cap in a puff of wind? Not likely! I never saw anything like it!"

So said Zach Fren, and in terms which testified to his absolute faith and made Mrs. Branican's heart leap. She was not the only one, then, to believe in John's return"! Another shared her conviction — and the other was the man who had saved her. It seemed to her an indication of Providence.

"Thank you, Zach Fren," said she, "thank you! You don't know the good you have done me! Tell me again — tell me again that Captain John survived the wreck — "

"He did! he did! Mrs. Branican. And the proof that he survived it is that one day or another he will be found! And if that is not a proof — "

And then Zach Fren gave a number of details as to the circumstances under which the wreckage had been fished up by the Californian. At last Mrs. Branican said to him, — "Zach Fren, I have decided to begin a new search immediately.""Well — and it will succeed this time — and I will go with it, if you will allow me."

"Will you agree to serve under Captain Ellis?"

"Willingly."

"Thank you, Zach Fren! It seems to me that with you on board the *Dolly Hope* there will be one chance more."

"I believe so, Mrs. Branican!" said the boatswain, winking his eye. "Yes! I believe so — and I am ready to start."

Dolly took Zach Fren's hand, she pressed it as if it were a friend's. Her imagination led her away, led her astray, perhaps, but it seemed as though this boatswain would succeed where others had failed.

However, as Captain Ellis bad observed — and although Mrs. Branican was convinced on the subject — it was necessary to make sure that the wreckage brought home by the Californian really did belong to the *Franklin*.

Ordered on by Mr. William Andrew, it soon arrived by railroad at San Diego, and was immediately taken to the shipyard. There it was submitted to the examination of the men who had built the *Franklin*.

The fragment met with by the crew of the Californian m off! the little island a dozen miles from the shore, was a piece of the stem, or rather of that carved cutwater which usually figures at the prow of sailing vessels. The fragment of wood had been much damaged, not by a long sojourn in the water, but by exposure to the weather. Hence the conclusion that it had remained for a long time on the reefs, against which the ship had been thrown, and then Been detached by some cause — perhaps by the action of a current, and drifted for many months or many weeks before it was noticed by the sailors of the Californian. But did it belong to Captain John's ship? Yes, for what remained of the carving resembled that which had ornamented the prows of the *Franklin*.

This was clearly made out at San Diego; the shipwrights had no doubt of it. The teak wood used for the prow had come out of the timber stores of the yard. They even found the traces of the iron band which fastened the cutwater of the stem, and the remains of a coat of red paint and a gold stripe on the foliage which had ornamented the bow.

And so this piece of wreck, brought home by the Californian, undoubtedly belonged to the ship which had been searched for in vain in the seas of Malaysia.

That point being settled, there had to be admitted the reasonableness of Captain Ellis's explanation, that as the *Franklin* had been sighted in the Java Sea south-west of Celebes, it followed that a few days later she had been driven through the Straits of Sunda, or some other channel opening into the Timor or Arafura seas, and had been wrecked on one of the reefs of the Australian coast.

The despatch of a vessel with orders to explore the seas between the Sunda Islands and the north coast of Australia was thus completely justified. Would this cruise succeed any better than that among the Philippines, Celebes and the Moluccas? There was reason to hope so.

This time Mrs. Branican thought of going out with the *Dolly Hope*. But Mr. William Andrew and Captain Ellis, as well as Zach Fren, dissuaded her, not without difficulty, from doing so. A cruise of this kind might be very long, and might be endangered by the presence of a woman on board.

We need not say that Zach Fren was engaged as boatswain of the *Dolly Hope*, and that Captain Ellis prepared his ship for sea with the least possible delay.

CHAPTER XIII - A CRUISE IN THE TIMOR SEA

THE *Dolly Hope* left the port of San Diego at ten o'clock in the morning of the 3rd of April, 1882. As soon as she was out of sight of the American coast, Captain Ellis steered south-west in a direction just a little lower than on his first cruise. In fact, he wished to take the shortest cut to the Arafura Sea through Torres Straits, beyond which the wreckage from the *Franklin*'s bow had been picked up.

On the 26th of April they sighted the Gilbert Islands, widely scattered in these regions, where the calms, of the Pacific at this time of the year make navigation so slow and difficult for sailing vessels. Leaving to the northward the Scarborough and Kingsmill groups, which make up this archipelago, situated about eight hundred leagues from the Californian coast to the south-east of the Carolines, Captain Ellis crossed the Vanikoro group, distinguishable fifteen leagues off by the lofty Mount Kapongo.

These green and fertile islands, covered throughout their extent by impenetrable forests, belong to the Fiji archipelago. They are surrounded by coral reefs which make approach to them very dangerous. It was on them that Dumont D'Urville and Dillon found the remains of the ships of La Perouse, the Recherche and Esperance, which left Brest in 1791, and, driven on the reefs of Vanikoro, lever returned.

In sight of this island, so sadly celebrated, a very natural feeling affected the crew of the *Dolly Hope*. Had the *Franklin* met with the fate of La Perouse's ships? And as it had happened to Dumont D'Urville and Dillon, would it happen to Captain Ellis to find only the remains of the lost ship? And if he did not discover the place of the catastrophe, would the fate of John Branican and his companions remain in a state of mystery?

Two hundred miles further the *Dolly Hope* crossed obliquely through the Solomon Islands, formerly called New Georgia. This archipelago comprises a dozen large islands, dispersed over an area of two hundred leagues in length and forty in width. Amongst them are the Carteret Islands, formerly called the Massacre Islands, the name sufficiently indicating the sanguinary scenes of which they had been the site.

Captain Ellis had no information to seek from the natives of this group and no investigation to make in the vicinity. He did not stop, and steamed on towards Torres Strait, no less impatient than Zach Fren to reach that part of the Arafura Sea where the wreckage had been recovered. It would be there that the search would be conducted with a minute care and indefatigable perseverance that perhaps might meet with success.

The shores of New Guinea were not far off. A few days after leaving the Solomon Islands the *Dolly Hope* sighted the Louisiade archipelago. They passed in the offing the islands of Rossel, of Entrecasteaux, Trobriand and a large number of islets covered with magnificent domes of cocoanut trees.

At length, after a passage of three weeks, the look-outs recognized on the horizon the high lands of New Guinea, and the peaks of Cape York projecting from the Australian coast which bound Torres Strait to the north and south.

This strait is extremely dangerous. Captains always avoid it if they can; and it seems that even marine assurance companies decline to guarantee against sea risks within it. A careful-note has to be taken of the currents which flow incessantly from the east to the west and bear the Pacific waters into the Indian Ocean. The shoals make navigation extremely perilous, and it can only be attempted during certain hours of the day when the position of the sun enables the breakers to be seen in the track of the surge.

It was when in sight of Torres Strait that Captain Ellis, in conversation with the mate and Zach Fren, asked the boatswain, —

"Is it the fact that it was in the latitude of Melville Island that the Californian picked up the wreckage of the *Franklin*?"

125

"Exactly," said Zach Fren.

"Then we must reckon nearly five hundred miles across the Arafura Sea after leaving the Strait?"

"That is so, captain, and I understand your difficulty. Given the regular currents which flow from east to west, it seems that if this piece of wreck was picked up off Melville Island, the *Franklin* must have been lost at the entrance of Torres Strait."

"Undoubtedly, Zach Fren, and we might reason that John Branican had been obliged to choose the dangerous road to Singapore; but I do not think so. Until I know more I shall persist in believing he crossed Malaysia, as we found in our first voyage, on account of his having been seen for the last time south of the island of Celebes."

"And as there is no doubt about that," said the mate, "it follows that Captain Branican entered Timor Sea down one of the straits dividing the Sunda Islands."

"That is incontestable," said Captain Ellis, "and I cannot understand how the *Franklin* got so far. Either she was disabled or she was not. If she was disabled it must have been from hundreds of miles west of Torres Strait that the currents bore her. If not, why should she return to this place when Singapore is in the opposite direction?"

"I do not know," said the mate. "If the wreckage had been found in the Indian Ocean it might be explained by a wreck having occurred either on the Sunda Islands or on the west coast of Australia."

"But," replied Captain Ellis, "as it has been recovered in the latitude of Melville Island, it shows that the *Franklin* was wrecked in that part of the Arafura Sea adjoining Torres Strait, or even in the Strait."

"Perhaps," said Zach Fren, "there are counter-currents along the Australian coast which floated the wreckage back. In that case the wreck might have taken place in the west of the Arafura Sea."

"We shall see," said Captain Ellis, "but in the meantime let us act as though the *Franklin* had been destroyed on the reefs of Torres Strait."

"And if we act wisely," repeated Zach Fren, "we shall find Captain John."

In short, this was the best thing to do, and it was done.

The width of Torres Strait is estimated at thirty miles. It would be difficult to imagine the swarm of islets and reefs, the position of which is hardly known to the best of hydrographers. There are at least some hundred of them at the level of the water for the most part, and the largest of them measuring no more than from three to four miles in circumference. They are inhabited by tribes of Andamans, who are much to be feared by the crews falling into their hands, as is shown by the massacre of the sailors of the Chesterfield and Hormuzier. By passing from one to the other in their light canoes, or flying proahs of Malay build, these natives can voyage without difficulty from New Guinea to Australia and from Australia to New Guinea. If Captain John and his companions had taken refuge on one of these islands it would have been easy for them to reach the Australian coast, then gain some settlement in the Gulf of Carpentaria or the Cape York peninsula, and thus return home without difficulty. But as none of them had reappeared, the only hypothesis admissible was that they had fallen into the hands of the natives, who were not the sort of savages to have respect for them; they would kill them without pity and devour them, and how could any trace be found of such a catastrophe?

So said Captain Ellis, and so said the sailors of the *Dolly Hope*. Such ought to have been the fate of the survivors of the *Franklin* if she had been lost in Torres Strait There remained, it is true, the chance that she had not entered the strait. But then how could they explain the fact of this fragment of cutwater having been met with off Melville Island?

Captain Ellis boldly entered among these dangerous channels, taking every measure that prudence required. With a good steamer, vigilant officers and brave crew, he might well reckon on traversing this labyrinth of reefs and keeping off the natives who might attempt to attack him.

When, for one reason or another, vessels enter Torres Strait, the mouth of which is furrowed with coral banks on the Pacific side, they generally keep along the Australian coast. But to the south of Papua there exists a rather large island, Murray Island, which had to be examined with some care.

The *Dolly Hope*, then, went on between two dangerous reefs, known as Eastern Fields and Boot Reef. And on the last, owing to the arrangement of the rocks having at a distance the appearance of a wrecked ship, it seemed as though the remains of the *Franklin* had been found, and in consequence there was some excitement, that did not last long owing to the steam launch soon discovering that there was nothing but a strange piling up of coral rocks.

Several canoes, mere trunks of trees hollowed out by fire or by the axe, and fitted with outriggers to give them stability, paddled by five or six natives, were perceived on approaching Murray Island. These natives contented themselves with shouting, or rather howling, like wild beasts. At half-steam the *Dolly Hope* made the round of the island without having to repel any attack. Nowhere did they see any trace of a wreck. On these islands and islets there was nothing but black natives of athletic build, with woolly hair, reddish in hue, shining skin, and with large, but not flat noses. By way of showing their hostile intentions they shook their spears, their bows, their arrows, as they gathered under the cocoanut trees which grow in thousands in the neighbourhood of the strait.

For a month, up to the 10th of June, after renewing his coals at Somerset, one of the ports of Northern Australia, Captain Ellis minutely examined the shores between the Gulf of Carpentaria and New Guinea. He put in at Mill- grave Island, Banks Island, Horn Island, Albany Island, and Booby Island, which is hollowed out in dark caverns, in one of which is the letter-box of Torres Strait. But sailors are not content with -depositing their letters in the box, the collection of which is not very regular, be it understood. A sort of international convention obliges the sailors of different countries to leave a store of coal and provisions on this Booby Island, and there is no fear of these being stolen by the natives, owing to the strength of the currents not permitting their frail vessels to land there.

Now and then, by pleasing them with presents of little value, it was possible to communicate with the mados or chiefs of these islands. In return they offered "kaiso," or tortoise-shell, and "incras," threaded shells which serve them for money. As they could not make themselves understood, and their language was unknown to those on the *Dolly Hope*, it was impossible to discover if they had any remembrance of a wreck taking place about the date of the *Franklin*'s disappearance. In any case it did not seem as though they had in their possession any objects, arms, or tools of American make. No ironwork or pieces of carpentry, or masts, or spars were found which could point to the demolition of a ship. And when Captain Ellis left these natives of Torres Strait, if he could not affirm that the *Franklin* had not been wrecked on the reefs, at least he had found no trace of her.

The next work was the exploration of the Arafura Sea, leading on to the Timor Sea, between the group of small Sunda Islands to the north and the Australian coast to the south. As to the Gulf of Carpentaria, Captain Ellis did not propose to visit it, for if a wreck took place on its coasts it would not remain unknown to the colonists in the neighbourhood. It was, on the contrary, on the coast of Arnheim Land that he first intended to explore. Then on the return, he would explore the northern part of the Timor Sea and the numerous channels of access to it between the islands.

This cruise along Arnheim Land, swarming with islands and reefs, did not take less than a month. It was accomplished with a zeal and a boldness nothing could discourage. But everywhere, from the western point of the Gulf of Carpentaria to the Gulf of Van Diemen, no information could be got. Nowhere could the crew of the *Dolly Hope* come across the remains of a wrecked. ship. Neither the Australian natives nor. the Chinese, who carry on the trepang trade in these seas, could throw any light whatever on the matter. But if the, survivors of the *Franklin* had been made prisoners by the Australian tribes of the region, tribes which are addicted to cannibalism, not one of them could have been spared except by a miracle.

On the 11th of July, on reaching the hundred and thirtieth degree of longitude. Captain Ellis began the exploration of Melville Island and Bathurst Island, which are separated from each other by only a narrow strait. Ten miles to the north of this group the wreckage of the *Franklin* had been recovered. As it had not been carried further west, it followed that it had not been taken from the reef until a short time before the arrival of the Californian. It was thus possible that the site of the catastrophe was not very far away.

The exploration lasted nearly four months, for it included not only the surroundings of these two islands, but also the neighbouring coast line of Arnheim Land up to Queen's Channel, and even the mouth of the Victoria River.

It was very difficult to continue the investigations inland, which would have risked much without any chance of success. The tribes inhabiting the northern territories of the Australian continent are very formidable. Recently, as Captain Ellis heard at one of the ports he put in at, there had been fresh acts of cannibalism in these parts. The crew of a Dutch vessel, the Groningen, deceived by the false signals of the natives of Bathurst Island, had been massacred and devoured by these wild beasts — is not that the only name they deserve? . Whoever became their prisoner might, perhaps, consider himself as destined to the most frightful of deaths.

But if Captain Ellis would have to give up all hope of knowing when and where the crew of the *Franklin* fell into the hands of these natives, it might still be possible for him to discover some trace of the wreck; and there was all the more reason for hoping that, as eight months had not elapsed since the Californian had found the fragment to the north of Melville Island.

Captain Ellis and his crew accordingly set to work to search the gulfs and creeks of the reefs on the coast, without troubling themselves about the fatigues or dangers to which they were exposed. This accounts for the duration of the exploration; it was very long, because it required to be very minute. Several times the *Dolly Hope* was in danger of running on the little-known breakers of these seas. Many times, too, she was on the point of being captured by the natives, who had to be driven off in their proahs by musketry when they were at a distance, and by axes when they tried to board.

But neither on Melville and Bathurst Islands, nor in Arnheim Land up to the mouth of the Victoria, nor in Torres Strait did the search yield anything. Nothing was discovered of the remains of a wreck, and no fragment of wreck was met with afloat by the *Dolly Hope*.

That was the position of affairs on the 3rd of November. What would Captain Ellis now do? Would he consider that his mission was ended — at least as far as the Australian coast was concerned, and the islands and inlets in its neighbourhood? Would he think of returning after exploring the small Sunda Islands in the north of the Timor Sea? In a word, did he think he had done all it was humanly possible to do?

The brave seaman hesitated, it will be understood, to look upon his task as ended, even after continuing it up to the Australian coast.

An, incident put an end to his hesitation. On the morning of the 4th of September he was walking with Zach Fren on the after part of the steamer, when the boatswain pointed out a few objects floating about half a mile from the *Dolly Hope*. These were not pieces of wood, fragments of planks, or trunks of trees, but huge clumps of vegetable matter, a sort of yellowish sargasso, torn from the ocean depths, and which followed the outline of the higher ground.

"That is curious," said Zach Fren. "May I lose my name if those weeds are not going west, even south-west! There must be a current taking them towards the Straits!"

"That's it!" said Captain Ellis, "and it ought to be a local current, unless it is the tide."

"I do not think so," said Zach Fren, "for at dawn I remember I saw a quantity of weeds drifting up the stream."

"Are you certain of that?"

"As certain as I am that we shall end by finding Captain John."

"Well, if the current exists," said Captain Ellis, "it may be that the wreckage of the *Franklin* came from the west, along the Australian coast."

"That is exactly as I look at it," said Zach Fren.

"Then we need not hesitate. We must continue our exploration across the Timor Sea, up to the extremity of Western Australia."

"Never was I more sure of anything, Captain Ellis, for it is beyond doubt that there is a current on this coast, the direction of which is very clear up to Melville Island. By supposing that Captain Branican was not wrecked west of this, we could explain how the piece of his vessel was brought where we picked it up on board the Californian."

Captain Ellis called the mate, and consulted with him as to the advisability of continuing the cruise more to the westward.

The mate was of opinion that the local current should be examined up to the point from which it started.

"We will go on to the west," answered Captain Ellis. "It is not doubt but certainty we must take back to San Diego — the certainty that nothing remains of the *Franklin* if she perished on the Australian coast."

In consequence of this determination, which was fully justified, the *Dolly Hope* went off to Timor to coal. After a stay in port of forty-eight hours, she came down towards Cape Londonderry at the angle of Western Australia.

Leaving Queen's Channel, Captain Ellis endeavoured to follow the outline of the continent from Turtle Point, where the current clearly showed that its direction was from west to east. It was not one of those effects of the tide which change with the ebb and flow, but a steady movement of the waters in this southern portion of Timor Sea. It was therefore necessary to steam up it, searching the creeks and reefs until the *Dolly Hope* found herself out in the Indian Ocean.

Arrived at the entrance of Cambridge Gulf, which washes the base of Mount Cockburn, Captain Ellis considered that it would be imprudent to venture with his vessel through this long strip of water bristling with reefs, and with its banks frequented by formidable natives. And so the steam launch, with a well-armed crew of six, was put under the orders of Zach Fren to explore the interior of the gulf.

"Evidently," said Captain Ellis to him, "if John Branican has fallen into the power of the natives in this part of the continent, it is not to be supposed that he and his crew have survived. But what we have to do is to find out if there still exist any remains of the *Franklin*, in case the Australians have wrecked her in Cambridge Gulf."

"And that would not astonish me with regard to these scoundrels!" said Zach Fren.

The boatswain's task was clearly stated, and he accomplished it conscientiously, being always on the alert. He took the launch to Adolphus Island, almost at the end of the gulf, and went round it, and discovered nothing that encouraged him to push his investigations any further.

The *Dolly Hope* then resumed her course beyond Cambridge Gulf, rounded Dussejour Cape, and went away to the north-west, along the coast which belongs to Western Australia. The islands were numerous, and the creeks cut into the shore capriciously, but neither at Cape Rhuliers nor Cape Londonderry did anything result to repay the crew for so many fatigues so gallantly undertaken.

The fatigues and dangers of this navigation became serious enough when the *Dolly Hope* had rounded - Cape Londonderry. On this crest, which is directly assailed by the great surges of the Indian Ocean, there exist few practicable refuges in which a disabled vessel could take shelter. And a steamer is always at the mercy of its engines, which may fail her in the violent pitching and rolling due to a boisterous sea. From this cape to Collier Bay in York Sound, and in Brunswick Bay there was nothing to be seen but a medley of islands, a labyrinth of shoals and reefs like those that swarm in Torres Strait. At Capes Talbot and Bougainville the coast is defended by such a tremendous surf that its vicinity is only practicable to the native boats, which are rendered almost uncapsizable by their outriggers. Admiralty Bay, opening between Cape Bougainville and Cape Voltaire, is so strewn with rocks that the steam launch was more than once in danger of being lost. But nothing could stop the ardour of the crew, and the bold sailors disputed among themselves as to who should take part in the perilous adventure.

Beyond Collier Bay Captain Ellis entered Buccaneer Archipelago, his intention being not to go beyond Cape Leveque at the end of King Sound to the north-west.

This was not on account of anxiety at the state of the weather, which tended to improve daily. In this part of the Indian Ocean, situated in the southern hemisphere, the months of October and November correspond to those of April and May in the northern. But Ellis could not keep on indefinitely, and his furthest point would be reached as soon as the shore current running east, and bringing the wreckage towards Melville Island, had ceased to make itself felt.

This was at last discovered towards the end of January, 1883, when the *Dolly Hope* had completed — unsuccessfully — the exploration of the large estuary of King Sound, into the extremity of which flows the Fitzroy River.

At the mouth of this important stream the steam launch was furiously attacked by the natives, and two men were wounded in the encounter, slightly, it is true; and it was only owing to Captain Ellis's coolness that this last attempt did not degenerate into disaster.

As soon as the *Dolly Hope* was out of King Sound, she stopped off Cape Leveque. Captain Ellis then held a consultation with the mate and - boatswain. After the charts had been carefully examined it was decided that the expedition should end here on the eighteenth parallel of northern latitude. Beyond King Sound the coast is clear, there are only a few islands, and that portion of Tasman Land which bounds the Indian Ocean still appears blank in the recently published atlas. There was no reason for going south-west, nor for visiting the neighbourhood of the Dampier Archipelago.

Besides, there only remained in the *Dolly Hope* a small quantity of coal, and the best thing to do was to make direct for Batavia, and fill up the bunkers. Then going east, she could regain the Pacific through Timor Sea, along the Sunda Islands.

The course was thus laid to the northward, and soon the *Dolly Hope* was out of sight of the Australian coast.

CHAPTER XIV - BROWSE ISLAND

THE region between the north-west coast of Australia and the western part of the Timor Sea contains no islands of importance. With difficulty geographers have noted a few islets. What is met with consists principally of curious shallow coral formations, known as banks and rocks and reefs and shoals — such as Lynher Reef, Scott's Reef, Seringapatam Reef, Korallen Reef, Courtier Shoal, Rowley Shoal, Hibernia Shoal, Sahul Bank, Echo Rock, etc. The position of these dangers is determined exactly for the most part, approximately in some instances. It is even possible that there remain to be discovered a certain number of those dangerous reefs which are at sea level. And so the navigation is not easy, and requires constant attention in these regions, which are often traversed by vessels coming from the Indian seas.

The weather was fine, the sea calm enough outside the breakers. The excellent engines of the *Dolly Hope* had in no way failed since the departure from San Diego, and her boilers worked splendidly. All the circumstances of weather and sea promised a favourable passage between Cape Leveque and Java. But this was the way home, and the only delays would be the stoppages Captain Ellis might make in exploring the small Sunda Islands.

For the first few days, after leaving Cape Leveque, nothing occurred worth mention. The most rigorous vigilance was imposed on the look-outs. Stationed in the foretop, they had to report as far off as possible the shoals and the reefs, which rarely rose above the water level.

On the 7th of February, about nine o'clock in the morning, one of the men in the foretop shouted, —

"Reef on the port bow!"

As this reef was not yet visible to the men on deck, Zach Fren went up the shrouds to reconnoitre its position for himself.

When he reached the top, the boatswain saw distinctly enough a rocky plateau about six miles off in the direction indicated. In reality it was neither a rock nor a shoal, but an islet in the shape of a saddleback, away to the north-west. Considering the distance, it was even possible that this islet was an island of some extent, if it was then visible end on.

A few minutes afterwards Zach Fren came down from aloft, and made his report to Captain Ellis, who gave the order to huff, so as to approach the said islet.

At noon, after taking the altitude, and finding his position, the captain had noted in the log-book that the *Dolly Hope* was in 14° 7' south latitude, and 133° 13' east longitude. This position being marked on the chart, coincided very nearly with the position of a certain island named Browse Island by modern geographers, situated about two hundred and fifty miles from York Sound, on the Australian coast.

As this island was not much out of his way, the captain resolved to coast along it, without any intention of stopping at it.

About one o'clock in the afternoon Browse Island was not more than a mile from the *Dolly Hope*. The sea, somewhat rough, broke noisily, and covered with spray a cape stretching out towards the north-east. The size of the island was not apparent, as it was being looked at obliquely. In any case, it looked like an undulating plateau, with no particular hill dominating its surface.

However, as there was no time to lose, Captain Ellis, after slowing a little, was about to give the order to go ahead full speed, when Zach Fren attracted his attention by saying, —

"Captain! Look there! Is that a spar on that cape?"

And the boatswain stretched out his hand in the direction of the cape, which ended abruptly: a rocky ridge.

"A spar! No! It looks to me like the trunk of a tree!" said Captain Ellis.

And taking his glasses, he looked at the object with more attention.

"You are right, boatswain," he said; "it is a spar, and I think I see a bit of bunting fluttered into tatters by the wind. Yes! yes! It ought to be a signal!"

"Then we bad better go and see!" said the boatswain.

"So I think," said Captain Ellis. And he gave the order to bear down on Browse Island carefully and at half-speed.

The order was instantly executed. The *Dolly Hope* began to approach the reefs which surrounded the island at a distance of a few hundred feet. The sea beat on them violently, not that the wind was strong, but that the current took the surge towards them.

Soon the details of the coast were apparent to the naked eye. The shore looked wild, arid, desolate, without a patch of verdure, with great gaping caverns in which the surf beat with the noise of thunder. At intervals a bit of yellowish beach broke the line of rocks, above which flew flocks of seabirds. But there was nothing to be seen of a wreck, neither fragments of spars nor vestiges of a hull. The spar at the extreme end seemed to be a portion of the bowsprit; but of this discoloured flag flying in rags in the wind it was impossible to recognize the colour.

"There have been shipwrecked people there!" said Zach Fren.

"Yes, there must have been!" said the mate.

"Undoubtedly," said Captain Ellis, "a vessel has been cast on that island."

"And what is none the less certain," said the mate, "is that the shipwrecked crew took refuge there, for they raised that signal mast, and perhaps they are there still, for it is rare for vessels bound to Australia or the Indies to pass in sight of Browse Island."

"I suppose, captain, you intend to go ashore here?"

"I do, if we can, but I have not yet seen a place to land. Let us begin by going round it before coming to a decision. If it is still inhabited by unfortunate shipwrecked people it is impossible for us not to be seen; and they may signal to us — "

"And if we see nobody, what is your plan?" asked Zach Fren.

"We will try and land as soon as landing is practicable," said Captain Ellis. "If it is not inhabited, the island may have some traces of a wreck, and that will be of more interest for us."

"And who knows?" murmured Zach Fren.

"Who knows? Do you mean that the *Franklin* may have been cast on Browse Island, quite out of the course she ought have followed?"

"Why not, captain?"

"Because it is quite unlikely," said Captain Ellis? "But although we ought not to stop for unlikelihoods, we will attempt a landing."

The plan of steaming round Browse Island was immediately put into execution.

Prudently keeping a cable length off the reefs, the *Dolly Hope* was soon round the different capes thrown out by the island towards the north. There was no change in the aspect of the shore, the rocks lay as if they had been crystallized in almost identical shapes, ridges roughly beaten by the surge, reefs covered with spray, and landing impracticable. In the background a few clumps of cocoa-nut trees rose on a rocky plateau, on which appeared no trace of cultivation. Of inhabitants there were none; of habitations there were none. Not a boat, not a fishing cane?. A desert sea, a desert island. A few flocks of gulls flew from one point to another, and gave the only life to this sad solitude.

If it was not the wished-for island of the castaway, in which the wants of existence were assured, it could at least offer a refuge to the survivors of a wreck.

Browse Island measures about six or seven miles round, as was discovered when the *Dolly Hope* reached the southern shore. In vain did the crew endeavour to discover a harbour, or in default of a harbour a creek among the rocks in which the steamer could be put in shelter for a few hours. It was soon seen that a landing could only be effected by means of the boats, and that a passage that would permit them to land was still to be found.

Soon the *Dolly Hope* was to leeward of the island. As the breeze then blew from the north-west, the surge beat less violently on the rocks. The shore describing a large hollow, formed a vast roadstead in which a vessel might anchor without risk until a change in the wind. It was decided that the *Dolly Hope* should remain there, if not at anchor, at least under half-steam, while the launch went ashore. There remained to be discovered a place where the men could set foot among the reefs which lay white in the long line of surf.

Searching the beach with his glasses, Captain Ellis finished by discovering a depression in the plateau, a sort of gap in the mass of the island, through which a brook rippled towards the sea.

After looking at it in his turn, Zach Fren affirmed that a landing could be effected at the foot of this gap. The coast seemed to be less steep there, and its profile was broken by rather a sharp angle. There was also visible a narrow passage through the reef on which the sea did not break.

Captain Ellis ordered out the launch, which in half an hour was under steam. He embarked in her with Zach Fren, a steersman", a man in the bow, the stoker and the engineer. As a matter of prudence two guns, two axes, and a few revolvers were put on board. During the captain's absence, the mate could handle the *Dolly Hope* in this open roadstead and attend to all the signals that might be made.

At half-past one the boat went off towards the shore, distant a good mile, and entered the channel, while thousands of gulls flew around, uttering deafening, strident cries. A few minutes afterwards she ran gently up to a sandy beach. Captain Ellis, Zach Fren and the two sailors jumped ashore, leaving the engineer and stoker in charge of the launch, which was to be kept under steam. Going up the gap through which the brook ran into the sea, all four stood on the crest of the plateau.

A few hundred yards off was a sort of rocky mound of curious form, the summit of which was a hundred feet above the beach.

Captain Ellis and his companions went towards the mound; they climbed it not without difficulty, and from the top could see over the whole island.

It was a broad oval, resembling a tortoise with the cape for the tail. In places a little vegetable soil covered the rock, which was of madreporic formation, like the atolls of Malaysia and the coral groups of Torres Strait. Here and there patches of verdure appeared, but there were more mosses than herbs, more stones than roots, more undergrowth than shrubs. Whence came the creek, the bed of which, visible for a part of its course, wound through the slopes of the plateau? Was it fed by some inland spring? That was not easy to discover, although the view extended up to the signal mast.

Standing on the top of the mound, Captain Ellis and his men looked around in every direction. No smoke rose in the air, no human being appeared. It followed, therefore, that if Browse Island had been inhabited — and there was no doubt of that — it was not likely to be so now.

"A miserable shelter for castaways," said Captain Ellis. "If their stay was a long one, I wonder how they managed to live."

"Yes," said Zach Fren. "It is almost a bare plateau.

Here and there only are a few clumps of trees. The rock is hardly covered with vegetable soil. But all the same, one is not too particular when shipwrecked! A bit of rock under your feet is always better than a hole with the sea over your head!"

"At first, yes," said Captain Ellis; "but afterwards?"

"Besides," said Zach Fren, "it is possible the castaways who took refuge on the island may have been promptly taken off by some vessel — "

"As it is equally possible that they succumbed to privations."

"And what makes you think that, captain?"

"That if they had left the island in some way they would have taken the precaution to strike the signal mast. It is, therefore, to be feared that the last of these unfortunates died before help arrived. But let us go up to the mast. We may perhaps find some trace of the nationality of the ship which was lost here."

Captain Ellis, Zach Fren and. the two sailors descended the mound and walked towards the promontory projecting towards the north. But they had scarcely taken a hundred steps before one of the men stopped to pick up something his foot had kicked against.

"Hallo! What is this?" he said.

"Give it to me," said Zach Fren.

It was a cutlass-blade like those which sailors carry in their belts in a leather scabbard. Broken at the handle, and full of dents, the blade had evidently been thrown away as useless.

"Well, boatswain?" said Captain Ellis.

"I am looking for some mark to show where this blade came from," replied Zach Fren.

It was possible it did bear a maker's name. But it was so rusted that it had first to be scraped. When Zach Fren had done this, he made out, not without difficulty, the words "Sheffield — England" inscribed on the steel.

The cutlass was thus of English origin. But to assert from that that the castaways on Browse Island were English was to be too positive. Why could not this weapon belong to a sailor of different nationality, since the manufactures of Sheffield arc spread over the whole world? If some other object were found, would this hypothesis be changed into certainty?

Captain Ellis and his companions continued on their way to the promontory. As there was no footpath, the walk was rather laborious. If it had been trodden by the feet of men, it must have been at a period too remote to be recognizable, for all trace had disappeared beneath the grass and moss.

After a walk of about two miles Captain Ellis halted near a clump of cocoa trees of anything but vigorous growth, and the nuts of which had fallen for some time, and were now nothing but dust and rottenness.

Up to there no other object had been found; but a few yards from the clump of trees, on the slope of a slight ' undulation it was easy to recognize traces of cultivation amid the scattered shrubs. What remained were a few yams and batatas almost returned to their wild state. A pickaxe lay under some thick briars, where one of the sailors discovered it accidentally. It seemed to be of American manufacture from the way it was hafted, and it was deeply eaten into by rust.

"What do you think of it, Captain Ellis?" asked the boatswain.

"I think," said the captain, "that we have not yet had enough to say anything about."

"Then, forward!" replied Zach Fren, motioning the men to follow him.

After descending the slopes of the plateau they reached the edge to which the northern promontory joined on. In this place a narrow sinuosity was cut back into the ridge, giving an easy access to the little sandy beach. This beach measured about an acre, and was enclosed by rocks of a beautiful red colour, on which the surf beat without cessation.

On the sand several objects were scattered about, showing that human beings had made a long stay at this point of the island, pieces of glass and crockery, iron bolts, preserve tins, the American origin of which was clear enough this time, and other things used at sea, a few fragments of chain, broken rings, ends of galvanized iron rigging, a fluke of a grapnel, several sheaves of blocks, a bent ring, a pump handle, bits of spars and yards, pieces of sheet iron, as to the origin of which the Californian sailors could make no mistake.

"It was no English ship that went down off here," said Captain Ellis. "It was an American."

"And you might say it was built in one of the Pacific ports," said Zach Fren, whose opinion was shared in by the two sailors.

But at the same time there was nothing to show that it was the *Franklin*.

And the question remained; what was" this ship which had sunk, and of which nothing of the frame or planking had yet been found? Had the crew reached .Browse Island in her boats?

No! And Captain Ellis soon had proof enough that the wreck had occurred on the reefs.

A hundred yards from the beach, amid a pile of pointed rocks and reefs at the water level, lay the melancholy ruin of a ship as thrown ashore and broken up by the sea, when the waves have beaten over it with the violence of a flood and in an instant, wood or iron, all is gashed to pieces, demolished, shattered and dispersed and carried by the surf among the rocks.

Captain Ellis, Zach Fren, and the two sailors, stood looking, not without deep emotion, at what the rocks still kept of the disaster. Of the hull there remained only a few misshapen curves, jagged timbers bristling with broken bolts, bent rails, a bit of the rudder, a few strakes of the deck, but nothing of the exterior upper works, nothing of the masts which had either been cut away by the sea, or since the wreck had been used for the camp on the island. There was not a piece of the frame intact, not a piece of the keel entire. Amid the rocks with their sharp edges like chevaux de frise the vessel had evidently been ground up until its remains could not be used.

"Let us look," said Captain Ellis, "and we may, perhaps, find a name, a letter, a mark which will tell us the nationality of this vessel."

"Yes 1 and pray God that it may not be the *Franklin* reduced to a state like that!" said Zach Fren.

But was there any such indication as the captain expected? Even supposing that the surf had left a part of the stern or of the bow, where the name of the ship is usually found, would not the weather and the spray have effaced it?

And nothing of it was left. The search was fruitless. And if some of the tilings on the beach were of American make, there was nothing to show that they belonged to the *Franklin*.

But if some of the castaways had taken refuge on Browse Island — and the signal mast at the end of the promontory showed that unmistakably — if, during a period, the length of which it was impossible to say, they had lived on this island, they had certainty taken shelter in some cave, probably near the beach, so as to be able to make use of the wreckage among the rocks.

One of the sailors very soon discovered the cave which had been occupied by the survivors of the wreck. It was in a huge mass of rock formed at the angle of the plateau and the beach.

Captain Ellis and Zach Fren ran up to the sailor who called them. Perhaps this cave contained the secret of the disaster? Perhaps it would reveal the name of the ship?

The only way in was through a narrow opening, very low, near which were the cinders of a fire outside, the smoke of which had blackened the rocky wall.

Inside the cave was about ten feet high, twenty feet deep and fifteen feet wide, large enough to hold twelve men. The only furniture was a bed of dry herbage, covered with a sail in tatters, a bench made of pieces of plank, two,stools of the same kind, and a rickety table. For utensils, there were a few plates and dishes of iron, three forks, two spoons, a knife, and three pannikins, all of them rusty. In a corner was a keg on the ground, evidently used for water from the creek.

On the table was a ship's lamp, dented and rusty, and' much too damaged for use. Here and there were a few cooking utensils, and more clothes in rags thrown on the bed.

"Poor creatures!" said Zach Fren. "To what an end they must have been reduced during their stay on this island."

"They had scarcely saved anything from the ship," said Captain Ellis, "and that shows with what violence she was thrown ashore! Everything had been broken, everything! How could they have got food? Doubtless from the little corn they saved, and salt beef, and the preserves they emptied to the last box! But what an existence, and how they must have suffered!"

Yes! and if we add what they might get by fishing, we shall have all the castaways could have procured for their wants. As to their being now on the island there seemed to be no chance. And if they had succumbed, it was probable that .the remains of him who died last would be found, although the closest search inside and outside yielded no result.

"It seems to me," said Zach Fren, "that these shipwrecked folks were taken off home."

"And why?" asked Captain Ellis. "Could they have built a boat big enough to go to sea out of the remains of the ship!"

No, captain, and they would not have had enough to make a canoe; but I rather think their signals must have been seen by some ship."

"And I cannot agree- to that."

"And why not?"

w Because if a ship had taken them off, the news would have spread all over the world, at least unless the ship that rescued them went down with all hands — and that is hot likely."

"Perhaps so!" said Zach Fren, who did not give in easily. "But if it was impossible for them to build a boat, there is nothing to prove that all the boats on board perished in the wreck and in that case — "

"Well, in that case," replied Captain Ellis, "as nothing was heard of a crew having been picked up somewhere near Western Australia, I think that the boat would have perished on the voyage from Browse Island!"

It would have been difficult to reply to this reasoning, as Zach Fren well knew, but not wishing to give up all hope he continued, —

"I suppose you intend to visit the other parts of the island?"

"Yes, to clear our conscience," said Captain Ellis, "and in the first place let us strike that signal mast so that ships need not be stopped, now that there is not a man to save."

The captain with Zach Fren and the sailors, came out of the cave and gave a last look round the beach; then again walking up the creek to the plateau, they went off towards the head of the promontory.

After turning aside a little, so as to skirt a sort of stony pool formed of rain-water, they went straight ahead.

Suddenly Captain Ellis stopped. At this point the ground .showed four undulations side by side. Probably this arrangement would not have attracted attention if a half rotten cross of wood had not been at the end of each little mound. These were graves, and this was the cemetery of the castaways.

"At last," said Captain Ellis, "shall we be able to learn?"

It would not be out of any want of respect due to the dead if they were to search these graves, and exhume the bodies they contained, and see the state in which they were, and search in the grave for some indication of their nationality.

The two sailors set to work, and digging into the ground with their knives, threw it up on each side. But a number of years must have elapsed since the corpses had been buried for the ground contained only bones. Captain Ellis had them covered up again and the crosses were replaced on the graves.

But it was necessary that the mystery of this wreck should be cleared up. If four human beings had been buried here, what had become of those who had rendered them the last duty? And when death had struck them in their turn, would not a skeleton be found on some other point of the island?

Captain Ellis had no hope in the matter.

"We shall not, then," he said, "learn the name of the ship lost on Browse island! We shall return to San Diego without having discovered the remains of the *Franklin* without knowing what has become of John Branican and his crew."

"Why should not this be the *Franklin*?" said one of the sailors.

"And why should it be?" asked Zach Fren. There was nothing in fact to show that it was the *Franklin* whose wreckage covered the reefs of Browse Island, and it seemed as though this second expedition of the *Dolly Hope* would no more succeed than the first had done.

Captain Ellis had remained silent with his looks cast on the ground where the poor castaways had found the end of their miseries, only with the end of their lives! Were they Americans as he was? Were they those of whom the *Dolly Hope* had come in search?

"To the flagstaff," he said.

Zach Fren and his men followed him as he descended the long rocky slope by which the promontory joined on to the island.

It took twenty minutes to walk the half mile which separated them from the flagstaff, for the ground was encumbered with stones and brambles.

148

When Captain Ellis and his men had reached the mast, they saw that it had been sunk deep in a rocky excavation, which explained how it was that it had resisted the storms for so long; and as had been seen with the glasses, this mast — the end of a bowsprit — had come from some ship.

The rag nailed to its summit was merely a bit of sailcloth torn in the breeze, without any indication of nationality.

At Captain Ellis' orders, the sailors were preparing to lower the mast when Zach Fren exclaimed, —

"Captain! Look there!"

"What is it?"

"That bell!"

On a still solid framework there was a bell with the clapper much rusted.

And so the castaways had not been contented with setting up the mast and fixing to it the flag, but had taken to it the bell, which they hoped could be heard by any ship passing in sight of the island. But did not this bell bear the name of the ship to which it belonged, according to the custom of all maritime nations?

Captain Ellis was walking towards the framework when he stopped.

At the foot of it lay the remains of a skeleton, or rather a mass of bones lay on the ground with a few rags among it.

There were, then, five survivors who had taken refuge on Browse Island. Four had died, and the fifth had remained alone.

Then one day he had left the cave, he had dragged himself to the end of the promontory, he had rung the bell to make it heard by a ship in the offing, and he had fallen at this spot never to rise again..

After giving orders to the two sailors to dig a grave for the bones, Captain Ellis made a sign to Zach Fren to follow him and examine the bell.

On the bronze, there were this name and number, deeply engraved and still legible —

Franklin.

1875.

CHAPTER XV - LIVING WRECKAGE

WHILE the *Dolly Hope* was carrying on this second campaign in the Timor Sea, and ending it in the way we know, Mrs. Branican and her friends and the families of the missing crew were sharing in all the anxieties of the attempt. What hopes attached to this little bit of wood picked up by the Californian, and belonging, without question, to the *Franklin*! Would Captain Ellis find the wreck of the ship on one of the islands, or on some point of the Australian continent? Would he find John Branican, Harry Felton, and the twelve sailors embarked under his orders? Would he bring back to San Diego one or many survivors of this catastrophe?

Two letters from Captain Ellis had arrived since the departure of the *Dolly Hope*. The first announced the useless result of the exploration among the channels of Torres Strait up to the Arafura Sea. The second announced that Melville and Bathurst Islands had been visited without finding any trace of the *Franklin*. Mrs. Branican was then informed that the search was to be continued along the Sea of Timor up to Western Australia, and among the numerous archipelagos bordering on Tasman Land. The *Dolly Hope* would then return, after searching the small Sunda Islands, and when no hope was left of finding any trace.

After this last letter there came a break. Several months elapsed, and now people were waiting from day to day for the *Dolly Hope* to be signalled by the semaphores of San Diego.

However, the year 1882 went by, and although Mrs. Branican had received no news of Captain Ellis, there was nothing surprising in that, for postal communications are slow and irregular across the Pacific Ocean, so that there was no reason for being anxious about the *Dolly Hope*, although they might be impatient to see her.

At the end of February, however, Mr. William Andrew began to think that the cruise of the *Dolly Hope* was unduly prolonged. Every day a certain number of people would go to Island Point, in the hope that the ship would be sighted in the Offing. And, far enough out as she might-be, and even though she might not make her number, the sailors of San Diego would recognize her from her look — just as they could tell a Frenchman from a German or a Yankee from a Britisher.

The *Dolly Hope* appeared at length in the morning of the 27th of March, nine miles off, coming along at full speed, under a fresh breeze from the north-west. In less than an hour she had entered the harbour, and dropped her anchor in the bay of San Diego.

The news Soon spread in the town, and the populace crowded on the quays, and on Island Point and Point Loma.

Mrs. Branican and Mir. William Andrew and a few other friends, hastening to enter into communication with the *Dolly Hope*, embarked on a tug to go out and meet her. The crowd, was possessed by some mysterious anxiety, and when the tug breasted the last wharf, on her way to the ship, there was not a sound. It seemed that if Captain Ellis had succeeded in this second attempt, the news would already have spread round the world.

Twenty minutes later Mrs. Branican, Mr. William Andrew and their companions were alongside the *Dolly Hope*.

A few minutes later they knew the result of the expedition It was oh the western boundary of the Timor Sea, on Browse Island, that the *Franklin* had been lost. It was there that the survivors of the wreck had taken refuge. It was there they had died.

"All?" said Mrs. Branican.

"All!" replied Captain Ellis.

The consternation was general when the *Dolly Hope* anchored in the middle of the bay with her flag a waft in sign of mourning, mourning for the crew of the *Franklin*.

The *Dolly Hope* had left San Diego on the 3rd of April, 1882, and returned on the 27th of March, 1883. Her cruise had lasted nearly twelve months, a cruise in which devotion never failed; but the only result had been to destroy the last hopes.

During the few minutes Mrs. Branican and Mr. William Andrew were on board, Captain Ellis had briefly informed them of the facts relative to the wreck of the *Franklin* on the reefs of Browse Island.

Although she now learnt that there existed no doubt as to the fate of Captain John and his companions, Mrs. Branican showed no change whatever Not a tear escaped from her eyes. She asked no questions. As the remains of the *Franklin* had been found on the island, as there remained none of the crew who had taken refuge there, what more could she ask at that time? The story of the expedition she could hear later. And so, having shaken hands with Captain Ellis and Zach Fren, she had sat down in the stern of the *Dolly Hope*, deep in her thoughts, and, in spite of so many irrefragable proofs, determined not to believe that she was yet "the widow of John Branican."

When the *Dolly Hope* cast anchor, Dolly returned to the front of the poop and asked Mr. William Andrew, Captain Ellis, and Zach Fren, to call on her that very day at Prospect House. She would expect them in the afternoon, so as to learn in detail all that had happened during the cruise in Torres Strait, the Arafura. Sea, and the Sea of Timor.

A boat took Mrs. Branican ashore. The crowd parted respectfully as she crossed the quay, and she directed her steps towards the upper quarter of San Diego.

About three o'clock in the afternoon Mr. William Andrew, Captain Ellis, and the boatswain presented themselves at the chalet, where they were immediately ushered into the drawing-room on the ground floor, in which Mrs. Branican was waiting for them.

When they had taken their places round a table on which was spread a chart of the northern Australian seas, "Captain Ellis," said Dolly, "will you tell me the story of your cruise?"

And then Captain Ellis spoke as if he had his eyes on the log-book, omitting no particular, forgetting no incident, and referring every now and then to Zach Fren for corroboration. He even told in due order of the operations in Torres Strait, in the Arafura Sea, at Melville and Bathurst Islands, among the archipelagos of Tasman Land, although they had been useless. But Mrs. Branican was interested in these details, and listened in silence, and fixed on the captain a look which her eyelids did not veil for an instant.

When the recital reached the episodes on Browse Island, it had to account for every hour and every minute after the *Dolly Hope* had seen the flagstaff on the cape. Mrs. Branican, without moving, but with just a slight trembling of the hands, saw in these different incidents, as if they were reproduced before her eyes, the landing of Captain Ellis and his men at the mouth "of the creek, the ascent of the knoll, the blade of the cutlass picked up off the ground, the traces of cultivation, the abandoned pickaxe, the beach with the fragments of wreckage, the remains of the *Franklin* among the heap of rocks where it could only have been driven by the most violent of storms, the cave which the survivors had inhabited, the discovery of the four graves, the skeleton of the last of the survivors at the foot of the flagstaff near the alarm bell. At this moment Dolly rose as though she heard the sound of the bell amid the solitudes of Prospect House.'

And then Captain Ellis, drawing from his pocket a locket rusted with being in the water, presented it to her.

It was Dolly's portrait, a half-faded photograph she had given to John at the *Franklin*'s departure, and which a fresh search had discovered in a dark corner of the cave.'

And if this locket showed that Captain John was one of the five survivors, was it not to be concluded that he was one of those who had succumbed to the long misery of destitution and abandonment?

The chart of the Australian seas was spread out on the table, the chart on which for seven years Dolly had so often. evoked the memory of

John. She asked the Captain to show her Browse Island, that point hardly perceptible, lost in the regions swept by the typhoons of the Indian Ocean.

"If we had arrived there a few years earlier," added Captain Ellis, "we might have found them still alive — John — his companions."

"Yes, maybe;" said Mr. William Andrew, "and the *Dolly Hope* should have gone there on - her first cruise. But who would have thought that the *Franklin* had been lost on an island in the Indian Ocean?"

"No one," said Captain Ellis, "considering the course he should have followed, and which he did follow, since the *Franklin* was seen- to the south of Celebes. Captain Branican must have lost control of his ship, which must have been borne through one of the Sunda Straits into the Timor Sea and driven on Browse Island."'

"There is no doubt," said Zach Fren, "that that is what happened."

"Captain Ellis," said Mrs. Branican, "in looking for the *Franklin* in the seas of Malaysia you did what you ought to have done. But it was to Browse Island that you should have gone first. Yes, it was there!"" — '''

Then taking part in the conversation, as if she wished to draw some hope from the figures, she said, —

"On board the *Franklin* there were Captain John; the mate Harry Felton, and twelve "sailors. You found on the island the remains of four men who had been buried, and the last died at the foot of' the flagstaff; What do yon think had become of the nine others?"

"We do not know," said Captain Ellis; "Yes, I know," said Mrs. Branican; "but what do you think became of them?"

"Perhaps they perished when the *Franklin* struck on the reefs of the island."

"You admit, then, that only five survived the wreck?"

"That, unfortunately, is the most probable explanation,' added Mr. William Andrew.

"That is not my opinion," said Mrs. Branican. "Why should not John, Felton, and twelve men have reached Browse Island safe and sound? Why should not nine of them have left it afterwards?"

"And how, Mrs. Branican?" said Captain Ellis.

"In a sloop built from the remains of the ship."

"Mrs. Branican," said Captain Ellis, "Zach Fren will tell you, as I do, that in the state in which we found those remains, it appeared to us to be impossible."

"But, one of their boats?"

"The boats of the *Franklin*, even supposing they were not all broken, could never have ventured a passage to the Australian coast or to the Sunda Inlands."

"And, besides," said Mr. William Andrew, "if nine of the men left the island, why did the five remain behind?"

"I add," said Captain Ellis, "that if they had any boat at all at their disposal, those who went away in her perished at sea or were the victims of the Australian aborigines, for they have never been heard of."

Then Mrs.' Branican, without showing a symptom of weakness, asked the boatswain, — " Zach Fren," said she, "do you think as Captain Ellis thinks?"

"I think," said Zach Fren, shaking his head, "that though it is possible for things to have been as he says, it is also possible for them to have been otherwise."

"And," said Mrs. Branican, "my opinion is that we have no absolute certainty as to what has become of the nine men whose remains were not found on the island. You and your crew, Captain Ellis, have done all that the most intrepid devotion could do."

"I should have liked to have done more, Mrs. Branican."'

"We will now leave you," said Mr. William Andrew, thinking the interview had lasted long enough.

"Yes, my friend," said Mrs. Branican, "I want to be alone. But whenever Captain Ellis, likes to come to Prospect House, I shall be happy to have a talk with him about John and his companions."

"I am. always at your orders," said the captain.

"And you also, Zach Fren," added Mrs. Branican; "do not forget that my house is yours."

"Mine?" said the boatswain, "but what will become of the *Dolly Hope?*"

"The *Dolly Hope?*" said Mrs. Branican, as if this question was of no importance.

"Your idea, my dear Dolly," said Mr. William Andrew, "is that, If an opportunity offers, of selling her?"

"Selling her?" answered Mrs. Branican, sharply, "selling her? No, Mr. Andrew, never."

Mrs. Branican and Zach Fren had exchanged looks; they understood each other.

From this day forwards Dolly lived in great retirement at Prospect House, where she had had brought the few things collected on Browse Island — the ship's lamp, the utensils, the fragment of canvas nailed to the flagstaff, the bell of the *Franklin,* &c.

The *Dolly Hope* was taken to the end of the harbour and laid up in charge of Zach Fren. The crew, well paid, were beyond reach of want for the future; but if ever the *Dolly Hope* went to sea on another expedition, they might be reckoned on.

Zach Fren did not forget to go often to Prospect House. Mrs". Branican was pleased to see him, to talk with him, to hear in detail all the incidents of his last cruise. Besides, the same way of looking at things made them understand one another better day by day; they did not believe that the last word had been said concerning the wreck of the *Franklin*, and Dolly would say to the boatswain, —

"Zach Fren, neither John nor his companions are dead."

"The eight? — that I don't know," the boatswain would answer, "but certainly Captain John is living!"

"Yes! Living! And where shall we go and look for him, Zach Fren? Where is he, my poor John?"

"He is where he is, and nowhere else, Mrs. Branican; and if we do not go there, we shall get news of him. I do not say it will be by post and a prepaid letter; but we shall receive it all right."

"John is living, Zach Fren!"

"If he were not, Mrs. Branican, should I ever have been able to save you? Would Heaven have permitted it? No. That would have been too bad."

And Zach Fren, with his manner of saying things and Mrs. Branican, with the obstinacy of her character, agreed to encourage a hope that neither Mr. William Andrew, nor Captain Ellis, nor any of their friends could continue to hold.

During 1883 nothing happened to direct public attention to the matter of the *Franklin*. Captain Ellis, in command of one of Andrews' ships, was again at sea. Mr. William Andrew and Zach Fren were the only visitors received at the chalet, and Mrs. Branican devoted herself entirely to her work at Wat House.

Now, about fifty poor children, some of them quite young, were being brought up in this asylum, which Mrs. Branican visited every day, looking after their health, their instruction, and their future.' The ample funds at the disposal of Wat House allowed of the children being as happy and comfortable as children could be who had lost father and mother. When they reached an age at which they could be apprenticed, Dolly placed them in the workshops and business houses of San Diego, where she continued to watch over them. This year, three or four sons of sailors had gone to sea under honest captains. Beginning as cabin boys, they would become apprentices between thirteen and eighteen years of age, then seamen, then boatswains, and, in this way, would be assured of a good trade for their manhood and a retreat in their old age. And thus the Asylum of Wat House was destined to become the nursery of the sailors who are an honour to the population of San Diego and the other ports of California.

In addition to these occupations, Mrs. Branican did not cease from being the benefactress of the poor. No one knocked in vain at the door of Prospect House. With the considerable income from her fortune, as controlled by Mr. William Andrew, she engaged in every good work, in which the families of the sailors of the *Franklin* had the greatest share. And did she not hope that these absent ones would one day return?

This was the one subject of her interviews with Zach Fren. What had become of the castaways of whom there was no trace on Browse Island? Why could not they have left it in a boat of their own making, although Captain Ellis thought otherwise? But so many years had since elapsed that it was madness to hope.

At night, in sleep troubled by strange dreams, Dolly would again and again see John appear to her. He had been saved from shipwreck and picked up in distant seas. The ship that was bringing him home was in the offing. John was on his way back to San Diego; and what was most extraordinary was that these illusions would persist, after she awoke, with such intensity that Dolly looked upon them as realities.

And, in the same way, Zach Fren continued obstinate. It might be thought that these ideas had been driven into his brain with a mallet as trenails are driven into a ship's frame. He also repeated that they had found five castaways instead of fourteen, that the nine had left Browse Island, and that no one could say it was impossible to build a boat out of the remains of the *Franklin*. But what had become of them after so long a time? Zach Fren could not say, and it was not without alarm that Mr. William Andrew saw him encouraging Dolly in these illusions. Was It not to be feared that this excitement was dangerous for a brain already smitten with madness? But when Mr. William Andrew took the boatswain to task om the subject, he only persisted in his ideas and said, —

"I will only swing to one anchor while its flukes are strong and its hold good."

Several years went by. In 1890, fourteen years had elapsed since Captain Branican and his *Franklin* had left the port of San Diego. Mrs. Branican was then aged thirty-seven. If her hair was going grey, if her warm colour was beginning to fade, her eyes were animated with the, same fire as before. It seemed she had lost nothing of her bodily and mental strength, of the energy which distinguished her, and she was only waiting for an opportunity of giving fresh proofs of it.

It was just as possible for her . as for Lady *Franklin* to organize expedition after expedition to spend her entire fortune in seeking to recover John and his companions. But where could she look for them? Was it not the general opinion that the maritime drama had had the same ending as the expedition of the illustrious British admiral? Had not the sailors of the *Franklin* succumbed on Browse Island as had the sailors of the *Erebus* and *Terror* in the ice of the Arctic seas?

During the long years which had brought no unravelling of the. mysterious catastrophe, Mrs. Branican had not ceased in her inquiries as to what had become of Len and Jane Burker. On this point also there was absolutely no proof. No letter had come to San Diego. Everything seemed to show that Len Burker had left America and was living under an assumed name in some foreign .country. To Mrs. Branican this was a very great sorrow added to so many others. This unfortunate woman, of whom she was so fond, how happy would she be to have her near her. Jane had been a devoted companion; but she was far away and none the less lost to Dolly than was Captain John.

The first six months of the year 1890 had gone by when San Diego newspaper reproduced in its number for the 26th of July an item of news of which the effect ought to have been, and was, immense, we may say, in both continents.

This news was quoted from the Sydney Morning Herald and the extract was as follows: —

"It will be remembered that the last researches made seven years ago by the *Dolly Hope,* with the object of rescuing the survivors of the *Franklin,* ended in failure. Since then it has been supposed that the shipwrecked crew had succumbed to the last man, either before reaching Browse Island or after leaving it. The mystery is, however, far from being solved. In fact, one of the officers of the *Franklin* has just arrived in Sydney. This is Harry Felton, the mate. He was met with on the banks of the Parru, one of the affluents of the Darling, almost on the frontier between New South Wales and Queensland, and he has been brought to Sydney. But he is in so weak a state that no information can be obtained from him, and it is feared that his death may take place at any moment. We give this information for the Denefit of those interested in the fate of the *Franklin*"

On the 27th of July, as soon as Mr. William Andrew heard the news, which reached San Diego by telegraph, he went to Prospect House, where Zach Fren happened to be at the time.

Mrs. Branican was at once shown the paper, and the only reply she made was, — "I start for Sydney."

"For Sydney?" said Mr. William Andrew. "Yes," answered Dolly, and turning to the boatswain, she said, —

"Will you accompany me, Zach Fren?"

"Wherever you go, Mrs. Branican."

"Is the *Dolly Hope* ready for sea?"

"No," said Mr. William Andrew, "and it will take three weeks to fit her out."

"Before three weeks I must be in Sydney," said Mrs. Branican. "Is there a mail boat due out to Australia?"

"The Oregon ought to leave San Francisco to-night."

"Zach Fren and I will be at San Francisco this evening."

"My dear Dolly," said Mr. William Andrew, "may Heaven give you back your husband!"

"It will give him back to me."

That night, at eleven o'clock, a special train, ordered by her, landed Mrs. Branican and Zach Fren in the capital of California.

At one o'clock in the morning the Oregon left San Francisco bound for Sydney.

CHAPTER XVI - HARRY FELTON

The steamer Oregon attained a mean speed of seventeen knots during her passage, which was favoured with superb weather — the usual weather in this part of the Pacific at this period of the year. The gallant ship shared in the impatience of Mrs. Branican, as Zach Fren said. We need scarcely say that the officers, passengers, and crew showed the brave woman that respectful sympathy of which her misfortunes, and the energy with which she bore them, made her so worthy.

When the Oregon was in 330 51' south latitude, and 148° 40' east longitude, the look-outs reported land. On the 15th of August, after a voyage of seven thousand miles, made in nineteen days, the steamer entered Port Jackson, between the high schistose cliffs forming the great gate opening on to the Pacific.

Leaving to the right and left the little bays dotted with villas and cottages, which bear the names of Watson, Vaucluse, Rose, Double, Elizabeth, the Oregon passed Sydney Cove and entered Darling Harbour, which is the port of Sydney, and ran alongside the quay.

To the first person who came on board — one of the custom-house officers — Mrs. Branican said, —

"Harry Felton?"

"He is alive," answered the officer, who had recognized Mrs. Branican.

Did not all Sydney know she was on board the Oregon, and was not she expected with the greatest impatience?

"Where is Harry Felton?" she asked.

"At the Marine Hospital."

Mrs. Branican, followed by Zach Fren, at once went ashore. The crowd received her with the same deference with which she was greeted at San Diego, and which she met with everywhere.

163

A carriage took them to the Marine Hospital, where they were received by the doctor on duty.

"Can Harry Felton speak? Is he conscious?" asked Mrs. Branican.

"No, madam," said the doctor. "The unfortunate man has not yet recognized any one. It seems that he cannot speak. Death may intervene at any time."

"Harry Felton must not die!" said Mrs. Branican. "He alone knows if Captain John or any of his companions are still alive. He alone knows where they are! I have come to see Harry Felton."

"I will take you to him at once," said the doctor.

A few moments afterwards Mrs. Branican and Zach Fren were in the room occupied by Harry Felton.

Six weeks before, some travellers were crossing the country of Ularara in New South Wales, on the lower boundary of Queensland. Reaching the left bank of the Parru River, they saw a man lying at the foot of a tree. Covered with clothes in rags, exhausted by privations, broken down by fatigue, this man could not be brought back to consciousness, and if his certificate as officer of the mercantile marine had not been found in one of his pockets, it would probably never have been known who he was.

It was Harry Felton, the mate of the *Franklin*. Where did he come from? From what distant and unknown part of the Australian continent had he set out? How long had he been wandering in the dreadful deserts of the centre of Australia? Had he been a prisoner of the natives, and had he escaped? If any of his companions remained, where had he left them? Was he the sole survivor of a disaster now fourteen years old? All these questions had, up to the present, remained without reply.

But it was a matter of considerable interest to know where Harry Felton came from, what his life had been since the wreck of the *Franklin* on the reefs of Browse Island — to know, in fact, the last word of this catastrophe.

Harry Felton was taken to the nearest station, that of Oxley, from which the railway brought him to Sydney. The Sydney Morning Herald, having the first news of his arrival, made it the subject of the paragraph we know, adding that the mate of the *Franklin* had not up to then been able to reply to the questions put to him.

And now Mrs. Branican was before Harry Felton, whom she would not have recognized. He was but forty-six years of age then, and he looked quite sixty. And this was the only man — almost a corpse — who could say what had become of Captain John and his crew.

The most assiduous care had been unable to ameliorate Harry Felton's condition — a condition evidently due to the terrible fatigues he had suffered during the weeks, during the months, perhaps, that his journey across Central Australia had lasted. The breath of life which still remained to him a fainting fit might deprive him of at any moment. Since he had been in the hospital he had hardly opened his eyes, and it was doubtful if he knew what was going on around him. He was supported by a little food, and this he did not even seem to notice. It was to be feared that excessive suffering might have annihilated his intellectual faculties, and destroyed in him the working of his memory, on which, perhaps, the safety of the castaways depended.

Mrs. Branican sat down at his bedside, watching his look, for a movement of his eyelids, the murmur of his voice, or the least indication it would be possible to seize. Zach Fren stood near her, alert for any spark of intelligence, like a sailor looking for a light through the mist on the horizon.

But the light did not shine neither that day nor the following day. Harry Felton's eyelids remained obstinately closed, and when Dolly lifted them she found only a look of unconsciousness.

But she did not despair, neither did Zach Fren, who said to her, —

"If Harry Felton recognizes his captain's wife, he will know how to make her understand, even though he may not speak."

Yes! It was important that he should recognize Mrs. Branican, and that, perhaps, might have a good effect on him. And things would have to be managed with great prudence while he was becoming accustomed to Dolly's presence. Little by little the recollection of the *Franklin* would return to his memory. He might express in signs what he could not say.

Although she was advised not to remain shut up in Harry Felton's room, Mrs. Branican refused to take an hour's rest or even go out for a breath of fresh air. She would not leave his bedside.

"Harry Felton may die, and if the only word I am waiting for escapes with his last breath, I must be here to hear it. I will not leave him."

Towards the evening a slight improvement seemed to take place. His eyes opened several times, but they did not look towards Mrs. Branican. And yet she leant over him and called him by his name, and repeated the name of John — of the captain of the *Franklin* — of San Diego! How was it these names did not recall to him the recollection of his companions? A word, he was only asked for one word — Living? Were they alive?

And all that Harry Felton had had to suffer before coming there, Dolly said to herself, that John had suffered also. Then the thought came to her that John had fallen on the way. But, no. John had not followed Harry Felton. He remained there with the others. Where? Was it with a tribe of the Australian coast? What was this tribe? Harry Felton alone could say, and it seemed that his intelligence was annihilated, that his lips had forgotten how to speak.

During the night his weakness increased. His eyes did not open again, his hand grew cold as if the little life that remained to him had retreated towards his heart. Was he, then, going to die without saying a word? And it entered Dolly's mind that she also had lost her memory and her reason for several years. As nothing could be obtained from her then, nothing could be obtained from this man — nothing of what he alone knew.

The day came. The doctor, very uneasy at the state of prostration, tried the most powerful remedies, which produced no effect. Harry Felton would die, and then Mrs. Branican would see, lost in the void, the hopes that his return had led her to "conceive. To the light he might have brought, there would succeed a darkness nothing could dissipate! And then all would be ended!

At Dolly's request the principal doctors of the city were gathered in consultation. But after examining the patient they declared themselves powerless.

"You can do nothing for this unhappy man?"

"Nothing," said one of the doctors.

"Not even a minute of intelligence, a minute of memory?"

And for that minute Mrs. Branican would have paid her whole fortune.

But what is not in the power of man is always in the power of God. It is to Him man should go when human resources fail.

As soon as the doctors had gone Dolly knelt, and when Zach Fren returned he found her in prayer by the side of the dying man.

Suddenly Zach Fren, who had bent over him to see if a breath escaped from his lips, exclaimed, —

"Look!"

Dolly, thinking the boatswain had found that life had gone, rose and murmured, — Dead?"

"No, not Look. His eyes are open. He is looking at us,"

Under the raised eyelids Harry Felton's eyes were shining with extraordinary brightness. His face had slightly regained its colour, and his hands moved. He seemed to have come out of the torpor in which he had been plunged for so long. And as he looked at Mrs. Branican, a sort of smile played round his lips.

167

"He has recognized me!" exclaimed Dolly.

"Yes!" said Zach Fren. "His captain's wife is near him, and he knows it. He is going to speak!"

"And if he cannot, may God grant he may make himself understood."

And taking his hand, which feebly returned her pressure, Dolly went near to him.

"John? John?" she said.

A movement of the eyes indicated that Harry Felton had heard her and understood.

"Living?" she asked.

"Yes!"

And this "Yes," so feebly uttered, Dolly had heard distinctly.

CHAPTER XVII - BY "YES "AND "NO"

Mrs. Branican at once called the doctor, who saw well enough that, in spite of the change in the patient's state of intelligence, it was only a last manifestation of life, and that death was near.

But the dying man seemed only to see Mrs. Branican. Neither Zach Fren nor the doctor attracted his attention. All that remained of the strength of his intellect was concentrated on his captain's wife.

"Harry Felton," asked Mrs. Branican, "if John is alive where did you leave him? Where is he?"

Harry Felton did not reply.

"He cannot speak," said the doctor, "but he might answer by a sign."

"If even by a look I would understand him," said Mrs. Branican.

"Listen!" said Zach Fren; "the questions ought to be put to him in a certain way, and, as we understand each other as sailors, let me put them. Let Mrs. Branican hold Felton's hand and not take her eyes off his. I will ask him. We will see ' yes' or ' no' by his eyes, and that will do."

Mrs. Branican leant over Harry Felton and took his hand.

If Zach Fren had, at the outset, asked him where Captain John was to be found, it would have been impossible to obtain a satisfactory reply, as that would have obliged Harry Felton to mention the name of a country, a county, or a town, which he probably could not do. Better to arrive gradually at the information by taking up the history of the *Franklin* from the day she had been last seen until the day Harry Felton had become separated from John Branican.

"Felton," said Zach Fren, in a clear voice, "you have near you Mrs. Branican, the wife of John Branican, the captain of the *Franklin*. You have recognized her?"

Felton's lips did not move, but a movement of his eyebrows, a feeble pressure of the hand, replied affirmatively.

"The *Franklin*," said Zach Fren, "was last reported south of the island of Celebes. You understand me. You understand me, Felton, do you not?"

Another look of affirmation.

"Well," continued Zach Fren, "listen to me, and, according as you open or shut your eyes, I shall know if what I am saying is right or wrong."

There was no doubt that Felton understood what Zach Fren said.

"When he left the Sea of Java, Captain John went into the Timor Sea?"

"Yes."

"By the Straits of Sunda?"

"Yes."

"Of his own free will?"

This question was followed by a negative sign of which there could be no doubt.

"No," said Zach Fren.

And this was what Captain Ellis had always thought. For the *Franklin* to leave the Java Sea for the Timor Sea she must have been obliged to do so.

"It was in a storm?" asked Zach Fren.

"Yes."

"A violent tornado caught you in .the Java Sea?"

"Yes."

"And drove you through the Straits of Sunda?"

"Yes."

"Perhaps the *Franklin* was disabled and dismasted, her rudder gone?"

"Yes."

Mrs. Branican, with her eyes fixed on Harry Felton, looked at him without saying a word.

Zach Fren, wishing to run through the different phases of the catastrophe, continued in these terms: —

"Captain John having been unable to take an observation for some days, did not know his position?"

"Yes."

"And after being swept for some days to the westward in Timor Sea, he was lost on the reefs of Browse Island?"

A slight movement showed the surprise of Harry Felton, who evidently did not know the name of the island on which the *Franklin* had been wrecked, and which no observation had enabled him to fix the position of in the Timor Sea.

Zach Fren continued, —

"When you left San Diego you had Captain John, yourself, and twelve men, fourteen in all. Were you fourteen after the wreck?"

"Yes."

"Some of the men perished, then, when the ship was cast on the rocks?"

"Yes."

"One? — two?"

An affirmative sign approved of this last number. So two sailors were missing when the men set foot on Browse Island.

At this moment, at the doctor's advice, a little rest was given Harry Felton, whom the interrogation was visibly tiring.

Then the questions having been resumed a few minutes afterwards, Zach Fren obtained information as to the way in which the twelve survivors had provided for the means of their subsistence. Without a part of the cargo, consisting of preserves and flour, which had been washed ashore, and without fishing, which became one of their chief resources, the castaways would have died of hunger. They had only very rarely seen ships pass out a t sea off the island. Their flag on the mast was never noticed, and they had no other chance of safety beyond this of a vessel taking them off.

When Zach Fren asked, —

"How long did you live on Browse Island? One year? — two years? — three years? — six years?"

It was to the last that Felton answered "yes "with a look.

And so from 1875 to 1881 Captain John and his companions had lived on this island. But how did they manage to leave it? That was one of the most interesting points which Zach Fren entered upon when he asked, —

"Did you build a boat with the remains of the ship?"

"No."

This is what Captain Ellis and the boatswain had agreed when they were exploring the site of the shipwreck. * It would not have been possible to build even a canoe with such fragments.

Arrived at this point, Zach Fren was rather embarrassed as to the questions he should ask as to the way the men had left Browse Island.

"You say," he said, "that no ship answered your signals?"

"No."

"Did a Malay proah, or a native Australian boat, come to the island?"

"No."

"Then a ship's boat came to the island?"

"Yes."

"Was the boat adrift?"

"Yes."

This point was cleared up at last, It was easy for Zach Fren to deduce the natural consequences.

"Did you make the boat seaworthy?"

"Yes."

"And Captain John used it to reach the nearest coast to leeward?"

"Yes."

But why had not the captain and all his companions embarked in this boat? That was what it was important to know.

"Doubtless the boat was too small to take twelve passengers?" asked Zach Fren.

"Yes."

"And seven of you went away — Captain John, you, and five men?"

"Yes."

And then they could clearly read in the dying man's look that he thought they could still save those who remained on Browse Island.

But, at a sign from Dolly, Zach Fren abstained from saying that the five sailors had succumbed after the captain's departure.

A few minutes' rest was given to Harry Felton, whose eyes remained closed, while his hand continued to clasp Mrs. Branican's.

And then her thoughts carried her to Browse Island, and she took part in these scenes. She saw John trying even the impossible for the safety of his companions. She heard him, he spoke to her, she encouraged him, she took passage with him. Where had this boat come ashore?

Harry Felton's eyes opened again, and Zach Fren began to question him.

"Then Captain John, you, and five men left Browse Island?"

"Yes."

"And the boat headed eastwards for the nearest land to the island?"

"Yes."

"The land was Australia?"

"Yes."

"Was she driven ashore by a storm during the voyage?"

"No."

"You landed in one of the creeks on the Australian coast?"

"Yes."

"In the neighbourhood of Cape Leveque?"

"Yes."

"Perhaps in York Sound?"

"Yes."

"As you landed did you fall into the hands of the natives?"

"Yes."

"And they took you away with them?"

"Yes."

"All?"

"No."

"Some of you perished as you landed?"

"Yes."

"Massacred by the aborigines?"

"Yes."

"One? — two? — three? — four?"

"Yes."

"There were only three, then, that the Australians took into the interior?"

"Yes."

"Captain John, you, and one of the sailors?"

"Yes."

"And this sailor, is he still with the captain?"

"No."

"He died before you left?"

"Yes."

"A long time ago?"

"Yes."

And so Captain John and Harry Felton were actually the only survivors of the *Franklin*, and now one of these had but a few hours to live.

It was not easy to obtain from Harry Felton information concerning Captain John, information it was desirable to have with extreme precision. More than once Zach Fren had to pause in his examination 5 then, when he resumed it, Mrs. Branican asked questions on questions, so as to know what had passed during the nine years, that is to say, since the day Captain John and Harry Felton had been carried off by the aborigines of the coast. In this way they learnt what the Australian nomads were doing. The prisoners had had to accompany them during their incessant peregrinations through the regions of Tasman Land, while leading a most miserable existence. Why had they been spared? Was it to obtain some services from them, or, if occasion offered, to obtain a high ransom for them from the English authorities? Yes, and this last important fact was definitely confirmed by Harry Felton. It was only an affair of ransom if they could reach the natives. A few other questions gave them to understand that Captain John and Harry Felton had been so Well watched during the nine years that they had not had a single opportunity for flight.'

At last a chance presented itself. A place had been chosen where the two prisoners could meet and escape together; but some circumstance, unknown to. Harry Felton, had prevented Captain John from coming to the rendezvous. Harry Felton had waited several days; .not wishing to escape alone, he had sought to rejoin the tribe, but it had moved off; then, resolved to deliver his captain if he could reach one of the villages of the interior, he had set out across the central regions, hiding to avoid falling again into the hands of the blacks, exhausted by the heat, dying of hunger and fatigue. For six months he had wandered until he had fallen unconscious on the banks of the Parru.

There, as we know, he was recognized by the paper she had on him; from there he had been brought to Sydney, where his life had been prolonged as if by a miracle, so that he might tell them what, for so many years, they had in vain sought to know.

And so Captain John still lived; but he was a prisoner of a nomad tribe which wandered in the deserts of Tasman Land.

And when Zach Fren had mentioned the different names of the tribes which frequent these territories, it was the Indas to which Harry Felton replied by the affirmative sign. Zach Fren even managed to learn that in the winter this tribe usually camped on the banks of the Fitzroy River, one of the streams running into Leveque Gulf, on the north-west of the Australian continent.

"There we will go and look for John!" exclaimed Mrs. Branican, "and there we shall find him."

And Harry Felton understood her, for his look grew animated at the thought that his captain would at last be saved — saved by her.

Harry Felton had now accomplished his mission. Mrs. Branican knew to what part of the Australian continent her investigation's should be directed. And he closed his eyes, having no more to say.

And that was the state to which had been reduced this man, so courageous and robust, by fatigue and privation, and chiefly by the terrible influence of the Australian climate, and, for having braved it, he was about to succumb when his miseries were near their end. Did not this await Captain John if he attempted to escape across the solitudes of Central Australia? And did not the same dangers menace those who went in search of this tribe of the Indas?

But this thought never occurred to the mind of Mrs. Branican. While the Oregon bore her towards the Australian continent she had conceived and organized the project of a new campaign; she would now put it into execution.

Harry Felton died at nine o'clock that night. For the last time Dolly had called him by his name. For the last time he had understood her. His eyes opened and this name escaped his lips — "John! John!"

Then the rattle came in his throat, and his heart ceased to beat.

That night as Mrs. Branican left the hospital she was spoken to by a boy who was waiting at the door.

He was an apprentice in the merchant service, employed on the *Brisbane*, one of the mail boats running between Sydney and Adelaide.

"Mrs. Branican!" said he, in a troubled voice.

"What do you want, my child?" answered Dolly.

"'Is Harry Felton dead?"

177

"He is dead."

"And Captain John?"

"He is alive; yes, alive!"

"Thank you, Mrs. Branican," said the apprentice.

Dolly hardly noticed the features of the boy, who went off without saying who he was or why he asked the question.

Next day Harry Felton was buried, and the sailors of the port and a part of the population of Sydney attended the funeral.

Mrs. Branican took her place behind the coffin, and followed to the grave him who had been the devoted companion and faithful friend of Captain John; and near her walked the young apprentice, whom she did not recognize among the crowd who had come to render the last honours to the mate of the *Franklin*.

PART TWO

CHAPTER I - ON THE VOYAGE

From the day M. de Lesseps severed the Isthmus of Suez it may be said that he made an island of the African continent. When the Panama Canal is finished, it will be quite as correct to say the same of North and South America. In fact, these immense territories are surrounded by water; but as they retain the name of continent, owing to their extent, it is logical to apply the description to Australia, or New Holland, which is similarly circumstanced.

Australia measures three thousand nine hundred kilometres in its greatest length from east to west, and three thousand two hundred in its greatest width from north to south. The product of these two dimensions yields an area of about four million eight hundred and thirty thousand square kilometres — about seven-ninths of the area of Europe.

The Australian continent is divided by the compilers of the most recent atlases into seven provinces, separated by arbitrary lines cutting each other at right angles, and taking no notice whatever of orographic or hydrographic conditions.

On the east, in the most populated part, are Queensland with its capital at Brisbane, New South Wales with its capital at Sydney, Victoria with its capital at Melbourne.

In the middle are Northern Australia and Alexandra Land, without capitals, and Southern Australia with its capital at Adelaide.

On the west is Western Australia, extending from north to south, with its capital at Perth.

It will soon be seen in what provinces, the most dangerous and least known of any on the continent, Mrs. Branican was about to adventure with that hope so vague, that thought almost unrealizable, of finding Captain John and rescuing him from the tribe who had kept him prisoner for nine years. And besides, was there not good reason to ask if the Indas had respected his life after the escape of Harry Felton?

Mrs. Branican's plan was to leave Sydney as soon as possible. She could reckon on the boundless devotion of Zach Fren, on the solid practical intelligence which characterized this confident, resolute man.. In a long interview, with the map of Australia before them, they had discussed the promptest and most efficient measures to be taken to assure the success of this new attempt. The choice of the point of departure was, it will be understood, of extreme importance, and this is what was finally decided upon: —

1. — A caravan provided with the best means of search and defence, and with everything required for a journey across the deserts of Central Australia, would be organized at the cost and by the effort of Mrs. Branican.

2. — The expedition should start as soon as possible, and to enable this to be done it was advisable to take it by the quickest roads, either on land or sea, to the terminus of the existing communications between the coast and the interior of the continent.

In the first place, the question of reaching the northwest coast, that is, the part of Tasman Land where the *Franklin*'s men had landed, was submitted and debated. But this roundabout way would have occasioned loss of time, and caused certain serious difficulties for the staff and material — and the staff would be numerous and the material considerable. -In short, there was nothing to show that in attacking the Australian continent on the west the expedition would more surely and more promptly meet with the tribe which held Captain John Branican prisoner; for the nomad aborigines wander in Alexandra Land as they do in the districts of Western Australia. And consequently the question was replied to in the negative.

In the second place they discussed the direction it was advisable to take at the outset of the campaign; this was evidently that which Harry Felton had had to follow during his crossing of central Australia. Though this direction was not known exactly, it was at least indicated by the point where the mate of the *Franklin* had been discovered, that is

181

to say, on the banks of the Parru at the boundary between Queensland and New South Wales, and in the north-west of the latter province.

Since 1770 — the period at which Captain Cook explored- New South Wales and took possession, in the name of the King of England, of the continent already discovered by the Portuguese Manuel Godenbho and the Dutchmen Verschoor, Hartog, Carpenter and Tasman — its eastern part has been largely colonized, developed, civilized. It was in 1787 that, when Pitt was prime minister, Commodore Phillip founded the convict settlement of Botany Bay, from which in less than a century there was to come a nation of more than three millions of people. Of all that goes to form the greatness and wealth of a country nothing is missing in that part of the continent; there are roads, canals, railways, connecting the innumerable districts of Queensland, New South Wales, Victoria and South Australia; and lines of steamboats ply from port to port on the coast.

Mrs. Branican was in Sydney, and this rich and populous capital would have afforded her all the resources required for the organization of the caravan, particularly as before leaving San "Diego she: had opened an account through Mr. William Andrew with the Central Australian Bank. She could easily have obtained the men, vehicles, saddle-horses, draught horses, and pack-horses required by an Australian expedition, even for one right across from east to west, a journey of two thousand two hundred miles. But ought Sydney to be the point of departure?

All things considered, and chiefly at the advice of the American consul, who was well up to date in Australian geography, Adelaide, the capital of South Australia, appeared more suitable as the base of operations. Following the telegraph line, which extends from Adelaide to the gulf of Van Diemen, that is to say, from south to north, close along the hundred and thirty-ninth meridian, the engineers had laid the first part of a railway which extends beyond the latitude reached by Harry Felton. This railway would permit of the expedition penetrating further and more quickly into those regions of Alexandra Land and Western Australia which few travellers had yet reached.

And so this third expedition in search of Captain John would be organized at Adelaide and taken as far as the railway ran, about four hundred miles to the northward.

And now in what way should Mrs. Branican travel from Sydney to Adelaide? If there had been a railroad without a break between the two capitals, there would have been no reason for hesitation. . A railroad does exist crossing the Murray on the Victorian frontier at Albury, and continuing by Benalla and Kilmore to Melbourne, and then on towards Adelaide; but it stops at Horsham, and beyond that the break in the line would have caused long delays.

And so Mrs. Branican decided to go to Adelaide by sea. This was a four days' voyage, and, adding forty-eight hours for the stoppage the boats make at Melbourne, she would reach the capital of South Australia after a six days journey along the coast. It is true that it was now August, which corresponds to February in the northern hemisphere. But the weather was calm and the wind in the north-west, so that the steamer would be under the shelter of the coast as soon as she was through Bass's Straits, And besides, as she had come from San Francisco to Sydney, Mrs. Branican had nothing to be uneasy about in a trip from Sydney to Adelaide.

The steamer *Brisbane* started next day at eleven in the morning. After stopping at Melbourne she would reach Adelaide on the morning of the 27th of August. Two cabins were engaged, and Mrs. Branican took the necessary steps for the transfer of the credit with the Sydney bank to the bank at Adelaide. The directors obligingly consented, and the transfer was effected without difficulty.

When she left the Marine Hospital, Mrs. Branican had gone to a hotel where she had taken rooms until her departure. Her thoughts were summed up in the one thought, "John is alive!" With her eyes obstinately fixed on the map of the Australian continent, her look lost amid the immense solitudes of the centre and north-west, a prey to the delirium of her imagination, she sought him, she found him, she saved him.

After their interview that day Zach Fren, understanding she would rather be alone, had gone for a walk in the streets of Sydney, which were unknown to him, And to begin with — as was not unnatural for a sailor — he had gone to look at the *Brisbane*, so as to make sure Mrs. Branican would be comfortable. The ship appeared to be comfortably fitted for a coasting voyage. Then he asked to see the cabins engaged for the lady. A boy took him to the cabin, where he made several changes with a view to make it more comfortable. Excellent Zach Fren! One would imagine he was preparing it for a long voyage!

As he was about to leave, the boy kept him back, and in rather an agitated voice asked, —

"Then it is quite certain that Mrs. Branican will go tomorrow to Adelaide?"

"Yes, to-morrow!" replied Zach Fren.

"On the *Brisbane*?"

"Undoubtedly."

"I hope she may succeed in her endeavour and find Captain John!"

"We will do our best, you may be sure."

"I do not doubt it."

"Are you one of the *Brisbane*'s crew?"

"Yes!"

"Well, then, good-bye until to-morrow."

During the last few hours he spent in Sydney Zach Fren went for a stroll along Pitt Street and York Street, which are bordered by fine buildings in reddish grey stone, and then he went into Victoria Park and Hyde Park, where stands the Cook monument. He visited the Botanic

Gardens, a lovely promenade situated by the side of the sea, where are gathered together the different trees of warm and temperate climes, oaks and araucarias, cactuses and mangosteens, palms and olives. In short, Sydney is well worthy of its reputation. It is the oldest of the Australian capitals, and if it is less regularly built than its juniors of Adelaide and Melbourne, it is richer in unexpected beauties and picturesque sites.

Next evening Mrs. Branican and Zach Fren went on board the steamboat. At eleven o'clock the *Brisbane* left the wharf and crossed the bay of Port Jackson. After doubling the Inner South Head she turned off to the south and kept along a few miles from the coast. During the first hour Dolly remained on deck, seated aft, looking at the shore, which appeared as confused masses through the mist. This was the continent into which she was about to penetrate, as if into an immense prison from which John had not yet emerged. For fourteen years they had been separated from each other.

"Fourteen years!" she murmured.

When the *Brisbane* had passed Botany Bay and Jervis Bay Mrs. Branican went below to rest. But next morning she was on deck with the dawn, just as Mount Dromedary, and a little behind it Mount Kosciusko, which belong to the system of the Australian Alps, appeared on the horizon.

Zach Fren had joined Dolly on the spar deck, and together they talked of the one thing in which they were both interested.

At this moment a sailor boy, hesitating and trembling, approached Mrs. Branican and asked her, on the captain's behalf, if there was anything she required.

"No, my child!" said Dolly.

"Ah!" said Zach Fren, "it is the brave lad I saw yesterday when I came on board the *Brisbane.*"

"Yes," said the boy.

"And what is your name?"

"Godfrey."

"Well, Godfrey, you see for certain that Mrs. Branican is on board your- steamboat and you are satisfied, I imagine?"

"Yes, and we are all on board. Yes! We all hope that Mrs. Branican's attempt will succeed, and that she will" rescue Captain John."

And as he spoke Godfrey looked at her with so much respect and enthusiasm that Dolly was greatly agitated. And then the boy's voice struck her. That voice she had already heard, and the remembrance of it returned to her.

"My child," said she, "did you not speak to me at the door of the hospital in Sydney?"

"I did."

"You asked me if Captain John was still alive?"

"I did!"

"You belong to the *Brisbane*?"

" Yes — for the last year," said Godfrey. "But if it please God, I shall soon leave her."

Then, probably not wishing or daring to say more, Godfrey retired to take Mrs. Branican's message to the captain.

"That is a boy who has the blood of a sailor in his veins!" said Zach Fren. "You have only to look at him to see that. He has a frank, clear, decided look. His voice is at the same time firm and gentle — "

"His voice!" murmured Dolly.

And by what illusion of the senses did she fancy she had just heard John speaking in the gentler tones of a voice not yet quite set by age!

And another remark she made — a remark still more significant. Probably she was mistaken, but the boy's features reminded her of John

186

— of John, who was no more than thirty when the *Franklin* had taken him away from her for so long.

"You see, Mrs. Branican," said Zach Fren, rubbing his fine large hands, "English or Americans, every one sympathizes with you! In Australia you find the same attentions as in America! It will be in Adelaide as in San Diego! All wish you the same as this young Englishman."

"Is he an Englishman?" asked Mrs. Branican, deeply impressed.

The voyage was very enjoyable during this first day. The sea was remarkably smooth, with the wind in the north-west blowing off the land. The *Brisbane* found it no rougher when she doubled Cape Howe at the angle of the Australian continent on her way to Bass's Straits.

Dolly spent the day almost entirely on the spar deck. The passengers showed her extreme deference, and also extreme eagerness to keep her company. They were anxious to see this woman whose misfortunes were so widely known, and who did not hesitate to brave so many perils and face so many fatigues in the hope of rescuing her husband, if Providence willed he still was living. In her presence no one dared to express a doubt on the subject. How could they do otherwise than share her confidence when they heard her inspired by such manly resolution and telling them all she was about to undertake? Unconsciously they followed her in imagination into the depths of Central Australia. And, in fact, more than one of them would have agreed to follow her otherwise than in thought.

But, as she replied to them, Dolly often interrupted herself, and her look assumed a singular expression, her eyes grew brighter, and Zach Fren was the only one who knew what was passing in her mind.

This happened whenever she saw Godfrey. The boy's bearing, his attitude, his gestures, the persistence with which he devoured her with his eyes, that sort of instinct which seemed to draw her towards him — all this took possession of her, agitated her, and so moved her that John and Godfrey became somehow mixed up together in her mind.

Dolly could not hide from Zach Fren that she noticed a striking resemblance between John and Godfrey. And Zach Fren did not see without anxiety Mrs. Branican abandon herself to an impression due to a purely fortuitous circumstance. He feared, not without reason, that this companion might recall too vividly the remembrance of the child she had lost. It was truly regrettable that Dolly should become so excited in the presence of this boy l

However, Godfrey had not come to her again. His duty did not call him to the after part of the steamer, which was exclusively reserved for first-class passengers. But from afar their looks often crossed, and Dolly had been on the point of calling him to her — yes! and at a sign Godfrey would have run to her. But Dolly did not make this sign, and Godfrey did not come.

That evening, as Zach Fren was escorting her to her cabin, she said, —

"Zach, I must find out who this boy is — to what family he belongs — the place of his birth. He may perhaps not be an Englishman."

"That is possible," said Zach Fren. "He may even be an American. And if you wish it I will go and ask the captain of the *Brisbane* — "

"No, Zach, no, I will ask Godfrey himself," said Mrs. Branican.

And Zach heard her say to herself in an undertone, —

"My child, my poor little Wat, would have been about his age now.""That is what I feared!" said Zach Fren to himself, as he went to his cabin.

"The next day, the 22nd of August, the *Brisbane*, which had passed Cape Howe during the night, continued the voyage under excellent conditions. The coast of Gipps Land, one of the chief provinces of the colony of Victoria, after curving to the south-east is terminated by Cape Wilson, the most southerly promontory of the continent. This coast is less rich in bays, ports, inlets, capes, geographically named, than the straighter section between Sydney and Cape Howe; and along it the plains stretch back out of sight to the line of mountains, which are too distant to be seen from the sea.

Mrs. Branican, having left her cabin in the- first rays of the morning, had resumed her place on the after part of the spar deck. Zach Fren had joined her almost immediately afterwards and noticed a very obvious change in her manner. The land, which extended towards the north-west, no longer attracted her attention. Absorbed in her thoughts, she hardly replied to Zach Fren when he asked her how she had passed the night.

Zach Fren said no more. The essential point was that Dolly had forgotten the singular resemblance between Godfrey and Captain John, and no longer thought of seeing him and questioning him. It was possible that she had changed her mind, and, in fact, she did not ask Zach Fren to bring her the boy, whose duty kept him in the steamer's bow.

After breakfast Mrs. Branican returned to her cabin, and did not appear on deck again until three or four o'clock in the afternoon.

At this time the *Brisbane* was running at full speed into Bass's Straits, which separate Australia from Tasmania, or Van Diemen's Land.

Nothing can be more indisputable than that the discovery of the Dutchman, Janssen Tasman, has been profitable to the English, and that this island, a natural dependency of the continent, has been a gain to the Anglo-Saxon race. Since 1642, the date of the discovery of the island, which is two hundred and eighty kilometres long, the soil of which is extremely fertile, the forests of which are enriched by superb trees, it is certain that colonization has advanced with rapid strides. From the earlier years of this century the English have ruled it, as they rule, obstinately, without the slightest thought for the native races. They have divided the island into districts, they have founded important towns, the capital Hobart, Georgetown, and many others; they have utilized the innumerable indentations of the cost for the .establishment of ports, at which their ships call in hundreds. All that is good. But of the black population which originally occupied this country, what remains? Doubtless these poor people were hardly civilized; they were even looked upon as the stupidest specimens of the human race; they were placed below the African negroes, below the Fuegians of Tierra del Fuego. If the annihilation of a race is the last word of colonial progress, the English colonists may boast of having brought their work to a good end. But, at the approaching universal exhibition at Hobart, if they wish to exhibit a few Tasmanians — there is not one left at this end of the nineteenth century.

CHAPTER II - GODFREY

The *Brisbane* passed through Bass's Straits during the evening. In this latitude the day closes in about five o'clock during the month of August. The moon entering her first quarter soon disappeared amid the mists of the horizon, and the coast scenery was veiled in deep obscurity.

That the steamer was passing through the straits was only apparent on board by the splashing of the short, choppy waves; currents and counter-currents striving impetuously with each other in this narrow channel, which is open to the waters of the Pacific.

Next morning, that of the 23rd of August, the *Brisbane* at dawn was off Port Phillip bay. Once in this bay shipping have no fear of bad weather, but the entrance requires careful and skilful manoeuvring, especially in rounding the long sandy point of Nepean on the one side, and that of Queenscliff on the other. The bay, which is well shut in, is cut up into several harbours, where ships of large tonnage find excellent anchorage — Geelong, Sand- ridge, Williamstown — the last two forming the port of Melbourne. The aspect of the coast is gloomy, monotonous, unattractive. There is little vegetation on the banks, and the shore looks like a newly dried-up marsh, which, in place of lagoons or ponds, has patches of hard, cracked mud. To the future the task is left of improving the surface of these plains, by replacing the few skeletons of trees by plantations, which the Australian climate will soon develop into superb forests.

The *Brisbane* ran alongside one of the Williamstown quays to disembark some of her passengers.

As she was going to stop there thirty-six hours, Mrs. Branican decided to spend the time in Melbourne. Not that she had business in the town, for it was at Adelaide only that she would be occupied in the preparations for an expedition which might perhaps reach the farthest limits of Western Australia; and having made up her mind to this, why did she leave the *Brisbane*? Was she afraid of being the object of too many and too frequent visits? But to escape these would it not have been enough for her to remain .in her cabin? Besides, to go down to one of the town hotels, where her presence would be immediately known, was not that to expose herself to the most persistent interviews, the most inevitable importunities?

Zach Fren could not understand Mrs. Branican's resolution. He saw that her manner was very different to what it had been at Sydney. There she had been most affable, now she. was much less communicative. Was it, as the boatswain thought, that the presence of Godfrey had too vividly reminded her of her child? Yes, and Zach Fren was not mistaken. The sight of the boy had troubled her so deeply that she felt the need of being alone. Did it not enter more into her thoughts to question him? Perhaps; although she had not done so the night before, notwithstanding she had expressed a-wish to do so. But now, if she wished to land at Melbourne, to spend the day there, it was not to avoid the inconveniences of a notoriety unhappily too real, but to escape — there is no other word for it — to escape from this fourteen-year-old boy to whom she was attracted by some instinctive force. Why, then, did she hesitate to speak to him, to ask what interested her concerning his nationality, his birth, his family? Did she fear that his replies — as was only too likely — would result in definitely destroying her imprudent illusions, a chimerical hope, to which she had abandoned herself in imagination, and which her agitation had revealed to Zach Fren?

Mrs. Branican, accompanied by the boatswain, landed during the first hour. As soon as she had set foot on the landing-stage she turned to come back.

Godfrey was leaning on the rail of the *Brisbanes* bow. Seeing her going away his face became so sad, he made such an expressive gesture, he seemed to wish her so imperiously to return on board, that Dolly was on the point of returning to Say to him, "No! I will not go!" But she controlled herself, made a sign to Zach Fren to follow her, and went off to the railway station, which puts the harbour in communication with the town.

Melbourne, in fact, is situated away from the sea shore, on the left bank of the river Yarra-Yarra, at a distance of two kilometres — a distance accomplished by the trains in a quarter of an hour. There stands this city, with its population of three hundred thousand inhabitants, the capital of the magnificent colony of Victoria, which holds nearly a million, and on which, since 1851, it may be said that Mount Alexander has poured all the gold from its beds.

Mrs. Branican, although she went to one of the least frequented hotels of the town, could not escape the curiosity — entirely sympathetic — which her presence everywhere aroused. And so she preferred to be in the company of Zach Fren to walk about the streets of the town, of which, owing to her strange pre-occupation, she saw nothing.

An American could not help being astonished or pleased in visiting an absolutely modern city. Although younger by a dozen years than San Francisco in California, Melbourne is like it, "only more so," as has been said. Wide streets crossing at right angles, squares without lawns or trees, banks in hundreds, offices where enormous business is done, a district in which the retail trade is concentrated, public buildings, churches, temples, university, museum, art gallery, library, hospital, town hall, schools which are palaces, palaces which, in some cases, would not be large enough for schools, a monument to Burke and Wills, who died in endeavouring to cross the continent from south to north; then along the roads and boulevards beyond the business quarter, a few passers-by, a certain number of strangers, chiefly Jews and Germans, who sell money as others self cattle or linen, and at a good price — to the joy of the heart of Israel.

But in business Melbourne, business men live as little as possible. It is in the suburbs, in the environs of the town, that the villas and cottages, and even princely dwellings, swarm, at St. Kilda, at Hoam, at Emerald Hill, at Brighton — and it is this, says M. D. Charnay, one of the most intelligent travellers who have visited the country, which gives

Melbourne the advantage over San Francisco. And already the trees of different kinds have grown large; sumptuous parks are covered with shade; and the running streams assure a healthy freshness for many months, so that there are few towns placed amid a more admirable frame of verdure.

Mrs. Branican gave but little attention to these magnificences, even when Zach Fren took her out of the town into the open country. Nothing indicated that this grand situation, with its distant views, had interested her. It seemed always as though she was possessed by some fixed idea, and was on the point of asking Zach Fren something she dared not put into words.

They returned to the hotel in the evening. Dolly had her dinner served in her room, and hardly touched it. Then she lay down, and slept but a half sleep, haunted by the images of her husband and her child. In the morning she remained in her apartment until the moment of departure. She wrote along letter to Mr. William Andrew, acquainting him with the departure from Sydney, and her approaching arrival in the capital of South Australia. She told him again of her hopes relative to the result of the expedition. And when he received this letter, to his great surprise and also anxiety, he would notice that, if Dolly spoke of John as if she were sure to find him alive, she also spoke of little Wat as if he were not dead. The excellent man would certainly ask himself if he had not again cause to fear for the sanity of this much-tried woman.

The passengers the *Brisbane* was to take to Adelaide had nearly all embarked when Mrs. Branican and Zach Fren returned on board. Godfrey was waiting for her return, and when he saw her coming his face lighted up with a smile. He rushed to the landing-stage, and was there when she set foot on the gangway.

Zach Fren was much annoyed, and his thick eyebrows were knitted in a frown. What would he not have given if the boy had left the steamer, or at least that he had not again met Dolly, in whom his presence revived the saddest of memories.

Mrs. Branican noticed Godfrey. She stopped for an instant and looked at him keenly; but she did not speak, and bowing her head, she went to shut herself up in her cabin.

At three o'clock in the afternoon the *Brisbane* cast off her warps, and started out to sea, rounding Queenscliff and steering for Adelaide, keeping out about three miles from the coast of Victoria.

The passengers who had come on board at Melbourne numbered about a hundred. For the most part they were inhabitants of South Australia returning home. There were a few strangers among them — one of them a Chinaman, aged from thirty to thirty-five, looking as sleepy as a mole, yellow as a lemon, round as a post, and as fat as a mandarin of three buttons. But he was not a mandarin. No! he was merely a servant in the employ of a personage who deserves to be described somewhat precisely.

Imagine a son of Albion, as "Britannic" as one can be, tall, thin, bony, a regular piece of osteology, all neck, all bust, all legs. This typical Anglo-Saxon, of from forty- five to fifty years of age, stood about six feet above seq-

level. A fair beard, which he wore uncut, and also fair hair, in which were a few streaks of yellowish gold; little ferret eyes, a nose pinched in at the nostrils, curved like the beak of a pelican or a heron, and of a length uncommon; a head on which the slightest observer of phrenology would easily have discovered the bumps of monomania and tenacity — made up altogether one of those heads which attract attention and provoke a smile when they are drawn by a clever artist.

This Englishman was clothed- in the traditional costume — a cap with a double peak, a waistcoat buttoned to the chin, a coat with twenty pockets, trousers of chequered cloth, high gaiters with nickel buttons, nailed shoes, and a check overcoat, which the wind wrapped round his body, revealing the thinness as of a skeleton.

Who was this original? No one knew, and on the Australian steamboats no one takes advantage of the familiarities of the voyage to ask who people are or whence they come. They are passengers, and as such they pass. No more. But the stewards could have told us that the Englishman had taken his cabin under the name of Joshua Meritt — shortly, Jos Meritt — of Liverpool (United Kingdom), accompanied by his servant Gin-Ghi, of Hong Kong (Celestial Empire).

For the rest, once he was on board, Jos Meritt went and sat down on one of the benches of the promenade deck, and did not leave it until lunch time.

He returned in about half an hour, left again at seven for dinner, reappeared at eight, looking all the time like a lay figure, with his two hands open on his knees, turning his head neither to the right nor the left, with his eyes looking straight in front, their gaze lost in the mists of the evening. Then at ten o'clock he regained his cabin at a geometrical pace, which the irregularities of the vessel's roll were unable to trouble.

During a part of the night Mrs. Branican, who had gone on deck about nine o'clock, remained in the after part of the *Brisbane*, although the temperature was rather low.

With her mind possessed, envisioned even (to employ the more exact expression), she could not sleep. Confined in her cabin she had need of a breath of fresh air, impregnated now and then by the penetrating odours of the Acacia flagrant, which distinguishes the Australian coast fifty miles out at sea. Was she thinking of meeting the sailor boy, speaking to him, questioning him, ascertaining from him — what? Godfrey having finished his watch at ten o'clock, would not come on duty again till two o'clock in the morning; and Dolly, much fatigued by a certain shock to her mind, regained her cabin.

In the middle of the night the *Brisbane* doubled Cape Otway at the extremity of the district of Polwarth. From this point she had to head N.W. to Discovery Bay, at the end of the conventional line traced on the hundred and forty-first meridian — the line which separates the colonies of Victoria and New South Wales from South Australia.

In the morning Jos Meritt was again to be seen on the bench on the spar deck, his customary place, in the same attitude, and just as if he had not left it the previous evening. As to Gin-Ghi he was sleeping in some corner.

Zach Fren was accustomed to the peculiarities Of his compatriots, for there is no lack of originals in the forty- two federated states included' under the formula U.S.A. However, he could not regard without a certain astonishment this successful type of human mechanism.

And what was his surprise when, approaching this long and motionless gentleman, he heard himself spoken to in rather a shrill voice.

"Boatswain Zach Fren, I believe?"

"The same," said Zach Fren.

"The companion of Mrs. Branican?"

"In person. I see you know — "

"I know — in search of her husband — lost for fourteen years. Good! Oh, very good!"

"What is very good?"

"Yes! Mrs. Branican! Very good! I also — I am on a search — "

"Your wife?"

"Oh! I am not married! Very good! If I had lost my wife I should not seek her!"

"Then it is for — "

"For finding — a hat."

"Your hat? You have lost your hat?"

"My hat? No! It is the hat I mean. Present my respects to Mrs. Branican. Good! Oh, very good!"

The lips of Jos Meritt closed and did not utter another syllable.

"He must be a lunatic," said Zach Fren to himself.

And it seemed to him to be loss of time talking to this gentleman.

When Dolly came on deck, the boatswain went to meet her, and they sat down almost in front of the Englishman, who moved no more than if he had been the god Terminus. Having asked Zach Freu to present his respects to Mrs. Branican, he apparently thought there was no necessity for his presenting them in person.

And besides, Dolly had not-remarked the presence of this curious passenger. She spoke for some time with her companion regarding the preparations for the journey, which were to be commenced as soon as they reached Adelaide.. Not a day, not an hour, was to be lost. It was important that the expedition should reach, and pass if possible, the central regions before they were parched by the intolerable heats of the torrid zone.

Among the dangers of different kinds, inherent to a search undertaken under such conditions, the most terrible would be probably due to the rigour of the climate, and. all precautions, should be taken to guard against it. . Dolly spoke much of Captain John, his robust temperament, his indomitable energy, which had permitted him — she did not doubt — to survive when others less vigorous, and not so hardy, had succumbed. But she made no allusion to Godfrey, and Zach Fren- was hoping she was no longer thinking of the boy, when she suddenly said, "I have not yet seen that boy to-day? Have you seen him, Zach?"

"No, madam," said the boatswain, whom the question evidently displeased.

"Perhaps I might do something for that child," continued Dolly.

And she affected to speak of him in a tone of indifference, which Zach Fren was not deceived by.

"This boy?" said he. "Oh! He has a good trade. He will get on. I see him a quartermaster in a few years. With zeal and good conduct — "

"That does not matter," said Dolly. "He interests me in one way. Look, Zach, at the extraordinary resemblance between him and my poor John. And then, Wat — my child — ought to be about his age."

And as she said this she became quite pale; and the look she gave Zach Fren was so questioning that he lowered his eyes. Then she added, —

"You will send him to me this afternoon, Zach. Do not forget. I wish to speak with him. This voyage will end to-morrow. We may never see each other again, and before I leave the *Brisbane* I wish to know — yes, to know — "

Zach Fren promised to bring Godfrey to her, and she retired.

The boatswain, in a state of great anxiety and even alarm, continued to pace the spar deck, until the steward rang the second breakfast bell. Zach then happened to run against the Englishman, who seemed to regulate his steps by the stroke of the bell, as he made towards the companion.

"Good! Oh, very good!" said Jos Meritt. "You have at my request conveyed my respects? Her lost husband — Good! Oh, very good!"

And he disappeared to reach the place he had taken at the dining-room table, the best be it understood, and the one nearest the kitchen, so that he could be served the first, and have the best choice.

At three o'clock the *Brisbane* was off Portland, the chief port of the Normanby district, where the Melbourne railway ends; then, rounding Cape Nelson, she crossed Discovery Bay, and steered almost due north along the coast of South Australia.

It was at this time that Zach Fren went to tell Godfrey Mrs. Branican desired to speak to him.

"Speak to me?" exclaimed the boy. And his heart - beat so furiously that he would have fallen had he not caught hold of the rail.

Godfrey followed the boatswain to the cabin where Mrs. Branican was waiting for him.

Dolly looked at him for some time as he stood upright with his cap in his hand. She was seated on a couch. Zach Fren, leaning near the door, watched both of them anxiously. He knew what Dolly was going to ask Godfrey, but he did not know what would be his replies.

"My child," said Mrs. Branican, "I want to know something about you, about the family to which you belong. If I ask, it is because I am interested in you — in your position. Will you answer my questions?"

"Willingly," said Godfrey, his voice trembling with emotion.

"How old are you?" asked Dolly.

"I do not know exactly, but I ought to be from fourteen to fifteen."

"Yes! - From fourteen to fifteen! And since when have you been at sea?"

"I went to sea when I was eight years old as a cabin boy; and for two years I have been an apprentice."

"Have you been any long voyage?"

"Yes, madam, across the Pacific to Asia — and across the Atlantic to Europe."

"You are not an Englishman?"

"No, madam, I am an American."

"But yet you are on an English steamer?"

"The ship on which I was apprentice was sold at Sydney. Finding myself without a ship, I came on the *Brisbane*, awaiting an opportunity to again get on an American ship."

"Good, my child," said Dolly, beckoning Godfrey to come nearer to her.

"And now," she asked, "I want to know where you were born?"

"At San Diego, madam."

"Yes! at San Diego!" repeated Dolly, without appearing surprised, as if she had expected the answer.

Zach Fren was much impressed with what he had just heard.

"Yes, madam, at San Diego," continued Godfrey. "Oh! I know you well! Yes, I know you. When I learnt you had come to Sydney I was very pleased. If you knew, madam, how much I am interested in all that concerns Captain John Branican —

Dolly took the boy's hand and held it for a few seconds without saying a word. Then in a voice which betrayed the wandering of her imagination, —

"Your name?" she asked.

"Godfrey."

"Godfrey is your baptismal name. But what is your family name?"

"I have no other name, madam."

"Your parents? "-

"I have no parents."

"No parents!" said Mrs. Branican. "Have you then been brought up — "

."At Wat House," replied Godfrey. "Yes! madam, and by your care. Oh! I have often seen you when you came to visit the children. You did not see me among all the little ones, but I saw you, and I wished J could kiss you. Then, as I had a taste for the sea, when I was old enough I became a cabin boy. And others of the Wat House orphans have gone

201

on ships, and we will never forget what we owe to Mrs. Branican — to our mother!"

"Your mother!" exclaimed Dolly, who started as if the name had resounded deep within her.

She drew Godfrey to her — she covered him with kisses — he kissed her again — he wept.

And in his corner Zach Fren, frightened at what he understood of the feelings he saw taking root in Dolly's heart, murmured, —

Poor woman! Poor woman! Where will she let herself be led?"

Mrs. Branican rose and said, —

"Go, Godfrey 1 Go, my child! I will see you again! I want to be alone!"

The boy looked at her for a last time and slowly withdrew.

Zach Fren was preparing to follow him, when Dolly stopped him by a gesture — " Remain, Zach!" Then, "Zach," said she, in a short, spasmodic way, which denoted the extraordinary agitation of her mind, "Zach, that child has been brought up with the children at Wat House. He was born at San Diego. He is from fourteen to fifteen years old. He resembles John feature for feature. He has his frank face, his resolute attitude. He has a taste for the sea like him. He is the son of a sailor. He is John's son. He is mine! We believed that the bay of San Diego never gave back the poor little creature. But he still lived; and he was rescued. Those who saved him did not know his mother. And his mother was I — I — then deprived of my reason. This child is not Godfrey, as he says, but Wat, my son! God has given him back to me before giving me back his father."

Zach Fren had listened to Mrs. Branican without daring to interrupt her. He understood that the unhappy woman could not speak differently. All the appearances compelled her to do so. She reasoned with the irrefutable logic of a mother. And the brave sailor felt his heart breaking, for these illusions it was his duty to destroy.

He must stop Dolly on this incline, which might lead her into a new abyss.

He did it without hesitating — almost brutally.

"Mrs. Branican," he said, "you are mistaken. I will not, I ought not to let you believe such things. The resemblance is but a chance. Your little Wat is dead. Yes, dead! He perished in the accident, and Godfrey is not your son."

"Wat is dead?" exclaimed Mrs. Branican. "And how do you know that? Who can prove it?"

"I can, madam!"

"You?"

"A week after the accident in the bay, the body of a child was thrown on the beach at Loma Point. I found it there. . I told Mr. William Andrew. Little Wat was recognized by him, and buried in the cemetery at San Diego, where we have often placed flowers on his grave."

"Wat! My little Wat — there — in the cemetery! And they never told me of it!" murmured Mrs. Branican.

"No, madam, no!" replied Zach Fren. "You were then out of your mind, and when you recovered your reason, four years afterwards, we feared — Mr. William Andrew feared — to renew your sorrows, and he was silent. But your child is dead, and Godfrey cannot be — he is not your son!"

Dolly fell back on the sofa. Her eyes were shut as if shadow had suddenly succeeded intense light.

At a sign she made, Zach Fren left her alone deep in her sorrows and remembrances.

On the morning of the next day, the 26th of August, Mrs. Branican had not yet quitted her cabin when the *Brisbane*, after running through Backstairs Passage, between Kangaroo Island and Jervis promontory, entered the Gulf of St. Vincent and cast anchor in Adelaide harbour.

CHAPTER III - A HISTORIC HAT

Of the three capitals of Australia, Sydney is the eldest, Melbourne the junior, and Adelaide the youngest. But if the last is the youngest, it can also be said to be the most beautiful. It was born in 1853, of a mother — South Australia — which had no political existence before 1837, and the officially recognized independence of which only dates from 1856. It is even probable that the youth of Adelaide will be indefinitely prolonged under an unrivalled climate, the healthiest on the continent, amidst a region which knows neither consumption nor endemic fevers, nor any kind of contagious epidemic. People die there occasionally, however; but, as has been wittily observed by M. D. Charnay, "that is the exception."

If the soil of South Australia differs from that of the neighbouring province in that it docs not contain auriferous deposits, it is rich in copper ore. The mines of Kapunda, Burra-Burra, Wallaroo and Moonta, discovered forty years ago, after attracting emigrants in thousands have made the fortune of the colony.

Adelaide does not stand on the shore of St. Vincent Gulf. Like Melbourne, it is situated a dozen kilometres inland, and a railway puts it in communication with the harbour. Its botanic garden rivals that of its second sister. Created by Schomburg, it possesses greenhouses which have no equal in the whole world, parterres of roses which are veritable parks, magnificent shades under the shelter of the most beautiful trees of the temperate and semi-tropical zones.

Neither Sydney nor Melbourne can enter into comparison with Adelaide for elegance. Its streets are wide, agreeably distributed, carefully kept. Some possess veritable monuments along their borders, such as King William Street. The post-office and the town-hall are worthy of notice from an architectural point of view. In the business quarter, Hindley and Glenell Streets are noisily animated with the throng of busy traders. And thereabouts gather a number of business men who seem to show only that satisfaction derived from business

205

wisely conducted, abundant, and easy without any of the cares it usually brings.

Mrs. Branican went to a hotel in King William Street, whither Zach Fren accompanied her. The mother, in her had just been cruelly tried by the annihilation of her last illusions. It seemed to be so likely that Godfrey was her son that she had naturally abandoned herself to the idea. The deception could still be read on her face, paler than usual, in her eyes, red with weeping. But, from the moment her hope had been so completely broken, she had not endeavoured to see the boy again, and had said no more about him to Zach Fren. There only remained the remembrance of the surprising resemblance to John.

And now Dolly was to set to work to begin without delay her preparations for her expedition. She was to appeal to all for help and devotedness. She would spend, if need be, her whole future in these new searches, in stimulating by considerable rewards the zeal of those who would unite their efforts to hers in a supreme attempt.

There was no lack of zeal in her cause. This colony of South Australia is essentially the country of bold explorers. Thence the most celebrated pioneers have started across the unknown territories of the interior. From there went Warburton, John Forrest, Giles, Sturt, whose routes intercross on the maps of this vast continent — routes which Mrs. Branican would cut obliquely with her own. It was thus that Colonel Warburton, in 1874, traversed Australia in its entire width from east to north-west at Nicholson Bay — that John Forrest, the same year, crossed it in an opposite direction, from Perth to Port Augusta — that Giles, in 1876, set out from Perth to Spencer Gulf, on the 25th degree of south latitude.

It had been agreed that the different elements of the expedition should be mustered, not at Adelaide, but at the terminus of the railway which runs northward, up to the latitude of Lake Eyre. Five degrees crossed in this way would be a gain of time and a saving of fatigue. Amid the districts furrowed by the orographic system of the Flinders Ranges, they could muster the number of vehicles and animals necessary for this campaign, the horses of the escort, the cattle for the transport of the victuals and camp effects. On these interminable deserts, these immense steppes of sand, deprived of vegetation, almost without water, provision had to be made for the wants of a caravan, which would comprise forty persons, counting the servants and the little escort for assuring safety to the travellers.

Her preparations Dolly made in Adelaide. She found a constant and firm friend in the governor of South Australia, who put himself entirely at her disposal. Thanks to him, thirty men well mounted, well armed, some of them natives, some chosen among the European colonists; accepted service under Mrs. Branican. She guaranteed them, very high pay for the whole campaign, and a bonus of-a hundred pounds apiece when it was over, no matter what the result might be. They were commanded by an old officer of the colonial police — Tom Marix, a robust and resolute fellow, aged about forty, whom the governor unhesitatingly recommended. Tom Marix had chosen his men with care, from among the strongest and most trustworthy of those who volunteered in great numbers. There was every reason, therefore, to trust to the devotedness of this escort, which was recruited under the best conditions.

The working staff of the expedition would be eventually under the orders of Zach Fren, and it would not be his fault if "men and beasts did not march squarely and roundly," as he said.

Above Tom Marix and Zach Fren, the true chief was Mrs. Branican, the soul of the expedition.

By means of the correspondents of Mr. William Andrew, a considerable credit had been opened for Mrs. Branican, at the Bank of Adelaide, and she could draw on it as she pleased.

The preparations being completed, it was agreed that Zach Fren should set out on the 30th at latest, for the station at Farina Town, where Mrs. Branican would rejoin him with the staff when her presence was no longer necessary at Adelaide.

"Zach," said she, "you will see that our caravan is ready to start at the end of the first week in September. Pay for everything, no matter at what cost. The provisions you can send on from here by railway, and we can put them on the drays at Farina Town. We must neglect nothing to ensure the success of our campaign."

"All shall be ready Mrs. Branican," said the boatswain. "When you arrive, all you will have to do will be to give the signal of departure."

One can easily imagine that Zach Fren did not fail in his task during the last few days he passed at Adelaide. In sailor style he worked away with such activity that on the 29th he' could take his ticket for Farina Town. Twelve hours afterwards, when the railway had deposited him at this terminal station of the line, he informed Mrs. Branican, by telegram, that a part of the stores of the expedition had already been collected.

Dolly, aided by Tom Marix, took as her share of the work all that concerned the escort, its armament, and its clothing. It was important for its horses to be carefully chosen, and the Australian breed furnished excellent animals, broken to fatigue, inured to climate, and of remarkable docility. While they were crossing the forests and the plains, there was no reason to trouble about their food, grass and water being available for them. But beyond, across the sandy deserts, they would have to be replaced by camels, and this would be done as soon as they reached Alice Spring. From that point onwards, Mrs. Branican and her companions would learn to struggle against the material obstacles which render the exploration of Central Australia so formidable.

The occupations to which this energetic woman had devoted herself, had rather distracted her attention from the later incidents of the voyage on the *Brisbane*. She was so absorbed in this display of activity, that she had not an hour of leisure. Of that illusion to which her imagination had for an instant abandoned her, of that ephemeral hope which the intervention of Zach Fren had broken in one word, there remained only the remembrance. Now she knew that her child slept in a corner of the cemetery of San Diego, and she could go and weep over his grave. But yet that boy's resemblance — and the images of John and Godfrey seemed to run together in her mind.

But since the arrival of the steamer, Mrs. Branican had not thought of the boy. If he had endeavoured to meet with her during the first days Which followed her landing, she knew it not. In any case it did not seem that Godfrey had presented himself at the hotel in King William Street, and why should he have done so? After her last interview with him, Dolly had shut herself up in her cabin, and had not sent for him again. Besides, Dolly knew that the *Brisbane* had gone back to Melbourne, and that, when she returned to Adelaide, the expedition would have started.

While Mrs. Branican was urging on her preparations, another personage was no less steadily busy in preparing for a similar journey. He had put up at a hotel in Hindley Street. An apartment in the front of the hotel, a bedroom looking on the interior court, united under one roof those singular representatives of the Aryan race and the Yellow race — the Englishman, Jos Meritt, and the Chinaman, Gin-Ghi.

Whence came these two types, one from furthest Asia, the other from furthest Europe? Where were they going? What did they do at Melbourne, and what were they going to do at Adelaide? In short, under what circumstances were this master and servant associated, to run about the world together? Let us be present at a conversation in which Jos Meritt and Gin-Ghi took part in the evening of the 5th of September, a conversation which will complete our brief explanation.

And, to begin with, if a few traits of character, a few eccentricities, the singularity of his attitudes, the way in which he expressed himself, have permitted us to glance at the profile of the Anglo-Saxon, it is as well to know also this Celestial in his service, who had retained the traditional vestments of the Chinese country, the shirt "han chaol," the tunic "ma coual," the gown "haol," buttoned on the flank, and the baggy trousers with the stuff belt. If he was called Gin-Ghi, he deserved the name, which properly means "lazy man." And he was a

209

lazy man, to a rare degree, in work as well as in danger. He would not take ten steps to execute an order, and he would not take twenty to avoid a peril. It follows that Jos Meritt had an unusual dose of patience for him to keep such a servant. It is true it was a matter of habit, for they had travelled together for five or six years. They had met each other at San Francisco, where the Chinese swarm, and Jos Meritt had made the Chinaman his servant only "on trial," as he said — a trial which would doubtless last until the final separation. It should be mentioned that Gin-Ghi was brought up at Hong-Kong, and spoke English like a native of Manchester.

And Jos Meritt hardly ever lost his temper, being of a phlegmatic temperament. If he threatened Gin-Ghi with the most frightful tortures in use in the Celestial Empire, where the Minister of Justice is literally called the Minister of Executions, he never gave him a slap. When his orders were not executed, he executed them himself. That simplified the situation. Perhaps the. day was not far distant when he would wait on his servant Probably the Chinaman thought so, and from his point of view that would only be equitable. It is true that while he was waiting for this agreeable reverse of fortune, Gin-Ghi was compelled to follow his master wherever his vagabond fancy might take him. On that point, Jos Meritt would stand no nonsense. He had carried on his shoulders Gin-Ghi's portmanteau rather than leave Gin-Ghi behind when the train or steamer was ready to start. Whether he liked it or not, the "lazy man "had to hurry up and be ready to sleep on the road with the most perfect laziness. In this way one had accompanied the other along thousands and thousands of miles, over the new and old continents; and it was in consequence of this system of continuous locomotion that they now found themselves in the capital of South Australia.

"Good! oh, very good!" Jos Meritt had said on this occasion. "I think our arrangements have all been made?" *

And we can hardly explain why he questioned Gin- Ghi in this way, for he had had to do everything with his own hands. But he never failed to do so, on principle.

"Ten thousand times finished," replied the Chinaman, who had not been able to drop the roundabout expressions held in honour by the inhabitants of the Celestial Empire.

"Our portmanteaux?"

"Are strapped." — ; "Our arms?"

"Are ready."

"Our boxes of provisions?"

"You yourself, Master Jos, took them to the railway station. And besides, what is the use of taking food when any day we may be eaten ourselves?"

"Be eaten, Gin-Ghi? Good! oh! very good 1 You arc always thinking of being eaten!"

"That will happen sooner or later, and it would not take much for us in the next six months to end our travelling in some cannibal's inside — me in particular!"

"You, Gin-Ghi!"

"Yes, for the excellent .reason that I am fat, while you, Master Jos, are lean; those fellows would always give me the preference.''

"The preference? Good! oh! very good!"

"And the Australian natives have a particular liking for the yellow flesh of the Chinese, which is all the more delicate owing to their feeding on rice and vegetables."

"That is why I have always advised you to smoke, Gin-Ghi," quietly replied Jos Meritt. "You know that cannibals do not like the flesh of smokers."

And this the prudent Celestial did, smoking not opium, but the tobacco with which Jos Meritt supplied him in abundance. The Australians, it seems, as well as their cannibalistic brothers of other countries, have an invincible repugnance to human flesh when it is impregnated with nicotine. That is why Gin-Ghi worked so conscientiously to make himself uneatable.

But was it true that he and his master were destined to figure at a cannibal banquet, and not in the position of guests? Yes, on certain parts of the African coast, Jos Meritt and his servant had nearly ended their adventurous existence in this fashion. Ten months before, in Queensland, west of Rockhampton and Gracemere, a few hundred miles from Brisbane, their peregrinations had taken them among the most ferocious of the native tribes. There, cannibalism is, so to speak, endemic. And so Jos Meritt and Gin-Ghi, fallen into the hands of the blacks, would certainly have perished had it not been for the intervention of the colonial police. Rescued in time, they had been able to regain the capital of Queensland, and then Sydney, whence the steamer had just brought them to Adelaide. And as that had not put a stop to this propensity of the Englishman to run the risk of being eaten together with Gin-Ghi, they were now preparing to visit the centre of the Australian continent.

"And all that for a hat!" said the Chinaman. "Ay ya! Ay ya! When I think of that, my tears fall like drops of rain on the yellow chrysanthemums."

"When you have finished dropping, Gin-Ghi," said Jos Meritt, frowning with his Britannic brows.

"But this hat, if you ever find it, Master Jos, will be only a rag."

"Enough, Gin-Ghi! Too much! I forbid your talking in that way of this hat and every other hat! You understand? Good 1 oh! very good! If you begin again, I shall have to administer forty or fifty cuts with the cane on the soles of your feet."

"We are not in China," retorted Gin-Ghi, impudently.

"I will stop your food!"

"That will make me thin."

"I will cut your pigtail off close to your crown."

"Cut off my pigtail?"

"I will put you on a tobacco diet."

"The god Fo protect me!"

"He will not protect you!"

And at this last threat Gin-Ghi became submissive and respectful.

But what was this hat they were talking about, and why did Jos Meritt spend his life running about after a hat?

This eccentric individual was, as we have said, an Englishman, of Liverpool, one of those inoffensive maniacs who do not only belong to the United Kingdom. They are met with on the banks of the Loire, the Elbe, the Danube and the Scheldt as well as in the regions watered by the Thames, the Clyde and the Tweed. Jos Meritt was very rich and well known in Lancashire and the neighbouring counties as an eccentric collector. It was not pictures, nor books, nor objects of art, nor nick-knacks, that, he collected at great effort and great cost. No! it was hats — a collection of historic head gear — men's hats, women's hats, four-cornered, three-cornered, two- cornered, petases, calashes, slouches, cocks, operas, helmets, floppeties, sailors, cardinals, burgundians, skulls, turbans, toques, caroches, caps, fezzes, shakoes, kepis, cidares, busbies, tiaras, mitres, tarbouches, schapskas, ottomans, mortar boards, Inca llantus, Mediaeval hermins, Sacerdotal infulas, Oriental smokers, Venetian doges, Baptismal chrisms, &c. &c. in hundreds, and more or less dilapidated, tattered, crownless and brimlcss. As may be imagined, he possessed many precious historical curiosities — the helmet of Patroclus when that hero was killed by Hector at the siege of Troy, the bonnet worn by Themis-tocles at the battle of Salamis, the caps of Galen and Hippocrates, the hat which the wind blew off Caesars head as he crossed the Rubicon, the head-gear of Lucrezia Borgia at each of her three marriages with Sforza Alphonso d'Este and Alfonso of Aragon, the hat of Tamerlane when he crossed the Sind, that of Genghis Khan, when he destroyed Bokhara and Samarcand, the cap of Elizabeth at her coronation, that of Marie Stuart when she escaped from Loch Leven, that of Catherine, when she was anointed at Moscow, the suroct of Peter the Great, when he worked in the shipyard at Saardam", the cocked hat worn by Marlborough at the battle of Ramillies, that of Olaus, King of Denmark, who was killed at Sticklestad, Gessler's cap to which William Tell refused to bow, the toque of William Pitt, when he entered the twenty-third year of his ministry, the cocked hat of Napoleon the First at the battle of Wagram, and a hundred others not less authentic. His greatest grief was at not having discovered the cap worn by Noah on the day the ark grounded on the summit of Mount Ararat, and the bonnet worn by Abraham, when the patriarch was about to sacrifice his son Isaac. But Jos Meritt did not despair of finding them some day. As to the headgear worn by Adam and Eve, when they were driven out of Eden, he had given up seeking for them, as historians worthy of credit had proved that the first man and woman went about bare-headed.

It will be seen from this brief description of the curiosities in Jos Meritt's museum in what utterly childish occupations he spent his life.. In no way doubting of the authenticity of his finds, he had travelled in every country, visited the towns and villages, ransacked every store and shop, interviewed the marine-store dealers and rag-men, and spent both time and money. The whole world he requisitioned to put his hand on some undiscoverable object, and after exhausting the stocks of Europe, Africa, Asia, America, and Oceania by himself, his correspondents, his agents, his commercial travellers, he had arrived here to explore the most inaccessible retreats of the Australian continent.

He had a reason for that — a reason which others might have considered insufficient, but which appeared serious enough for him. Having been informed that the nomads of Australia wore hats — in what a state of dilapidation we may imagine — 'knowing from another source that cargoes of this old rubbish were regularly exported to the coast- towns, he had concluded that he might perhaps get "a good thing or two," in the language of antiquarian collectors. He was in fact a prey to a fixed idea, tormented by the desire which possessed him, which threatened to drive him quite mad, for he was half mad already. This time he was after a hat which he believed would be the gem of his collection.

What was this marvel? By what ancient or modern maker had this hat been turned out? On what head of royalty, nobility, bourgeoisie, or commonalty had it been placed and under what circumstances? Whatever it was, owing to valuable information, and by following the trail with the ardour of a Chingachgook or a Renard Subtil, he had arrived at the conviction that the said hat, after a long series of vicissitudes, ought to be ending its career on the cranium of some notable of an Australian tribe in doubly justifying his title of "cover chief." If he succeeded in discovering it, Jos Meritt would pay whatever was asked for it, or he would steal it if he could not purchase it. It would be the trophy of the campaign which would take him to the north-east of the continent; and not having succeeded in his first attempt, he was prepared to brave the very real dangers of an expedition into Central Australia. That is why Gin-Ghi was again about to risk finishing his life in the jaws of cannibals — and what cannibals! The most ferocious of those whose teeth he had hitherto braved! But it is as well to note that the servant was so attached to his master — the attachment of two mandarin ducks — as much by interest as affection, that he would not leave him.

"To-morrow morning we leave Adelaide by the express," said Jos Meritt.

"At the second watch?" replied Gin-Ghi.

"At the second watch, if you like; and see that everything is ready for our departure."

"I will do my best, Master Jos; but I beg you to observe that I have not ten thousand hands like the goddess Kwanin!"

"I do not know if the goddess Kwan-in has ten thousand hands," replied Jos Meritt; "but I know that you have two, and I desire you to use them in my service."

"Until I am eaten!"

"Good! Oh! Very good!"

And doubtless Gin-Ghi did not use his hands more actively than usual, preferring to leave the work to his master; and on the morrow the two oddities left Adelaide, and the train took them full speed towards the unknown, where Jos Meritt hoped to discover the hat which he required for his collection.

CHAPTER IV - THE TRAIN TO ADELAIDE

A FEW days later Mrs. Branican also left the capital of South Australia. Tom Marix had just completed the escort, which consisted of fifteen white men who had been in the local militia, and fifteen natives who had been in the service of the colony in the governor's police. This escort was intended for the protection of the caravan against the nomads, and not for fighting the tribe of the Indas. It would not do to forget what Harry Felton said: it was better to rescue Captain John at the cost of a ransom than to take him by force from the natives who held him prisoner.

Provisions in sufficient quantity for the victualling of forty persons for a year filled two of the trucks unloaded at Farina Town. Every day a letter from Zach Fren, dated from the station kept Dolly informed of all that passed. The cattle and horses bought by him were mustered there under the charge of the drivers. The vehicles which were at the railway station were ready to receive the boxes of provisions, the bales of clothing, the utensils, ammunition, tents, in a word all that composed the baggage of the expedition. Two days after the arrival of the train the caravan could begin its march.

Mrs. Branican had fixed her departure from Adelaide for the 9th of September. In a last interview she had with the governor of the colony he had not hidden from the intrepid woman the dangers she was about to face.

"The dangers are of two kinds, Mrs. Branican," he said, "those that come from the ferocious tribes in the regions over which we have no control, and those resulting from the very nature of those regions. Denuded of all resources, notably deficient of water, for the rivers and wells are already dry from the drought, terrible sufferings are in store for you. On this account it might have been better had you started six months later at the end of the hot season — "

"I know that," said Mrs. Branican, "and I am prepared for all. Since my departure from San Diego, I have studied the Australian continent, reading again and again the narratives of travellers who have been through it; Burke, Stuart, Giles, Forrest, Sturt, Gregory, Warburton. I have been able to get the account of the intrepid David Lindsay, who from September, 1887, to September, 1888, crossed Australia from Port Darwin in the north to Adelaide in the south. No! I am fully aware of the dangers of the enterprise. But I must go where duty calls me."

"The explorer David Lindsay," replied the governor, "only journeyed through regions that were known, for the telegraph line crosses them. And he only took with him a young native and four pack horses. You, on the contrary, Mrs. Branican, are in search of nomad tribes, and will be obliged to take your caravan away from the line, to venture into the north-west of the continent as far as the deserts of Tasman Land or De Witt Land — "

"I will go wherever it may be necessary," said Mrs. Branican. "What David Lindsay and his predecessors have done was in the interest of civilization, of science, or of trade. What I will do is to rescue my husband, now the only survivor of the *Franklin*. After his disappearance, and against the opinion of everyone, I maintained that John Branican was alive, and I was right. For six months, for a year if necessary, I will travel in these territories, convinced that I shall find him, and I shall again be right. I trust to the zeal of my companions, and our motto will be, 'Never behind!'"

"That is the Douglas motto, and I have no doubt it will lead you to the same end — "

"Yes! With the help of God!"

Mrs. Branican took leave of the" governor, after thanking him for the assistance he had rendered her since her arrival at Adelaide, That evening — the 9th of September — she left the capital of South Australia.

The railways of Australia are well managed; comfortable carriages run without jolting, and the permanent way is firm and level. The train consisted of six carriages, including the two baggage trucks. Mrs.

Branican occupied a reserved compartment with a woman named Harriett, half English half native, whom she had taken into her service. Tom Marix and the men of the escort occupied the other compartment.

The train only stopped to take in water and coals, and made but short stoppages at the principal stations. The duration of the journey was thus shortened by about a quarter.

Beyond Adelaide the train steamed towards Gawler through the district of the same name. On the right of the line rose a few wooded heights which dominate this part of the colony. The mountains of Australia are not distinguished by their altitude, which rarely exceeds two thousand metres, and they are generally situated on the edge of the continent. A very old geological origin is attributed to them, their composition consisting chiefly of granite and the Silurian rocks.

This part of the country is very varied and cut into by gorges, obliging the railroad to make numerous curves, sometimes along narrow valleys, sometimes through thick forests where the multiplication of the eucalyptus is truly exuberant. A few degrees further on, when it enters the central plains, the railway continues in the imperturbable straight line .which is the characteristic of the modern iron road.

Beyond Gawler, where a branch runs off to Great Bend, the great river Murray describes a sudden curve towards the south. The train, after leaving and skirting the boundary of the Light district, reaches the Stanley district in the thirty-fourth degree of latitude. If it had not been night, a view might have been had of the top of Mount Bryant, the highest of the orographic cluster extending along the east of the line. From that point the elevations of the ground are more to the west, and the line skirts the irregular base of the chain, the principal summits of which are Mounts Bluff, Remarkable, Brown and Ardon. Their extreme ramifications die out oh the shores of Lake Torrens, a vast sheet of water doubtless in communication with Spencer Gulf which deeply indents the Australian coast.

Next morning at sunrise the train passed in sight of the Flinders Ranges, of which Mount Serle forms the farthest projection of any importance. Through the windows of her carriage Mrs. Branican looked out over these regions so new to her. This, then, was Australia which has so justly been called the Land of Paradoxes, whose centre is a vast depression below the level of the ocean, where the streams for the most part rise in sands and are lost before they reach the sea, where the humidity is as absent in the air as in the soil, where multiply the strangest animals the world knows, where wander the ferocious tribes which frequent the centre and the west. There to the north and west extend the interminable deserts of Alexandra Land and Western Australia, amid which the expedition was to search for traces of Captain John. What clue would she find to guide her when she had advanced beyond the towns and villages and was reduced to the vague indications obtained by the bedside of Harry Felton?

And with regard to this a difficulty had been suggested to Mrs. Branican. Was it likely that Captain John during the nine years he had been held prisoner by the Australian blacks had never found an opportunity of escape? To this objection Mrs. Branican had but one reply; that, according to Harry Felton, he and his companion had only had one chance of escape during this long period — the chance of which John had been unable to avail himself. With regard to the argument based on the statement that it was not the custom of the natives to respect the lives of their prisoners, it was clear that they had done so in the case of the survivors of the *Franklin*, and Harry Felton had proved it. Besides, was there not a precedent in the case of the explorer, William Classen, who had disappeared for thirty-eight years, and who was still believed to be with one of the tribes in Northern Australia? Well! was not that exactly the fate of Captain John, inasmuch as in addition to mere hypothesis, there was the formal declaration of Harry Felton? There were other travellers, too, who had never reappeared, though there was nothing to show they had succumbed. Who knows if these mysteries would not some day be cleared up?

However, the train ran along rapidly, without stopping at the smaller stations. If the railroad had curved a little more towards the west it would have skirted the shore of Lake Torrens, which is in the form of a bow — a long narrow lake near which begin the first undulations of the Flinders Ranges. The weather was warm. The temperature was the same as in the northern hemisphere in the month of March in the countries along the thirtieth parallel, such as Algeria, Mexico, or Cochin China. There was to be feared a heavy rain or even one of those violent storms the caravan would pray for in vain when it was well out on the plains of the interior. This was the state of the weather when Mrs. Branican, at three o'clock in the afternoon, reached the station at Farina Town.

There the railroad stops, and the Australian engineers are busy carrying it further northwards in the direction of the Overland Telegraph Line which extends to the shore of the Arafura Sea. If the railroad continues to follow it, it will have to bend off towards the west so as to pass between Lake Torrens and Lake Eyre. On the contrary, it will have to keep to the east of the lakes if it does not leave the meridian which passes through Adelaide.

Zach Fren and his men were mustered at the railway station when Mrs. Branican descended from her carriage. They welcomed her with much sympathy and respectful cordiality. The brave boatswain was deeply affected. Twelve days, twelve long days! without having seen the widow of Captain John, such a thing had not happened since the last return of the *Dolly Hope* to San Diego. Dolly was very happy to again find her companion, her friend, Zach Fren, whose devotion to the very last she could reckon upon. She smiled as she pressed his'-hand — and she did not often smile.

This station of Farina Town is of recent origin. Even on modern maps it does not appear. One recognizes in it the embryo of one of those towns which English' or American railways produce on their passage as trees produce fruits; but they ripen -quickly, these fruits, thanks to the ready practical genius of the Saxon race. And-such of these stations as are still but villages show in their general plan in the arrangement of their squares, and roads, and boulevards that they will become towns in a very short time.

Such was Farina Town, forming at this time the terminus of the Adelaide Railway.

Mrs. Branican had no occasion to remain long at the station. Zach Fren had shown himself as intelligent as he was active. The material of the expedition which he had mustered comprised four bullock drays and their drivers, and two buggies, drawn by a pair of good horses, with their drivers. The drays had already received many of the camp fittings which had been sent on from Adelaide. When the railway trucks had disgorged their contents they would be ready to start, and this would be an affair of twenty four or thirty-six hours.

From the very first Mrs. Branican examined this material in detail. Tom Marix approved the measures' taken by Zach Fren. With such an outfit they would easily reach the extreme boundary of the region where the; horses and cattle find the pasture necessary for their food, and above all things water, which is rarely met with in the deserts of the centre.

"Mrs. Branican," said Tom Marix, "while we follow the: telegraph line the country will give us food, and our animals will not have much to endure. But, beyond, when the caravan turns to the westward, we shall have to replace the horses and bullocks by pack and riding camels. These animals alone can stand the burning regions and find enough in the wells, which are often several days' march apart."

"I know it, Tom Marix," said Dolly, "and will trust to your experience. We will reorganize the caravan as soon as we reach Alice Spring, where I hope to be as soon as possible."

"The camel drivers have been gone four days with the drove of camels," added Zach Fren, "and they will be waiting for us at the station."

"And then," said Tom Marix, "the real difficulties of the expedition will begin."

"We shall know how. to overcome them," said Mrs. Branican.

And so, in conformity with the plan carefully decided upon, the first part of the voyage, consisting of about three hundred and fifty mile?, would be accomplished with horses, buggies and bullock drays. Of the thirty men of the escort the whites, to the number of fifteen, would be mounted; but these thick forests, these capriciously hilly regions, not, allowing of long stages, the blacks would without difficulty be able to follow the caravan on foot. When the. new start was made from Alice Spring, the camels would be reserved for the whites on duty as scouts, collecting information from the wandering tribes or discovering the wells scattered over the face of the desert.

It should be mentioned here that explorations undertaken across the Australian continent have been managed in this way ever since camels have been so advantageously introduced into Australia. Travellers of the time of Burke, Stuart, and Giles would have had much less to undergo had they had these animals at their disposal. It was in 1866 that Mr. Elder imported from India a sufficiently large number, with their equipment of Afghan camel drivers; and the breed has prospered. Thanks to their employment, Colonel Warburton was able to bring to a satisfactory conclusion his bold expedition which set out from Alice Spring and reached Rockburn, on the coast of De Witt Land. If David Lindsay had afterwards succeeded in crossing the continent from north to south with pack-horses, it was because he had only occasionally left the district through which the telegraph line runs and found the water and grass which so frequently fail in the Australian solitudes.

And with regard to these hardy explorers who did not hesitate to brave every sort of peril and fatigue, Zach Fren was led to say, —

"You know, Mrs. Branican, we are anticipated in our advance on Alice Spring?"

"Anticipated, Zach?"

"Yes, madam. Do you not remember that Englishman and his Chinese servant, who were on the *Brisbane* from Melbourne to Adelaide?"

"I do," said Dolly. "But did not they land at Adelaide? Did they not stop there?"

"No, madam; three days ago, Jos Merritt — that is his name — arrived at Farina Town by railway. He even asked me for information concerning our expedition, as to the road we were going to take, and contented himself with replying, 'Good! Oh, very good!' while his Chinaman shook his head and seemed to say,' Bad! Oh, very bad!' and next morning they left Farina Town, going northwards."

"And how did they travel?" asked Dolly. "They travelled on horseback, but when they reached Alice Spring they were going to change their means of transport."

"Is the Englishman an explorer?"

"He does not look it; I thought the gentleman was crazy."

"And did he not say why he was venturing into the Australian desert?"

"No, madam. But alone with his Chinaman I do not suppose he" intends to risk much danger beyond the inhabited portion of the province. We shall probably find him at Alice Spring!"

Next day, the nth of September, at five o'clock in the afternoon, the last preparations were completed. The drays had received their load of provisions in sufficient quantity for the necessities of the long journey. This consisted of preserved meats and vegetables of the best American brands, flour, tea, sugar, salt, and the contents of the medicine chest. The reserve of whiskey, gin and brandy filled a certain number of kegs, which would later on be placed on the backs of the camels.

A large stock of tobacco figured among the articles of consumption — a stock all the more indispensable as it was required not only for the staff, but as a medium of exchange with the natives, among whom it is used as currency. With tobacco and brandy whole tribes in Western Australia could be bought. A large reserve of this tobacco, a few rolls of printed calico, a number of objects of Birmingham manufacture formed the ransom destined for the purpose of the freedom of Captain John.

As to the camp necessities, the tents, the coverings, the boxes containing the clothes and linen, all that belonged to Mrs. Branican and the woman Harriett, the. belongings of Zach Fren and the captain of the escort, the utensils required for the preparation of the food, the paraffin used for cooking, the ammunition, consisting of ball cartridges and shot cartridges for the guns carried by Tom Marix and his men, all this found its "place on the bullock drays.

The preparations being over, nothing remained but to give the signal of departure. Mrs. Branican, impatient to be off, fixed the departure for the morning. It was decided that at daybreak the caravans would leave Farina Town, and go along the route of the telegraph line. The drivers and escort made up a force of forty men, enrolled under the command of Zach Fren and Tom Marix; and all were told to be ready first thing in the morning.

That evening, about nine o'clock, Dolly and the woman Harriett with Zach Fren had just gone into the house they occupied near the railway station. The door was shut, and they were about to retire to their rooms when a gentle knock was heard.

Zach Fren returned to the door, opened it, and could not restrain an exclamation of surprise.

Before him, with a little bundle under his arm and his cap in his hand, stood the boy from the *Brisbane*.

In truth, it seemed that Mrs. Branican had guessed who it was. Yes! And how can we explain it? Although she had no expectation of seeing this boy, had she remembered that he wished to be near her? Anyhow, his name escaped instinctively from her lips, —

"Godfrey!"

Godfrey had arrived about half-an-hour before by the train from Adelaide.

A few days before the departure of the mail boat he had asked the captain of the *Brisbane* to pay him his wages and had left the ship.

Once on shore, he had made no attempt to present himself at the hotel in King William Street, where Mrs. Branican was staying. But how many times had he seen her! How many times he had followed her, without her seeing him, without his seeking to speak to her!

Hearing all about the preparations, he knew that Zach Fren had gone on to Farina Town to organize a caravan; and, as soon as he learned that Mrs. Branican had left Adelaide, he took the train and resolved to find her.

What, then, did Godfrey want, and what was the object of this proceeding?.

What he wanted Dolly soon ascertained.

Godfrey, admitted into the house, found himself in Mr:. Branican's presence.

"Is it you, my child! You, Godfrey!" she said, taking his hand.

"It is he, and what does he want?" growled Zach Fren, with very obvious vexation, for the boy's presence seemed to him extremely regrettable.

"What do I want?" said Godfrey. "I want to go with you, madam; to go with you as far as you go, and never to leave you! I want to go in search of Captain Branican, to find him, to bring him back to San Diego, to his friends, to his country."

Dolly could only restrain herself with difficulty. The child's features, his voice, were all John — her well-beloved John!

Godfrey fell on his knees, and stretched out his hands to her, and beseechingly said, —

"Take me, madam, take me!"

"Come, my child, come!" said Dolly, clasping him to her breast.

CHAPTER V - ACROSS SOUTH AUSTRALIA

The departure of the caravan took place on the 12th of September in the early morning.

The weather was fine, the heat being tempered by a gentle breeze. A few light clouds moderated the ardour of the solar rays. In this thirty-first degree of latitude at this time of the year, the warm season had fairly set in on the Australian continent. The explorers knew only too well how formidable was its intensity when there was neither rain nor shade to cool the central plains.

It was regrettable that circumstances had not allowed Mrs. Branican to undertake her expedition five or six months later. During the winter the ordeal of such a journey would have been more supportable. The cold season, during which the thermometer sometimes goes down to freezing-point, is less to be feared than the hot one, which raises the mercurial column above forty degrees centigrade. Previously to the month of May the vapours dissolve into abundant showers, the creeks revive, the wells fill. There is no need of travelling for days in search of brackish water under a burning sky. The Australian desert is more fatal to caravans than the desert of Africa; the Sahara has its oases, the Australian desert has none.

But Mrs. Branican had no choice of place or time. She went because she had to go; she would risk these terrible chances of climate because she had to risk them. The finding of Captain John and his rescue from the natives admitted of no delay, even if she were to succumb in the endeavour as Harry Felton had succumbed. It Is true that the privations which this unfortunate man had borne were not in store for this expedition, which was organized in such a way as to overcome all difficulties, at least such as were probable.

We know the composition of the caravan, which, since Godfrey had joined it, consisted of forty-one persons. The following was the order of march adopted north of Farina Town, through the bush and along the creeks, where there was no obstacle to bar the progress.

At the head went the fifteen Australians, clothed in trousers and shirt of striped cotton, wearing straw hats, and with naked feet as usual. Armed each of them with a gun and revolver, and with a cartridge belt round their waist, they formed the vanguard under the leadership of a white man who acted as scout.

After them in a buggy drawn by two horses, driven by a native coachman, went Mrs. Branican and the woman Harriett. A hood fitted to the light vehicle, so as to be raised or lowered, afforded shelter from rain or storm.

In a second buggy were Zach Fren and Godfrey. However much Zach had resented the boy's arrival, he had soon taken a great liking to him when he saw how fond he was of Mrs. Branican.

The four bullock drays came next, driven by the four teamsters, and the progress of the caravan was regulated by the pace of these animals, whose introduction into Australia is of recent date, and which are valuable auxiliaries in matters of transport and agriculture.

On the flanks and in the rear of the little troop rode Tom Marix's men, dressed like their leader, with their trousers tucked into their boots, a linen jacket and belt, a white-cloth cap, a light mackintosh slung over their shoulders, and armed like their native companions. These men, being mounted, were to be of service in reconnoitring the road, choosing the halting places at noon, or for the camp at night when the second stage of the day's work neared its end.

In this way the caravan was in a position to travel twelve or thirteen miles a day over rough ground, occasionally through patches of thick forest where the drays could only get along slowly. In the evening the task of pitching the camp fell to Tom Marix, who was accustomed to that sort of thing. Then all would rest during the night and start at sunrise.

The journey between Farina Town and Alice Spring, about three hundred and fifty miles, promised to be free from serious danger or fatigue, and would probably occupy thirty days. The station where the caravan would have to be remodelled, in view of the exploration of the western desert, would thus be reached during the first third of the month of October.

On leaving Farina Town the expedition for a certain number of miles followed the works in progress for the prolongation of the railway, and then to the westward entered the Williouran Ranges, taking the direction already staked out by the posts of the Overland Telegraph Line.

On the road Mrs. Branican asked Tom Marix, who was riding near the buggy, for a few particulars regarding this line.

"It was 1870," said Tom Marix, "sixteen years after the declaration of the independence of South Australia, that the colonists had the idea of making this line between Port Adelaide and Port Darwin, from the south to the north of the continent. The works were carried on with such activity that they were finished by the middle of 1872."

"But," said Mrs. Branican, "had not the continent to be explored right through?"

"Just so," said Tom Marix, "and ten years before, in 1860 and 1861, Stuart, one of our most intrepid explorers; had crossed it, and pushed out reconnaissances east and west."

"And who was the originator of this line?" asked Mrs. Branican.

"An engineer as bold as he is intelligent, Mr. Todd, the

director of posts and telegraphs, one of our fellow-citizens whom Australia honours as he deserves."

"Did they find the material here for the work?"

"No," said Tom Marix; "they had to bring from Europe the insulators, the wire, and even the posts for the line. The colony ought really to be in a position to furnish the material for any industrial enterprise."

"Did the natives let the works go on without interfering with them?"

"At first they did rather more than interfere with it, Mrs. Branican. They destroyed the stores, taking the wire for the sake of the iron, and using the posts for making axes out of. Along eighteen hundred and fifty miles there were constant encounters with the Australians, although they were always beaten off. They returned to the charge again and again, and I think the affair would have had to be given up if Mr. Todd had not had an idea, not only ingenious, but of genius. He seized a few chiefs of the tribes and gave them a few electric shocks, and this so frightened them that neither they nor their comrades ever dared go near the thing again. The line was then finished and is now at regular work."

"Is it not guarded?" asked Mrs. Branican.

"Yes, by the black police as we call them in this country."

"And does not this police ever go into the central or western regions?"

"Never, or at least very seldom. There are so many scoundrels, bushrangers and others to look after in the inhabited districts."

"But why have they not thought of putting the black police on the track of the Indas, when they know that Captain Branican has been their prisoner for fifteen years?"

"You forget, madam, that we did not know it, and that you yourself only knew it from Harry Felton a few weeks ago."

"That is so," said Dolly, "a few weeks ago!"

"Besides," said Tom Marix, "I know that the black police have had orders to explore in Tasman Land, and that a strong detachment is to be sent there, but I am afraid — "

Tom Marix stopped. Mrs. Branican did not notice his hesitation.

Resolved as he was to fulfil to the end the duties he had undertaken, he had, it should be said, very great doubts as to the result of the expedition. He knew how difficult these wandering tribes of Australia are to get hold of, and had no share in Mrs. Branican's ardent faith, nor

231

Zach Fren's conviction, nor Godfrey's instinctive confidence. However, we may repeat, he would do his duty. On the evening of the 15th at. the turn of the Deroy Hills the caravan camped at the town of Boorloo. To the north rose the summit of Mount Attraction, beyond which extend the Illusion Plains. From this connection of - names it may be thought that while the mountain attracts the plain deceives. Anyway, Australian cartography offers many of these designations, which are at the same time physical and moral.

It is at Boorloo that the telegraph line runs off at almost a right angle towards the west. Twelve miles away it crosses Cabanna creek. But what is a simple matter for aerial lines stretched from post to post, is more difficult for a body of travellers on foot and horseback. It was necessary to find a ford. The boy would not leave to others the task of discovering it. Throwing himself resolutely into the rapid, tumultuous river, he found a shallow place by which the drays and carriages could reach the left bank without getting over their axles.

On the 17th the caravan camped on the last spurs of Mount North-West, which rises about twelve miles to the south.

The country being inhabited, Mrs. Branican and her companions received a cordial welcome at one of the large farms, which had several thousand acres under tillage. The raising of sheep in considerable flocks, the growing of corn on the wide, treeless plains, the cultivation on a large scale of sorghum and millet, immense fallows ready for sowing during the coming season, practical forestry, plantations of olive trees and other species suitable for these warm latitudes, many hundreds of beasts of labour and draught, the staff required for such enterprises, a staff submitted to quasi-military discipline which reduces men almost to a state of slavery — all this can be met with on these estates, which yield the wealth of the colonics of the Australian continent. If Mrs. Branican's caravan had not been amply provisioned at the start, she would here have obtained everything she wanted, thanks to the generosity of the rich farmers, of the free-selectors, the proprietors of these agricultural stations.

These large industrial establishments are increasing. Immense tracts, which the absence of water rendered unproductive, are being brought into cultivation, and the ground then being crossed by the caravan a dozen miles south of Lake Eyre was intersected by liquid streams from the newly dug artesian wells, which yield three hundred thousand gallons a day.

On the 18th of September, Tom Marix camped for the night on the southern point of South Lake Eyre, a considerable sheet of water joining North Lake Eyre. On its wooded banks was a flock of those curious water-fowl of which the jabiru is the most remarkable specimen, and a few flocks of black swans, with a few cormorants, pelicans, and herons.

A curious geographical arrangement is that of these lakes. They extend from the south northward — Lake Torrens, the curve of which is followed by the railway, Little Lake Eyre, Great Lake Eyre, Lakes Frane, Blanche, Amadeus — and are sheets of salt water, the old natural basins in which linger the remains of an inland sea. t In fact, geologists are inclined to admit that the Australian continent was formerly divided into two islands, at a period not very remote. It has been observed that the coast of the continent has a tendency to rise above sea-

level, and there seems to be no reason for supposing that the centre is not subject, to a similar continuous elevation. The old basin will thus close in time, and bring about the disappearance of these lakes, which lie between the hundred and thirtieth and hundred and fortieth degrees of latitude.

From the point of South Lake Eyre to the station of Emerald Spring, where they arrived in the evening of the 20th of September, the caravan advanced about seventeen miles across a country of magnificent forest, the trees of which reached two hundred feet in height.

Accustomed as Dolly was to the forest marvels of California, amongst others its gigantic sequoias, she could not but have admired this astonishing vegetation if her thoughts had not been far away in the north and west, among the arid deserts, where the sandy hills barely support a few miserable shrubs. She saw nothing of those giant ferns of which Australia possesses the most remarkable species, nothing of those enormous masses of eucalyptus, with weeping foliage, grouped on the gentle undulations of the ground.

It is a curious fact that brushwood is absent from the foot of these trees; the ground is clear of briars and thorns, and their lower branches are not thrown out below twelve or fifteen feet from the ground. All that remains is a golden-yellow grass, which is never dried up. Animals have destroyed the young shoots, and fires lighted by the squatters have cleared away the bushes. Consequently, although there are no roads cut through these vast forests — so different to the African forests, in which you can travel for six months without reaching the end — there is no difficulty in moving about. The buggies and drays passed easily between the trees and under the high roof of their foliage.

Besides, Tom Marix knew the country, having several times crossed it when in command of the Adelaide colonial police. Mrs. Branican could not have trusted to a safer or more devoted guide. No leader of an escort could have joined so much zeal to so much intelligence.

And, to help him, Tom Marix found an auxiliary, young, active, determined, in the lad who had so ardently attached himself to Dolly; and it is not to be wondered at that he shared in the ardour of this boy of fourteen years. Godfrey talked of going alone, if necessary, into the interior. If any traces of Captain John were discovered, it would be difficult, even impossible, to keep him back. Everything about him — his enthusiasm when he spoke of the captain, his assiduity in consulting the maps of Central Australia, in taking notes, in gaining information during the halts, instead of giving himself over to rest after the fatigue of the day — all denoted in this impassioned soul an effervescence which nothing could temper. Very strong for his age, hardened already to the hardest trials of a sailor's life, he was often ahead of the caravan and out of sight. If he remained in his place it was only at Dolly's precise orders. Neither Zach Fren nor Tom Marix, although Godfrey showed much friendship for them, could get from him what she got by a look. Abandoning herself to her instinctive feelings in the presence of this child, who was John's physical and mental portrait she felt for him the affection of a mother. If Godfrey was not her son, if he was not so according to the laws of nature, he could at least be so by adoption. Godfrey should not leave her again. John would love him as she loved him, and with the same love.

One day, after an absence during which he had been some miles in advance of the caravan, —

"My child," she said, "I want you to promise me not to go so far away without my consent. When I see you go I am quite uneasy until you come back. You leave us for hours without any news of you."

"It is necessary I should collect information," said the boy. "There was a report of a tribe of wandering natives encamped on Warmer Creek. I wanted to see the chief of the tribe, to question him." .

"And what did he say?" asked Dolly.

"He had heard of a white man coming from the west and making for Queensland."

"Who was he?"

"I understood at last that he was talking of Harry Felton, and not of Captain Branican. But we shall find him — yes, we shall find him! Ah! I love him as I love you, who are a mother to me!"

"A mother!" murmured Mrs. Branican.

"But I know you, while Captain John I have never seen; and without that photograph you gave me, which I always carry about with me — the portrait which speaks to me, which seems to answer me — "

"You will know him one day, my child," said Dolly, "and he will love thee as I love thee."

On the 24th September, after having camped at Strangway Spring, beyond Warmer Creek, the expedition halted at William Spring, forty-two miles to the north of Emerald Station. It will be seen from this qualification of "spring "that the water system is of great importance in the districts crossed by the telegraph line. The hot season was already far enough advanced for these springs to be drying up, and it was not difficult to find fords by which the creeks could be crossed with the teams.

At the same time, the strong vegetation gave no signs of decreasing. If the villages were only met with at longer intervals, the farms still succeeded each other from stage to stage. Hedges of spiny acacia, which scented the air, mingled with a few sweetbriars, formed the impenetrable enclosures. In the forests, now more scattered, European trees, such as the oak, the plane, the willow, the poplar, the tamarind, were taking the place of the eucalyptus and the gum-trees which are called "spotted gums" by the Australians.

"What sort of a tree is that?" asked Zach Fren the first time he saw some fifty of these gums in a clump. "It looks as if their trunks were painted in all the colours of the rainbow."

"What you take for a coat of paint," said Tom Marix, "is the natural colour. The bark of those trees colours according to whether the vegetation is early or late.- Some are white, some are pink, some are red. Look! there is one with the trunk striped with blue, another with' yellow plates."

"One more drollery to distinguish your continent, Tom Marix."

"Drollery, if you like; but believe me, Zach, you arc paying my countrymen a compliment in repeating that their country resembles no other. And it will not be perfect — "

"Until there remains not a single native; that is understood!" replied Zach Fren.

It was equally noticeable that, in spite of the insufficient shelter of these trees, the birds gathered there in great numbers. There were magpies, parrots, cockatoos of startling whiteness, laughing birds (which, according to M. D. Chamay, would be more appropriately called sobbing birds), red-necked tandalas, whose cackle is inexhaustible, flying squirrels (amongst others the polatouche, which sportsmen" attract by imitating the cry of nocturnal birds), birds of paradise, and especially the rifle bird, of velvet plumage, which is held to be the finest specimen of Australian ornithology; and, finally, on the surface of the lagoons or swampy places, pairs of cranes, and lotus birds the conformation of whose feet permits of their running on the leaves of the water-lily.

In addition, there was an abundance of hares, and there was no harm in knocking them over, to say nothing of partridges and wild ducks, which enabled Tom Marix to economize with the provisions of the expedition. This game was plainly grilled or roasted every evening at the camp- fire. Occasionally, too, iguana eggs were dug up, which are excellent, and better than the iguana with which the blacks of the expedition regaled themselves.

The creeks still yielded perch, a few long-nosed pike, and a number of those mullets so active as to jump over the fisherman's head, and in addition to these were myriads of cols. At the same time, a constant look-out had to be kept for crocodiles, which arc very dangerous in their aquatic surroundings.- From all of which it follows that lines or nets are articles with which the traveller in Australia should be furnished, in accordance with the expressed recommendation of Colonel Warburton.

On the morning of the 29th the caravan left Umburn Station and entered on hilly ground, very rough for the Walkers. Forty-eight hours afterwards, to the west of Denison Ranges, it-reached the Peak Station, recently established for the requirements of the telegraphic service.

From a detailed account of the journeys of Stuart, given by Tom Marix, Mrs. Branican learnt that it was from this point that the explorer had started for the north, through country almost unknown before.

After this station, for a distance of some sixty miles, the caravan had a foretaste of the fatigues in store for them in the Australian desert. Very arid ground had to be traversed up to the banks of the Macumba River, and beyond, for about the same distance, a no less wearisome stretch to Lady Charlotte Station.

On these vast undulating plains, varied here and there by a few clumps of trees with discoloured foliage, game, if it can all be called so, did not fail. There leapt the kangaroo, of a small species known as the wallaby, which escaped at many an enormous bound. There ran the opossums of the bandicoot and dyasuran varieties, which nestle — that is the word — at the top of the gum trees. Several pairs of cassowaries were seen with as proud and defiant a look as an eagle, but with the advantage over the king of birds, that their flesh is fat and nourishing and Very like beef. The trees were bunga-bungas, a kind of araucaria, which in the western regions of Queensland attain a height of two hundred and fifty feet. These pines, which are trees of more moderate height, yield a large nutritious kernel, which is eaten by the Australians.

Tom Marix warned his, companions against a possible meeting with some of the bears which take up their abode in the hollow trunk of the gum trees. And this did happen, but these plantigrades, called by the name of "potorous," were no more formidable than the long" clawed marsupials.

As to the natives, the caravan had hardly met with any up to then. In fact, it is to the north, and cast, and west of the Overland Telegraph Line, that the tribes wander from camp to camp.

In traversing these more and more barren countries, Tom Marix would have to profit by the peculiar instinct of the bullocks yoked to the drays. This instinct, which seems to have become developed in the breed since its introduction to the Australian continent, causes these animals to move towards the creeks in which they can satisfy their thirst. It is seldom that they are deceived, and the men have only to follow them. And their instinct in another matter is under certain circumstances of great value.

In fact, on the morning of the 7th of October, the bullocks of the leading dray suddenly stopped, and were immediately imitated by the other teams. The drivers prodded them with their goads, but could not make them advance a step.

Tom Marix noticing this, at once rode up to Mrs. Branican's buggy.

"I know what it is," he said; "if we have not yet met with blacks on our road, we are now crossing one of the tracks they arc accustomed to take, and our bullocks have scented the trail and refuse to go beyond."

"And why?" asked Dolly.

"The reason we do not really know," said Tom Marix, "but the fact is no less indisputable. What I believe is, that the first cattle imported into Australia were badly treated by the natives, and recollection of the ill-treatment has been retained and transmitted from generation to generation."

Whether this peculiarity of atavism, pointed out by the chief of the escort, was or was not the reason of their mistrust, it is certain that the cattle could not be prevailed upon to continue their advance. They had to be unyoked and turned round, and then, with blows of the whip and goad, backed for about twenty yards, so as to cross the path contaminated by the passage of the blacks. And when they were again yoked up the drays resumed their journey to the north.

When the caravan arrived on the borders "of the Macumba River, everyone found plenty to slake his thirst with. It is true the water was already low, owing to the great heat. But where there was not water enough to float a skiff, there was enough to satisfy forty men and twenty cattle.

On the 6th the expedition crossed Hamilton Creek on the half-covered stones which strewed its bed; on the 8th, Mount Hammersley was left to the east; on the 10th, in the morning, a halt was made at the station of Charlotte- town, after accomplishing three hundred and twenty miles since leaving Farina Town.

Mrs. Branican then found herself on the border between South Australia and Alexandra Land, also called the Northern Territory. This is the country discovered by the explorer Stuart in 1860, when he followed the hundred and thirty-first meridian up to the twenty-first degree of latitude.

CHAPTER VI - AN UNEXPECTED MEETING

Tom Marix had asked Mrs. Branican for a rest of twenty-four hours at Lady Charlotte Station. Although the journey had been accomplished without obstacles, the heat had fatigued the cattle. The journey to Alice Spring was a long one, and it was important that the drays should be certain of reaching its end.

Dolly gave in to the reason advanced by the chief of the escort, and the best arrangements possible were made. A few shanties form the station, the population of which was tripled for a day by the caravan's arrival. It was therefore necessary to camp. But the squatter, who owned a large farm in the neighbourhood, came to offer Mrs. Branican more comfortable hospitality, and he was so pressing that she accepted his invitation to. Waldek Hill, where very suitable lodgings were placed at her disposal.

This squatter was only the tenant of one of those vast domains called "runs" in Australia. These runs comprise no less than six hundred thousand hectares, and even more, particularly in the colony of Victoria. Although that at Waldek Hill was not quite as large as this, yet it was of considerable, size. .Surrounded by paddocks, or enclosures, it was specially devoted to the raising of sheep — requiring a certain number of men, shepherds employed in looking after the flocks, and savage dogs whose barking resembled that of the wolf.

The nature of the ground determines the choice of the station when a run is to be formed, the preference being given to the plains in which the salt-bush grows. These bushes with nutritive juices, in some ways resembling the asparagus, in others the aniseed, are greedily sought after by the sheep, who belong to the pig-face variety. As soon as the land has been found fit for pasture, it is put under grass. Then cattle are put on it to take the first growth, while the sheep, which are more difficult to feed, take the second growth.

It will not be forgotten that it is to the wool produced by the sheep that the great wealth of the Australian colonies is due; and there are no less than one hundred millions of these representatives of the ovine race.

On the run at Waldek Hill, around the- principal house and the huts of the men, were large ponds well supplied with water from a creek, and used for the washing of the sheep before shearing. In front of these were the sheds in which the squatter stored the woolpacks before sending them off to Adelaide.

At the time the operation of shearing was in full swing. For some days a gang of wandering shearers had, according to custom, come to work at this lucrative trade.

When Mrs. Branican, accompanied by Zach Fren, had passed the barriers, she was struck with the astonishing animation that reigned within the enclosure. The men at piece work did not lose a moment, and, as the most skilful could shear a hundred fleeces a day, they were sure of earning a sovereign in that time. The snipping of the large shears in the hands of the shearer, the bleating of the sheep when they received some ill-directed blow, the shouting of the men one to another, the coming and going of those engaged in carrying the wool to the sheds, made up a curious scene. And above this tumult rose the shouts of the little boys, "Tar! tar!" as they carried the bowls of tar with which to wash the wounds made by the unskilful shearers.

Over all this there have to be overseers to ensure the work being properly done. And some of these were at Waldek Hill, independently of those engaged in keeping the accounts, that is to say, a dozen men and women who thus obtained their living.

And what was Mrs. Branican's surprise — more than surprise, stupefaction — when she heard her name pronounced a few yards behind her.

A woman had just run up. She had thrown herself on her knees, with her hands stretched out, and looking appealingly, —

It was Jane Burker — Jane, aged less by years than by trouble, grey-haired, pale of face, almost unrecognizable, but whom Dolly recognized.

"Jane!" she exclaimed.

She had risen, and the two cousins were in each other's arms.

What then had been the life of the Burkers for the last twelve years? A miserable life — and even a criminal life, at least so far as regards the husband of the unfortunate Jane.

When he left San Diego in-a hurry to escape from the pursuit of his creditors, Len Burker had taken refuge at Mazatlan, one of the ports on the west coast of Mexico. As will be remembered, he left at Prospect House the mulatto No, with orders to watch over Dolly Branican, who had not at that time recovered her reason. But shortly afterwards, when the unhappy maniac had been placed in the asylum of Doctor Brumley, owing to the influence of Mr. William Andrew, the mulatto having no more occasion to remain at the chalet, had escaped to rejoin her master, whose retreat she knew.

It was under an assumed name that Len Burker had been in hiding at Mazatlan, where the Californian police had been unable to find him, for he had only remained a few weeks in that town. Two or three thousand piastres — all that remained of what he had run through, and all that remained of the little fortune of Mrs. Branican — was all that he possessed. To begin business again in the United States was no longer possible, and he resolved to leave America. Australia appeared to offer an opportunity of again tempting fortune before he was reduced to his last dollar.

Jane, always under the complete dominion of her husband, had not strength of mind enough to resist him. Mrs. Branican, her only relative, was now deprived of reason. As far as Captain John was concerned, there was no longer any doubt as to his fate. The *Franklin* had perished with all hands. John would never return to San Diego. Nothing could henceforth save Jane from the destiny to which Len Burker was

243

dragging her, and under these conditions she accompanied him to the Australian continent.

Len Burker had landed at Sydney. There he spent all he had in launching forth into new speculations, in which he made fresh dupes, and displayed more ability than he had done at San Diego. And then he ventured on other speculations, in which he lost the few profits he made at the outset.

Eighteen months after he had taken refuge in Australia, Len Burker had had to leave Sydney. A prey to poverty bordering on destitution, he was compelled to seek his fortune elsewhere. But matters were no more favourable to him at Brisbane, whence he soon escaped to take refuge in the most out-of-the-way districts of Queensland.

Jane followed him. Resigned to her fate, she was even reduced to work with her hands for money to assist in the payment of the household expenses. Harshly treated by the mulatto, who continued to be Len Burker's evil genius, she had many times thought of running away from this miserable life, and putting an end to its vexations and humiliations! But that was beyond her weak, indecisive character. The poor dog is beaten, and yet dare not leave its master's house!

At this time Len Burker had learnt from the newspapers of the attempts that were being made to discover the survivors of the *Franklin*. The two expeditions of the *Dolly Hope*, undertaken by Mrs. Branican, had informed him of the new state of affairs: 1:Dolly had recovered her reason after a period of four years, during which she had remained in Doctor Brumley's asylum; 2. During that period her uncle Edward Starter had died in Tennessee, and the enormous fortune she had inherited from him had enabled her to organize these two expeditions in the seas of Malaysia and on the coasts of Northern Australia. As to their definitive result, it had been settled that the remains of the *Franklin* had been found on Browse Island, and the last survivor of the crew had died on that island.

Between Dolly's fortune and Jane, her sole heiress, there now remained but a mother who had lost her child, a wife who had lost her husband, and whom a combination of misfortunes had shaken in her sanity. So said Len Burker to himself. To resume family intercourse with Mrs. Branican was impossible. To ask for assistance through the mediation of Jane he was afraid, for he was still wanted by the police, and at the mercy of an extradition treaty which would have handed him over to punishment. But if Dolly died, by what means could he prevent her fortune failing to reach Jane, that is to say, himself?

It will not have been forgotten that about seven years had elapsed between the return of the *Dolly Hope*, after her second expedition, up to the meeting with Harry Felton, which had revived the question of the *Franklin* disaster.

During this period Len Burker's life had become more miserable than ever. From the illegal acts he had committed without remorse, he had glided down the slope of criminality. He had now no fixed home, and Jane had been compelled to submit to her wandering life.

The mulatto, Nô, was dead; but Mrs. Burker received no benefit from the death of the woman whose influence had been so fatal to her husband. As the companion of a criminal, she was obliged to follow him over these vast territories, where so many crimes remain unpunished. After the exhaustion of the gold-mines of the colony of Victoria, and the-dispersal of thousands of diggers, who found themselves without work, the country was invaded by a population little accustomed to submission and respect for the law on the diggings; and now there was a formidable class of the unclassed, of people without standing, known in the districts of South Australia under the name of "larrikins." These scoured the country, indulging their criminal propensities, and driven from the towns by the police.

Such were the companions,with whom Len Burker associated when his notoriety forbade him access to the towns. Then, as he was gradually driven out into the less protected regions, he associated with the gangs of wandering scoundrel', among others with the ferocious bushrangers, who date from the early years of colonization, and whose race is not yet extinct.

To that step in the social ladder Len Burker had descended. During the last few years, in how many cases he had taken part in robbing farms, in highway robbery, in all the crimes that justice was impotent to repress, he alone could tell. Yes, he alone; for Jane, almost always abandoned in some village, was not admitted into the. secret of his abominable actions. And perhaps blood had been shed by the hand of the man she no longer respected, but whom she would never betray.

Twelve years had elapsed when the reappearance of Harry Felton renewed the public excitement. The news was spread by the newspapers, and notably by the numerous journals of Australia. Len Burker learnt it as he read a number of the Sydney Morning Herald in a little village in Queensland, where he had then taken refuge after a matter of pillage and incendiarism which, thanks to the intervention of the police, had not turned out precisely to the advantage of the bushrangers.

At the same time as he learnt the facts regarding Harry Felton, Len Burker learnt that Mrs. Branican had left San Diego to come to Sydney and put herself in communication with the mate of the *Franklin*. Almost immediately came the rumour that Harry Felton had died after giving certain indications relative to Captain John. Then, a few days later, Len Burker was informed that Mrs. Branican had landed at Adelaide, with the object of organizing an expedition, in which she would take part, and which had for its object the visiting of the deserts of the centre and northwest of Australia.

When Jane heard of her cousin's arrival on the continent her first feeling was to run away and seek a refuge with her. But Len Burker had guessed her intentions, and, owing to his threats, she dare not carry out her plan.

Then it was that the scoundrel, without hesitating, resolved to make the best of the position. The hour was decisive. To meet Mrs. Branican on the road, to again ingratiate himself with her by means of calculated hypocrisy, to accompany her amid the Australian solitudes, nothing could be less difficult, or tend more surely to his object. It was hardly probable that Captain John, even admitting that he still lived, would be discovered among the wandering natives, and it was possible that Dolly would succumb in the course of this dangerous campaign. All her fortune would then revert to Jane, her only relative. Who knows? There are such profitable opportunities when one has the talent for originating them.

Be it understood Len Burker was careful not to tell Jane of his intention to renew his relations with Mrs. Branican. He separated from the bushrangers, though prepared to call on them for their good offices later on, if he had need of them. Accompanied by Jane, he left Queensland, making for Lady Charlotte station, which is only about a hundred miles away, and through which the caravan must necessarily pass on its way to Alice Spring.

And that is why," for the last three weeks, Len Burker had been at Waldek Hill, where he fulfilled the duties of overseer. There he was waiting for Dolly with his mind fully made up to shrink from no crime in his attempt to get possession of her fortune.

On her arrival at Lady Charlotte station Jane suspected nothing. And what were her feelings in the irresistible and thoughtless movement to which she yielded, when she found herself in the presence of Mrs. Branican, and thus helped on Len Burker's plans far more than he had ever hoped.

Len Burker was then forty-five years of age. Having aged but little, he was still erect and vigorous, and still had the fugitive, false look, and the features stamped with dissimulation, which inspired distrust in him. Jane appeared to be quite ten years older, her colour all faded, her hair white at the temples, her body crushed down. But her look, almost extinguished by misery, lighted up when she saw Dolly.

After clasping her in her arms Mrs. Branican had taken Jane into one of the rooms put at her disposal by the squatter of Waldek Hill. There the two women could abandon themselves to their feelings. Dolly only remembered the cares with which Jane had surrounded her at the chalet of Prospect House. She had nothing to reproach her with, and she was ready to pardon her husband if he would consent to separate them from one another no longer.

They talked for some time. Jane only told her what she could of her past life without compromising Len Burker, and Mrs. Branican was very reserved in questioning her on the subject. She felt how much the poor creature had suffered and was still suffering. Was not that enough to render her worthy of all her pity, of all her affection? The position of Captain John, the unshakable assurance that she would soon recover him, the efforts she was making to succeed in doing so, that is what she spoke of above everything, and then of the child she had lost — of little Wat. And when she recalled the remembrance always, living in her, Jane became so pale, her face underwent such an alteration, that Dolly believed the unfortunate woman was about to faint.

Jane managed to recover herself, and then had to tell of her life since the fatal day on which her cousin had gone toad up to the time when Len Burker was compelled to leave San Diego.

"Is it possible, my poor Jane," said Dolly, "is it possible that during these fourteen months, when you were taking such care of me, that there came a lucid interval to my mind? Is it possible that I had no recollection of my poor John? Is it possible that I never pronounced his name, nor that of our dear little Wat?"

"Never, Dolly, never!" murmured Jane, who could not restrain her tears.

"And you, Jane, you my friend, you who are of my blood, you never read my mind? You never noticed neither in my words nor my looks that I was conscious of the past?"

"No, Dolly!"

"Well, Jane, I am going to tell you what I have told nobody else. Yes — when I returned to sanity — yes — I had a presentiment that John was alive, that I was .not a widow, and it seemed to also — "

"Also?" said Jane.

Her eyes filled with inexplicable terror, her looks wild with fright; she waited, for what Dolly was about to say.

"Yes, Jane," continued Dolly, "I had the feeling that I was still a mother!"

Jane rose, her hands beat the air as though she would chase away some horrible image, her lips worked without her being able to articulate a word. Dolly, absorbed in her own thoughts, did not observe this agitation, and Jane had begun to resume her self-possession when her husband appeared at the door of the room.

Len Burker remained in the doorway looking at his wife, and seeming to say to her, — "What have you been saying?"

Jane fell back utterly powerless before this man — the invincible domination of a strong spirit over a weak one. Jane was annihilated under Len Burker's look. Mrs. Branican understood. The sight of Len Burker recalled the past, and reminded her of what Jane must have endured from him. But this revolt of her heart lasted but a moment. Dolly was resolved to sacrifice her recrimination, to overcome her repulsion, in order to be no more separated from the unfortunate Jane.

"Len Burker," she said, "you know why I have come to Australia. It is a duty to which I shall devote myself until I see John, for John is alive. As chance has placed you in my road, as I have again found Jane, the only relative left to me, leave her to me and allow her to come with me, as she desires."

Len Burker did not at once reply. Knowing what there was against him, he wished Mrs. Branican to complete her proposal by asking him to join the caravan. But, as Dolly remained silent, he had to take the initiative.

"Dolly," said he, "I will answer without circumlocution to your offer, and I will add that I expected it. I will not refuse, and I willingly consent that my wife should remain with you. Ah! life has been hard for both of us since mischance forced me to leave San Diego. We have suffered much during the fourteen years which have elapsed, and you see fortune has not favoured me on Australian soil, as I am reduced to work for my bread from day to day. When the shearing is over at Waldek Hill I do not know where I shall get other work. And, as also it will be painful for me to part with Jane, I, in my turn, ask you to permit me to take an active part in your expedition. I know the natives of the interior, with whom I have had some experience, and I can be of some use to you. Do not doubt it, Dolly, I shall be happy to join my efforts to those of your companions, and help you to deliver John Branican."

Dolly saw that this was the condition on which Len Burker would consent to leave her Jane. There was no disputing with such a man; besides, if he really meant what he said, his presence would not be useless, inasmuch as. for a number of years, his wandering life had led him through the central regions of the continent. Mrs. Branican thus had to reply, but coldly enough, —

"That is agreed, Len Burker; you shall be one of us, and get ready to start, for we leave Lady Charlotte station first thing to-morrow morning."

"I will be ready," said Len Burker, who retired without having dared to offer his hand to Mrs. Branican.

When Zach Fren learnt that Len Burker was to join the expedition he showed very little satisfaction. He knew the man, he knew from Mr. William Andrew how this solemn personage had abused his functions in dissipating Dolly's patrimony. He knew under what conditions this faithless trustee, this broken broker, had had to leave San Diego; he had no doubt whatever but that his life had been suspicious during the fourteen years he had been in Australia. But, at the same time, he said nothing, looking upon it as a fortunate circumstance that Jane was near

Dolly. But in his heart he resolved to keep a good lookout on Len Burker.

The day ended without other incident. Len Burker was not again seen, but was busy in his preparation for departure after arranging with the. squatter of Waldek Hill. The arrangement gave rise to no difficulty, and the squatter even undertook to provide him with a horse, so that he might be in a state to follow the caravan to Alice Spring, where the re-organization was to take place.

Dolly and Jane remained together during the afternoon and evening at Waldek Hill. Dolly avoided speaking of Len Burker, and made no allusion to what he had been doing since his departure from San Diego, feeling that he had done things Jane could not mention.

During this evening neither Tom Marix nor Godfrey, who were collecting information among the natives whose huts were in the neighbourhood, came to Waldek Hill. It was early in the morning that Mrs. Branican had an opportunity of introducing Godfrey to Jane, telling her he was her adopted son.

Jane was extraordinarily struck with the resemblance which existed between Captain John and the boy. Her impression was, indeed, so profound that she scarcely dared to look at him. And how can we express what she felt when Dolly told her all about Godfrey, how she had met him on the *Brisbane*, how he was a child found in the streets of San Diego, how he had been brought up at Wat House, how he was about fourteen years old.

Jane sat listening to this story motionless and dumb, pale as death, her heart scarcely beating in the intensity of her anguish.

And when Dolly left her alone, she fell on her knees and clasped her hands. Then the life came back to her features, and her face was as if transfigured.

"Him! him!" she screamed, "him! Near her! God, then, has willed it so!"

A moment afterwards Jane had left the house at Waldek Hill, and, crossing the interior yard, was rushing towards the hut where she lived, to tell her husband everything.

Len Burker was there packing a portmanteau with the few articles of clothing and other objects he was going to take on his journey. Jane's arrival in this extraordinary state of trouble made him jump back.

"What is the matter?" he said, sharply. "Speak! Will you speak? What is the matter?"

"He is alive!" said Jane. "He is here! Near his mother — him we thought — "

"Near his mother — alive — him?" said Len Burker, who was thunderstruck at the revelation.

lie understood too well to whom this word "him" applied.

"Him!" said Jane, "him! The second child of John and Dolly Branican!"

A short explanation will be sufficient to relate what had taken place fifteen years before at Prospect House.

A few months after taking up their abode at the chalet, Mr. and Mrs. Burker had noticed that Dolly, then for some weeks out,of her mind, was in a situation of which she herself was ignorant. Narrowly watched by the mulatto, No, and in spite of Jane's supplications, Dolly was, so to speak, sequestered, withdrawn from the sight of her friends and neighbours under the pretext of her malady. Seven months later, while still insane and without even a trace of memory, she had brought into the world a second child. At this time, when Captain John's death was generally admitted, the birth of this child interfered with Len Burker's plans regarding Dolly's future fortune. He had, therefore, resolved to keep the birth secret. It was in view of this eventuality that for several months the servants had been sent away from the chalet, and visitors refused admittance, which Jane, compelled to yield to her husband, was unable to prevent. The child, when only a few hours old, had been abandoned by No on the highway, where it was fortunately found by a passer-by, who took it to a hospital. Later on, after the opening of Wat House, it was taken there, and thence at eight years it came out to go to sea as a cabin boy. And now all is explained, the resemblance of Godfrey to Captain John, his father, the instinctive feelings continually experienced by Dolly — Dolly a mother without knowing it!

"Yes, Len," said Jane. "It is his son! . And we must confess everything — "

But at the thought of a recognition which would endanger the plan on which his future reposed, Len Burker made a threatening gesture, and oaths escaped from his lips. Seizing the unfortunate Jane by the hand, and looking into her eyes, he said in a low voice, —

"For Dolly's sake as well as for Godfrey's sake, I advise you, Jane,-to be silent."

CHAPTER VII - NORTHWARDS

There could be no mistake; Godfrey was, indeed, the second child of John and Dolly Branican. The affection Dolly felt for him was merely the mother's instinct. But she did not know that the boy was her son, and how could she ever discover it, if Jane, afraid of the threats of Len Burker, were compelled to remain silent in order to assure Godfrey's safety? To speak was to put the boy at the mercy of Len Burker, and the scoundrel who had once before abandoned him, would know how to get rid of him during this perilous expedition. It was therefore necessary that the mother and son should continue to be ignorant of the tie which attached them to each other.

When he saw Godfrey, and compared the facts relative to his early life, and assured himself of the striking resemblance the boy bore to John, Len Burker had no doubt as to his identity. And thus, when he had made up his mind that John Branican was irretrievably lost, this is what had come about. Well! Woe to Godfrey if Jane spoke! But Len Burker was not uneasy. Jane would not speak.

On the 11th of October, the caravan resumed its journey after a day's rest. Jane took her place in the buggy occupied by Mrs. Branican. Len Burker moved about on rather a good horse, sometimes in front, sometimes behind, talking with Tom Marix about the districts through which he had travelled along the telegraph line. He did not" seek the company of Zach Fren, who showed a marked dislike to him. And he avoided Godfrey, the sight of whom annoyed him. When the boy came to take part in the conversation between Dolly and Jane, Len Burker retired so as to have nothing to do with him.

As the expedition advanced, the aspect of the country gradually changed. Here and there were a few farms devoted entirely to the raising of sheep, extensive prairies stretching away out of sight, groups of trees, gum trees or eucalyptus, forming a few isolated clumps in no way resembling the forests of South Australia.

On the 12th of October, at six o'clock in the evening, after a long stage which the heat rendered very tiring, Tom Marix pitched the camp on the bank of Finke River, not far from Mount Daniel, whose summit rose to the westward.

Geographers are now agreed in considering this river Finke — called the Larra-Larra by the natives — as the principal stream in the centre of Australia. During the evening Tom Marix called Mrs. Branican's attention to this subject, while Zach Fren, Len and Jane Burker were in her company under one of the tents.

"The question is," said Tom Marix, "if Finke River pours its waters into the vast Lake Eyre, which we left beyond Farina Town. To settle this question the explorer David Lindsay devoted the end of the year 1885. After reaching the station of The Peak, which we passed, he followed the river to the place where it is lost in the sands to the north-east of Dalhousie. But he was led to believe that in the floods of the rainy season its waters ran into Lake Eyre."

"And how long is Finke River?" asked Mrs. Branican.

"It is estimated as not being less than nine hundred miles," replied Tom Marix.

"Shall we follow it far?"

"Only for a few days, for it makes several bends and turns off westward through the James Ranges."

"But I knew this David Lindsay you are speaking of," said Len Burker.

"You knew him?" said Zach Fren, in a tone which denoted a certain amount of incredulity.

"And what is there astonishing in that?" said Len Burker. "I met Lindsay just as he reached Dalhousie. station. He was on the West Queensland frontier, which I was visiting on account of a Brisbane house."

255

"That," said Tom Marix, "is the way he went. Then having reached Alice Spring and rounded the MacDonnell Ranges, he made a complete exploration of the, Herbert River, and struck up towards the Gulf of Carpentaria, where he finished his second voyage from south to. north across the Australian continent."

"I will add," said Len Burker, "that David Lindsay was accompanied by a German botanist of the name of Dietrich. Their caravan consisted of a few camels for. transport purposes. That, Dolly, I believe, is how you are going to have yours beyond Alice Spring, and I am sure you will succeed as David Lindsay succeeded."

"Yes, we will succeed, Len," said Mrs. Branican.

"No one doubts that!" added Zach Fren.

In short it appeared to be true that Len Burker had met David Lindsay under- the circumstances he said, and, besides, Jane corroborated him. But if Dolly had asked him for what Brisbane house he was then travelling, he would have been rather embarrassed.

During the few hours that Mrs. Branican and her companions passed on the banks of Finke River, they indirectly had news of the Englishman Jos Meritt and Gin Ghi, his Chinese servant. Both were then about a dozen stages ahead of the caravan, and they were gradually gaining on them along the same road.

It was from the natives that the news came regarding this famous collector of hats. Three days before Jos Meritt and his servant had stopped in the village of Kilna, a mile from the station.

Kilna contains many hundred blacks, men, women and children, who live in shapeless bark huts. These huts are called "villums "in the Australian language, and it is worth while to note the singular resemblance of this native word to the words villa and villages of Latin derivation.

These natives were worth looking at. Some of them were tall, well-built fellows, lithe and strong, and of indefatigable constitution. For the most part they are characterized by the peculiar depressed facial angle common to savage races; the eyebrows are very prominent, the hair is waved rather than woolly, with a narrow forehead retreating under its locks, the nose is flat, the nostrils large, the mouth is enormous and the teeth like those of wild animals. The usual large bodies and thin legs were not noticed among these men, making them quite exceptional among Australian negroes.

Where did the natives of this fifth part of the world come from? Did there formerly exist, as some learned men — too learned, perhaps — have stated, a Pacific continent, of which there remain only the summits in the form of islands scattered over the surface of that vast ocean? Are these Australians the descendants of the numerous races who peopled this continent at a remote epoch? Such theories are likely enough as mere hypotheses. But if the explanation is correct, it must be admitted that the aboriginal race has considerably degenerated, mentally and physically. The Australian has remained a savage in manners and tastes, and with his ineradicable habits of cannibalism — at least among certain tribes — he is on the lowest step of the human ladder, and hardly above the carnivora. In a country where there are no lions or tigers or panthers, it can be claimed that he replaces them in a man-eating point of view. The ground these Australians leave uncultivated; they barely clothe themselves with a rag; they have not the simplest culinary utensils; their weapons are the most rudimentary, their spears being of wood hardened at the point; their axes are of stone, and they have the nolla-nolla, a kind of mace of very hard wood, and the famous boomerang of the helicoidal form, which makes it return to the thrower after it has been hurled forward by a vigorous hand. The Australian black, we repeat, is a savage in every sense of the word.

To such beings nature has given the woman most suitable to them — the "lubra " — strong enough to stand the fatigue of the wandering life; submit to the most laborious work, and carry the younger children and the materials for the camp. These unfortunate creatures are old at twenty-five years of age, and not only old but hideous, chewing the leaves of the pituri, which over-excite them during their interminable marches, and help them to Support the long abstinences from food.

And, will it be believed? Those who have dealings with the European colonists in the towns are beginning to follow the European fashions. Yes! They must have gowns and trains to their gowns; they must have hats and feathers in their hats. The men even cannot do without European headgear, and gratify their tastes by ransacking the shops of the sellers of old clothes.

Doubtless Jos Meritt had heard of the remarkable voyage made by Carl Lumholtz in Australia; and probably remembered this paragraph from the hardy Norwegian who stayed for six months among the wild cannibals of the north-east: —

"I met the two natives half-way. They had made themselves look very fine; one of them strutted about in a shirt, the other wore a woman's' hat. These things were thought a great deal of by the Australian negroes, and had passed from one tribe to another, from the more civilized, who live in the neighbourhood of the colonists, to those who have never had any intercourse with the whites. Many of my men used to borrow the hat, and were quite proud of taking their turn in wearing-it. One of them who walked in front of me hi puris naturalibus, sweating under the weight of my gun, was really an absurd sight in this hat, which he wore crossways. What travels this hat had made during its long voyage from the country of the whites to the mountains of the blacks!"

Jos Meritt must have known of this, and perhaps it would be among some Australian tribe, on the head of some chief of the northern or north-western territories, that he would find this remarkable hat>'the search for which had sent him, at the risk of his life, among the cannibals of the Australian continent. But it should be noted that, if he had not succeeded among the natives of Queensland, he might meet with more success among the natives of Kilria, and so had resumed his adventurous peregrinations into the central desert.

On the 13th of October Tom Marix gave the signal to start at sunrise. The caravan resumed its usual order of march. It was a great satisfaction for Dolly to have Jane near her. The buggy, which carried them, and in which they could be alone, permitted of their exchanging their thoughts and confidences. Why should Jane have to journey to the end without daring to speak? Occasionally, when she saw the mutual affection, maternal and filial, which manifested itself every moment, by a look, a question, a word, between- Dolly and Godfrey, it seemed to her that her secret was about to escape her. But Len Burker's threats returned to her mind, and from fear of losing the boy, she even affected a certain quasi-indifference towards him which Mrs. Branican did not notice without vexation.

We can easily imagine how she felt when Dolly said to her one day,

—

"You can understand, Jane, that with this very striking resemblance, and the instincts I felt so persistent within me, I had believed that my child had escaped death without Mr. Andrew or any of his friends knowing of it; and, hence, I thought that Godfrey was our son, John's son and my son. But no! Poor little Wat now lies in the cemetery at San Diego."

"Yes, it was there we laid him, dear Dolly," said Jane. "There is his grave among the flowers."

"Jane, Jane," exclaimed Dolly, "if God did not give me back my child He will give me back his father; He will give me back John."

On the 15th of October, at six o'clock in the evening, after leaving Mount Humphries behind, the caravan halted on the bank of Palmer Creek, one of the affluents of the Finke River. This creek was then almost dry, it being fed, like most of the streams in these regions, solely by the rains. It was thus very easy to cross, as was also Hughes' Creek, three days afterwards, thirty-four miles to the northward.

In that direction the Overland Telegraph Line stretches it: aerial wires — the threads of Ariadne, which lead from station to station.

259

Occasionally a few groups of houses were met with, and more rarely farms, where Tom Marix, by paying well, could procure fresh meat. Godfrey and Zach Fren went out in search of news. The squatters were only too glad to give news concerning the wandering tribes that frequent these territories. Had they ever heard of a white man kept as a prisoner among the Indas to the northward or westward? Did they know if any travellers had recently ventured across these distant regions? The replies were in the negative. No trace, not the vaguest, could be discovered to put them on the track of Captain John. And hence the need of haste to reach Alice Spring, from which the caravan was still eighty miles away at least.

After leaving Hughes' Creek progress became more difficult. The country was very mountainous, the road lay through narrow gorges, one after the other, cut through by hardly practicable ravines, which wound among the ramifications of the Water House ranges. Tom Marix and Godfrey were ahead, seeking out the best passes. The travellers on foot and horseback easily found a passage, even the buggies were drawn through without difficulty by the horses, and there was no need to be anxious about them; but the heavily laden drays could only be dragged along by the bullocks at the cost of extreme fatigue. The main thing was to avoid accidents, such as the breakage of wheels or axle-trees, which would take a long time to repair, if they did not necessitate the abandonment of the vehicle.

It was in the morning of the 19th of October that the caravan entered these territories, where the telegraph wires could no longer retain their rectilinear direction. The character of the ground had already caused them to incline towards the West, and this direction Tom Marix took.

But if the region offered a capriciously irregular surface, unfitted for a quick and steady advance, it had again become thickly wooded owing to the vicinity of the mountain masses. These "brigalow scrubs "had continually to be skirted, being impenetrable thickets consisting, for the most part, of the prolific family of acacias. On the banks of the streams were clumps of casuarinas as stripped of leaves as if the winter wind had shaken their branches. At the mouth of the gorges were a few of those calabash trees the trunks of which thicken out in the form of a bottle, and which the Australians call bottle-trees. In the same way as the eucalyptus, which empties a well when the roots reach into it, the calabash tree pumps up all the humidity from the ground, and its spongy wood is so impregnated with it that the starch it contains can be used for the nourishment of cattle.

Marsupials live in great numbers under the brigalow shrubs, among others the wallabies, which are so swift in their flight that often the natives, when they wish to catch them, are obliged to surround them with a circle of flame by setting light to the grass. In certain places were swarms of kangaroo rats, and those giant kangaroos which the whites hunt only for the pleasure of hunting, inasmuch as you must be a negro, and an Australian negro, to care to be fed on their coriaceous flesh. Once or twice Tom Marix and Godfrey managed to shoot two or three couples of these animals, the speed of which is that of a horse at a gallop. It need not be said the tail of these kangaroos makes excellent soup, which everyone enjoyed at the evening meal.

That night there was an alarm. The camp was troubled by one of those invasions of rats common in Australia at the time these rodents migrate. No one could sleep without risking being bitten, and no one did sleep.

Mrs. Branican and her companions departed in the morning, that of October 22. At sundown the caravan, had reached the last spurs of the MacDonnell ranges. Henceforward the travelling conditions would be much more favourable. Forty miles more, and the first part of the campaign would end at Alice Spring.

The expedition resumed its march at dawn on the 23rd. Immense plains extended up to the horizon. A few undulations varied the view. Clumps of trees relieved the monotonous aspect. The drays could easily follow the narrow road traced at the foot of the telegraph poles, which runs from station to station, situated at long distances apart. It is almost incredible that the line, which is very slightly guarded in these desert countries, could be respected by the natives. And to the observations made with regard to this, Tom Marix replied, —

"These nomads, I have said, were electrically punished by our engineer, and they believe that the thunder runs along the wires, and take care not to touch them. They even believe that the two ends are attached to the sun and the moon, and that those big balls would fall on their heads if they tried to drag them down."

At eleven o'clock, according to custom, the first stage of the journey came to an end. The caravan stopped near a clump of eucalyptus, the leaves of which, falling like the crystal pendants of a lustre, gave hardly any shadow. A creek flowed by, or rather a thread of water, hardly enough to wet the pebbles in its bed. On the opposite bank the ground rose abruptly and barred the surface of the plain for a length of many miles from east to west. Behind these could still be seen the distant profile of the MacDonnell ranges-above the horizon.

The midday halt generally lasted till two o'clock. In this way there was avoided the necessity of journeying during the warmest part of the day. Properly speaking, it was a halt,-not an encampment. All that Tom Marix did was to unyoke the bullocks and unsaddle the horses. These animals fed on the spot. No tents were pitched; no fires lighted. Cold venison or tinned meat served for the second meal, which had been preceded by the breakfast at sunrise.

Everyone had come,- as usual, to sit or lie on the grass with which the hillside was covered. After the first half hour, the drivers and the men of the escort, white and black, had satisfied their hunger and were asleep until the time of departure.

Mrs. Branican, Jane, and Godfrey, formed a group apart. The native servant, Harriett had brought them a basket containing a few provisions. As they were eating they were talking of their arrival at Alice Spring. The hope which had never abandoned Dolly the boy shared to the full, and, even if there had been no room for hope, nothing could have shaken their convictions. Both were full of faith in the success of the campaign, their fixed resolution being not to leave Australian soil until they had satisfied themselves of the fate of Captain John.

Len Burker, pretending to cherish the same ideas was not unsparing of his encouragements when he had the opportunity. - That entered into his game, for it was his interest that Mrs. Branican should not return to America while he was forbidden to go there. Dolly, suspecting nothing of his odious plots, was very grateful for his support During the halt, Zach Fren and Tom Marix had a talk with regard to the new formation of the caravan after leaving Alice Spring. A serious question this. Was it not then that there-would commence the real difficulties of an expedition across Central Australia?

It was about half-past one when a dull noise was heard to the northward. It seemed liked a prolonged uproar, a continuous roll borne from the distance up to the encampment.

Mrs. Branican, Jane, and Godfrey, who had stood up, began to listen.

Tom Marix and Zach Fren had just come near them and were also listening.

What is the meaning of that noise?" asked Dolly.

"A storm, doubtless," said the boatswain.

"It is more like the beating of the waves on the beach,' said Godfrey.

However, there was no sign of a storm, and the atmosphere disclosed no electric intensity. As to any outburst of furious waters, that could only be produced by a sudden inundation due to the creeks being too full. But when Zach Fren would have explained the phenomenon in this way, Tom Marix replied, —

"An inundation in this part of the continent, at this time, after such a drought? Be assured, it is impossible!"

And he was right.

After violent storms, there occasionally come floods caused by the excessive abundance of the pluvial waters, and the liquid sheets will spread themselves over the low lands, and they often do in the wet seasons; but at the end of October this hypothesis was inadmissible.

Tom Marix, Zach Fren, and Godfrey climbed the slope of the hill and looked away northward and eastward.

There was nothing in view over the immense extent of gloomy desert plain; but, just above the horizon, there was a cloud of strange shape, which could not be confused with the mists the long heat had accumulated on the peripheric line between the earth and sky. It was not a cloud of mist in the vesicular state, it was rather an agglomeration of those outlined volutes caused by the discharges of artillery. As to the noise which came from the cloud of dust — and how could they doubt it was a cloud of dust? — it increased rapidly, and seemed to have a regular beat, a sort of colossal gallop echoed by the elastic ground of the immense prairie. Whence did it come?

"I know — I have seen it before — it's sheep!" said Tom Marix.

"Sheep?" replied Godfrey, laughing. "If those are only sheep — "

"Do not laugh, Godfrey!" said the chief of the escort; "there are, perhaps, thousands and thousands of sheep who are seized with panic. If I am not mistaken, they will pass us like an avalanche and destroy everything on their passage."

Tom Marix did not exaggerate. When these animals go mad from some cause or other, which occasionally happens in these runs, nothing can stop them; they destroy the fences and escape. An old proverb says, "The king's carriage stops before the sheep," and it is the case that a flock of these stupid beasts will be annihilated rather than give way; but, if they are annihilated, they also annihilate when they precipitate themselves on anything in their enormous masses. And this was what had happened.

The cloud of dust covered a space of between two and three leagues, and there could not be less than a hundred thousand sheep, which a blind panic was hurling down the caravan road. Coming from north to south they were opening out like a flood on the surface of the plain, and would not stop until they fell exhausted by their madness.

"What is. to be done?" asked Zach Fren.

"To get into shelter as well as we can along the foot of the hill," said Tom Marix.

There was nothing else to do, and the three went down. Insufficient as were the precautions indicated by Tom Marix, they were at once put into execution. The avalanche of sheep was but two miles from the encampment. The cloud rose in great spirals into the air, and from the cloud came a tumult of formidable bleatings.

The drays were run into shelter against the slope. The horses and cattle were compelled by their riders and drivers to lie on the ground so as to better resist the assault which might pass over without reaching them. The men leant against the slope. Godfrey placed himself near Dolly so as to protect her more efficaciously, and they waited.

Tom Marix went up the edge of the hill to look out over the plain, which was rolling like the sea under a strong breeze. The flock came along with a great noise and at great speed, and stretched over a third of the horizon.

As Tom Marix had said, the sheep could be counted by hundreds of thousands. In less than two minutes they would be in the encampment.

"Look out!" said Tom Marix.

And he slipped rapidly down the hill to where Mrs. Branican, Jane, Godfrey, and Zach Fren were huddled together.

Almost immediately the first line of sheep appeared on the crest. They did not stop, they could not stop. The animals at the head fell — some hundreds — in a heap, when the ground failed them. To the bleatings

265

were added the neighing of the. horses, the bellowing of bullocks now terror-stricken. Everything' was effaced amid a thick cloud of dust, while the avalanche poured over the hill in irresistible impulse — a regular torrent of sheep.

It lasted five minutes. The first who got up were Tom Marix, Godfrey, and Zach Fren and they saw the frightened mass with the last lines undulating towards the south.

"Up, up!" exclaimed the chief of the escort.

Everyone arose. A few contusions, a little confusion in the drays — that was all the damage amounted to, thanks to the shelter of the slope.

Tom Marix, Godfrey, and Zach Fren at once climbed the hill again.

To the south the flying flock was disappearing behind a curtain of sand. To the north extended the plains with footprints all over its surface.

Suddenly Godfrey exclaimed, "There, there! look!"

Fifty yards from the hill two bodies lay on the ground — two natives, doubtless, carried away, thrown down, and probably killed by this flight of sheep.

Tom Marix and Godfrey ran towards these bodies.

What was their surprise! Jos Meritt and his servant, Gin-Ghi, were there, motionless, unconscious.

But they still breathed, and with a little attention soon recovered from this rough assault. They had scarcely opened their eyes than they got on their feet, although covered with bruises.

"Good! Oil, very good!" said Jos Meritt. Then he turned round. "And Gin-Ghi?" he asked.

"Gin-Ghi is here — or rather what remains of him!" replied the Chinaman, rubbing his back. "Decidedly too many sheep, my master Jos, a thousand and ten thousand times too many!"

"Never too many legs, never too many chops, Gin-Ghi; then never too many sheep!" said the gentleman. "It is a pity we did not catch one as they went by — "

"Console yourself, Mr. Meritt," said Zach Fren; "at the foot of the slope there are a few hundred at your service."

"Very good! Oh, very good!" concluded the phlegmatic personage solemnly.

Then he addressed his servant, who after rubbing his back was now rubbing his shoulders, — "Gin-Ghi!"

"Master Jos!"

"Two chops for this evening," he said; "two chops — underdone!"

Jos Meritt and Gin-Ghi then related what had passed. They were travelling about three miles in advance of the caravan when they were surprised by this charge of sheep. Their horses took flight and they could not stop them. Thrown off and trodden on, it was a miracle they were not killed, and it was a lucky chance also that Mrs. Branican and her companions arrived in time to help them.

And so, after having escaped this very serious danger, a start was made, and at six o'clock in the evening the caravan reached Alice Spring.

CHAPTER VIII - BEYOND ALICE SPRING

Next day was October 24, and Mrs. Branican was busy in rearranging the expedition in view of a campaign that would probably be long, difficult, and dangerous, inasmuch as it would be in the almost unknown regions of Central Australia.

Alice Spring is but a station on the Overland Telegraph Line, consisting of some twenty houses and hardly worth the name of a village.

In the first place Mrs. Branican went in search of the head of the station, Mr. Flint. He might, perhaps, have some information regarding the Indas. Did this tribe of Western Australia, among whom Captain John was kept prisoner, ever come down into these central regions?

Mr. Flint had no information on the subject except that the Indas occasionally moved about in the west of Alexandra Land. He had never heard of John Branican. As to Harry Felton, all that he knew was that he had been found about eighty miles east of the telegraph line on the Queensland frontier. According to him, the best thing to do was to follow the instructions the unfortunate man had given just before he died, and take the expedition obliquely across the regions of Western Australia. He hoped that it would end favourably, and that Mrs. Branican would succeed where he, Flint, had failed six years before in searching for Leichardt — a project which the inter-tribal wars of the natives had soon compelled him' to abandon, he put himself at Mrs. Branican's disposal to provide her with all the resources of Alice Spring, and that, he added, was what he had done for David Lindsay when that traveller stopped there in 1886, before starting for Lake Nash and the eastern spurs of the MacDonnell ranges.

At this period the part of the Australian continent which the expedition was preparing to explore on the way north-westwards was as follows: —

At two hundred and sixty miles. from the station of Alice Spring, on the hundred and twenty-seventh meridian, runs the rectilinear frontier which from south to north separates South Australia, Alexandra Land, and Northern Australia, from that colony known as Western Australia, of which Perth is the capital. It is the largest, the least known, and the least populated of the seven great divisions of the continent. In reality, it is only geographically surveyed along the coasts, which comprise Nuyts Land, Leeuwin Land, Vlaming Land, Eendraght Land, De Witt Land, and Tasman Land..

Modern cartographers indicate in the interior of this territory, the distant solitudes of which the wandering natives are the only people to traverse, three distinct deserts.

1. — To the south the desert comprised between the thirtieth and twenty-eighth degree of latitude, explored by Forrest, in 1869, from the coast up to the twenty-third meridian, and which Giles traversed in its entirety in 1875.

2. — The Gibson Desert, between the twenty-eighth and twenty-ninth degrees, the immense plains of which were crossed by Giles during the year 1876.

3. — The Great Sandy Desert, comprised between the twenty-third degree and the northern coast, which Colonel Warburton crossed from east to north-west in 1873, at the cost of the dangers we know of.

It was through this region that Mrs. Branican's expedition was to carry on its search. Colonel Warburton's itinerary was the one it was best to follow after the information given by Harry Felton. From the station at Alice Spring to the shore of the Indian Ocean, the journey of this bold explorer had occupied not less than four months out of the fifteen between September, 1872, and January, 1874. How much time would the one take which Mrs. Branican and her companions were about to attempt?

Dolly requested Zach Fren and Tom Marix not to lose a day, and, very actively helped by Mr. Flint, they were enabled to obey her orders.

Under the guidance of the Afghan drivers, the camels, to the number of thirty, had been at Alice Spring for a fortnight after having been bought at a high price on account of Mrs. Branican.

The introduction of camels into Australia dates only from the last thirty-two years. It was in 1860 that Mr. Elder imported a few from India. These useful animals are abstemious and robust, and of very rough appearance, but arc capable of bearing a load of one hundred and fifty kilogrammes and travelling forty kilometres in twenty- four hours "at their own pace." Besides, they can remain a week without eating, and without drinking for six days in winter and three days in summer. They have consequently been called upon to render the same services in this arid continent as in the burning regions of Africa. There as here they endure almost with impunity the privations due to want of water or to excessive heat. The Desert of the Sahara and the Great Sandy Desert, are they not traversed by the corresponding parallels of the two hemispheres?

Mrs. Branican had thirty camels, twenty for riding and ten for the packs. There were more males than females, most of them being young and in good condition as regards strength and health. Just as the escort had Tom Marix for its chief, so the animals had for chief the oldest male camel, whom the others willingly obeyed. He directed them, mustered them at the halts, and prevented them running off with the females. With him dead or ill the troop was in danger of disbandment, and the drivers would be powerless to keep good order. It was therefore natural that this valuable animal should be assigned to Tom Marix, and these two chiefs — the one carrying the other — had their place assigned to them at the head of the caravan.

It goes without saying that the horses and bullocks which had brought the expedition from Farina Town to Alice Spring had to be left with Mr. Flint, with whom they will be found with the buggies and drays on the return. There was every likelihood that the expedition would return to Adelaide along the road marked by the posts of the Overland Telegraph Line.

Dolly and Jane were to occupy a "kihitka," a sort of tent almost identical with that of the Arabs, and which was borne by one of the strongest camels. They could find, shelter from the rays of the sun behind the thick curtains, and even obtain protection against the rains which the violent storms discharge — too rarely, it is true — on to the central plains of the continent.

Harriett, the. waiting woman to Mrs. Branican, accustomed to the long journey of the nomads, preferred to follow on foot. These huge beasts, with two humps, seemed rather more adapted for carrying packages than human creatures.

Three saddled camels were reserved for Len Burker, Godfrey, and Zach Fren, who would soon learn to accustom themselves to their rough jolting gait. Besides, there was no question of adopting another rate of travel, as a portion of the expedition was to be unmounted. The trot would only become necessary when it was required to advance in front of the caravan to discover some well or spring during the crossing of the Great Sandy Desert.

As to the whites of the escort, it was for them that the other fifteen saddle camels were required. The blacks destined to lead the ten pack camels would journey on foot the twelve or fourteen miles of which the two daily stages would consist; that would not be too much for them.

In this way the caravan was reorganized in view of the inherent difficulties of this second period of the voyage. All had been arranged, with Mrs. Branican's approval, to be equal to the exigencies of the campaign, long as it might be, with due consideration for the beasts and the men. Better provided with the means of transport, better furnished with victuals and camp effects, working under conditions more favourable than had ever been those of the Australian explorers, there was some ground for hoping that it would attain its object.

It remains to be said what was to become of Jos Meritt. Was that gentleman, with his servant Gin-Ghi, to remain at Alice Spring? If he left it, would it be to continue along the telegraph line northwards?

271

Would he not rather go to the east or the west in search of the native tribes? That was when the collector would have a chance of discovering the undiscoverable hat, the track of which he had been on for so long. But now that he was deprived of his mount, dispossessed of his baggage, denuded of his provisions, how could he continue his journey?

On many occasions Zach Fren had questioned Gin-Ghi about this. But the Celestial had replied that he never knew what his master would do, and that even his master did not know himself. It was certain, however, that Jos Meritt would not consent to remain behind so long as his monomania remained unsatisfied, and he, Gin-Ghi, native of Hong-Kong, was no nearer seeing the country "where the young Chinamen, clothed in silk, gather with their pointed fingers the flower of the water-lily."

It was now, however, the eve of departure, and Jos Meritt had said nothing of his plans, when Mrs. Branican was informed by Gin-Ghi that the gentleman requested the favour of a private interview.

Mrs. Branican, glad to be of as much service to this eccentric individual as possible, replied that she begged he would come to Mr. Flint's house, where she had stayed since her arrival at the station.

Jos Meritt went there immediately — it was in the afternoon of October 25 — and as soon as he had sat himself down in front of Dolly, began as follows, —

"Mrs. Branican! Good! Oh, very good! I have no doubt — no — I do not doubt for a moment that you will find Captain John, and I am just as certain of putting my hand on the hat to the discovery of which I have devoted all the efforts of a very active life. Good! Oh, very good! You of course know why I have come to ransack the most secret regions of Australia?"

"I do know, Mr. Meritt," replied Mrs. Branican, "and on my part I do not doubt that some day you will be repaid for so much perseverance."

"Perseverance? Good! Oh, very good! The reason is that the hat, you see, is the only one in the world!"

"And you want it in your collection?"

"Regrettably, and I would give my head to be able to put it on!"

"Is it a man's hat?" asked Dolly, who was interested, more out of kindness than curiosity .in the innocent hobby of this maniac.

"No, madam, no. A woman's hat. But what woman's! You will excuse me if I keep the secret of her name and position, for fear of exciting competition. Think, madam, if anybody else — "

"Then you have some clue?"

"Clue? Good! Oh, very good!, I have ascertained from much correspondence, inquiry, and peregrinations, that this hat has emigrated to Australia, after exciting vicissitudes, and that, descended from high places — yes, very high places! it now graces the head of the sovereign of a native tribe."

"But this tribe?"

"One of those wandering in the north or west of the continent. Good! Oh, very good! If necessary, I will visit them all, I will ransack them all. And as it is of no consequence which I begin with, I ask your permission to follow your caravan to the Indas."

"Willingly, Mr. Meritt," replied Dolly, "and I will give orders, if possible, two extra camels shall be procured."

"One will do, one for my servant and myself; that will be quite enough. I will ride the animal, and Gin-Ghi can walk,"

"You know we start to-morrow morning, Mr. Meritt?"

"To-morrow? Good! Oh, very good! I am not the man to delay you, Mrs. Branican. But it is understood, is it not, that I have nothing to do with anything concerning Captain John? That is your business. My business is my hat."

"Your hat, it is understood, Mr. Meritt!" replied Dolly.

Thereupon Jos Meritt retired, declaring that this intelligent, energetic, and generous woman deserved to discover her husband as much at least as he himself deserved to set hands on the jewel whose conquest would complete his collection of historic head-gear.

Gin-Ghi received orders to be in readiness for the morning, and had to be busy in packing up the few things which had escaped disaster after the affair of the sheep. As to the animal which the gentleman was to share with his servant, in the manner stated above, Mr. Flint managed to procure it, and that was worth a "Good! Oh, very good!" on the part of the very grateful Jos Meritt.

On the morning of the 26th of October, the signal for departure was given, after Mrs. Branican had taken leave of the chief of the station. Tom Marix and Godfrey took the head of the whites of the escort, who were mounted. Dolly and Jane took their seats in the kibitka, having Len Burker on one side, Zach Fren on the other. Then came, majestically astride between the two humps of his camel, Jos Meritt, followed by Gin-Ghi. Following these were the pack-camels and the blacks forming the second half of the escort.

At six o'clock in the morning the expedition, leaving the Overland Telegraph Line and Alice Spring to the west, disappeared behind one of the outliers of the MacDonnell Ranges.

In Australia during the month of October the heat is excessive; and consequently Tom Marix had .decided to travel only during the early hours of the day — from four to nine o'clock in the morning — and during the afternoon from four to eight o'clock. Even the nights began to be suffocating, and long halts were needful to acclimatize the caravan to the fatigues of the central regions.

They were not yet in the desert, with the aridity of its interminable plains, its creeks entirely dry, its wells containing only brackish water when the dryness of the soil has not completely exhausted them. At the base of the mountains extends that varied region where the ramifications of the MacDonnell and Strangways Ranges rise in an entanglement, and across which runs the telegraph line curving to the north-west. This direction the caravan had to abandon, so as to bear more to the westward, almost along the parallel of the tropic of Capricorn. This was almost the same route Giles had followed in 1872, and it cut that of Stuart twenty-five miles northward of Alice Spring.

The camels went very slowly over this hilly country. A few threads of creeks watered it here and there. Under the shelter of the trees running water could be found, fairly fresh, of which the animals drank sufficient to last them for many hours.

Skirting the scattered thickets, the sportsmen of the caravan, whose duty it was to provide the venison, were able to bring down several kinds of game — rabbits among others.

It will be remembered that the rabbit of Australia is what the locust is to Africa. These too prolific rodents will finish by eating up everything if care is not taken. Up to then the men of the caravan had rather despised them from an alimentary point of view, as real game abounds in the plains and forests of South Australia! There would be time enough to take to this rather insipid meat when the hares, the partridges, the bustards, the ducks, the pigeons and other fur and feather gave out. But on this river in the region of the MacDonnell Ranges they had to be content with what they could get, and that meant these rabbits, which were in swarms.

And in the evening of the 31st of October when Godfrey, Jos Meritt and Zach Fren were together, conversation worked round to these animals, the destruction of which cannot come too soon. And Godfrey having asked if there had always been rabbits in Australia, Tom Marix said, —

"No, my boy. They Were imported about thirty years ago. That was a nice present they made us! The animals have so multiplied as to devastate the country. Certain districts are so infested that neither sheep nor cattle can be raised on them. The fields are riddled with their holes

275

like a colander, and the grass is eaten off down to the roots. It is absolute ruin, and I am ready to believe that it will not be the colonists who will eat the rabbits, but the rabbits who will eat the colonists."

"Have they not used any strong measure to get rid of them?" said Zach Fren.

"Useless measures," said Tom Marix, "for the numbers increase instead of diminishing. I know a man who spent forty thousand pounds in the destruction of the rabbits that ravaged his run. The Government has put a price on their head as they have done with tigers and serpents in British India. Bah! It is like a hydra; the heads spring up as fast as you cut them down, and even in greater numbers. Strychnine has been used, which has poisoned them in thousands, and nearly started a plague in the country. Nothing has succeeded."

"Have I not heard," said Godfrey, "that a French scientist, Monsieur Pasteur, proposed to destroy these rodents by giving them a disease?"

"Yes, and the means might have been efficacious. But it failed — to be used, although a reward of twenty thousand pounds was offered with that object in view. Queensland and New South Wales have just set up a wire fence eight hundred miles long to protect the east of the continent against the invasion of the rabbits. The rabbit is really a calamity!"

"Good! Oh, very good! Quite a calamity!" said Jos Meritt," like the Yellow race, which will end by invading the five parts of the world. The Chinese are the rabbits of the future."

Luckily Gin-Ghi was not there, for he would not have allowed to pass, without protest, this offensive comparison to the Celestials. Or rather, he would have shrugged his shoulders and laughed the peculiar laugh of his race, which is merely a long, noisy inspiration.

"And so," said Zach Fren, "the Australians have given up the battle?"

"And in what way can they continue it?" asked Tom Marix.

"It seems to me," said Jos Meritt, "that there is one sure way of getting rid of these rabbits."

"And what is that?" asked Godfrey.

"To get the British Parliament to pass an Act that only beaver hats should be used in the United Kingdom and its dependencies. Then, as beaver hats are always made of rabbit skin — good! Oh, very good!"

And in that way Jos Meritt finished the sentence with his usual exclamation.

Meanwhile, until the British Parliament passed the Act, the best to be done was to feed on the rabbits shot on the journey. There would be so many fewer in Australia, and there could be no harm in knocking them over.

The other animals were of no use for food; but a few were seen of a peculiar species of great interest to naturalists. The one was an echidna of the monotreme family — an animal with a snout in the form of a beak, with horny lips, a body bristling with quills like a hedgehog, whose chief food consists of the insects it catches with its threadlike tongue stretched out of its burrow. The other was an ornithorhyncus, with the mandibles of a duck, and fur of a ruddy brown, covering a small body measuring a foot in length. The animals of both these species have the peculiarity of being ovoviviparous; they are hatched from eggs, and when they come out of the eggs they are fed from the breast.

One day Godfrey, who distinguished himself among the sportsmen, was lucky enough to sight and shoot an "ilrri," a sort of kangaroo, which being only wounded, managed to get away among the neighbouring thickets. The boy had little to be sorry for, as, if Tom Marix was to be believed, the marsupial has no value beyond that due to the | difficulty of getting near him. It was not the same with a "bungari," an animal of large size, with a blackish coat, who was climbing among the higher branches in marsupial fashion, hanging on with his cat-like claws and swinging his long tail. This animal is

277

essentially nocturnal and hides himself so artfully among the branches that it is difficult to see him.

Tom Marix observed that the bungari is excellent game, the meat being very much superior to that of kangaroo when grilled over the embers. Unfortunately there were no means of testing this, and it was probable that bungaris would become rarer and rarer as they approached the desert. Evidently, as they advanced westwards, the caravan would be reduced to live entirely on its own resources.

However, in spite of the difficulties of the ground, Tom Marix managed to maintain the required rate of from twelve to fourteen miles a day — the rate on which the advance of the expedition was based. Although the heat was already very great — thirty to thirty-five degrees centigrade in the shade — the expedition bore it very comfortably. During the day, it is true, there were still occasional groups of trees under which they encamped under acceptable conditions. And there was no lack of water, although there was little more than a streamlet in the bed of the creeks. The halts regularly took place from nine o'clock till four o'clock in the afternoon, giving sufficient rest to the men and animals after the fatigue of the journey.

The country was uninhabited. The last runs had been left behind. There were no more paddocks, no more enclosures, no more of those numerous sheep, which the short, dry grass could not feed. And only a few natives were met with on their way to the stations of the Overland Telegraph Line.

On the 7th of November, in the afternoon, Godfrey, who was about half a mile in advance, signalled the presence of a horseman. This horseman was following a narrow path at the foot of the MacDonnell Ranges, whose base consists of quartz and metamorphic grit. Noticing the caravan, he put his spurs to his horse and came up to it at a gallop.

The camp had just been pitched under some slender eucalyptus trees, a group of two or three, giving but little shade. A little creek Went curving by, fed by springs in the central chain, and the roots of the eucalyptus had drunk up all the water.

Godfrey brought the man into the presence of Mrs. Branican. She began by offering him a bumper of whiskey, for which he seemed very grateful.

He was an Australian white, aged about thirty-five, one of those splendid horsemen, accustomed to the rain, which glides off their shining skin as if off a waterproof, accustomed to the sun, which has no more to brown on their thoroughly browned faces. He was a travelling postman, and fulfilled his duties with zeal and good humour, traversing the districts of the colony, distributing the letters, carrying the news from station to station, and to the villages scattered east and west of the telegraph line. He was then returning from Emu Spring, a station on the southern slope of the Bluff Ranges, after crossing the region extending up to the MacDonnell hills.

The postman, who belonged to the class of "rough men," might be compared to the typical .good fellow, such as the old postillion in France. He knew how to endure hunger and thirst. Sure of a cordial welcome wherever he stopped, even when he had no letter to draw from his bag, resolute, brave, strong, his revolver in his belt, his gun slung on his shoulder, mounted on a swift, powerful horse, he travelled night and day with no fear of misadventure.

Mrs. Branican took pleasure in talking to him, in asking him fur information concerning the native tribes with whom he had come in contact.

The postman replied simply and obligingly. He had heard — like everybody else — of the wreck of the *Franklin*; but he did not know that an expedition, organized by John Branican's wife, had left Adelaide to explore the central regions of the Australian continent. Mrs. Branican told him that, according to the revelations of Harry Felton, it was among the people of the tribe of the Indas that Captain John had been kept as prisoner for fourteen years.

"And in your journeys," she asked, "did you ever come into contact with natives of that tribe?"

"No, madam, although the Indas have occasionally come near Alexandra Land," replied the postman, "and I have often heard of them."

"Perhaps you can tell us where they are now?" asked Zach Fren.

"With the wandering tribes that is difficult. One season they arc here, another there — "

"But where were they last?" asked Mrs. Branican.

"I can tell you," said the postman, "that six months ago the Indas were in the north-west of Western Australia, on the banks of the Fitzroy River. The natives of Tasnian Land are often in those regions. You know what it means to get there; you will have to cross the deserts of the centre and the west, and I need not tell you what risks you run. After all, with courage and energy, one can go far. Then be prepared for it, and a pleasant journey to you, Mrs. Branican!"

The postman accepted another large glass of whiskey, and even a few tins of provisions he slipped into his holsters. Then, mounting his horse, he disappeared round the last spur of the MacDonnell Ranges.

Two days afterwards the caravan passed the last outlier of the chain dominated by the summit of Mount Liebig. It was now on the edge of the desert, one hundred and thirty miles north-west of Alice Spring.

CHAPTER IX - MRS. BRANICAN'S JOURNAL

The word "desert" recalls to the mind the Sahara, with its immense sandy plains dotted with fresh and green oases. However, the central regions of the Australian continent have nothing in common with the northern regions of Africa, unless it is the rarity of water. "The water is in the shadow," say the natives, and the traveller is reduced to run from spring to spring, often situated at considerable distances from each other. However, although the sand, whether extending in immense plains or relieved by hills, covers a large part of the Australian soil, this soil is not absolutely barren. Shrubs adorned with little flowers, a few scattered trees, gum trees, acacias or eucalyptus, make it look rather more cheerful than the nakedness of the Sahara. But these trees, these shrubs, yield neither edible fruits nor leaves for the caravans, which are obliged to carry their victuals with them; and animal life is but poorly represented in these solitudes by the flight of birds of pas-age.

Mrs. Branican kept with perfect regularity and exactitude her journal of the journey. A few extracts from this journal will inform us more clearly than a simple narrative, regarding the incidents of this toilsome journey. They will reveal also Dolly's ardent soul, her firmness under trial, her unshakable and never-despairing tenacity, even at the moment when the greater part of her companions despaired around her. And from them we shall see of what a woman is capable when she devotes herself to the accomplishment of a duty.

"10th November. — We left our camp at Mount Liebig at. four o'clock in the morning. The postman gave us valuable information. It agreed with that of poor Felton. Yes, it is in the north-west and more specially on the banks of the Fitzroy River that we must look for the tribe of the Indas. Nearly eight hundred miles to cross! We will cross them. I will get there, even if I get there alone, even if I become the prisoner of this tribe. At least, I shall be with John!

"We will go north-west, almost on Colonel Warburton's track. Our road will be almost the same as his up to Fitzroy River. May we not have to undergo the trials he underwent, nor leave behind us any of our companions dead of exhaustion! Unfortunately, the circumstances are not favourable. It was in the month of April that Colonel Warburton had left Alice Spring, which answers to the month of October in North America, that is to say, towards the end of the warm season. Our caravan, on the contrary, started from Alice Spring at the end of October, and we are in November, that is to say, at the beginning of the Australian summer. The heat is already excessive, being nearly thirty-five degrees centigrade in the shade. And for that all we can do is to wait for a cloud to pass over the sky or for some shelter under a group of trees.

"The order of march adopted by Tom Marix is very practical. The duration and the times of the stages are well proportioned. Between four and eight o'clock in the morning we do our first stage; the second stage lasts from four o'clock to eight o'clock in the evening, and we rest during the night. In this way we avoid travelling during the burning noon. But what time is lost, what delay! Even supposing we meet with no obstacle, it will take us quite three months to reach the Fitzroy River.

"I am well satisfied with Tom Marix. Zach Fren and he are two resolute men on whom I can depend in all circumstances.

"Godfrey frightens me with his impassioned nature. He is always in front and often out of sight. I can scarcely keep him with me, and yet this boy loves me as if he were my son. Tom Marix has been lecturing him on his temerity. I hope he will benefit by it.

"Len Burker is almost always in the rear of the caravan, and seems to seek the company of the blacks of the escort rather than that of the whites. He has been long acquainted with their tastes, their instincts, their customs. When we meet with natives he is very useful, for he speaks their language well enough to understand them and be understood. Would that my poor Jane's husband had seriously reformed, but I am afraid he has not! His look has not changed; he has one of those looks without frankness, which turn away from you."

"13th November. — There is nothing new during the last three days. What a comfort and consolation it is to have Jane near me! What a deal we have to say to each other in the kibitka when we are both shut in. I have made Jane share in my conviction; she no longer doubts that I shall find John. But the poor woman is always sorrowful. I have not said anything to her regarding the time when Len Burker forced her to follow him to Australia. Can quite see she could not tell me everything. It seems sometimes as though she was about to tell me something, but Len Burker watches her, and when she sees him, when he approaches, her manner changes and her face becomes uneasy. She is afraid of him. It is certain that this man is her master, and at a gesture from him she would follow him to the end of the world.

"Jane appears to have a great affection for Godfrey, and when the dear boy comes near our kibitka to talk to us she dare not say a word to him; not even to answer him. Her eyes turn away from him, she lowers her head. One would say she is in pain in his presence.

"To-day we crossed a long, marshy plain during the morning stage. We met with a few pools of water, brackish water, almost salt. Tom Marix told us these marshes are the remains of ancient lakes which were formerly connected with Lake Eyre and Lake Torrens, forming a sea which divided the continent. Fortunately we had some fresh water at our camp last night, and our camels quenched their thirst abundantly.

"It appears that many of these lagoons are found, not only in the low ground, but also in the more elevated regions.

"The ground is damp; the feet of the camels leave a sticky mud after treading in the saline crust which covers the pools. Sometimes the crust resists the pressure, and when the foot comes down roughly and breaks through there is a splash of liquid slime.

"We had great trouble in getting across the marshes, which extend for twelve miles towards the north-west.

"We have met with snakes since our departure from Adelaide. They are widely spread in Australia, and are in great numbers on the surface of these lagoons, which are dotted with dwarf trees and shrubs. One of the men of our escort was even bitten by one of these venomous reptiles, which are about three feet long, brown in colour and hair. I am told the scientific name is Trimesurus ikaheca. Tom Marix at once cauterized the wound with a pinch of powder dropped on the man's arm and lighted. The man, who was a white, did not even utter a cry. I held his arm during the operation. He thanked me. I gave him an extra glass of whiskey. We have reason to believe the wound will not end fatally.

"We must take care where we tread. Even on a camel one is not completely out of the reach of these snakes. I am always afraid that Godfrey will commit some imprudence, and I tremble when I hear the blacks shouting ' Vin'dohe!' which is the word for snake in the native language.

"This evening, while pitching tents for the night, two of our natives killed a reptile of large size. Tom Marix said that if two-thirds of the snakes which swarm in Australia are venomous, there are only five species whose venom is dangerous to man. The snake they have just killed measures twelve feet long; it is a sort of boa. Our Australians wished to cook it for supper. And we had to let them.

"This is what they did.

"They dug a trough in the sand and a native put into it a lot of stones he had previously warmed up in a fire, and then they strewed fragrant leaves. The snake, with its head and tail cut off, was laid, in this trough and covered with similar leaves, the heat being given by the hot stones. The earth is covered in and beaten down thick enough to prevent the steam of the cooking from escaping.

"We watched this culinary operation not without disgust; but, when the snake was cooked and taken out of this improvised oven, we agreed that its flesh exhaled a delicious odour. Neither Jane nor I cared to taste it, although Tom Marix assured us that, though the white flesh of these reptiles is a little insipid, their liver is a very savoury morsel.

"'It has been compared,' he said, 'to the finest among the game birds, particularly the hazel grouse.'

"' The hazel grouse! Good! Oh, very good! Delicious, the hazel grouse !So said Jos Meritt.

"And after being served with a little piece of the liver, he returned for a larger one, and he would have ended by eating the lot. What would you have?

"There was no need to ask Gin-Ghi. A good slice of smoking snake flesh, which he ate like an epicure, put him in the best of humours.

"'Ai ya!' he exclaimed with a long sigh of regret, ' with a few Ning Po oysters and Tao Ching wine one would think we were in Tie-Coung-Yuan.'

"Godfrey and Zach Fren, mastering their repugnance, took a few slices of snake. They thought it rather nice; I preferred to trust to their word.

"The reptile was devoured to the last bit by the natives of the escort. They did not even leave the few drops of grease the animal had yielded while it was being cooked.

"During the night our sleep was troubled by a dreadful howling from some distance off. It was a pack of dingoes. -

The dingo might be called the Australian jackal, for he is half dog and half wolf. He has a yellowish or reddish brown fur, and a long ornamental tail.' Fortunately these dingoes kept to howling and did not attack the encampment. In a very large number they might be dangerous."

"19th November. — The heat is becoming more and more overwhelming, and the creeks we meet with arc almost entirely dry. We have to dig down into their beds if we want a little water to fill our kegs. Before long we shall have to trust entirely to the springs, for the creeks will have disappeared.

"I am obliged to notice that there exists a truly inexplicable antipathy, almost instinctive, between Len Burker and Godfrey. Never do they address a word to each other. It is certain they avoid each other as much as possible.

"I was talking about this to Godfrey one day.

"'You do not like Len Burker?' I said.

"' No," said he," and do not ask me to like him.'

"'But he is a connection of mine,' I said; 'he is my relative, Godfrey, and if you were to like me — '

"' Mrs. Branican, I like you, but I shall never like him.'

"Dear Godfrey! what is then the presentiment, the secret reason which makes him speak thus?"

"27th November. — To-day we have seen a large stretch, an immense monotonous steppe, covered with spinifex. This is a spring herb appropriately called the vegetable porcupine. We have had to get through the clumps, which are sometimes five feet high, and the sharp thorns might have wounded our camels. The spinifex is already of a yellow colour and unfit for the animals to feed on. When they are young and green, camels do not refuse to eat them. But that is not the case now, and our only anxiety was to get along without being pricked by the bushes.

"Under these circumstances our progress was very painful. We must get accustomed to it though, for we have hundreds of miles to go over these spinifex plains. It is the shrub of the desert, the only one that will grow on the barren lands of the centre of Australia.

"The heat is gradually increasing, and there is no shade. Our men on foot are visibly suffering from this excessive temperature. And will it be believed that, five months later, according to Colonel Warburton, the thermometer may sink below freezing point, and the creeks will be covered with ice an inch thick?

"Then the creeks are numerous; now, however deep the bed may be, we cannot find a drop of water.

"Tom Marix has given orders to the mounted men to give up their mounts occasionally to their companions on foot. This measure has been taken with the object of satisfying the complaints of the blacks. I see with regret that Len Burker was their spokesman in this matter. Certainly the men had cause to complain; to march on foot among tufts of spinifex in a temperature hardly supportable in cither evening or morning is extremely fatiguing. But in any case it was not for Len Burker to excite their jealousy against the squadron of whites. He interfered with what did not concern him, and I told him so..

' What I did, Dolly,' he replied, 'was in the interest of all.'

"' That I wish to believe,' I replied.

"'The burden should be justly shared — '

"' Leave that to me, Mr. Burker,' said Tom Marix, who intervened in the discussion. ' I will take what measures I think necessary.'

"I saw that Len Burker went off with ill-disguised vexation and gave us an evil look. Jane noticed it, but her husband's eyes fixed on hers, and the poor woman turned away her head.

"Tom Marix promised me to do all he could to save the men of the escort, white and black, from having to complain again."

"5th December. — During our halts we are much tormented by white ants. These insects swarm in myriads. They are invisible under the fine sand, and it requires the pressure of the foot to make them appear on the surface.

"'My skin is hard and horny,' said Zach Fren, 'a regular shark skin, but these ants make nothing of it.'

"The truth is that the skin of animals is not thick enough to resist the bite of their mandibles. We cannot lie down without being immediately attacked. To escape these insects we must get out in the rays of the sun, and they are so hot we can hardly support them, so that it is only changing one evil for another.

"The one who seems less ill-treated than any of us by these insects is the Chinaman. Is he too indolent for their importunate stings to triumph over his indolence? I do not know; but, while we are fidgeting and writhing about half mad, the privileged Gin-Ghi, stretched in the shade of a spinifex bush, never moves, and sleeps peacefully as if these wretched insects respected his yellow skin.

"Jos Meritt is just as patient, although his long body offers his assailants a huge field to devour. He never complains. Automatically and regularly his two lips open and shut again, and mechanically slaughter thousands of ants, and he is content to say, looking at his servant quite free from any bite, —

"' These Chinese are really exceptionally favoured by nature. Gin-Ghi!'

"' Sir!'

"' We shall have to change skins.'

"' Certainly,' said the Celestial, ' if we change places at the same time.'

"' Good! Oh, very good! But to begin the change of skin, one of us must be skinned first, and I will begin on you.'

"' Ah, we will talk of that at the third moon,' said Gin- Ghi.

"And he resumed his sleep at the fifth watch, to use his poetic language; that is to say, at the moment the caravan was about to resume its journey."

"10th December. — This torment only eases when Tom Marix gives the signal for departure. It is lucky that the ants do not think of climbing up the legs of the camels. Our walkers are never free from these insupportable insects.

"Besides, during the march, we are almost devoured by enemies of another kind and no less disagreeable. These are the mosquitoes, which constitute one of the most formidable plagues of Australia. At their sting, particularly during the rainy season, cattle, as if they were struck by an epidemic, grow thin, waste away, and even die, without it being possible to save them.

"But what would we give to be here in the rainy season. It is nothing, this plague of ants or mosquitoes, after the tortures of thirst caused by the heats of our Australian November. The want of water brings about the annihilation of all the intellectual faculties and all the physical strength. And our reserves are being exhausted and our kegs sound empty. We filled them at the last creek, and what they contain now is but a warm liquid, thick and shaken about, and it does not quench the thirst. Our position will soon be that of the Arab stokers on board the steamers in the Red Sea, the miserable men who fall half-fainting in front of the boiler fires.

"What is no less alarming is that our camels begin to crawl instead of keeping up their usual pace. Their necks are stretched out towards the horizon around the long, wide, level plain broken by no undulation or variation of the ground. Always the vast steppe covered by arid spinifex growing from its roots deep down in the sand. There is not a tree in sight, not a trace by which we can discover the presence of a well or a spring."

"16th December. — In two stages our caravan has not moved nine miles to-day. For some days I have-noticed that our day's work has become less and less. Notwithstanding their strength, our camels advance but wearily, particularly those carrying the packs.

"Tom Marix is in a rage when he sees the men stop before he has given the signal to halt. He goes up to the pack camels and hits them with his whip, the lash of which has but little effect on the skin of these rugged animals.

"Jos Meritt, with that dryness which never leaves him, said with regard to this, —

"' Good! Oh, very good. Mr. Marix! But I will give you a bit of advice; it is not the camel you should whip, but its rider.'

"And certainly Tom Marix would not have been displeased to follow the advice if I had not interfered. To the fatigues our men have to undergo we must have the prudence at least not to give them ill-treatment. Some of them might desert. I am afraid that that will happen, particularly if the idea occurs to any of the blacks; but Tom Marix assures me there is no danger."

"From the 17th lo the 27th December. — The journey continues under these conditions. During the first days of the week the weather changed with the wind, which blew briskly. A few clouds came up from the north in the form of rounded volutes, as if they were huge bombs which a spark had exploded. That day, the 23rd, the spark came. A flash cleft the sky. Noisy claps of thunder of rare intensity were heard without the prolonged roll which the "echoes give out in mountainous countries. At the same time the atmospheric currents were set free with such violence that we could not keep on the camels. We had to get down and even to lie on the ground. Zach Fren, Godfrey, Tom Marix, and Len Burker had much difficulty in saving our kibitka from being blown away. As to camping under these circumstances or raising our tents among the tufts of spinifex, it was Impossible to think of it. In an instant all the things would have been scattered, torn, and rendered useless.

"' This is nothing,' said Zach Fren, rubbing his hands; a storm is soon over.'

"'Hurrah for the storm if it brings us water!' said Godfrey.

"Godfrey was right. 'Water, water!' Is our cry. But will it rain? That is the question.

"Yes, that is all the question, for an abundant rain would be for us like the manna of the desert. Unfortunately, the air is so dry — as we can see by the curious sharpness of the thunder-claps — that the water of the clouds might remain in a state of vapour and not dissolve in rain. But It would have been difficult to imagine a more violent storm or a more deafening exchange of flashes and thunderings.

"I have been able to observe what I had heard regarding the Australian aborigines during these storms. They had no fear of being struck, they did not shut their eyes at the lightning, nor did they tremble at the thunder. In fact, the blacks of our escort uttered exclamations of joy. They were in no way affected like every other living creature when the air is charged with electricity at the moment when this electricity is manifested by the tearing asunder of the clouds in the heights of the sky.

"Assuredly, the nervous organization of these primitive beings cannot be very sensitive. Perhaps, after all, they greeted in the storm the flood it might send them. And in truth, the waiting for this was quite a Tantalus' task.

"' It is really water,' said Godfrey to me, ' good, pure water, the water of the sky, which is hanging over our heads! There is the lightning cleaving the clouds, and yet nothing falls.'

"' A little patience, my child,' I replied; ' let us not despair.'

"' That is it,' said Zach Fren. ' The clouds are thickening, and coming down at the same time. Ah! If the wind would only drop, this poise would soon end in cataracts!'

"It was to be feared that the storm would sweep away the mass of vapour towards the south without giving us a drop of water.

"About three o'clock in the afternoon it seemed that the northern horizon had begun to clear, and that the storm would soon end. This would be a cruel deception.

"' Good! Oh, very good!'

"Jos Meritt had uttered his usual exclamation. Never was this phrase of approval more appropriate. The Englishman had stretched out his hand and found it moistened with a few large drops.

"We had not to wait long for the deluge. We had to be quick in getting into our mackintoshes. Then without losing a minute we were ready to receive the beneficent shower. Everything was laid out on the ground, even blankets, towels and sheets, from which we could squeeze the water when they were soaked — the water for the camels to drink.

"But the camels were soon able to quench the thirst which tortured them. Streamlet and pools were quickly formed between the tufts of spinifex. The plain threatened to be transformed into a vast marsh. There was water for everybody. We were at first delighted at this abundant flood, which the dried ground absorbed like a sponge, and the first drops of which the sun, which had reappeared on the horizon, turned into vapour.

"Our reserve was assured for many days. There was a possibility of resuming our daily stages, with the men revived in body and. soul, and the animals firmly set on their feet again. The kegs were filled to the bung. Everything that could hold anything was used as a recipient. The camels did not neglect to fill the interior pouch, with which nature has provided them, and in which they can provision themselves with water for some time. And surprising as it may be, this pouch contains about fifteen gallons.

"Unfortunately these storms are rare, at least at this period of the year when the summer heat is at its greatest.

It is, therefore, a fortunate chance on which it would be imprudent to reckon for the future. The storm hardly lasted three hours, and the burning beds of the creeks soon absorbed the waters of the sky that had been poured into them. The springs, it is true, derived more benefit from the storm, and we shall have to congratulate ourselves if it has not been merely local. Let us hope it has refreshed the Australian plain for hundreds of miles round."

"29th December. — Following almost the same route as Colonel Warburton, we have now reached Waterloo Spring, one hundred and forty miles from Mount Liebig. Our expedition has now reached the hundred and twenty- sixth degree of longitude. It has just covered the conventional straight line running from, south to north which divides the neighbouring colony from that vast portion of the continent called Western Australia."

CHAPTER X - A FEW MOKE EXTRACTS

Waterloo Spring is not a town; it is not even a village. A few native huts, abandoned at this time, and that is all. The wandering natives only stop while the rainy season feeds the watercourses of this region — so that they stay there for a certain time. Waterloo in no way justifies the addition of the word 'Spring,' which is common to all the stations in the desert. No spring flows up from the ground, and if, as we have said, we meet "in the Sahara with fresh oases sheltered by trees, and watered by running streams, it is in vain we seek such things in the Australian desert."

Such is the observation entered in Mrs. Branican's journal, from which we will make a few more extracts. Better than more precise description, they are of a nature to make the country known, and show in all their horror the trials in store for the daring explorers who venture into it. They will, also help us to appreciate the mental strength and indomitable energy of their author, her unshakable resolution to attain her object at the cost of no matter what sacrifice.

30th December. — We have to stay a day at Waterloo Spring. These delays make me miserable, when I think of the distance which still separates us from the valley in which flows the Fitzroy. And "who knows if we may not have to seek beyond this valley for the tribe of Indas. Since Harry Felton left him, what has been the existence of my poor John? Did the natives avenge on him the flight of his companion? It will never do to think of that. The thought would kill me.

"Zach Fren tries to reassure me.

"'Inasmuch,' he says, 'as Captain John and Harry Felton were the prisoners of these Indas for so many years, they must have some interest in keeping them, as Harry Felton led you to think. These natives must have recognized in the captain a white chief of great value, and they are waiting for an opportunity of surrendering him for a ransom in proportion to his importance. In my opinion the flight of his companion would not have made the position of Captain John any worse.'

"Would to God it is so!

"Today ends the year 1890. Fifteen years ago the *Franklin* left San Diego. Fifteen years! And it is four ' months and five days only since our caravan left Adelaide! This year, which begins for us in the desert, how will it end?

"My companions would not allow the day to pass without offering me their good wishes for the new year. My dear Jane embraced me, a prey to the keenest emotion, and for a long time I held her in my arms. Zach Fren and Tom Marix came to shake hands with me. I know that I have in them two friends who would die for me. Our people all surrounded me, tendering their affectionate felicitations. I say all, to the exclusion, however, of the blacks of the escort, whose discontent is shown on every occasion. It is clear that Tom Marix only keeps them in order with great trouble.

"Len Burker spoke to me with his habitual coolness, assuring me of the success of our enterprise. He had no doubt that we should attain our object. At the same time he asked if we were doing well in making for the Fitzroy River. The Indas, as far as his knowledge goes, are nomads, who are most frequently met with in the regions neighbouring on Queensland, that is to say in the east of the continent. It is true, he added, we are going where Harry Felton left his captain, but how were we to know that the Indas had not moved off, etc. etc.

All this is said in a tone which inspires no confidence, the tone certain people adopt when, they speak without looking at you.

But it was Godfrey whose greeting most affected me, He had made a nosegay of the little wild flowers that grow among the tufts of spinifex. He offered it me with such good grace, and said such loving things to me, that the tears came into my eyes. As I embraced him, and as his kisses replied to mine, why did the thought occur to me that my little Wat would be just his age, that he would be just like him.

Jane was there, she was so affected, and became so pale in Godfrey's presence that I thought she was going to faint. But she recovered and her husband took her away; I dared not keep her.

We resumed our journey to-day at four o'clock in the afternoon, the sky being overcast. The heat is a little more bearable. The saddle-camels and pack camels, sufficiently rested from their fatigue, are going better. We even have had to check them so that the men on foot can follow them.

15th January. — For some days we have kept on at this increased speed. Two or three times the rain has fallen rather abundantly. We have not had to suffer thirst, and our reserve has been completely replenished. The most serious of all questions is this of water, and it is also the most alarming when we are travelling across these deserts. It means constant anxiety. In fact the springs appear to be few on the road we are following. Colonel Warburton noticed this on his journey which ended on the west coast of Tasman Land.

We are now living on our provisions, and on them only. It is not worth reckoning on what we can shoot, for the game has all fled from these miserable solitudes. A few flocks of pigeons are all we see, and these we cannot get near. They only rest among the tufts of spinifex after a long flight when their wings can no longer support them. Nevertheless our food is assured for many months, and on that point I am at ease. Zach Fren carefully sees that the food, the preserves, the flour, tea, coffee, etc. are distributed with method and regularity. We ourselves have to share with the rest; there are no exceptions. The blacks of the escort cannot complain that we are treated better than they are.

Here and there flit about a few sparrows dispersed over these regions, but they are not worth the trouble and fatigue of going after.

All the time there are these myriads of white ants, making our halting hours miserable; as to mosquitoes, the country is too dry for them to annoy us. We shall find them in the damp places, as Tom Marix observes. Well, we had better have their bites; and we shall not pay too dearly for the water which attracts them in thousands.

We reached Mary Spring, ninety miles from Waterloo, on the 23rd of January.

A group of slender trees rises in this place, a few eucalyptuses, which have exhausted the water in the ground and are evidently suffering.

"Their foliage hangs like tongues dry with thirst," said Godfrey.

And the comparison was very good.

I notice that this young-, ardent and "resolute boy has lost nothing of the gaiety of his age. His health is not affected as I feared it would be, for he is just at the age when a lad begins to shape into a man. And this incredible likeness which troubles me. It is the same look when his eyes are fixed on mine, the same intonations when he speaks to me. And he has a way of saying things, of expressing his thoughts, which reminds me so of my poor John.

One day I drew Len Burker's attention to this peculiarity.

"No, Dolly," he replied, "it is a pure illusion on your part. I confess I am in no way struck with this resemblance. In my opinion it only exists in your imagination. It matters little, after all, and if it is for that reason you take so much interest in this boy — "

"No, Len," I replied, "if I feel such a lively affection for Godfrey, it is that I have seen his enthusiasm in what is the only object of my life, the finding and rescuing of John. He begged me to take him with me, and, touched by his persistence, I consented. And besides, he is one of my San Diego children, one of those poor boys without father or mother who have been brought up at Wat House. Godfrey is like a brother of my little Wat."

"I know, I know, Dolly," Len Burker replied, "and to a certain extent I understand you. May Heaven grant you will not have cause to repent of an act in which your sentiment has had more share than your reason."

"I do not like to hear you talk like that, Len Burker," I replied with vivacity. "Such observations wound me. What have you to complain of about Godfrey?"

"Oh! nothing, nothing as yet. But who knows? later on, perhaps, he will abuse the affection which is a little too pronounced regarding him. A child is picked up, no one knows whence he comes or who he is, what blood runs in his veins — "

"It is the blood of brave and honest men, I will answer for it!" I exclaimed. "On board the *Brisbane* he was liked by all, by his masters and his comrades, and the captain himself told me Godfrey had never had to be spoken to. Zach Fren, who knows him well, appreciates him as much as I do. Tell me, Len Burker, why you do not like this boy?"

"I — Dolly? I do not like him or dislike him; I am quite indifferent to him, that is all. My friendship I do not give to the first comer, and I think only of John and his rescue from the natives."

If Len Burker wished to give me a lesson, I did not accept it, for he aimed badly. I do not forget my husband for this child, but I am happy in thinking that Godfrey joins his efforts to mine. I am sure that John would approve of what I have done, and what I intend to do in the future for this boy.

When I told Jane of this conversation the poor woman bowed her head and said nothing.

For the future I shall say nothing. Jane will not and cannot say Len Burker is in the wrong. I understand this reserve; it is her duty.

29th January. — We have reached the shore of a small lake, a kind of lagoon, which Tom Marix believes to be White Lake. It justifies its name of White Lake, for in place of the water, which has evaporated, a layer of salt occupies the bed. Again a remnant of that interior sea which once separated Australia into two large islands.

Zach Fren made up our stock of salt, but we should have preferred drinking water.

There are in these parts a large number of rats, smaller than the ordinary rats. We have to provide against their attacks during our halts. They are so voracious that they gnaw everything within range.

But the blacks in no way despise them as food. They caught a few dozen of them, prepared them, cooked them, and regaled themselves with the objectionable meat. We shall have to run very short of provisions before we have recourse to that food. Heaven grant we may never be reduced to that!

We are now on the borders of the desert known as the Great Sandy Desert.

During the last twenty miles the ground has been gradually changing. The tufts of spinifex are fewer and this meagre vegetation is disappearing. Is the soil so barren that it cannot support this not very exacting, vegetation? Who would not believe it if he saw the immense plain undulating with a few hillocks of red sand, and without any trace of the bed of a creek? One would suppose it never rained on these territories devoured by the sun, not even in the winter.

Amid this mournful aridity, this disquieting dryness, there is not one of us who has not been seized with the most mournful presentiments. Tom Marix shows me these desolate solitudes on the map; it is nearly a blank space crossed by the routes of Giles and Gibson. Towards the north, that of Colonel Warburton shows clearly the uncertainties of his march by the numerous turns and zigzags necessitated by his search for springs Here his men were ill, exhausted, and almost dead; there his camels were decimated, his son dying. Better not read the account of his journey if we wish to follow him — the bravest recoiled. But I have read it and I will read it again. I must not let myself be frightened. What this explorer did for the study of the unknown regions of the Australian continent, I will do to find John. The only object of my life is that, and I will accomplish it!

2d February. — For the last five days we have had to shorten our-stages. So much more time lost on the long road we are travelling. It is extremely regrettable. Our caravan, retarded by hilly ground, is incapable of following the straight line. The ground is very hilly and oblige us to ascend and descend some very steep slopes. In many places it is cut up into sand-hills round which the camels have to work, as they cannot climb them. There are also some sandy hills a hundred feet high, at intervals of six or seven hundred feet; the men on foot sink into the sand, and the advance becomes more and more laborious.

The heat is overwhelming. It is impossible to imagine the intensity with which the sun darts down its rays. They are arrows of fire which pierce you in a thousand places. Jane and I can hardly remain under the shelter of our kibitka. What must our companions endure during the morning and evening stages? Zach Fren, strong as he is, buffers much from these fatigues, but he does not complain; he has lost nothing of his good humour, this devoted friend whose existence is bound up with mine!

Jos Meritt bears up with a quiet courage, a resistance to privation, one is tempted to envy. Gin-Ghi, less patient, complains without its having any effect on his master. And when one thinks that this eccentric man is suffering all this for the sake of a hat!

"Good! Oh! very good!" he replies, when anything is said about this. "But also what a rarity of a hat!"

"Some old mountebank's rag!" said Zach Fren, shrugging his shoulders.

"Some old .rubbish you would hot even wear on your feet!" retorted Gin-Ghi.

Between eight o'clock and four o'clock it would be impossible to move a step. We camp anywhere; we put up two or three tents. The men of the escort, black and white, stretch themselves where they can in the shade of the camels. The worst of it is that the water is beginning to fail. What will become of us if we meet with only dry springs? I know Tom Marix is very uneasy, although he tries to hide his uneasiness. He is wrong, he would do better to tell me everything, I could bear everything, and I should not be afraid.

14th February. — Eleven days have passed during which we have had but two hours' rain. We could hardly replenish our kegs after the men had had enough to satisfy their thirst, and the animals had taken enough for their store. Under these circumstances we have reached Emily Spring, which is quite dry. Our camels are exhausted; Jos Meritt docs not know what to do to get his earner along. He will not strike it, however, and merely appeals to its feelings. I heard him say, —

"Look here, you poor brute, if you are in pain, at least you have no grief!"

But the poor brute did not seem to understand the distinction.

We will resume our journey more uneasy than we have ever been.

Two camels arc sick. "They are crawling along, and will not be able to last. The provisions carried by the pack camel have been shifted on to a saddle camel.

Luckily the male camel, ridden by Tom Marix, has kept its strength up to now. Without him, the others, more particularly the females, would disband, and nothing would stop them.

We have found it necessary to leave behind the two which fell sick. To leave them to die of hunger and thirst, a prey to a long agony, would have been more inhuman than to end their misery at a blow.

The caravan journeys on and turns round a sand-hill. There are two reports. Tom Marix returns to rejoin us, and the journey continues.

What is more alarming is that the health of two of our people gives us much uneasiness. They have been seized with fever, and we have dosed them well with sulphate of quinine, with which the medicine-chest is well supplied. But a burning thirst devours them. Our store of water is exhausted, and nothing indicates that we are in the proximity of a spring.

The invalids are on their backs on two camels which their companions lead by the hand. Man cannot be left behind like camels. We must look after them; it is our duty, and we will not fail in it. But this pitiless temperature is gradually devouring them.

Those of us who stand fatigue best, who can bear excessive heat without suffering, are the blacks of our escort.

But though they have less to bear, their discontent increases daily. In vain Tom Marix busies himself in tranquillizing them. The most excited keep apart when we halt, and talk together, and the signs of an approaching revolt are only too evident.

During the 21st, all, with one accord, refused to continue the journey to the north-west, giving as a reason that they were dying of thirst. The reason was only too well founded. For twelve hours there had not been a single drop-of water in our kegs. We are reduced to alcoholic drinks, the effect of which is deplorable, as they get into our heads.

I had to personally intervene among these obstinate natives. I had to make them understand that to stop under such conditions was not the way to put an end to their sufferings.

"What we want," said one of them, ""is to go back."

"Back? Whereto?"

"To Mary Spring."

"To Mary Spring! "I answered, "there is no water there, and you know it."

"If there is no water at Mary Spring," replied the black, "we may find it a little further up, near Mount Wilson, in the direction of Sturt Creek."

I looked at Tom Marix. He went to look at the special map of the Great Sandy Desert. We consulted it. In fact, north of Mary Spring there is a somewhat important watercourse which might not perhaps be entirely dry. But how could the native have known of the existence of this watercourse? I interrogated him on the subject. He hesitated at first, and at last told me Mr. Burker had spoken to him about it. It was from him that the proposition of heading for Sturt Creek had come.

I am much annoyed that Len Burker has had the imprudence — was it only imprudence? — to instigate a part ◁ f the escort to return towards the east. It will riot only lead to delay, but to a serious modification of our route, which will take us a long way from Fitzroy River.

I told him what I thought rather strongly.

"What would you have, Dolly?" he replied. "Better submit to delays and go a little way round, than to obstinately follow a road where there arc no wells."

"In that case, Mr. Burker," said Zach Fren, sharply, "you should have spoken to Mrs. Branican, and not to the blacks."

"You are carrying on with the blacks in such a way," said Tom Marix, "that I have no control over them. Are you in command of them. Mr. Burker.' or am I?"

"I think that observation is rather unseemly, Tom Marix," said Len Burker.

"Unseemly or not, it is justified by your proceedings, sir, and you would do well to think over it."

"I take orders from nobody here but from Mrs. Branican — "

"Be it so, Len Burker," I replied; "but for the future, if you have any observations to make, I' beg you will make them to me and not to others."

"Mrs. Branican," said Godfrey, "shall I go on in advance of the caravan in search of a well? I am sure to find one."

"A well without water!" muttered Len Burker, shrugging his shoulders.

I can easily imagine what Jane must have suffered as she heard this discussion. Her husband's conduct, which was so prejudicial to the good feeling which ought to exist among our people might be the cause of serious difficulty. I had to support Tom Marix in obtaining the consent of the blacks not to persevere in their intention of returning to the rear. We succeeded after considerable difficulty. But they declared that if we did not find water in twenty- four hours, they would return to Mary Spring in order to reach Sturt Creek.

22nd February — What terrible sufferings we have had during the two days which followed. The state of our two sick companions has become worse. Three camels fell, never to rise again, their heads stretched out on the ground, their bodies swollen, and incapable of making any movement. We had to shoot them. Two of these were saddle animals and one was a pack camel. Now four of the whites of the escort have to travel on foot.

And there is not a human creature in this Great Sandy Desert, not an Australian in these regions of Tasman Land to give us any information as to the position of the wells. Evidently our caravan has diverged from Colonel Warburton's route, for the colonel never had such long stages without being able to replenish his store of water. Often, it is true, the springs were half-dry and contained only a muddy, warm and barely drinkable liquid. But we must be content.

To-day, at last, at the end of our first stage, we were able to slake our thirst. It was Godfrey who discovered a spring near Emily Spring.

In the morning of the 23rd the brave boy went off some miles in advance, and two hours afterwards we saw him returning in all haste.

"A well! a well!" he shouted, as far off as we could hear him.

At this cry our little world received new life. The camels hurried on. It seemed as though our Godfrey had said to them, —

"Water! water!"

An hour afterwards the caravan halted under a group of trees with dried foliage which shaded the well. Luckily they were gum trees and not eucalyptuses, which would have dried it up to the last drop.

But such wells a very few men would empty in an instant. The water is not abundant and soon loses itself in the sands. The wells have not been made by the hands of man, they are merely natural cavities formed during the rainy season. Rarely are they more than five or six feet deep — just enough for the water, shaded from the solar rays, to escape evaporation and remain during the long heats of summer.

Sometimes these wells are without the group of trees to distinguish them, and then it is only too easy to pass near them without noticing them. A careful look-out has consequently to be kept, as Colonel Warburton very justly observes. This we remembered.

This time Godfrey had made a fortunate find. The well, at which we encamped at eleven o'clock in the morning, contained more water than was required for our camels and our reserve. The water was limpid, for it was filtered through the sand, and it had retained its freshness owing to the cavity being at the foot of a sand-hill and shaded from the direct rays of the sun.

It was with delight that we refreshed ourselves, and we had to warn our companions to drink with moderation, lest they should make themselves ill.

One cannot imagine the beneficent effect of water after a long torture from thirst. The result is immediate, the most exhausted are revived, strength returns instantly, and courage with the strength. It is more than to live again, it is to be born again.

Next day, at four o'clock in the morning, we resumed our journey, and travelled north-west so as to reach Joanna Spring, about one hundred and ninety miles from Mary Spring.

These few notes extracted from Mrs. Branican's journal are enough to show that her energy had not abandoned her for an instant. We must now resume the account of this journey, for which the future had in reserve such eventualities impossible to foresee, and so serious in their consequences.

CHAPTER XI - INDICATIONS AND INCIDENTS

As we have seen from the last lines of Mrs. Branican's journal, courage and confidence had returned to the men of the caravan. Never had they been short of food, and the provisions would last for many months. Water alone had been wanting for a few stages; but the well discovered by Godfrey had yielded more than they wanted, and they started from it in good spirits.

It is true they always had to face an overwhelming heat, to breathe the fiery air of the surface of these interminable plains, without trees and without shade. And the travellers who can bear this excessive temperature are not very numerous, particularly if they are not natives of Australia. Where the native resists, the foreigner succumbs. The man has to be made to suit this murderous climate.

The hills of red sand, with their long undulations and symmetrical ripples, continued. The ground was so hot that the whites could not walk on it with naked feet. The blacks were accustomed to it, and should have had no reason to complain of it; but they did complain, and their ill-will showed itself every day more clearly. If Tom Marix had not had to keep the escort at its full strength, in ease he had to defend the caravan against some wandering tribe, he would have "assuredly asked Mrs. Branican to dismiss the blacks from her service.

Every day he saw the difficulties inherent to such an expedition increasing, and when he said to himself that these fatigues were undergone and these dangers faced for nothing, it was only natural that he could not completely hide his thoughts. Zach Fren, however, was the only one to discover this.

"Truly, Tom," said he one day, "I should not have thought you were the man to be discouraged."

"Me discouraged! You are mistaken, Zach, at least in the sense that I shall fail in the courage that will make me fulfil my undertaking. It is not crossing the desert I am afraid of, but, after we have crossed it, to have to cross it back again without having succeeded."

"Do you think, Tom, that Captain John has died since Harry Felton left him?"

"I know nothing about it, Zach, and you know no more."

' I know it as well as I know that a ship goes to starboard when you put her helm to port."

"There, Zach, you talk like Mrs. Branican and Godfrey. You take your hopes for certainties. I hope you are right. But if Captain John is alive, he is in the power of the Indas, and where are the Indas?"

"They are where they are, Tom, and that is where the caravan will go if we box the compass for the next six months. If we cannot find them on one tack, we will try them on the other; but we will get them at last."

"If we were at sea, yes; but then we should know the port to which we were bound. But in these regions who knows where they will go?"

"We shall not know by despairing."

"I am not despairing, Zach."

"Perhaps not, Tom; but, worse than that, you will soon lead people to suppose so. The man who does not hide his anxiety makes a bad captain and discourages his crew. Take care of your face, Tom, not for Mrs. Branican's sake, for nothing can shake her, but for the whites of our escort. If they are going to make common cause with the blacks —"

"I will answer for them as I answer for myself — "

"And I will answer for you, Tom! But don't let us talk of hauling down the flag while the masts are standing."

"Who is going to talk of that, unless it is Len Burker?"

"Oh, ah, Tom! If I had been captain he would have been down in the hold long ago with a shot at each foot J But as it is, look after him; I have got my eye upon him."

Zach Fren was right in keeping an eye on Len Burker. If the expedition broke up, he would be the cause of it. He it was who excited to disorder the blacks of the escort on whom Tom Marix had thought he could trust. This was one of the things which might imperil the success of the campaign. But, even if it had not existed, Tom Marix retained hardly the trace of an illusion as to the possibility, of meeting with the Indas and rescuing Captain John.

But if the caravan did not go quite at a venture in making for the Fitzroy River, there was one circumstance which might compel the Indas to leave Tasman Land, and that was the chance of war. It is seldom that there is peace between the tribes, which number from two hundred and fifty to three hundred souls. There are inveterate hatreds, blood rivalries, and these are kept alive with all the more passion owing to war among cannibals being a sort of hunting enterprise. The enemy is not only the enemy, he is edible game, and the victor eats the vanquished. Hence, battles, pursuits, retreats, which may take the natives long distances. It was, therefore, of importance to know if the Indas had left their territories, and the only way to do this was to catch an Australian coming from the north-west.

This was the great object of Tom Marix, assiduously assisted by Godfrey, who, in spite of the recommendations and even the injunctions of Mrs. Branican, was often out scouting for miles. When he was not looking for some well he was looking for some blacks, but as yet without success. The country was deserted, and, in fact, what human being, however degraded he might be, would be able to exist without the mere necessities of existence; To venture beyond the telegraph line was to expose himself to the terrible experiences we have described.

At last, on the 9th of March, at half-past nine in the morning, there was heard a call in the distance — a call consisting of these two syllables, Coo-cch!

"There are blacks somewhere about," said Tom Marix.

"Blacks!" said Dolly.

"Yes, madam, that is the way they call to each other."

"Let us get up with them," said Zach Fren.

The caravan advanced a hundred yards, and Godfrey signalled two blacks among the sand-hills. To get hold of them was not easy, for the Australians run away from the whites as soon as they see them. These tried to hide themselves among some tufts of spinifex. But the escort managed to surround them, and they were brought before Mrs. Branican.

The one was about fifty; the other was his son, aged twenty. Both were on their way to Lake Woods station on the telegraph line. A few presents of cloth and some cakes of tobacco soon pacified them, and they were quite ready to answer the questions put to them by Tom Marix, their replies being at once translated for the benefit of Mrs. Branican, Godfrey, Zach Fren, and their companions.

'The Australians were at first asked where their were going, which was not of much interest But Tom Marix asked them where they came from, and this deserved serious attention.

"We come from there — far — very far," answered the father, pointing to the north-west.

"From the coast?"

"No. From the interior."

"From Tasman Land?"

"Yes. From Fitzroy River."

It was to this river, as we know, that the caravan was bound.

310

"Of what tribe are you?" asked Tom Marix.

"Of the tribe of the Goursis."

"Is that a wandering tribe?"

The native did not understand what that meant.

"Does your tribe go from camp to camp," asked Tom, "or does it live in a village?"

"It lives in the village of Goursi," said the son, who seemed fairly intelligent.

"Is this village near the Fitzroy?"

"Yes. Ten long days "from where it enters the sea."

This was in King's Sound into which the Fitzroy flows, and it was there that the voyage of the *Dolly Hope* had ended in 1883. The ten days showed that the village of Goursi was about a hundred miles from the coast.

This was at once pointed out by Godfrey on the map of Western Australia — a map which showed the course of the Fitzroy for two hundred miles from its source in the interior of Tasman Land.

"Do you know the tribe of the Indas?" asked Tom Marix.

The looks of father and son kindled at the name.

"Evidently these tribes are enemies; they are at war with each other," said Tom Marix to Mrs. Branican.

"That is very likely," said Dolly, "and perhaps these Goursis can tell us where the Indas are now. Ask them, Tom Marix and get a reply as precise as possible. On that reply the success of our efforts may depend."

Tom Marix put the question, and the elder of the blacks replied without hesitation that the tribe of the Indas was then on the upper course of the Fitzroy.

"How far are they from the village of Goursi?" asked Tom Marix.

"Twenty days towards the rising sun," said the younger.

This distance, on reference to the map, put the camp of the Indas about two hundred and eighty miles from the place then reached by the caravan. And the information agreed with that previously given by Harry Felton.

"Your tribe is often at war with the Indas?" asked Tom Marix.

"Always!," replied the son.

And his emphasis and gesture indicated the strength of their cannibal hatreds.

"And we will pursue them," added the father, "and they will be beaten when the white chief is no longer there to give them his advice."

We can imagine what were the feelings of Mrs. Branican and her companions when Tom Marix translated this reply. This white chief, for so many years a prisoner of the Indas — who could doubt that it was Captain John?

And at Dolly's suggestion Tom Marix questioned the two natives closely. They could give but very little precise information regarding this white chief. But they were able to say that three months ago, during the last terrible fight between the Goursis and the Indas, he was in the power of the latter.

"And without him," said the young Australian, "the Indas would be only women."

That this was an exaggeration on the part of the natives it mattered little. All that was wanted was known. John Branican and the Indas were less than three hundred miles away to the north-west. They would be met with on the banks of the Fitzroy.

As the camp was about to break up Jos Meritt detained for a moment the two men whom Mrs. Branican was about to send away with "more presents. And then the Englishman begged Tom Marix to ask them a

312

question relative to the hat of ceremony worn by the chief of the tribe of the Goursis and the chief of the tribe of the Indas.

In truth, as he awaited their reply, Jos Meritt was no less excited than Dolly had been during the examination of the natives.

He had reason to be satisfied, had the worthy collector, and the "Good! Oh, very good!" flashed from his lips when he learnt that hats of foreign manufacture were not uncommon among the peoples of the North-West. These hats were habitually worn by the principal Australian chiefs when they took part in grand ceremonies.

"You understand, Mrs. Branican," said Jos Meritt, "that to find Captain John is all very well, but to set hands on the historic treasure I have been hunting for through the five quarters of the globe is still better — "

"Evidently!" replied Mrs. Branican.

"You heard, Gin-Ghi?" added Jos Meritt, turning to his servant.

"I heard," said the Chinaman, "and when we have found this hat — "

"We will return to England, we will return to Liverpool, and then, Gin-Ghi, with a lovely black hat on your head, and a red silk robe, draped with a macoual of yellow silk, you will have nothing else to do than to show my collection. Are you satisfied?"

"As the haitang flower which opens in the breeze when the rabbit of Jade descends towards the west," replied Gin-Ghi, poetically.

But at the same time he shook his head as if as little convinced of his future happiness as if his master had told him he would become a Mandarin of Seven Buttons.

Len Burker had been present at the conversation between Tom Marix and the two natives, whose language he understood; but he had taken no part in it. Not a question relative to Captain John had come from him. He listened attentively, noting in his memory the information regarding the present position of the Indas. He saw on the map the spot the tribe probably occupied on the upper course of the Fitzroy river; he calculated the distance the caravan would have to travel to get there, and the time it would take.

It would be a matter of some weeks if no obstacle arose, if the means of locomotion did not fail, if the fatigues of the journey and the sufferings due to the heat of the climate were happily surmounted. And so Len Burker, feeling that the preciousness of this information would give courage to all, was in a terrible rage. What! The deliverance of Captain John was to be accomplished, and, thanks to the ransom she was bringing, Dolly would rescue him from the Indas?

While Len Burker was reflecting on this chain of events, Jane saw his brow become clouded, his eyes grow bloodshot, and his whole physiognomy betray the detestable thoughts which agitated him. She was terrified, she had a presentiment of an approaching catastrophe, and at a moment when her husband's eyes were fixed on hers she felt herself fainting.

The unhappy woman had divined what was passing in the mind of this man, who was capable of every crime to make sure of the fortune of Mrs. Branican.

Len Burker said to himself that, if John and Dolly met, his whole future was ruined. It would mean, sooner or later, the discovery of Godfrey's relationship to them. The secret would end by escaping from his wife, unless he made it impossible for her to speak; but it was necessary Jane should be alive for the fortune to reach her after Mrs. Branican's death.

It was thus necessary to separate Jane and Dolly, and, with the object of making away with John Branican, reach the Indas before the caravan.

With an unscrupulous and resolute man like Len Burker this plan was quite possible, and besides, circumstances soon helped him.

That day, at four o'clock in the afternoon, Tom Marix gave the signal of departure, and the expedition resumed its march in the usual order. The past fatigues were forgotten. Dolly had communicated to her companions the energy which animated her. They were nearing their object. Success appeared beyond doubt. The blacks of the escort seemed to obey willingly, and probably Tom Marix would have been able to reckon on their help to the end if Len Burker had not been there to incite the spirit of treason and revolt.

The caravan, at a good rate of advance, had almost resumed the route of Colonel Warburton The heat increased and the nights were stifling. On. this plain, without a single clump of trees, no shade could be found but in the shelter of the sand-hills, and this shade was very narrow owing to the almost verticality of the solar rays.

And yet in this lower latitude than the tropical line, that is to say, well within the torrid zone, it was not so much the excesses of the Australian climate the men had to suffer most from, but there was the more serious question of water, which was daily present. Wells had to besought for at great distances, and that interfered with the route, which was lengthened by a thousand deviations. Oftenest it was Godfrey, always ready — sometimes it was Tom Marix, always indefatigable — who took this duty. Mrs. Branican never saw them ride off without a sinking at the heart. But nothing could be hoped for from the storms which are extremely rare at this time of the year. On the sky, which was clear from one horizon to the other, there was not the sign of a cloud. Water could only come from the ground.

When Tom Marix and Godfrey had discovered a well if. was towards it that the caravan went. The stage was resumed, the animals, were urged on by this goad of thirst; and what was it that they oftenest found? A muddy liquid at the bottom of a cavity swarming with rats. If the blacks and the whites of the escort did not hesitate to drink, Dolly, Jane, Godfrey, Zach Fren, and Len Burker had the prudence to wait until Tom Marix had cleared out the well, thrown away the dirt on the top, and dug in the sands for less impure water. Then they drank; and then the kegs were filled which were to yield enough to last till the next well was reached.

So the journey went on for eight days, from the 10th to the 17th of March, without any incident, but with an increase of fatigue which could not last much longer. The state of the two sick men did not improve, and a fatal issue was feared. With five camels short, Tom Marix was embarrassed by his transport difficulties.

He began to be very uneasy, and Mrs. Branican was quite as much so, although she let nothing appear. The first on the march, the last to halt, she afforded an example of the most extraordinary courage joined to a confidence nothing could shake.

And what sacrifices would she not have made to avoid these incessant delays, to shorten this interminable journey!

One day she asked Tom Marix why he did not make direct for the upper course of the Fitzroy, where the information given by the blacks placed the last encampment of the Indas.

"I thought of that," said Tom Marix, "but it is always this question of water which stops me and troubles me, Mrs. Branican. In going towards Joanna Spring we are sure of meeting a certain number of the wells reported by Colonel Warburton."

"And are there not any in the regions to the north?"

"It is possible, but I am not certain; and besides, we must admit the possibility that these wells may now be dry, while, by continuing to the west, we are sure of reaching Oakover River, where Colonel Warburton halted. This river is a running stream, and we shall be sure of renewing our supplies at it before reaching the valley of the Fitzroy."

"Quite so, Tom Marix," said Mrs. Branican, "and as we can do no better, let us make for Joanna Spring."

This was done, and the fatigues of this part of the journey exceeded anything the caravan had had to bear up to then. Although the summer season was still in its third month, the temperature maintained an intolerable average of forty degrees centigrade in the shade, and by this the shade of the night must be understood. In fact, a cloud would have been sought for in vain in the higher zones of the sky, just as a tree would have been vainly sought for on the surface of this plain. The advance was through an atmosphere that suffocated; the wells did not contain enough water for the needs of the expedition; not a dozen miles were traversed at a stage; the men on foot crawled along; the attention that Dolly, assisted by Jane and the woman Harriett, although weak themselves, gave to the sick men, did them good. What ought to be done was to stop, encamp in some village, take a long rest, wait till the. temperature became more clement. And nothing of that sort was possible.

In the afternoon of the 17th of March two more pack camels were lost, one of them laden with the articles of barter intended for the Indas. Tom Marix had to transfer these loads to saddle camels, and this necessitated dismounting two more whites of the escort. These brave fellows did not complain, and accepted without a word this increase of fatigue. How different to the blacks, who complained unceasingly and caused Tom Marix the most serious uneasiness! Was it not to be feared that some day these blacks would be tempted to abandon the caravan, probably after pillaging it?

At last, in the evening of the 19th of March, near a well the water of which was six feet under the sand, the caravan stopped about five miles from Joanna Spring. It had been impossible to continue the stage beyond this.

The air was of extraordinary heaviness; it burnt the lungs as if it came from a furnace. The sky was very clear and of a hard blue, such as it is in certain Mediterranean regions when the mistral is about to burst, and its aspect was strange and threatening.

Tom Marix regarded this state of the atmosphere with an anxiety that did not escape Zach Fren.

317

"You scent something," said the boatswain, "and something you don't like?"

"Yes, Zach," replied Tom Marix, "I expect a simoom like those which ravage the deserts of Africa."

"Well, wind will bring wet, I suppose?" said Zach Fren.

"Not at all, Zach; it will bring a dryness worse than now, and in the centre of Australia no one knows of what a wind like that is capable."

This observation, coming from so experienced a man, was enough to give great anxiety to Mrs. Branican and her companions.

Precautions were then taken in view of the threatening tempest. It was nine o'clock in the evening. The tent had not been pitched, being useless in these burning night amid the sand-hills of the plain. After quenching their thirst from the kegs, the people took their share of provisions which Tom Marix had just distributed. Scarcely any thought of satisfying their hunger; what they wanted was fresh air, and the stomach suffered less the organs of respiration. A few hours sleep would have done them more good than many mouthfuls of food; was it possible to sleep amid an atmosphere so stifled that it seemed to be rarefied?

Up to midnight nothing unusual took place. Tom Marix, Zach Fren, and Godfrey took it in turns to mount guard. Sometimes one, sometimes the other, got up to look at the horizon towards the north. This horizon was of a clearness, and even of a purity, that boded ill. The moon, setting at the same time as the sun, had disappeared behind the hills. Hundreds of stars shone around Southern Cross which glitters at the Antarctic pole of world.

About three hours after midnight this illumination the firmament was blotted out. A sudden darkness enveloped the plain from one horizon to the other.

"Look out! look out!" shouted Tom Marix.

"What is the matter?" asked Mrs. Branican getting up suddenly.

Near her, Jane and the woman Harriett, Godfrey,; Zach Fren tried to look through the darkness, camels stretched on the ground raised their heads and uttered hoarse cries of terror.

"But what is it?" asked Mrs. Branican.

"The simoom!" replied Tom Marix.

And those were the last words that were heard. Space was filled with such a tumult that the ear could no more perceive a sound than the eyes could see a ray of light amid the thick darkness.

It was indeed the simoom, as Tom Marix had said, one of those sudden storms which devastate the Australian deserts. An enormous cloud had risen in the south and swooped down on to the plain, a cloud formed not only of sand, but of cinders whirled up from the ground calcined by heat.

Around the encampment, the sand-hills were in motion like the surge of the sea, and broke, not in liquid spray, but in impalpable dust which blinded, deafened and stifled. It seemed as though the plain would be levelled by the storm which had broken on the surface. If the tents had been up, not a rag of them would have been left.

Everyone felt the irresistible torrent of air and sand which passed them like a hail of musketry. Godfrey held on to Dolly by both hands, not wishing to be separated from her if this formidable attack swept the caravan towards the north.

And this was what in- fact happened, and no resistance was possible.

During this hour's torment — an hour which sufficed to change the aspect of the country, by displacing the hills and changing the general level of the soil — Mrs. Branican and her companions, including the two invalids of the escort, were driven along for a space of four or five miles, rising only to fall again, and sometimes spun round like straws in a whirlwind. They could neither see nor hear, and risked being lost for

319

ever. And in this way they reached the neighbourhood of Joanna Spring, near the banks of Oakover Creek, at the moment when, clearing from the last mists, the day had begun to break under the rays of the rising sun.

All were present to the roll-call? All?

No.

Mrs. Branican, the woman Harriett, Godfrey, Jos Meritt, Gin-Ghi, Zach Fren, Tom Marix, the whites remaining at their post were there, and with them four saddle camels; but the blacks had disappeared — disappeared with the twenty other camels, those that carried the provisions and those that carried Captain John's ransom.

And when Dolly called Jane, Jane did not answer.

Len and Jane Burker were not there.

CHAPTER XII - THE LAST EFFORTS

THIS disappearance of the blacks, with the saddle cars and the pack camels, made the situation nearly desperate for Mrs. Branican and those who remained faithful to her.

"Treason "was the word pronounced first by Zach Fren; the word repeated by Godfrey. Treason was only evident under the circumstances. Such was the opinion of Tom Marix, who did not forget the malign influence exercised by Len Burker over the natives of the escort. Dolly would still have doubted. She could not believe in so much duplicity, in so much infamy.

"Len Burker could not have been swept away as it were?"

"Swept away with the blacks,'' said Zach Fren, "at same time as the camels with our provisions!"

"And my poor Jane!" murmured Dolly, "separated from me without my noticing it."

"Len Burker would not even let her remain with you," said Zach Fren, "the scoundrel!"

"Scoundrel! Good! oh! very good!" said Jos. "If all that is not treachery I will give up the search — the historic hat which — " and he turned to Gin-Ghi. "What do you think, Gin-Ghi?"

"Ai ya, Master Jos! I think I would rather a thousand and ten thousand times never have set foot in so comfortless a country!"

"Perhaps so!" replied Jos Meritt.

Treachery was so obvious, in short, that Mrs. Branican had to give in.

"But why have deceived me?" she asked; "what have I done to Len Burker? Did I not forget the past? Did I not receive them like my relations, him and his unhappy wife? And he abandons us, he leaves us without resources, he has stolen from me the price of John's freedom! But why?"

No one knew Len Burker's secret, and no one could answer Mrs. Branican. Jane alone could have revealed what she knew of her husband's abominable plans, and Jane was not there.

It was only too true, however, that Len Burker had just put in execution a plan he had long prepared, a plan which seemed to have every chance of success. Under promise of being well paid, the blacks of the escort had easily listened to him. At the height of the storm, while two of the natives had dragged off Jane without its being possible to hear her screams, the others had pushed northwards with the camels around the encampment.

No one had seen them amid the profound obscurity, deepened by the whirlwinds of dust, and before the day Len Burker and his accomplices were several miles to the east of Joanna Spring.

Jane being separated from Dolly, her husband had no further .fear that, tortured by remorse, she would betray the secret of Godfrey's birth. Besides, deprived of provisions and the means of transport, there was reason to believe that Mrs. Branican and her companions would perish in the solitudes of the Great Sandy Desert.

In fact, at Joanna Spring the caravan was still three hundred miles from the Fitzroy. In the course of this long journey how could Tom Marix provide for the wants of the expedition reduced as it now was?

Oakover Creek is one of the chief affluents of Grey River, which flows into the Indian Ocean by one of the estuaries in De Wilt Land.

On the banks of this river, which the excessive heat never dries up, Tom Marix would find the same shade, the same country which Colonel Warburton eulogizes with such a burst of joy.

There verdure and running waters take the place of t interminable plains of sand-hills and spinifex! But Colonel Warburton, arrived at this point, was almost sure of attaining his object, for he had only to descend to the creek to the settlement of Rockborne on the coast, it was not so with Mrs. Branican. The situation would, on the contrary, become worse on traversing the arid region which separate the Oakover from the Fitzroy.

The caravan now only consisted of twenty-two persons out of the forty-three which left Alice Spring — Dolly and the native woman Harriett, Zach Fren, Tom Mari Godfrey, Jos Meritt, Gin-Ghi, and with them; the fifteen whites of the escort, of whom two were seriously ill. There were only four camels, the others having been carried off by Len Burker, including the male which served as guide, and the one that carried the kibitka. The brute whose good qualities Jos Meritt appreciated so much had also disappeared, and this obliged the Englishman to travel on foot like his servant. In the matter of provisions there remained a very few tins of preserves found in a box, which one of the camels had let fall. There was no flour, nor coffee, nor tea, nor sugar, nor salt; no alcoholic drink no medicines; and how could Dolly attend to them who were suffering from the fever? It was absolute destitution in a country in which no supplies could be had.

At once Mrs. Branican called the men together. The valiant woman had lost nothing of her energy, which was really superhuman, and by her encouraging words managed to raise the spirits of her companions. What she pointed out to them was their nearness to the object of the expedition.

The journey was resumed and under such painful conditions that the most confident of the men could not hope it would end well. Of the four camels that remained, two had been reserved for the sick, whom they could not abandon at Joanna Spring, one of those uninhabited stations of which Colonel Warburton found so many in his journey. But would these poor fellows be strong enough to bear being taken to the Fitzroy, whence it might be possible to send them down to some settlement on the coast? This was doubtful, and Mrs. Branican's heart almost broke at the idea that two more victims would be added to those already due to the loss of the *Franklin*. But Dolly did not give up her plans. No; she would not even delay her search. Nothing would stop her in the accomplishment of her duty, even if she alone remained.

Leaving the right bank of Oakover Creek, the bed of which was crossed at a ford about a mile above Joanna Spring, the caravan went north-north-east. In taking this direction Tom Marix hoped to strike the Fitzroy at the nearest bend it makes before running into King's Sound.
—

The heat was more bearable. It required the most urgent persuasion, almost the command, on the part of Tom Marix and Zach Fren, before Dolly would ride one of the camels. Godfrey and Zach Fren walked along at a good pace; so did Jos Meritt, whose long (legs were as' rigid as a pair of stilts, and when Dolly offered him her mount he declined, saying, —

"Good! Oh! very good! An Englishman is an Englishman, madam, but a Chinaman is a Chinaman, and I do not see why you should not make the same offer to Gin-Ghi — only I forbid him to accept it."

And so Gin-Ghi went on foot, not without grumbling, thinking of the distant delights of Sou-Teheow, the city of the flower-boats, the town adored by the Celestials.

The fourth camel was used by Tom Marix or Godfrey when they went ahead reconnoitring. The water taken from Oakover Creek would soon be consumed, and then the well question would again become serious.

Leaving the banks of the creek, the journey continued towards the north over a gently undulating plain furrows by sand-hills, extending to the extreme limits of the horizon. The tufts of spinifex were in closer clumps, and different shrubs, made yellow by autumn, gave the region a monotonous aspect. An opportunity might occur of shooting some game. Tom Marix, Godfrey, and Zack Fren, who never laid aside their weapons, had fortunately kept their guns and revolvers, and would know how to use them. It is true there was very little ammunition and it would have to be used with great care.

The advance continued for some hours; a morning stage and an afternoon stage. The bed of the crops which furrowed this territory were only strewn with calcined pebbles among the vegetation discoloured by drought. The sand showed not the least trace of humidity. It was thus necessary to find a well, and to find one within twenty-four hours, as Tom Marix had no more water at his disposal.

And so Godfrey went off right and left of the route in search of one.

"My child," said Mrs. Branican, "be careful! Do not run into danger."

"Run into danger!" said Godfrey, "when it concerns you and Captain John!"

Owing to his devotion, and owing also to a certain instinct which guided him, a few wells were discovered when occasionally exploring several miles from the track.

Thus if sufferings from thirst were not quite spared, then at least they were not excessive in this part of Tasman Land between Oakover Creek and Fitzroy River. What added to their fatigues were the insufficient means of transport, and the meagre rations now reduced to a few preserves, the want of tea and coffee, the want of tobacco so painful to the men of the escort, the impossibility of adding a few drops of alcohol to the brackish water. After two hours on the road the strongest were attacked by lassitude, exhaustion, and misery.

And then the camels found scarcely anything to drink among the brushwood which yielded no edible twig or leaf. There were none of those dwarf acacias, the gum of which is nutritious and sought for by the natives during these periods of drought. Nothing but the thorns of the slender mimosas and the tufts of spinifex. The camels, with their heads thrust forward, their bodies limp, dragged their feet along, and fell on their knees, and it was only by great efforts they could be kept on their legs.

On the 25th, in the afternoon, Tom Marix, Godfrey, and Zach Fren managed to obtain a little fresh food; some migrating pigeons flew by in flocks. Very wild and very quick in escaping from among the mimosa clumps, they were not easy of approach. But a few were shot. They could not but be excellent, and they were so in reality, and the famished travellers appreciated them as if they were the most savoury game. They were grilled in front of a fire of dry roots, and for a few hours Tom Marix was able to save the preserves.

But what was food for the man was not food for the camels. And in the morning of the 26th, the one that carried the sick, men fell heavily to the ground and had to be abandoned, as nothing could get him to resume the journey.

To Tom Marix fell the task of finishing him by a bullet in the head. Then, not wishing to lose the flesh, which represented food for some days, although the animal was very much emaciated by privation, he set to work to cut him up in Australian fashion. Tom Marix was not unaware that every part of the camel could be used as food. With the bones and some of the skin which they boiled in the only pot they had left, they obtained a soup which was well received by the famished stomachs; the brains, the tongue, the cheeks, properly cooked, afforded more substantial nourishment. Even the flesh cut into thin strips and quickly dried in the sun was kept, as were also the feet which are the best part of the animal. It was a pity there was no salt, for the salted flesh would have kept better.

The journey was continued under these conditions at the rate of a few miles a day. Unfortunately the sick men grew no better, more owing to the want of remedies than the want of attention. All would not reach the spot to which every effort of Mrs. Branican was directed, to this Fitzroy River where the misery would in a certain degree be relieved.

And in fact, on the 26th of March and the following day the two men succumbed to their prolonged exhaustion. They were natives of Adelaide, one being only twenty-five years of age, the other being fifteen years older, and death had struck them both on this journey through the Australian desert.

Poor fellows! They were the first that perished at this work, and their companions were very painfully affected. Was not the same fate awaiting all, since Len Burker's treachery, abandoned amid these regions, where even the animals could not find means of subsistence?

And what could Zach Fren reply when Tom Marix said to him, —

"Two men dead to save one, without reckoning those who are still to go!"

Mrs. Branican gave free vent to her grief, in which everyone shared. She prayed for these two victims, and their grave was marked by a little cross which the heat of the climate would soon reduce to dust.

The caravan resumed its journey.

The three camels that remained would mount the most tired of the men in turn, so as not to delay their companions, and Mrs. Branican refused to reserve one of the animals for her own use. During the halts the camels were used in searching for wells, sometimes by Godfrey, sometimes by Tom Marix, for not a solitary native was met with from whom information could be obtained. This appeared to indicate that the tribes had moved into the north-east of Tasman Land. In that case the Indas would have to be followed down the valley of the Fitzroy, a very serious matter, inasmuch as it would add several hundred miles to the length of the journey.

In the beginning of April Tom Marix noticed that the provisions were nearly exhausted. It consequently became necessary to sacrifice one of the three camels. A few days' food being assured, they would doubtless be able to reach Fitzroy River, from which the caravan could not be more than fifteen stages away.

The sacrifice being indispensable, they had to resign themselves to it. The animal least fit for service was chosen. It was killed, cut up, and reduced to strips which, dried in the sun, possessed fairly nutritive properties after being cooked for some time. The other parts of the animal, including the heart and the liver, were carefully put by.

Meanwhile Godfrey managed to kill several brace of pigeons — a poor addition, it is true, to the food of twenty- people. Tom Marix also noticed that clumps of acacia began to reappear on the plain, and it was possible to use the seeds as food if they were first roasted on the fire.

Yes! It was time they were at the Fitzroy River, to find there the supplies they had vainly demanded from this accursed country. A delay of a few days, and the majority of the expedition would not have strength to reach it.

On the 5th of April there remained none of the provisions, and none of the camel meat. Mrs. Branican and her companions were reduced to a few acacia seeds.

In fact Tom Marix hesitated to sacrifice the two last camels. In consideration of the distance he had still to traverse he could not make up his mind to kill them. But he would have to do so that very evening, for nobody had had anything to eat for fifteen hours. . But just as they stopped one of the men ran up shouting, —

"Tom Marix! Tom Marix! the two camels have just fallen."

"Try to get them up."

"It is impossible."

"Then we must kill them at once."

"Kill them?" answered the man. "But they are dying if they are not already dead."

"Dead!" exclaimed Tom Marix. And he could not restrain a gesture of despair, for the flesh of these animals is intractable unless they are killed.

Followed by Mrs. Branican, Zach Fren, Godfrey Jos Meritt, Tom Marix went to the spot where the animals had just fallen.

There, stretched on the ground, they were shaking convulsively, foaming at the mouth, their limbs contracting, their stomachs panting. They were about to die, and not of a natural death.

"What has happened to them?" asked Dolly. "This not fatigue: that is not exhaustion."

"No," replied Tom Marix, "I fear it is the effect of some noxious plant."

"Good! Oh! very good! I know what it is," Jos Meritt; "I have seen it in the eastern colonies... Queensland. These camels have been poisoned."

"Poisoned?" repeated Dolly.

"Yes," said Tom Marix, "poisoned."

"Well," continued Jos Meritt, "since we have no more supplies, we must follow the example of the camels, unless we die of hunger. What would you have? The country has its usages, and the best thing is to conform to them."

The gentleman said these words in such a tone of irony that with his eyes enlarged by hunger, and his lips thinner than ever, he was quite alarming to look at.

Thus the two camels were dying of poison, and that poison — for Jos Meritt was right — was due to a spray of poisonous nettles, somewhat rare on the plains of the north-west; this is the Moroides laporlea, producing a scent like raspberry, with the leaves bristling with sharp edges. Even their contact causes intense and lasting pain; fruit is a deadly poison, if not treated with the juice of Colocaria macrorhisa, another plant generally grown in the same localities as the Moroides.

The instinct which prevents animals from touching hurtful substances had been this time overcome, and the two animals had not been able to resist feeding on these nettles, and were dying in horribie suffering.

How the two following days passed neither Mrs. Branican nor any of her companions can remember. They had to abandon the two dead animals, for an hour afterwards they were in a state of complete decomposition, so rapid is the effect of the vegetable poison. Then the caravan, crawling along towards the Fitzroy, tried to make out the country that surrounds the valley. Would they all reach it? No, and some were asking to be killed on the spot, so as to be spared the most frightful agony.

Mrs. Branican went from one to the other. She tried to cheer them up. She begged them to make a last effort. The end was not far off. A few more marches. Beyond was safety. But what could she get from these unfortunates?

On the 8th of April, in the evening, no one had strength enough to pitch the camp. The unfortunates crept to the foot of the spinifex to chew the dusty leaves. They could not speak — they could not go beyond. They had fallen at this last halt.

Mrs. Branican still refused to give way. Kneeling near her, Godfrey fixed his eyes on hers. He called her "mother I mother!" like a child begging of her who bore him not to let him die.

And Dolly standing amid her companions swept the horizon with a look, and shouted, "John! John!"

As if it was from Captain John that the last help could come.

CHAPTER XIII - AMONG THE INDAS

The tribe of the Indas, composed of several hundreds of natives, men, women and children, at this time occupied the banks of the Fitzroy River, about one hundred and forty miles from its mouth. These natives had returned from the regions of Tasman Land which are watered by the upper course of the river. For some days the chances of their wandering life had brought them within five-and- twenty miles of that part of the Great Sandy Desert, where the caravan had reached its last halt, after a chain of misery exceeding the power of man to bear.

It was among these Indas that Captain John and his mate, Harry Felton, had lived for nine years. With the aid of the events which are to follow, we are able to narrate their history during this long period, and complete the story told by Harry Felton on his death-bed.

Between the years 1875 and 1881 — it will not have been forgotten — the crew of the *Franklin* had taken refuge on an island in the Indian Ocean, Browse Island, situated about two hundred and fifty miles from York Sound, the nearest point on the coast which rounds off the Australian Continent on the north-west. Two of the sailors had been lost during the storm, and the shipwrecked men, to the number of twelve, had lived for six years on this island, without any means of leaving it, when a boat drifted on to the shore.

Captain John, wishing to use this boat for the common Safety, put it in a state to reach the Australian mainland, and prepared it for a voyage of some weeks. But as the boat could only hold seven passengers, Captain John and Harry Felton embarked in it with five of their companions, leaving five others on Browse Island, to wait until a ship was sent to them. We know how these unfortunates died before they were rescued, and under what circumstances Captain Ellis discovered their remains during the second cruise of the *Dolly Hope* in 1883.

After a dangerous passage through these detestable regions of the Indian Ocean, the boat reached the continent in the latitude of Cape Leveque, and entered the gulf into which flows the Fitzroy. But misfortune willed it that Captain John should be attacked by the natives, an attack in which four of his men were killed in defending themselves.

These natives, belonging to the tribe of the Indas, dragged away into the interior Captain John, Harry Felton and the sailor who escaped the massacre. The sailor, who was wounded, could not be cured of his wounds. A few weeks later, John Branican and Harry Felton were the only survivors of the wreck of the *Franklin*.

Then commenced for them an existence which at first was seriously menaced. . As we have said, these Indas, like all the sedentary or wandering tribes of Northern Australia, are fierce and sanguinary. The prisoners made in their incessant tribal wars are pitilessly killed and eaten. There is no more inveterate custom than cannibalism among these aborigines, who are veritable wild beasts.

Why were Captain John and Harry Felton spared? That depended on the circumstances.

We are not unaware that among the natives of the interior and the coast, a state of war is perpetuated from generation to generation. The sedentaries attack village after village, destroying and taking prisoners. So it is with the nomads; they pursue their enemies from camp to camp, and their battles always end with the most frightful scenes of cannibalism. These massacres will inevitably bring about the destruction of the Australian race as surely as the proceedings of the Anglo-Saxons, which, under certain circumstances, have been of unavoidable barbarity. How can we describe such acts? Blacks chased by the whites as if they were game, with all the refined emotions derivable from this kind of sport, fires widely spread so that the inhabitants would no longer be spared their bark "gunyos" which serve them for dwellings. The conquerors have even gone almost as far as poisoning them with strychnine, so as to destroy them more rapidly. We have only to quote this sentence from the pen of an Australian colonist; "All the men I meet on my pasturages I shoot, because they are cattle-slayers; all the women because they bring cattle-slayers into the world, and all the children because they will become cattle-slayers!"

We can thus understand the hatred the Australians have vowed against their executioners, a hatred which is hereditary. It is seldom that the whites who fall into their hands are not massacred without mercy. Why then had the survivors of the *Franklin* been spared by the Indas?

If the sailor had not died soon after he was taken prisoner, he would very probably have suffered the usual fate. But the chief of the tribe, a native named Willi, had had dealings with the colonists on the coast, and knew enough to notice that Captain Branican and Harry Felton were two officers, out of whom he might make something in two ways. As a warrior, Willi could make use of their talents in his contests with his rivals; and as a trader, who knew how to trade, he saw the possibility of a lucrative speculation in the shape of a substantial ransom for the two prisoners, who consequently had their lives respected, although they had to submit to a wandering existence, which was all the more painful from the constant watch the Indas kept over them. Never out of sight day or night, never allowed far away from the camp, they had tried now and then to escape at the risk of their lives, but all in vain.

In the meantime their advice was asked with regard to the frequent tribal encounters, and their advice was valuable to Willi, who derived much advantage from it, owing to its always assuring him the victory. Thanks to his successes, his tribe had become one of the most powerful in the country of Western Australia.

These natives of the north-west are apparently a cross between the Australians and the Papuans. Like the recongeners, the Indas have long and curly hair; their colour is not so dark as that of the natives of the southern districts, who seem to be a more vigorous race; their height is not so great, and rarely exceeds fifty-two inches. The men are more strongly built than the women; if their forehead is somewhat retreating, their superciliary arches are rather prominent — which, if ethnologists are to be believed, is a sign of intelligence; their eyes, the iris of which is dark are remarkably brilliant in the pupil; their hair, very brown in colour, is not woolly like that of the African negroes; their skulls are not large, and nature has not given them too much in the way of brains. They are called blacks, although they have nothing of the Nubian black in them; they are chocolate, if we may coin a word which exactly describes their general colour.

The Australian negro is gifted with an extraordinary keenness of scent, which rivals that of the best dogs of the chase. They will recognize the traces of a human being or any animal by the mere smell of the ground or of the vegetation. Their auditory nerve is also of extreme sensibility, and they can even distinguish, it would appear, the sound of ants working in the interior of an ant-hill. There would be a certain amount of justice in classifying these natives among the order of climbers, for there is no gum tree too high or too smooth for them to climb by means of a reed of flexible rattan, to which they give the name of "kamin," and by the prehensile conformation of their great toes.

As we have already noted with regard to the natives of Finke River, the Australian woman is short-lived, and rarely reaches forty years of age; the men attaining about twelve more in certain districts of Queensland. These unfortunate creatures have as their share the roughest work of the household; they are slaves, under the yoke of their pitiless masters, compelled to carry the bundles, the utensils, the weapons, and to seek for the edible roots, and lizards, worms and snakes which form the food of the tribe. But it is as well to mention that they take affectionate care of their children, whom the fathers hardly trouble themselves about, for the child is a burden to the mother, who is thereby prevented from giving her exclusive attention to the cares of this nomad existence; hence among some tribes the blacks have cut off the woman's breasts in order to make it impossible for them to give their children nourishment. And yet, horrible as the custom may be, and discordant as it may appear with the precautions taken to diminish the numbers — these little beings in time of famine are eaten in certain tribes where cannibalism is still carried to excess.

Among the Australian blacks, who are scarcely worthy of being called human, life is concentrated as one sole object. "Ammeri! arnmeri!" recurs incessantly in the native speech, the word meaning "hungry." The most frequent gesture of these savages consists in slapping the stomach, which is only too often empty. In these lands, without game and without cultivation, the people eat at all hours of the day and night, when an opportunity offers, on account of this constant fear of a near and lengthy fast. And, after all, what food is there for these aborigines — the most miserable, assuredly, of all those whom nature has scattered over the globe? A sort of coarse cake called "damper," made of a little flour Without yeast, and cooked, not in an oven, but under glowing embers — honey, which they sometimes collect by felling the tree, at the summit of which the bees have established their hives — " kadjerah," a kind of white porridge, made by the" pounding of poisonous palm-roots, from which the poison has been extracted by delicate manipulation — eggs of the jungle birds laid in the ground — which the heat hatches artificially — and of the pigeons, peculiar to Australia, which hang their nests from the end of the tree branches — and, finally, certain kinds of the larvae of beetles, some gathered among the boughs of the acacia trees, others dug up from the rotten deposits about the roots of the thickets. And that is all.

In this hourly struggle for existence, we have the explanation of cannibalism, with all its horrible monstrosities. It is not a sign of natural ferocity, but the. consequence of the commanding necessity to which the Australian is given to escape dying Of hunger.

At the lower course of the Murray, and among the tribes of the north, it is the custom to kill the children, and feed on them, and to the mother is given the joint of a finger of each child she is forced to hand over to these cannibal feasts. It is dreadful to think that when the mother has nothing else to eat, she has to devour her own child, and yet travellers have heard these miserable women talk of this abomination as if it were a most natural act.

But at the same time it is not hunger alone which forces the Australian to cannibalism; they have a decided taste for human flesh, the flesh they call "talgoro,"

"the meat that speaks," according to one of their horribly realistic expressions. If they do not gratify this taste on the people of their own tribe, they none the less do it by man- hunting. Their incessant wars had no other object than talgoro, which they eat fresh; as well as preserve for future use. It is stated by Dr. Carl Lumholtz, that during his daring journey across the North-Eastern Provinces, the blacks were continually discussing this food question, saying that "for Australians there was nothing like human flesh," but this was not so much the flesh of the white man, which had a saltish after-taste that was very disagreeable.

There is another motive which predisposes these tribes to exterminate each other. The Australians are extraordinarily credulous. They are terrified at the voice of the "Kvin'gan," an evil spirit which haunts the fields and the gorges of the mountainous districts, although this voice is merely the melancholy call of a charming bird, one of the most curious in Australian ornithology. But if they believe in the existence of a superior and wicked being, according to the best authorities, no native ever says a prayer, and not a trace can be found of religious practices.

In reality they are very superstitious, and as they firmly believe their enemies can kill them by witchcraft, they are eager to destroy them; and this, added to the habit of cannibalism, exposes these countries to constant depopulation.

It may as well be noted, in passing, that some of the Australians respect their dead; they wrap the body in strips of foliage or bark, and deposit it in a shallow grave, with the feet towards the east, unless they bury it upright, as they do among certain tribes. The grave of a chief is then covered by a hut, the entrance to which is towards the rising sun. It should also be said that among certain tribes the strange belief prevails that blacks are re-incarnated as whites, and, according to the observations of Carl Lumholtz, the language of the country has the same word for the spirit of a man, and a man of white colour. According to another native superstition, the animals have formerly been human creatures — which is metempsychosis the wrong way round.

Such are the tribes of the Australian continent destined evidently to disappear, as have also the natives of Tasmania. Such were the Indas, into whose hands had fallen John Branican and Harry Felton.

After the sailor's death, John Branican and Harry Felton had had to follow the Indas in their continual peregrinations in the central and north-western regions. Sometimes attacking hostile tribes, sometimes attacked by them, they obtained an incontestable superiority over them, thanks to the advice of their prisoners, by which Willi profited. Hundreds of miles were traversed from King's Sound to Van Diemen's Gulf, between the Fitzroy Valley and that of the Victoria, and even on the plains of Alexandra Land. In this way Captain John and his mate travelled across countries unknown to geographers, which are left blank on modern maps, east of Tasman Land, and Arnheim Land and the' confines of the Great Sandy Desert.

Although these interminable journeyings appeared extremely laborious to them, the Indas made nothing of it. This was their usual mode of life, taking no notice of either distance or time, of which they have hardly a notion. In fact an event which could only take place within five or six months would be described by a native in all good faith as taking place in two or three days, or the next week. They have no notion of age; and know of no time but the hour that exists. It would seem as though the Australian belongs to a special division in the scale of beings — as do certain animals of the country.

In these customs John Branican and Harry Felton were obliged to conform. To these fatigues due to the daily movements, they had to submit. With this food, often so insufficient, and always so repugnant, they had to be contented. To say nothing of those frightful scenes of cannibalism, the horrors of which they never could mitigate, after the battles in which the enemies fell in hundreds.

And in thus submitting, the intention of Captain John and Harry Felton was to lull the vigilance of the tribe to sleep until an opportunity for flight presented itself. That an escape into the deserts of the north-west had its chances we have seen in the case of the mate of the *Franklin*. But the two prisoners were watched so closely that opportunities of flight were extremely rare, and hardly one presented itself during the nine years. Once only — the very year preceding Mrs. Branican's expedition — escape might have succeeded, and that under these circumstances.

After a series of battles with the tribes of the interior, the Indas were in camp on the shores of Lake Amadeus, in the south-west of Alexandra Land. It was not often they advanced so far into the centre of the continent. Captain John and Harry Felton, knowing they were within three hundred miles of the Overland Telegraph Line, thought the opportunity was favourable, and resolved to take advantage of it. After reflection it seemed best to escape separately, and meet a few miles from the camp. Outwitting the vigilance of the aborigines, Harry Felton was fortunate in gaining the spot where he was to wait for his companion. Unfortunately John had been summoned to Willi, who required him to attend to a wound he had received in the last engagement. John could not get away, and Harry Felton waited for him in vain for some days. Then, thinking he might reach one of the villages in the interior, or on the coast, and there organize an expedition for the deliverance of his captain, Felton set off towards the south-west. But such were the fatigues, privations and misery he had to undergo, that four months after his departure he fell dying on the banks of the Parroo, in the Ulakara district of New South Wales. Taken to the hospital at Sydney, he had lingered for some weeks and then died, after being able to tell Mrs. Branican what he knew concerning Captain John.

It was a terrible trial for John to be without his companion, and his energy of mind had to equal his physical energy, or he would have given way to despair. To whom now could he talk of what had been so dear to him — his country, San Diego, the loved creatures he had left there, his courageous wife, his son Wat growing up far from him, and whom he would never probably know, Mr. William Andrew, and all his friends, in fact? For nine years John had been the prisoner of the Indas; and how many years would roll by before his liberty was restored to him? However, he never lost hope, being sustained by the hope that he would succeed in reaching one of the towns of the Australian coast, and that Harry Felton would do all that was humanly possible to rescue his captain.

During the early period of his captivity John had learnt to speak the native language, which by the logic of its grammar, the precision of its terms, the delicacy of its expressions, seemed to show that the Australian aborigines must at one time have enjoyed a certain amount of civilization. He had often spoken to Willi of the advantages he would gain by leaving his prisoners free to return to Queensland or South Australia, where he would be in a position to send him any ransom that might be required. But Willi was not of a trusting nature, and would not entertain the idea. If the ransom arrived he would give John and his mate their liberty. As to trusting to their promises, judging probably that others were like himself, he would never consent to it.

It naturally followed that Harry Felton's escape, which made him furiously angry, rendered Willi more severe towards Captain John. He stopped him from moving about during the halts or marches, and put him under the guard of a native, who had to answer for him with his life.

Long months elapsed, and the "prisoner had received no news from his companion. Was there not every probability that Harry Felton had died on the journey? If the fugitive had succeeded in reaching Queensland or Adelaide, would he not have already made some attempt to rescue him from the Indas?

During the first three months of the year 1891 — that is to say at the beginning of the Australian summer — the tribe had returned to the Fitzroy Valley, where Willi generally passed the hottest period of the summer season, and where he found the requisite resources for his tribe.

The Indas were there in the first days of April, and their camp occupied a bend of the river, into which flowed a small affluent from the northern plains.

Since the tribe had taken up their quarters here, Captain John, knowing they were near the coast had thought of reaching it. If he could do so, it would not perhaps be impossible for him to take refuge in one of the stations more to the south, where Colonel Warburton had ended his journey.

John had resolved to risk everything to put an end to this hateful life, even if he died in the attempt.

Unfortunately a change in the plans of the Indas nipped in the bud the prisoner's hopes. During the first fortnight in April it was evident that Willi was preparing to depart so as to fix his winter encampment on the upper part of the river.

What had happened, and to what was to be attributed this change in the habits of the tribe?

Captain John managed to learn, but not without some trouble: the tribe was to move further east, because the black police had been reported on the lower course of the Fitzroy.

It will not have been forgotten that Tom Marix had spoken about these black police, who, since Harry Felton's revelations, had been ordered into the north-west territories.

These police are much feared by the natives, and display a keenness of which we can have no idea when they are in pursuit of them. They are commanded by a captain called a "mani," having under his orders a sergeant, thirty white men and eighty blacks mounted on good horses, and armed with guns, swords and pistols. Known under the name of the native police, they are sufficiently strong to guarantee the security of the inhabitants of the regions they visit at different times. Pitiless in their repression of the aborigines, they are blamed by some in the name of humanity, and approved by others in the name of public safety. They are most active in their movements, and journey from place to place with incredible rapidity. The natives fear to meet them, and that is why Willi, when he learnt they were in his neighbourhood, was preparing to ascend the course of the Fitzroy.

But what was a danger for the Indas might be the safety of Captain Branican. If he could join a detachment of this police, his deliverance was assured and his return home certain. When the camp was being struck could he not find it possible to elude the vigilance of the natives?

Willi, it would seem, had some suspicion of the prisoner's plans, for on the morning of. the 20th of April the door of the hut in which John was confined was not opened at the usual hour. A native was on guard close to the hut. To the questions John put to him he made no reply. When he asked to be taken to Willi they refused to comply with his request, and the chief did not even come to visit him.

What had happened? Were the Indas hastening their preparations- to leave their encampment? It was probable, and John heard them rushing about in front of the hut, where Willi had sent him some food.

A whole day went by, then another. No change took place in his position. The prisoner was narrowly watched all the time. But during the night of the 22nd and 23rd of April he noticed that the noise outside had ceased, and he wondered if the Indas had definitely abandoned their project of camping on Fitzroy River.

At daybreak next morning the door of the hut suddenly opened.

A man — a white — appeared before Captain John.

It was Len Burker.

CHAPTER XIV - LEN BURKER'S GAME

Thirty-two days had passed since the night of the 22nd of March, when Len Burker had separated from Mrs. Branican and her companions. The simoom so fatal to the caravan, had given him an opportunity of executing his plans. Dragging away Jane, and followed by the blacks of the escort, he had driven in front of him the healthy camels, and among them those which carried Captain John's ransom.

Len Burker found himself in more favourable circumstances than Dolly for meeting the Indas in the valley watered by the Fitzroy. Already during his wandering life he had had frequent intercourse with the Australian nomads, with whose language and customs he was acquainted. The ransom he had stolen assured him a warm welcome from Willi, and Captain John, once rescued, would be in his power, and then —

On abandoning the caravan Len Burker had hastened north-west, and at sunrise he and his companions were many miles away.

Jane implored her husband, and begged of him not to abandon Dolly and her people in the desert; she reminded him it was another crime added to that committed at Godfrey's birth, and besought him to atone for his abominable conduct in taking the child from its mother by joining his efforts to those being made for the rescue of Captain John.

Jane gained nothing. It was in vain. To prevent Len Burker from advancing towards his object was in no one's power. A few days more and he would have reached it. Dolly and Godfrey dead of privation and misery, John Branican disappeared, Edward Starter's inheritance would pass into the hands of Jane, that is to say into his own, and he would know how to use those millions well.

Nothing was to be expected from this rascal. He ordered his wife to be silent, and she had to yield, knowing well that if he had not need of her to enter into possession of Dolly's fortune, he would have abandoned her long ago, and perhaps worse. As to getting away and attempting to reach the caravan, how could she think of it? What would have become of her, all alone? Besides, two of the blacks had orders not to leave her for an instant.

We need not dwell on the incidents which Len Burker met with on his journey. Neither camels nor provisions failed him. In this way he was able to make long stages as he approached the Fitzroy with men accustomed to the life, and who had suffered less than the whites since the departure from Adelaide.

In seventeen days, on the 8th of April, Len Burker had reached the left bank of the river, on the very day that Mrs. Branican and her companions made their last halt.

On the river bank Len Burker met with a few natives, and obtained information from them regarding the position of the Indas.

Learning that the tribe had followed the valley more to the westward, he resolved to go down it so as to enter into communication with Willi.

The task was not difficult. During the month of April, in this part of Northern Australia, the climate is less excessive, however low it may be in latitude. It was evident that if Mrs. Branican's caravan could reach the Fitzroy its miseries would be at an end in a few days. She could enter into communication with the Indas, for scarcely eighty-five miles then separated John and Dolly from each other.

When Len Burker was certain that he had only two or three days more to travel he stopped. To take Jane with him among the Indas, to bring her face to face with Captain John, to run the risk of being denounced by her, did not at all suit him. By his orders a halt was organized on the left bank, and, in spite of her supplications, there the unfortunate woman was left in charge of the two blacks.

When that was done, Len Burker and his companions continued their journey towards the west, with the saddle camels and the two beasts laden with the articles of barter.

It was on the 20th of April that Len Burker met the tribe who were then in a state of alarm at the neighbourhood of the black police, whose presence had been reported a dozen miles down the river. Willi was already preparing to leave his camp to seek refuge in the upper- regions of Arnheim Land, which belongs to the province of Northern Australia.

-

At this moment, by Willi's orders, and with a view to prevent any attempt at escape on his part, John was shut up in a hut, so that he could learn nothing of the communications entered into between Len Burker and the chief of the Indas.

These communications occasioned no difficulty. Len Burker had had previous acquaintance with these natives. He knew their chief, and had only to treat concerning the amount of Captain John's ransom.

Willi was disposed to surrender the prisoner for a ransom. The display of what Len Burker had brought in fabrics, toys, and, above all, in the stock of tobacco that was offered, favourably impressed him. But, like an experienced merchant, he required a higher price, as he could not separate without regret from a man of as much importance as Captain John, who for so many years had lived with the tribe and rendered it such valuable services, etc. etc. Besides, he knew that the Captain was an American, and he was not ignorant that an expedition had been formed with a view of obtaining his deliverance — which Len Burker confirmed by observing that he was the chief of the expedition. Then, when he learned that Willi was easy at the presence of the black police on the lower arse of the Fitzroy, he took advantage of the circumstance to urge him to complete the bargain without ay. In fact, for his own interest it was necessary that Captain Branican's rescue should remain secret, and if he t him away from the Indas there was every probability his actions remaining unknown. The final disappearance of John Branican could not be imputed to him, and the men of his escort could not keep silent on the matter would know how to make sure of their silence. It follows that as the ransom was accepted by Willi the bargain was concluded on the 22nd of April. That very evening the Indas abandoned their camp and went away the Fitzroy River.

That is what Len Burker had done, that was how he had attained his object, and now we have to see how he drifted by it.

It was about eight o'clock in the morning when the door of the hut opened and John Branican found himself Len Burker's presence.

Fourteen years had elapsed since the day when the Captain had given him the last shake of the hand at the departure of the *Franklin* from San Diego bay. He didn't recognize him, but Len Burker was struck with the le change that had taken place in him. He had, of course, aged — he was then forty-three — but less than could believed after so long a stay among the natives; he J the same well-marked features, the same resolute look,; fire of which was not at all dulled, and his hair was as thick, although it had whitened. He had remained strong and robust, and better, perhaps, than Harry Felton lid have borne the fatigues of a journey across the Australian desert — fatigues to which his companion had succumbed.

When he saw Len Burker, Captain John stepped back.

It was the first time he had found himself face to face with a white since he had been the prisoner of the Indas. It was the first time a stranger had come to say a word to him.

"Who are you?" he asked.

"An American of San Diego."

"Of San Diego?"

"I am Len Burker."

"You!"

Captain John threw himself on Len Burker. He took him by the hands, he clasped him in his arms. What! This man was Len Burker. No! It was impossible. It was only an appearance. John had not clearly heard.

He was under the influence of some hallucination." Len Burker —
Jane's husband —

And at that moment John hardly thought of the antipathy with which
Len Burker had formerly inspired him, of the man whom he had so
justly suspected.

"Len Burker?" he repeated.

"Myself, John."

"Here — in these parts! Ah, you also, Len — you have been taken
prisoner."

How could John in any other way explain the presence of Len Burker
in a camp of the Indas?

"No!" quickly replied Len Burker. "No, John, I came here to ransom
you from the chief of this tribe — to rescue you — "

"To rescue me!"

Captain John could only control himself by a violent effort. It seemed
that he had. gone mad, that his reason was at the point of leaving him.

Then when he had become master of himself he thought of darting out
of the hut. He dared not. Len Burker had spoken of his deliverance. But
was he free? And Willi? And the Indas?

"Speak, Len, speak!" said he, crossing his arms as if he would keep
his chest down.

Then Len Burker, faithful to the plan he had formed to tell him only a
part of the story, and attribute to himself all the merit of this campaign,
began to relate the facts in his way, when John, in a voice strangled by
emotion, cried, —

"And Dolly? Dolly?"

"She is living, John."

"And Wat, my child?"

346

"Living — both of them — at San Diego."

"My wife — my son!" murmured John, his eyes filling with tears.

Then he added, —

"Now speak — Len — speak! I have strength to listen to you."

And Len Burker, coolly looking him in the face all the time, said, —

"A few years ago, John, when no one had any further doubt about the loss of the *Franklin* my wife and I had to leave San Diego and America. Business matters called me to Australia, and I came to Sydney, where I started an office. Since our departure Jane and Dolly never ceased their correspondence, for you know the affection they bore each other, an affection which neither time nor distance could weaken.

"Yes! I know!" replied John. "Dolly and Jane were friends, and the separation must have been cruel to them."

"Very cruel, John," said Len Burker, "but after some years the day came when this separation was about to end. About eleven months ago we were preparing to leave Australia for San Diego, when an unexpected piece of news put an end to our plans of departure. We then learnt what had become of the *Franklin*, in what parts she had been lost, and at the same time the rumour spread that the sole survivor of the wreck was the prisoner of the Australian tribe, and that was you, John."

"But how did you know that, Len? Was it through Harry Felton?"

"Yes, the news was brought by Harry Felton.

Almost at the end of his journey your companion had been met with on the banks of the Parroo, in the south of Queensland, and brought to Sydney — "

"Harry — my brave Harry!" exclaimed Captain John. "Ah! I knew well he would never forget me! As soon as he got to Sydney he organized an expedition — "

"He is dead!" said Len Burker; "dead of the fatigues he had endured."

"Dead!" said John. "My God — dead! Harry Felton — Harry!"

And the tears flowed from his eyes.

"But before he died," continued Len Burker, "Harry Felton related all that occurred after the wreck of the *Franklin*, the wreck on Browse Island, your reaching the west of the continent. It was at his bedside that I — I learnt this from his lips — all. And' as his eyes closed, John, he uttered your name."

"Harry, my poor Harry!" murmured John, as he thought of the terrible miseries to which the faithful companion had succumbed, whom he would never see again.

"John," continued Len Burker, "the loss of the *Franklin*, of which there had been no news for fourteen years, made a considerable sensation. You may judge of the effect produced by the news that you were alive, and that Harry Felton had left you a few months before a prisoner with a northern tribe. I immediately telegraphed to Dolly, informing her that I was getting ready to rescue you from the hands of the Indas, for it could only be a question, of ransom after what Harry Felton had said. Then, having organized a caravan, of which I took the command, Jane and I left Sydney. That was seven months ago. It has taken us all that time to teach the Fitzroy. At last here we are at the camp of the Indas."

"Thanks, Len, thanks!" said Captain John. "What you have done for me — "

"You would have done for me under similar circumstances," replied Len Burker.

"Certainly! And your wife, Len, this courageous Jane, who has not feared to face such fatigue — where is she?"

"Three days' march up the river with two of my men," replied Len Burker.

"I will go and see her."

"Yes, John, and if she is not here it is because I did not wish her to accompany me, not knowing what sort of welcome the natives would give our little caravan — "

"But you did not come alone?" asked John.

"No; I had my escort, composed of a dozen blacks. We arrived in the valley two days ago — "

"Two days?"

"Yes, and I have spent them in concluding my bargain. The Willi thought much of you, my dear John. He knew your importance, or rather your value. It took a lot of talking to obtain your liberty in exchange for the ransom — "

"Then I am free?"

"As free as I am."

"But the natives?"

"They have all gone off with their chief, and are no longer in the camp."

"Gone?" exclaimed John.

"Look!"

Captain Branican bounded out of the hut. On the bank of the river there were only the blacks of Len Burker's escort: the Indas were there no longer.

It will be seen what was true and what was false in Len Burker's story. Of Mrs. Branican's madness he had said nothing. Of the fortune which had fallen to Dolly through Edward Starter's death he had said nothing; nothing .of the voyages of the *Dolly Hope* in the sea of the Philippines and Torres Straits during the years 1879 and 1882; nothing of what had passed between Mrs. Branican and Harry Felton on his deathbed; nothing of the expedition organized by this intrepid woman, now abandoned in the Great Sandy Desert, the whole credit of which the .unworthy Len Burker had taken to himself.

It was he who had done all, he who, at the risk of his life, had delivered Captain John!

And why should John doubt the truth of the story? Why should he not thank with effusion him who after so many perils had just snatched him from the Indas, and who was going to take him home to his wife and child?

This he did, and in terms which would have touched a less hardened being. But remorse had never troubled Len Burker's conscience, and nothing would hinder him from carrying out his criminal projects. Now John Branican would go with him to the camp where Jane was waiting for him. Why should he hesitate? And during this journey Len Burker would find an opportunity of getting rid of him, without being suspected by the blacks of his escort, who could not afterwards bear witness against him.

Captain John was impatient to set out, and it was agreed that the departure would take place that very day. His great wish was to see Jane, the devoted friend of his wife, to talk to her about Dolly and his son, about Mr. William Andrew, and all those he would meet again at San Diego.

They started during the afternoon of the 23rd of April. Len Burker had provisions for several days. During the journey the Fitzroy would yield the water necessary for the little caravan. The camels on which John and Len Burker were mounted would permit them to get several stages in advance of their escort. That would facilitate Len Burker's designs. It would not do for Captain John to reach the camp, and he would not reach it.

At eight o'clock in the evening Len Burker pitched his . camp on the left bank of the river for the night. He was still too far off to put into execution his plan of getting on in advance of his escort, amid regions where dangers were always to be feared.

At daybreak the march was resumed.

The following day was divided into two stages, divided by a halt of two hours. It was not always easy to follow the course of the Fitzroy, the banks of which were often cut into by deep ravines, and sometimes barred by inextricable masses of gum trees and eucalyptus, obliging the caravan to go round them.

It was a hard day's march, and after their meal the blacks went to sleep.

A few moments later Captain John was plunged in a deep slumber.

Here was an opportunity of which Len Burker might take advantage, for he was not asleep. To kill John, drag his body about twenty yards, and throw it into the river — it seemed as though circumstances had united to facilitate the perpetration of the crime. Then in the morning Captain Branican would be sought for in vain.

About two o'clock Len Burker got up noiselessly, and crept towards his victim, knife in hand. He was just about to strike when John awoke.

"I thought you called me," said Len Burker.

"No, my dear Len," replied John, "just as I awoke I was dreaming of my dear Dolly and our child."

At six o'clock John and Len Burker resumed their journey along the Fitzroy.

During the midday halt Len Burker resolved to accomplish his purpose, for they would reach the camp that night He proposed to John to ride on in advance of the escort.

John agreed, for he was anxious to get to Jane and be able to speak to her more intimately than he had done to Len Burker.

The two were starting when one of the blacks descried a white advancing with a certain amount of precaution, about a hundred yards off.

351

An exclamation escaped Len Burker.

He had recognized Godfrey.

CHAPTER XV - THE LAST ENCAMPMENT

IMPELLED by a sort of instinct, and almost unconscious of what he did, Captain John had rushed up to the boy.

Len Burker had remained immovable, as if his feet were nailed to the ground.

Godfrey was face to face with him — Godfrey, the son of Dolly and of John! Then Mrs. Branican's caravan had not succumbed P She was, then, a few miles away — a few yards away, perhaps — unless Godfrey was the sole survivor of those the scoundrel had abandoned?

In any case, this meeting, so unexpected, must shatter Len Burker's plan. If the boy spoke, he would say that Mrs. Branican was at the head of this expedition. He would say that Dolly had dared a thousand fatigues, a thousand dangers, amid the Australian deserts to bring help to her husband. He would say that she was there — that she was following him up the course of the Fitzroy.

And she was there.

On the morning of the 22nd of March, after Len Burker had abandoned her, the little caravan had resumed its march towards the north-west. On the 8th of April, as we know, the poor people, exhausted from hunger and tortured by thirst, had fallen half dead.

Sustained by her superior strength, Mrs. Branican had endeavoured to revive her companions, imploring them to continue their advance, to make a last effort to reach the river, where they might obtain relief. It was as if she were speaking to corpses, and even Godfrey was unconscious.

But the soul of the expedition survived in Dolly, and Dolly did what her companions could not do. Towards the north-west was their course; it was towards the northwest that Tom Marix and Zach Fren had stretched their sinking arms. Dolly set off in that direction.

Across the plain, which stretched away out of sight towards the west, without food, without the means of transport, what could this energetic woman hope? Was her object to reach the Fitzroy, to seek assistance among the whites of the coast, or among the wandering natives? She did not know, but she struggled on for some miles — twenty in three days. Then her strength failed her; she fell, and she would have died if help had not arrived providentially, as one may say.

At this time the black police were out on the boundary of the Great Sandy Desert. Leaving thirty of them near the Fitzroy, their chief, the mani, had started off on a reconnaissance into these parts with sixty of his men.

He it was who fell in with Mrs. Branican. As soon as she recovered consciousness she was able to tell him where her companions were, and she took him to them. The mani and his men revived the poor fellows, whom they would not have found alive twenty-four hours later.

Tom Marix, who had known the mani in Queensland, told him what had happened since they left Adelaide. The officer was acquainted with the object of the expedition in these distant countries of the north-west, and, as Providence had brought him to its help, he offered to join it. When Tom Marix asked him about the Indas, he replied that they were then on the banks of the Fitzroy, about sixty miles off.

There was no time to lose if they wished to spoil Len Burker's plans, whom the mani was already after for some bush ranging crime in Queensland. He did not doubt that if Len Burker succeeded in rescuing Captain John, who had no reason to mistrust him, it would be impossible to get on his track.

Mrs, Branican might reckon on the mani and his men, who shared their provisions with her companions and lent them their horses. The party set off that evening, and in the afternoon of the 2ist of April were in sight of the heights of the valley, near the seventeenth parallel of latitude.

Here the mani picked up his men who had been on the watch along the Fitzroy. They told him that the Indas were then in camp a hundred miles further up the river. It was important to come up with them as soon as possible, although Mrs. Branican had no objects of exchange with which to ransom her husband. But the mani, reinforced by his whole detachment, assisted by Torn Marix, Zach Fren, Godfrey, Jos Meritt, and their companions, would not hesitate to employ force to rescue Captain John from the Indas. But when they reached the native camp it had been abandoned. The mani followed up the natives, halt by halt, and it was in this way that, on the 25th of April, Godfrey, who had gone on half a mile in advance, found himself suddenly in Captain John's presence.

Len Burker had begun to recover himself, looking at Godfrey without uttering a word, waiting for what the boy was going to do or say.

Godfrey had not even seen him. He could not take his eyes off the captain. Although he had never seen him, he knew his features from the photograph Mrs. Branican had given him. No doubt was possible. This man was Captain John.

On his part, John looked at Godfrey with an emotion none the less extraordinary. Although he could not imagine who the boy was, he devoured him with his eyes, he held out hands to him, he called him with a trembling voice — yes, he called him as if he were his son.

Godfrey threw himself into his arms, exclaiming, —

"Captain John!"

"Yes, I; it is I!" said Captain John. "But you, my child, who are you? Whence do you come from? How come you know my name?"

Godfrey could not reply. He became frightfully pale as he caught sight of Len Burker, and could not conceal the horror he felt at seeing the scoundrel.

"Len Burker!" he exclaimed.

Len Burker, after reflecting on the consequences of this meeting, could not but congratulate himself. Was not this a lucky chance which had given him over both Godfrey and John? Was it not incredible luck to have at his mercy both father and child? Turning to the blacks, he made a sign to them to separate John and Godfrey, and seize them.

"Len Burker!" repeated Godfrey.

"Yes, my boy," answered John. "It is Len Burker, who has saved me — "

"Saved!" said Godfrey, "No, Captain John, no. Len Burker has not saved you! He wants to destroy you, he ran away from us, he stole your ransom from Mrs. Branican — "

At this name John answered with a cry, and, seizing Godfrey's hand, said, "Dolly? Dolly?"

"Yes. Mrs. Branican, Captain John — your wife, who is close by here!"

"Dolly?" said John.

"This boy is mad!" said Len Burker, approaching Godfrey.

"Yes! mad!" murmured Captain John. "The poor child is mad!"

"Len Burker!" said Godfrey, trembling with passion, "you "are a traitor; you are a murderer! And this murderer is here, Captain John, to make away with you after abandoning Mrs. Branican and her companions."

"Dolly! Dolly!" exclaimed Captain John. "No — you are not mad, my boy! I believe you! I believe you! Come! come!"

Len Burker and his men threw themselves on John and Godfrey, who, taking a revolver from his belt, shot one of the blacks in the chest. But John and he were seized, and the blacks were dragging them towards the river.

Fortunately the report was heard. Shouts came in reply from a few hundred yards down stream, and almost immediately the mani and his men, Tom Marix and his companions, Mrs. Branican, Zach Fren, Jos Meritt and Gin-Ghi came running up.

Len Burker and his blacks were not strong enough to make any resistance, and a moment afterwards John was in Dolly's arms.

The game was up for Len Burker. If they captured him he could expect no mercy; and, followed by his blacks, he fled up the river.

The mani, Zach Fren, Tom Marix, Jos Meritt and twelve of the police went off in pursuit.

How can we paint the feelings, how can we describe the emotion which overflowed in the hearts of Dolly and John? They wept, and Godfrey shared in their embraces, their kisses, and their tears.

So great was Dolly's joy and so much had she suffered, that her strength abandoned her and she fainted away.

Godfrey knelt near her and helped Harriett to revive her. John did not know it, but they knew that once before Dolly had lost her reason through excess of grief. Would she now lose it under excess of joy?

"Dolly! Dolly!" said John.

And Godfrey, taking her hands, called, "Mother! mother!"

Dolly's eyes opened. Her hand clasped that of her husband, whose joy was overflowing, and who held out his arms to Godfrey, saying, —

"Come, Wat! Come, my son!"

But Dolly could not have him thus mistaken in believing that Godfrey was his child.

"No, John!" said she, "no, Godfrey is not our son. Our poor little Wat is dead — dead soon after you left us."

"Dead!" exclaimed John, still keeping his eyes on Godfrey.

Dolly was about to tell him of the misfortune which had befallen fifteen years before, when there was the sound of a shot in the direction taken by the mani in pursuit of Len Burker.

Had justice been done on the rascal, or had he added another to his long list of crimes?

Almost immediately they all came into view on the bank of the Fitzroy. Two of the police were holding up a woman from whom the blood was flowing from a large wound and reddening the ground.

It was Jane.

What had happened was this.

Notwithstanding the swiftness of his flight, the pursuers had not lost sight of Len Burker, and a few hundred yards only separated them from him when he stopped as he caught sight of Jane.

During the evening before this wretched woman had managed to escape, and she had fled along the Fitzroy. She went as chance led her, and when the first shot was heard she was not a quarter of a mile from the spot where John and Godfrey had just met. She hastened her pace and immediately found herself in presence of her husband, who was running towards her.

Len Burker, seizing her by the arms, would have dragged her away with him. At the thought that Jane would again meet Dolly, and reveal the secret of Godfrey's birth, his anger reached its height. And as Jane resisted he stabbed her.

The next moment there was the report of a gun, accompanied by these words — appropriate enough on this occasion, —

"Good! Oh! very good!"

It was Jos Meritt, who had coolly aimed at Len Burker and" rolled him over into the water of the Fitzroy.

And that was the scoundrel's end, shot dead in the heart by the hand of the gentleman.

Tom Marix ran towards Jane, who still breathed, but feebly. Two of the police took the unhappy woman between them and brought her to Mrs. Branican.

Seeing Jane in this state, Dolly uttered a heartrending shriek. Leaning over the dying woman, she tried to listen to the beating of her heart, to feel the breath escaping from her mouth. But Jane's wound was mortal, the knife had been driven into her lungs.

"Jane! Jane!" said Dolly, loudly.

At this voice, which recalled the only love she had ever known, Jane opened her eyes, looked at Dolly, and smiled as she murmured, —

."Dolly! dear Dolly!"

Suddenly life came into her look. She had just seen Captain John.

"John — you — John!" she said, but so feebly they could hardly hear her.

"Yes, Jane!" said the captain, "it is I — I, whom Dolly has come to save."

"John — John is there!" murmured she.

"Yes — with us, Jane," said Dolly. "He will leave us no more. We will take him back with you, with you — there — "

Jane heard no longer. Her eyes seemed to be looking for someone, and she uttered the name, —

"Godfrey! Godfrey!"

And anguish was depicted on her features, already drawn with agony.

Mrs. Branican made a sign to Godfrey, who came near.

"Him! Him! At last!" said Jane, rising with a last effort.

Seizing Dolly's hand, —

"Come near, Dolly! come near!" she said. "John and you listen to what I have still to tell you."

And they leant over her so as not to lose any of her words.

"John, Dolly," she said, "Godfrey — Godfrey who is there — Godfrey is your child."

"Our child!" murmured Dolly. And she became as pale as if she were dying, the blood having violently flowed back to her heart.

"We have a son no longer," said John, "he's dead."

"Yes!" said Jane, "little Wat — over there — in San Diego Bay. But you had a second child, and that child is Godfrey."

In a few sentences, broken by the gaspings of death, she told them what had happened after John's departure; of Godfrey's birth at Prospect House, of Dolly deprived of reason, a mother without knowing it, of the little child abandoned by Len Burker's orders, found a few hours afterwards, brought up afterwards at Wat House under the name of Godfrey.

And Jane added, —

"If I am guilty of not having had the courage to tell you all, Dolly, forgive me — forgive me, John!"

' Do you need forgiveness, Jane — you, who have just given us back our child?"

"Yes — your child!" said Jane. "Before God — John, Dolly, I swear it — Godfrey is your child."

And seeing them both clasp Godfrey in their arms, Jane smiled with happiness, and the smile died away with her last breath.

CHAPTER XVI.

THE END.

We need not linger over the Incidents with which this adventurous journey across the Australian continent came to an end, nor dwell on the different conditions which marked the return to Adelaide.

At the outset the question was discussed: Should they make for the Settlements on the coast by going down the Fitzroy — among others that of Rockbourne — or should they go to Prince Frederick harbour in York Sound? But some time might elapse before a ship visited the coast, and it seemed preferable to return by the route they had come. Escorted by the black police, abundantly supplied with provisions by the mani, having at its disposal the saddle and pack camels recovered from Len Burker, the caravan had nothing to fear from anything it might meet.

Before they started, the body of Jane Burker was laid in a grave dug at the foot of a group of gum trees. Dolly knelt at the grave and prayed for the poor woman's soul.

Captain John, his wife, and their companions left the camp on the Fitzroy on the 25th of April, under the direction of the mani, who offered to accompany them as far as the nearest station of the Overland Telegraph line.

Everyone was so happy that none felt the fatigues of the journey, and Zach Fren, in his joy, said to Tom Marix, — "Well, Tom, we have found the captain!"

"Yes, Zach, but to what was it due?"

"To Providence having put the helm down, and we should always reckon on Providence."

However, there was a black spot on Jos Meritt's horizon. If Mrs. Branican had found Captain John, the famous collector had not found the hat, the search after which had cost him so much trouble and sacrifice. To be just within range of the Indas, and not enter into communication with this Willi, who was perhaps wearing the historic head-gear-what misfortune! Jos Meritt found some consolation, it is true, in hearing from the mani that the fashion of European head-coverings had not extended to the people of the north-west, contrary to what Jos Meritt had already observed among the natives of the north-east. Thus his desideratum could not be realized among the tribes of Northern Australia. On the other hand, he could congratulate himself on the splendid shot with which he had disembarrassed the Branican family of "that abominable Len Burker," as Zach Fren called him.

The return was made as rapidly as possible. The caravan had no more to suffer from thirst, for the wells were already replenished by the heavy showers of autumn, and the heat was not insupportable. Acting on the mani's advice, they headed direct for the regions crossed by the telegraph line, where there was no scarcity of well- provisioned stations nor of means of communication with the capital of South Australia. Thanks to the telegraph, it was soon known all over the world that Mrs. Branican had brought her daring expedition to a successful end.

It was in the latitude of Lake Wood that Dolly and her companions reached a station on the Overland Telegraph line. There the mani and the black police took leave of John and Dolly Branican. They did not depart without having received the cordial thanks they deserved, to be followed by the reward the captain would send them as soon as he reached Adelaide. There was now no more to do than to pass south through Alexandra Land to Alice Spring, where the caravan arrived on the 19th of June, after a seven weeks' journey.

There, under the care of Mr. Flint, the chief of the station, Tom Marix recovered the means of transport he had left behind, the cattle, the drays, the buggies, the horses for the distance remaining to be traversed. And on the 3rd of July the expedition reached the railway at Farina Town, and the next day arrived in Adelaide.

What a welcome awaited Captain John and his courageous wife! The whole town turned out to receive them, and when Captain John Branican appeared between his wife and child on the balcony of the hotel in King William Street,,the cheers were so terrific that, according to Gin-Ghi, they might have been heard at the other end of the Celestial Empire.

The stay at Adelaide was not of long duration. John and Dolly were eager to return to San Diego, to see their friends and take up their abode at Prospect House, where happiness awaited them. They parted from Tom Marix and his men, who were liberally rewarded, and whose services could never be forgotten.

Neither did they forget that character, Jos Meritt, who also resolved to leave Australia with his faithful domestic.

But how about the hat he had not found? Did he find it? Where? In a royal palace, where it was kept with all the respect which was its due. Yes! Jos Meritt, led astray on a false scent, had been running about the five parts of the world in vain to find a hat which was all the time in Windsor Castle, as he learned six months later. It was the hat worn by Her Gracious Majesty at the visit of King Louis Philippe in 1845, and he must have been mad at the very least, to have supposed that this masterpiece of a Parisian milliner would have finished its career on the woolly cranium of an Australian savage!

The peregrinations of Jos Meritt consequently ceased, to the extreme joy of Gin-Ghi, but to the extreme displeasure of the celebrated curio-hunter, who returned to Liverpool, much amazed that he had not been able to complete his collection by the acquisition of the only hat of its kind in the world. Three weeks after leaving Adelaide, where they embarked on the *Abraham Lincoln*, John, Dolly, and Godfrey Branican, accompanied by Zach Fren and the woman Harriett, arrived at San Diego.

There Mr. William Andrew and Captain Ellis received them amid the inhabitants of that generous city, proud of having recovered Captain John, and. welcoming in him one of the most glorious of its children.

The End

Printed in Great Britain
by Amazon.co.uk, Ltd.,
Marston Gate.